PENGUIN BOOKS

THE MAGNATES

Susan Crosland was born in Baltimore, Maryland, the daughter of a Pulitzer Prize-winning newspaperman. She began her own career in journalism when she came to London, writing for the *Sunday Express*, where she quickly became known for her vivid and penetrating profiles of the rich and powerful. Two selections of her *Sunday Times* profiles have been published as books: *Behind the Image* (under the name Susan Barnes) and *Looking Out, Looking In*. For thirteen years she was married to Anthony Crosland, who was the British Foreign Secretary at the time of his sudden death. She is the author of the celebrated biography, *Tony Crosland*, and of the best-selling novels *Ruling Passions* and *Dangerous Games* (Penguin, 1992). She lives in London.

SUSAN CROSLAND

THE MAGNATES

PENGUIN BOOKS

PENGUIN BOOKS

Published by the Penguin Group
Penguin Books Ltd, 27 Wrights Lane, London W8 5TZ, England
Penguin Books USA Inc., 375 Hudson Street, New York, New York 10014, USA
Penguin Books Australia Ltd, Ringwood, Victoria, Australia
Penguin Books Canada Ltd, 10 Alcorn Avenue, Toronto, Ontario, Canada M4V 3B2
Penguin Books (NZ) Ltd, 182–190 Wairau Road, Auckland 10, New Zealand

Penguin Books Ltd, Registered Offices: Harmondsworth, Middlesex, England

First published in Great Britain by Orion 1994
Published in Penguin Books 1995
1 3 5 7 9 10 8 6 4 2

Printed in England by Clays Ltd, St Ives plc

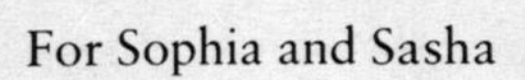

PART I

PROLOGUE

Baked earth rose steeply at one side of the road twisting through the cordillera. At the road's outer edge an escarpment fell away to the ravine below, a patchwork of colours – emerald-green of sugar-cane, lime-green of corn, rust-red of earth waiting for the rains to come. Sometimes Mexican children appeared at the road's edge, seemingly from nowhere, standing alone with one or two others, their opaque eyes watching cars and trucks intermittently thread their way. Even in late afternoon the sun raised blisters on the tarmac.

A car hurtling round a bend careened along the outer shoulder as the road kept twisting. A woman's voice cried: 'Look out!' Rammed brakes, tearing of gears, scream of tyres. The car veered, shuddered, veered again before it shot over the edge and lurched down the escarpment. Doors burst open when it hit the mesquite. Then it turned on one side and came to a rest.

On the road above lay the body of a small girl.

ONE

Zoë angled two mirrors so she could manage a French braid. She bit her lower lip as she began at her crown and criss-crossed her hair, interweaving a wide gold ribbon. The phone rang. Goddammit. Now she'd have to start the whole process again.

'Have I caught you at a bad moment?'

'Yes – since you ask. I'm trying to make myself look both spellbinding and intelligent.'

'That shouldn't be hard. Where're you going?'

'To the British Embassy. A dinner for big wheels, including my boss, if you please. And now I'm going to be late because I have to start my dumb hair all over again.'

'Why didn't you tell me you'd be there? So will I. See you soon.'

They'd never been at the same dinner party. But of course his wife would be with him, and that thought added to her nervousness as she began the braid again. She glanced at the clock on her dressing-table. Oh God.

It wasn't as if she went to one of the capital's high-powered dinners five nights a week. At twenty-eight she'd made a real mark as a feature writer on the *Washington Express*, and she could have been asked to a garden party at the British Embassy. But it was unusual to be included at this kind of shindig. She was only invited, she knew, because of her friendship with the Ambassador's American wife.

So here she was, Zoë Hare, about to sally forth if she ever got her idiot braid finished.

Miles Brewster lifted his chin to adjust his black tie. Tall, spare, broad-shouldered, he was good-looking in the way typical of east-coast Americans from English stock – sandy hair, freckled skin, tawny eyes. Flipping down the corners of his collar, he hardly saw himself in the mirror. His mind was on whether he would bid for one of Britain's two most famous newspapers.

Now forty-two, he'd spent twenty years building up his media empire. His most recent takeover, the *Washington Express*, was the jewel. Now he wanted a gem on the other side of the Atlantic.

He tried to avoid business calls on social occasions. But tonight he'd told his secretary to phone him at the Embassy if the information he needed to go ahead came through.

Marigold Brewster took a good deal longer than her husband to prepare for the dinner party. The ravishingly pretty and amusing daughter of a Surrey solicitor, she was thirty-seven, an English beauty with red-gold hair, green eyes and luscious breasts which she displayed as much as decorum permitted.

When she first met Miles at a Long Island house party, she was a titled widow. (The earl was seventy when they married.) Miles was not the easiest of guests. If the talk was about something that interested him, well and good, but he was bored by chitchat, when he would withdraw into himself. From the start Marigold sensed how to pique his interest and draw him out.

By the end of that summer five years ago, she was no longer a countess. But she had something far more valuable to her than an English title – a passport to anywhere in the world as the wife of America's foremost media magnate.

Senator Peter Stainsley and his wife looked fondly at each

other in the tall mirror over her dressing-table. She had just fastened a sapphire and moonstone brooch on her evening dress. He had given it to her six months before. She always knew when Peter had embarked on a liaison because that was when, out of the blue, he gave her a carefully chosen piece of jewellery.

They had married young, and he was not much more than thirty when he won his Senate seat. Now thirty-eight, he was an extremely competent and highly regarded member of the Senate Armed Services Committee.

Both took it for granted that tonight wouldn't be a purely social affair. Most Washington dinners they attended were networks for power-broking.

Brushing back his straight auburn hair without parting it, Lord Scrope was satisfied with the man he saw in the mirror. At forty-six his body had thickened without the muscles turning to flab. Physically or in a test of wills, few would take him on.

He'd returned to his suite at the Willard Hotel with just twenty minutes to spare before setting off for the Embassy. Throughout his rise from garage-chain owner to media baron, Gerald Scrope never liked hanging about any place too long. Yesterday he'd flown from London to New York to check up on a few far-flung divisions of Scrope Opportunities Ltd. He liked to descend on his employees without prior warning.

Even the British Ambassador had learned only that morning of Lord Scrope's intention to be in Washington overnight. Of course Lord Scrope was added to the dinner guests. Of course he knew his greatest rival would be there.

He half-grinned as he turned from the mirror. He wanted to watch Miles Brewster's face when he discovered the surprise Gerald Scrope had in store for him.

At 7.25 precisely, the British Ambassador, James Wharton, straightened his black tie, adjusted his starched collar beneath his ruddy boyish face and slipped into the dinner jacket cut by his Savile Row tailor in London. He was staggered by the effort needed to tear his mind away from the letter he'd received that morning in the overnight bag from London, the corner of the envelope sternly embossed: The Prime Minister.

Glancing automatically at his watch – 7.27 – he gave a rap-rap at his wife's dressing-room. Silence. Opening the door he saw she was lying in her bath at the other end of the room, her feet resting on the edge of the tub, oily bubbles floating on the water's surface, her pretty plump breasts protruding through the foam. She was day-dreaming about her lover.

The chestnut curls twisted to the crown of her head were held by a butterfly clip. Her hair was naturally curly and would bounce into a shoulder-length bob – if she ever removed the butterfly grip.

'You will be on time, Jancie, won't you? You know these things matter to our guests,' said the Ambassador.

'Fuck the guests,' Jancie Wharton replied equably, swooshing the water in glistening eddies as she recrossed her ankles.

At the same moment Zoë was trotting down the four flights of her apartment house so she wouldn't arrive late.

TWO

The British Embassy in Washington was the most majestic of the national showcases lining the sweep of Massachusetts Avenue known as Embassy Row. Created by the last great English country-house designer, Sir Edwin Lutyens, it stood in stately symmetry, brick walls with white columns soaring to a pediment.

James Wharton glanced at his watch. He had mentioned the Prime Minister's letter to no one. It drew him like a magnet. He closed the library door behind him and unlocked a drawer in his desk. After a few minutes he refolded the letter and returned it to what now seemed a furtive hiding place rather than his own ambassadorial desk. He squared his shoulders. He would allow no one this evening to guess he had suffered the most grievous blow of his life. At exactly 7.45 he strolled into the drawing-room to await his guests.

Three minutes later Miles and Marigold Brewster were announced. At once Miles saw something wasn't right. He'd got to know James well in the time they'd overlapped in Washington. James prided himself on his fitness at forty, working out on the Embassy's squash court, testing himself at weekends behind the wheel of his forty-foot yacht. Tonight he looked shrunk. However hard James tried to conceal it, his square face revealed uncertainty. Yet Miles didn't ask if something was wrong. He would have detested it if someone had asked the same thing of him.

'Where's Jancie?' said Marigold as she and James touched cheeks. 'I do hope she doesn't have another migraine.'

'Just a faulty sense of time,' he replied coolly. He'd felt slightly uncomfortable when her cloud of hair brushed his face. Marigold had that apparently poreless English skin which looks like porcelain. Her emeralds matched her eyes and were the perfect foil for her hair. The spectacular stones of the necklace – the same green as the silk of her *décolleté* gown – set off the milky skin. Most people were bowled over by her beauty. But James found something too considered in the perfection with which she invariably presented herself.

He turned to Miles. 'I'm not sure what view you take of one of my guests this evening,' he said as a footman handed round a tray, and Marigold took a glass of champagne.

'I'd better have a stiff whisky then,' said Miles good-temperedly, helping himself to a tumbler three-quarters filled with Scotch and very little soda. He had a distinctive voice – huskiness with a crack in it. People who'd only heard it once recognised his voice if he phoned, before he said his name. 'Male or female?'

'Male and distinctly macho,' James replied. 'It's Gerald Scrope, better known these days as Lord Scrope. He flew in from London yesterday. He's casting his eye over American publications which might take his fancy. I suppose you know one another?'

'Merely by reputation.' Miles smiled drily. 'Lord Scrope can cast his eye as much as he likes at my publications – it's a free country. He won't hook any of them.'

'Senator Peter Stainsley and Mrs Stainsley,' intoned the butler.

The man and woman entering the drawing-room imparted the sense of being very much a couple. Miles was glad they were here too. He liked them both, their air of shared self-confidence and the way neither Stainsley felt the need to make a show of calling the other 'darling' every second sentence.

By eight o'clock sixteen guests had been introduced, and the Ambassador was moving from group to group, making sure things were going smoothly. He was talking with Peter Stainsley when he saw the Senator's face flush as he looked towards the door. At the same moment the butler announced: 'Miss Zoë Hare.'

She made a striking figure, standing alone in a room where most guests knew each other and had arrived with someone. The dark hair drawn back from her widow's peak and temples emphasised the oval of her face. The cream silk dress, belted with gold mesh, was simplicity itself. Certainly she looked dramatic. And she was doing her best to appear self-sufficient and casual as she moved her eyes around the room in search of Jancie.

James hurried over to greet her warmly.

'Do you know the Secretary of State? Or Marigold Brewster?' he asked. 'Let me introduce you.' And putting his arm protectively through Zoë's he steered her across the room. When Miles broke away from his group to say hello to his employee, James said to him, laughing: 'You must wait until dinner. I've put you beside each other.' As they passed Peter Stainsley's group, the Senator and Zoë exchanged a pleasant formal smile.

Beneath Reynolds's portrait of Lady Anstruther, the Secretary of State was holding forth, a large bourbon in one hand, while beside him Marigold sipped her champagne, looking more imperious than the varnished Lady Anstruther. When James made the introductions, Marigold smiled cordially and said in her attractive deep voice, the accent clipped: 'It's not often I have the pleasure of meeting any of the girls who work for Miles.'

Zoë felt the blood rush to her face.

James lifted his brows. 'Secretary of State, this is Zoë

Hare, whom you will know already as a distinguished feature writer on the *Express*,' he said.

'Good evening,' said Zoë. 'And excuse me but my favourite woman in Washington has just come in,' she added, and quickly started across to where the Ambassadress had at last appeared. At that moment Zoë felt her stocking laddering at the back. 'Goddammit,' she muttered to herself, certain the immaculate Mrs Brewster would spot the ladder growing wider by the second as it snaked down the left calf of one of 'the girls who work for Miles'.

James looked at his watch.

When Zoë and Jancie touched cheeks, the social ritual contained real affection. They'd liked each other from the moment they met, soon after the Whartons were posted to Washington. When Zoë arrived at the Embassy to interview the Ambassador's American wife, she discovered Jancie was a quick-witted, unaffected woman who understood the frailties and strengths of politicians and media, and wasn't overly impressed by her seat in the front row of the circus. Each liked the directness of the other. Not long afterwards, Zoë dropped a line to Jancie suggesting they have lunch, this time off the record, just for the fun of it. Soon they were close friends.

'I've just been put in my place by the boss's wife,' Zoë said drily. 'If you'd decided to have a migraine tonight, I might have gone upstairs to join you.' She looked more closely at Jancie. 'What's the matter?'

To the other guests the tardy Ambassadress looked charming when at last she appeared. Only Zoë – and James – saw the petulance of Jancie's mouth as she smiled.

'It's getting worse,' Jancie muttered, and then erupted in a stream of words to Zoë. 'I know it makes me sound like a goddam spoiled brat, which I am not, by the way, but I now can hardly bear it when James says' – she mimicked his precise voice – '"You will be on time, Jancie, won't you. You know these things matter to our guests." It's not that I have anything against his goddam guests. Tonight I think of them as my guests too. Some are even my friends. It's just that I am expected to be the Concerned, Charming, Perfect Hostess as a *duty*. If he ever said: "I know much of this is a pain in the ass, but will you do it out of love for me?" then I would do it gladly. You know I love him very much. It's this *duty* thing that drives me straight up the goddam wall.'

The tirade was spoken at top speed in a low voice. Having delivered herself of her resentment and been understood, Jancie now looked around the room, petulance gone from her face. 'OK, buster, here we go.' Whereupon she gracefully, if belatedly, began the rounds of the assembled guests.

At that minute the footman intoned: 'The Lord Scrope.'

Every American journalist knew about Gerald Scrope's climb to power. Zoë watched James hurry across the room to welcome his final guest, the Ambassadress moving at a more leisurely pace towards the figure standing stock-still as he surveyed the room. He could have been sizing up bankers in a boardroom or cattle at a market. His eyes, so deep a blue they seemed almost navy, were intent but otherwise unreadable.

Watching them shake hands, Zoë was struck by how Lord Scrope seemed to dominate James physically, even though James was taller. Lord Scrope's square head and full-frontal stance were strangely aggressive. The crude vitality emanating from him was that of a middleweight boxer. Standing with his legs slightly apart, on the balls of his feet, he was spoiling for a fight. Zoë wanted to know him better.

Nor was she alone. Marigold Brewster was in the last group to whom the Ambassador introduced his final guest. For a brief moment Lord Scrope glanced boldly at the titian hair, the emerald necklace, the breasts half-bared, before he returned his hard gaze to Marigold's face. He gave a curt nod which could have been a social greeting or an auction bid. Excited, uneasy, she recognised the tremor that passed through her. Abruptly he turned away.

The guests began moving towards the terrace for dinner.

THREE

The terrace overlooked the rose garden. Two tables, each laid for ten, sparkled with Stourbridge goblets and Georgian silver on gleaming white damask. As people looked for their seats, Zoë found Peter Stainsley at her elbow.

'How nice to see you again, Zoë,' he said affably.

'Always a pleasure to see you, Senator,' she replied, her eyes dancing.

'Have you met my wife?' he asked. 'You're sitting at the same table.'

The woman just taking her seat looked up confidently and gave Zoë a friendly smile as Peter introduced them. Zoë warmed to her immediately.

'I enjoyed the piece you wrote about Peter,' she said to Zoë. 'You're the first journalist to capture his personality.'

Normally early June would be too uncomfortable to eat outside, but this year the long sultry summer was slow to clamp down. James Wharton liked the image of gathering public figures in a quintessentially English romantic setting – everything punctiliously planned yet relaxed.

He was not a career diplomat: he was an eminent British journalist who was an expert on defence. Many were surprised when he was appointed to the plum Washington post, the personal choice of the Prime Minister. But James turned out to be a superb ambassador. He saw himself as the modern 'Renaissance man', the all-rounder who likes to present himself informally. Tonight should have been perfect. But whenever his secret knowledge pushed itself to the front of his consciousness, he felt the knot tighten in his stomach.

'Do you ever miss journalism?' Marigold asked him.

She had jabbed the wound. James could see the black letters embossed on that envelope.

'I haven't missed journalism for a minute during this job,' he answered carefully. 'But when my appointment here comes to an end, I'll enjoy moving on to a different career – leaping off one track on to another.' This time his face revealed no anxiety. Not for nothing had James been to Eton.

'Miles loves doing that – leaps as he likes on to a newspaper or television station or whatever,' replied Marigold. 'You know, he enjoys managing the television side of things, but the newspaper world is where his heart is. That's where you *influence* people. But then no one knows that better than you, James,' she added.

She was right. But he said nothing.

'I'll bet you spend nil time with TV news presenters – except at parties,' she continued, 'and hours and hours briefing journalists. No?'

He remained uncharacteristically silent.

'I'm hoping Miles will buy a London paper next,' she went on. 'I long to spend more time in London, don't you?'

At that moment James hated her. However unwittingly, everything she said rubbed salt in the sore. When the rattle of china began as the footmen removed the soup plates – how James loved the Royal cipher painted on each Minton plate – he turned with relief to the Secretary of State's wife on his other side, no matter that she was famously dull.

Miles had guessed he could count on James to put him between two women he'd get on with. Jancie was on one side, Zoë on the other.

He spent the soup course in conversation with Jancie.

He always responded to her quirky sharpness. At the same time he could see she was hardly Britain's ideal ambassadress since she'd become obsessed with Simon Fleet.

When Miles took over the *Washington Express*, the British-born Fleet was already its foreign editor, a skilled newshound with a nose for finding a story. Miles liked Fleet's work, but he didn't care much for the man.

Three times over the crab bisque, Jancie had introduced Simon Fleet's name into the conversation. She savoured it, Miles saw, and inwardly he winced for both Whartons. There was no reason to doubt the general assumption that Fleet was a shit in his relations with women.

When the second course came and Miles turned to Zoë, she determined to conceal quite how curious she was about him. She seldom even glimpsed him at the *Express*, where most of his time was spent in his suite up in Corporate. The newsroom was two floors below. The editor handled the day-to-day business of running the *Express*, but he always went upstairs to Corporate to discuss the next day's paper with Miles. On the rare occasions when Miles came down to the newsroom, a *frisson* passed among the journalists. But their actual contact with him was superficial.

He's sort of the same colour all over, Zoë thought as she looked at him now, hair, freckles, eyes.

Everyone had heard he was lousy at chitchat, so she started off with shop talk about how various papers were handling the latest White House crisis.

'Tell me,' he suddenly said after a minute or two of that. 'As we live in a sexually schizophrenic age, do you find being a woman an advantage or disadvantage when interviewing male politicians?'

She was so unprepared for him to be personal that she had to stop and think.

Maybe she'd turn out as uncommunicative as he was supposed to be, Miles thought.

Then she looked at him and gave a big smile. He noticed the grey eyes with their sooty lashes, the curves of the full-lipped mouth.

'Well, it certainly isn't a deathblow,' she replied.

He waited.

'I can ask the male politician personal questions he'd resent coming from another guy,' she went on. 'The chemistry's different. Chemistry plays a helluva big role in interviews.'

When she turned back to her beef Wellington, he glanced at her profile. He liked the pronounced bridge of her nose. He wondered if she had broken it, perhaps as a child. Looking away – he didn't want to sit there staring at her – he too was silent for a minute. Then he said:

'Do male politicians you're interviewing ever make a play for you?'

Zoë burst out laughing. This guy was meant to be so reticent.

'It's unusual,' she replied. 'Usually they're too busy projecting the image they want conveyed to the public. And of course in today's climate, it'd be taking a real risk: if I decided to mention Congressman So-and-So had patted my knee, it could land his career in real trouble.' She paused before adding: 'But once the interview's over and the piece is published, occasionally the person calls me for a date – though I have to tell you that's never happened after I've given someone a tough time.'

Miles smiled. 'Sure. Like your interview with the senator from Ohio who sees himself as God's spokesman. Did you know he phoned me the moment the first edition was on the streets? He said the story must be pulled "*immediately*" – before the second edition came out – because you'd distorted what he said.'

That crack in his voice was like the sound of breaking walnut husks, she thought.

He liked the way her whole face lit up when she laughed.

'The editor told me there was a little commotion about that piece,' she said, 'but he didn't mention you were involved.' But then, like any editor, he would have preferred to keep it quiet that the senator had gone over his head to complain to the paper's owner.

'I told the senator he'd have to shove it,' said Miles. 'To be more exact, I said I was sorry he felt the piece was unfair, but you had too high a reputation for fairness for me to ask the editor to pull it.'

Zoë smiled inwardly at his choice of words. Everyone at the paper knew when Miles Brewster 'asked' it was the same thing as an order.

At James's table, Marigold had taken her time in turning to her other partner. Glancing down at her necklace, she saw the pendant had shifted slightly to one side. With a tapered finger she nudged the shimmering jewel until it rested where the twin curves of her breasts began. Then she turned in her chair.

Lord Scrope's eyes were on the pendant, one side of his mouth drawn up in a sardonic smile. She knew he'd seen her preparing herself for him. She felt her face warm with embarrassment. His gaze moved further down. She saw how the slicked-back auburn hair grew from a forehead grooved with two deep horizontal lines, reddish brows over the short straight nose. Unhurriedly, he moved his gaze up to the emeralds again, and at last the hooded eyes looked directly into Marigold's face.

'We should get to know each other, Mrs Brewster,' he said.

The words were spoken in an orotund formal manner,

but the accent had the flat vowels of the south London garage mechanic.

For a moment she looked at him without replying. She saw the contours of his face had the well-fed beefiness of a man who can indulge himself and does, yet the wide mouth – lips defined as if drawn with a sharp pencil – made Marigold think of a wolf. Though clean-shaven, the heavy jaws had a darkish hue. She'd always harboured a taste for rough trade.

'It's surprising we haven't met before,' she said archly. 'You and Miles have interests in common.'

'Common interests don't make you mates,' said Gerald Scrope. 'Your husband and I got where we got by different roads. Something tells me he thinks he's better than me.'

He said this with no display of rancour. He might have been talking about two men unknown to him and Marigold.

She laughed. 'And do you feel superior to him?' she asked.

But Gerald had applied himself to the main course. He was greedy and particular about his food. If the pastry case was properly flaky, beef Wellington was one of his favourite dishes, and when a footman had held out the platter, he saw at a glance that the British Embassy chef's reputation was deserved, and took two portions. He ate with systematic relish before turning back to Marigold and replying to her question:

'If your husband and I met on neutral territory, I'd have him by the nuts every time.'

At once Marigold's mood changed.

'Not a very impressive boast when the other man has a leg messed up. Or perhaps you didn't know,' she said coldly.

'You think too narrowly, Mrs Brewster,' Gerald replied. 'I thought you'd interpret things less literally.'

She was now very angry, and as her breathing quickened, he looked down at the pendant trembling with the rise and fall of her breasts. His insolence was insufferable, yet if she rose to his bait, it would simply add to his bloody cockiness, damn his eyes.

Still watching the effect he continued: 'A less conventional person would know I'm not talking about a physical fight.'

He looked up to her face again.

'And you seem to think I can't read, Mrs Brewster.'

He gave an odd smile.

'Every profile written about Miles Brewster mentions his leg. People say it's where he gets his urge for power. Personally, I find that psycho stuff hot air. You don't need a special reason to want power. You just got to want it. And you got to be prepared to put it first all the time. Always.'

As she looked at him, Marigold's expression became absorbed.

'I feel superior to your husband because when it comes to a fight between us – and it will – I'll win. I'm smarter than he is.'

'That's a view you may have to alter,' said Marigold sharply, her initial attraction to Gerald Scrope once again erased. No one ever insulted Miles's intelligence, let alone addressed the insults to her.

'You take everything personally,' said Gerald. 'That's a mistake. It makes you miss the point. I didn't say there's anything wrong with your husband's IQ. I said I'm smarter. I had to be. From day one, if anything went wrong in Miles Brewster's life, he had Papa to fall back on.'

Gerald pronounced 'Papa' with a crude mockery of an educated accent.

'Maybe he never actually asked Papa for help. Everyone

knows Miles Brewster has guts. But he always knew Papa was there. That makes all the difference in life. It means you can take your eye off the ball occasionally. If you got to make every inch on your own, you got to watch the ball twenty-five hours a day – even in your sleep. I wouldn't be having this conversation with you, Mrs Brewster, if I didn't want something out of it.'

He resumed eating his beef Wellington. When he looked up again, his eyes fastened on a footman who'd appeared at the other table to say something to Miles. As Miles pushed back his chair to get up, there was a brief clumsiness, like a stumble, as he got to his feet. But Gerald saw the limp was hardly perceptible as Miles crossed the terrace in his long-limbed gait and for a moment was silhouetted against the lights of the ballroom within. Even after he disappeared from view, Gerald continued to watch the open door.

Five minutes later Miles reappeared in the doorway. Returning to his seat, he glanced at the other table and his eyes met Gerald's. Lord Scrope's were now inscrutable. Miles Brewster's were cold with dislike.

When they all had moved back to the drawing-room, something made Zoë look over to the fireplace where Gerald stood, balloon glass of brandy in one hand, a cigar in the other. He was watching Miles saunter towards him. Even at a distance Zoë sensed a leashed violence in Gerald's head-on stance. Any semblance of casualness in Miles disappeared when he stopped three feet away, each man in his own space taking the measure of the other.

'My, my, what an odd coincidence, Lord Scrope,' Miles said in a tight voice. 'You and I meet for the first time this evening. Before dinner is over, my editor at the *Express* phones to say the AP wants me to comment on a bulletin they've just received. Well, what do you know. It seems you claim to be able to read my mind.'

Holding his cigar between thumb and forefinger, Gerald drew on it unhurriedly, exhaling a thin stream of smoke through lips nearly clamped.

'*You* announce,' Miles went on, 'that I intend to bid for the *London Dispatch*.' His voice had taken on a hard edge that carried to other guests.

Conversation petered out around the room. Sitting on a sofa, Marigold broke off chatting with the National Gallery director, and both leant forward, eager to watch what would follow. Zoë was astonished at the openness of the hostility.

'According to this bulletin, Lord Scrope, you will bid for the *London Dispatch* in order to – how did you so nicely express it? – "For the purpose of shutting out what would be an unhealthy influence on Britain." Enlighten me as to what you find so unhealthy about my influence.'

It was the studied insolence with which Gerald exhaled another stream of smoke that made Miles want to hit him.

At last Gerald replied: 'Your newspapers keep strumming the old guitar, saying market values ain't enough – the strong should help the weak. In the old days that Sir Galahad stuff had a certain charm. But the weak always knew it was rubbish. All the weak have ever wanted, Mr Brewster, is to be strong enough to push everyone else around. Strength is what it's all about. If Britain is going to be strong, hearts and flowers can't come into the deal. We don't want Sir Galahad galloping around. That's point one.'

'Let's have point two,' said Miles.

'Point two. You got this thing about hands-across-the-sea. If I get my way – and I will, Mr Brewster – Britain will have a prime minister who says the hell with Anglo-American joint policies unless they happen to suit Britain. I'd lift Britain's arms embargo on Arabi tomorrow, and if

America-the-Beautiful says that ain't nice, too bad. I'm not interested in bogus self-righteousness. Trade is what matters – and British deals should be in British interests, full stop. That's what my newspapers in Britain pound out every day. If you take over the *Dispatch*, you'll be preaching that morality crap.'

He gave a parody of a smile.

'Nothing personal. I'd feel the same about anyone who gives a bum steer to the new Britain.'

He returned the cigar to his lips and with deliberate slowness pulled on it.

Peter Stainsley, standing a few feet away, opened his mouth to try and defuse the situation, then thought better of it. In the silence a tray crashed in another room.

Miles smiled faintly. 'If you won your bid for the *London Dispatch*, Lord Scrope – and you have a problem with the Monopoly and Mergers Commission – my guess is you'd revamp it as a down-market tabloid, sandwiching your political messages between tits and bums. I've got nothing against breasts and buttocks but not in a market bazaar – Britain's news-stands are already awash with them. And there's a lot wrong with the messages you shove between them.'

Gerald nodded slowly, as if sizing up his opponent.

'I'll tell you another thing, Lord Scrope,' Miles went on. 'When I arrived here this evening, I hadn't decided to bid for the *Dispatch*. This is hardly the ideal moment to invest in Britain. But it's a funny thing.' He gave a short laugh. 'You know you've whetted my appetite.'

Marigold's eyes shone like her pendant as she watched her husband and Gerald Scrope throw down the gauntlet. Jancie catalogued the scene in her mind to tell Simon Fleet. Zoë's face was rapt: she enjoyed watching well-matched opponents snarl. And she was intrigued by the contrast between them – Miles Brewster with the assurance peculiar to his background, Lord Scrope a strangely compelling thug.

Miles ended the confrontation as abruptly as it began. Turning away from Gerald he said lightly to the Ambassador: 'James, you were going to show me the Stubbs you're so proud of.'

The Ambassador to Washington had the pick of the British government's art collection. Only a week earlier, James had told Miles of his pleasure and pride at the prospect of having the Stubbs horse adorn his walls.

When they reached the next room, James said: 'Look, Miles. Something has come up for me. It's personal. Is there any time we could meet tomorrow?'

'Have your secretary call mine first thing. She'll fix up something.'

Miles had closed off his anger. He turned his attention to the painting. James pretended an interest he no longer felt.

When they went back to the drawing-room, the guests were starting to go. Miles glanced around, wanting to say goodnight to Zoë before he and Marigold left. It was easy to pick her out: she was standing with her back to him, the gold-ribboned French braid like a club touching the base of her neck.

He found himself looking directly into the face of the man she was talking with. It was Gerald Scrope. They were standing alone, and something about Zoë's stance implied her interest was wholly concentrated. Miles felt his face flush with unexpected resentment.

His sixth sense made Gerald glance over Zoë's shoulder and meet Miles's eyes. For a full minute the two men looked at each other stonily.

FOUR

She could feel his pulse slowing back to normal. How many miles did a man have to run to equal the strain he put on his heart in a single act of love? Three? Thirty? A lot, anyhow. Zoë was glad she wasn't a man. Half-seeing she gazed over the bed's footboard to the window framing a pale afternoon sky.

Her apartment was on the fourth floor of one of the smaller new developments on the Virginia side of the Potomac River. It cost her most of her salary, but she loved it. One of the things she liked best was its privacy. So did Senator Peter Stainsley. Washington remained a small town in many ways: there were few public places where a senior-ranking senator would not be recognised by someone.

'The perfect couple,' he said.

'Referring to our common interest in politics, no doubt,' she replied, laughing.

'Which reminds me,' he said, propping himself on an elbow. 'Do you mind if I make a phone call, Zoë?'

'Help yourself.'

He leaned over her to take the handset from the table on her side, and they both watched the plastic cord spiral over her still damp breasts as he lay back again, holding the phone above him while he dialled his office.

'I'll be late for the Committee session,' he said. 'Anything I need to know in the meantime?'

When he finished she took the phone from him. 'Allow me,' she said formally, restoring it and then turning contentedly to him again, one arm across his chest, liking the feel of his sweat-soaked skin against hers.

She found lying in bed and talking afterwards was one of the most enjoyable stages of making love.

So did Peter. Along with the perpetual demands on his time, being in the public eye meant he had continually to keep his guard up. Only at Zoë's apartment did he feel he could let it down. They talked about their separate hopes and disappointments. They dissected someone both knew. They exchanged confidences about some past relationships. He noticed how when she mentioned an insignificant flirtation or an unsuccessful pass, she might throw in the man's name if it was familiar to Peter: he loved to hear how another politician comported himself when pursuing a woman. But she was vague about any previous experience in bed.

She had begun her affair with Peter six months earlier. Each love affair had its unique combination of passion and intimacy, but it had to be with the right man.

'Don't you ever have moments in the middle of the night when you feel lonely?' Peter asked, turning his head on the pillow to look at her.

'Don't say that,' she replied sharply. 'I can't stand that word being applied to me. It suggests I must be lonely for just anyone. The company of someone who bores me is what I find depressing; *that's* when I feel really lonely.'

They watched the cotton-wool clouds float across the square of blue. Had they been standing at the window they'd have looked down on the Potomac, the capital sprawling on the other side and merging into Maryland on the horizon. Off to the left were the familiar landmarks – the Capitol's gleaming dome and the Washington Monument, even the Lincoln Memorial, Zoë's favourite, just in view before the river bent again.

'In a way,' she said suddenly, 'I wish I hadn't met your wife.'

He turned again to look at her.

'I liked her. The only time we talked was when you introduced us. But she was across the table from me, and during dinner I looked at her sometimes. She has a really good face. If she had been nasty or just boring, I could have told myself it must be awful to have a wife like that.'

Peter said nothing.

Zoë had never had an affair with a married man before. She knew she was not Peter's first infidelity, and usually that kept her from feeling guilt. They both took pains to make sure the truth of their friendship would not be discovered. Zoë knew someone on the *Express* who was hell-bent on her lover's wife knowing about her, but Zoë thought this horrible and sadistic. She saw her relationship with Peter as an enclosed interlude in their lives. If, despite herself, she ever imagined being his wife, she banished the thought: she would never try to break up his marriage.

'Of course I've been curious about her. Whenever I see a photograph of you both, I always examine her face, the way she's dressed, how she looks at you. But she was someone that had nothing to do with me. She had to do with you. If you chose to be unfaithful to her, that was your business, not mine – so long as it didn't get back to your wife.'

Her eyes followed two little clouds move like plump twins in one side of the frame and out the other.

'But meeting her makes her become my business too – not very much, but a little,' she said.

'No it doesn't,' said Peter. 'My marriage is my business. It has nothing to do with you. The guilt is mine alone. Certainly not yours.'

Early on in his marriage, Peter had convinced himself that an infidelity, so long as it was discreet, not only didn't harm his marriage but probably made it better. A *modus vivendi* evolved without discussion: he never spoke of his extra-marital activities; his wife never asked. That's the way she preferred it. In most respects it was a good marriage, and both took trouble to see it remained so.

He and Zoë were together once a week at most. He didn't stay late. Sometimes, like today, they met in a restaurant for lunch – easy to explain away, as lunching with a journalist was a regular feature in any politician's schedule. Other times, Zoë picked up something on her way home from work, and they had it with a bottle of wine at the gateleg table in her living-room, looking down on the Potomac. Or Peter bought crab cakes from a fish store nearby. Residents let themselves in the main door with their security keys, and an entryphone system allowed guests to be buzzed in. Once Peter found himself sharing the elevator with another person, so he got off at the wrong floor and walked up to the fourth. After that, he always used the stairs. His motto: when taking a big risk, reduce small risks which attend it.

'What *did* happen to Miles Brewster's leg?' Zoë asked unexpectedly.

'All anyone knows is that it was a car accident in Mexico. Some time in his twenties. Drink was involved. A child was killed. The Mexican girl with Miles was paralysed for life. It's the bad act in his past.'

She was quiet, thinking.

'For an absolute man, that's hard to take,' Peter went on.

'How do you mean?'

'An absolute man sets higher standards for himself than most of us. He keeps to them – whatever. And when he fails to do so, the regret is terrific. Miles never talks about it. It'd be better if he did. His silence makes people think his conduct must have been worse than has ever come out.'

He turned again to look at her. With his free hand he reached for hers.

But Zoë disengaged her hand, rolling away from him so she could see her bedside clock. Her appointment on Capitol Hill was in less than an hour. She turned back again to touch Peter's face. This was the poignant part, each time the regret they couldn't lie together a little longer.

He collected his clothes from where he'd dropped them. If he found a taxi right away, he'd miss hardly any of the Committee's session on Arabi and the arms embargo.

From the bathroom Zoë called out: 'Say goodbye before you leave.'

He guessed she was already thinking about her interview ahead.

He was wrong. She was thinking about 'the bad act' in Miles's past. She was thinking about her parents. They were killed in a car crash.

Others imagined Zoë must have been a lonely child, living with her grandparents on that isolated, run-down farm on Lake Champlain where it swelled wide as it swept north to Montreal. Two miles of water were between the stone shore of the Hare farm in Vermont and the railway town at the foot of the Adirondack mountains in up-state New York. Certainly her childhood developed a taste for solitude. But she never thought of it as loneliness. It was like being suspended in an enchanted land.

The house had been built in the late nineteenth century and kept spruce for most of the next, the land tilled and tended. Perhaps it was because Mr Hare had what his wife called 'a poet's nature', but when Zoë was growing up the duck-egg blue paint of the house had been left to peel away until so few slivers clung to the clapboard that it looked grey, with the Federal green flaked off the shutters. (At the end of her third year on the *Express*, she had saved enough to help get the place painted again.) Yet the house had always retained its calm assurance, its cupola rising jaunty above it.

Of the once flourishing livestock, two fat brown horses and a Jersey cow called Fern were still there in Zoë's childhood. Fern's nut-brown coat, black velvety face and long eyelashes gave her a charm which made other cows nonentities for Zoë. Once a visiting cousin had used Fern's black switch of a tail to vault on to her bony back, and as Fern careened off clumsily, trying to dislodge her rider, Zoë had raced after them and pulled the youth to the ground, furious at the affront to Fern's dignity.

Soon after her twelfth birthday she began swimming alone further and further into the lake where it stretched two miles wide, first to the gleaming red buoy bobbing where the deepest waters began, then further, flipping on her back to rest, sometimes slipping her shoulder straps down so the sun warmed her breasts still small and pointed, her hair fanned out, then over again and on into the vastness of the lake.

On the long summer evenings, her grandmother packed a picnic supper, and the three of them made their way down a rough path, its perennial struggle with the nettles never won, to the immense rocks, smooth, sloping to the water's edge. There Emmy waited, the rope from her bow tied round a silver birch stunted by winter's battering. Sometimes Zoë rowed, and when the lake was shiny and still she knew how to dip the oars without a splash, and the only sound was the distant rattling of the train which passed on the far side of the lake. Often she felt a deep thrill within, which she didn't understand.

They cooked on the stone barbecue she and her grandfather built anew each spring. Most evenings they ate their supper in near silence, sitting on the primeval rocks, the lake lapping at their feet, each caught in a private dream as they watched the swollen sun change from gold to scarlet, flaming the sky into carmine sheets above its reflection.

Best of all, she sometimes thought, were the hours spent in the high-ceilinged music room where her grandfather's collection of Indian artefacts was housed. All that remained of the room's earlier musical manifestation was a phonograph – called the Victrola – with a tuba-like speaker and a crank. Here her day-dreams reached daily heights of excitement. In pre-pubescent years her favourites among the scratchy ancient twelve-inch records were 'Song of the Volga Boatmen', Sousa's military marches, the triumphal march from *Aida*; her fantasies briefly interrupted while she rewound the Victrola. By the time she was twelve, it was the love duet from *Tristan und Isolde* which produced that feeling inside her, along with the worn records of Ella Fitzgerald's heart-breaking croons, or the early love songs of The Beatles.

Often she looked at the framed family photographs that stood on a worn leather-topped table in the middle of the room. For years she had studied the picture of a little girl walking hand in hand with a laughing young woman on one side and a debonair young man in striped shirt-sleeves and seersucker trousers on the other. Her grandmother said it was taken in New York's Central Park only days before the couple died in a car crash. He had just been made the *New York Times* bureau chief in London. They were driving home from a dinner given for them before they were to fly to England with Zoë. His parents took the two-year-old child back to the Vermont farm. As long as she could remember, Zoë had known that photograph and its story. Sometimes she thought she actually remembered walking in the park, hand in hand with her mother and father.

FIVE

Of all the rooms he loved in the British Embassy, this one he loved best. James locked the door behind him. He sat down at his uncluttered desk, fresh blotter in the outsize tooled-leather holder, narcissi blooming in an eighteenth-century Staffordshire jug. Morning's golden light filtered through the sash windows behind him.

He was an attractive, decent, highly intelligent man of forty, middle height, muscular, with pleasant features, and when he pressed his lips in disapproval of another's infractions it made his wife think of a schoolboy disappointed in the waywardness of the world around him. He'd been a senior boy at his school and he retained that sense of responsibility and honour and a certain priggishness. His ideal weekends were those spent at the wheel of his racing yacht in strong force gales on the Chesapeake Bay, one other man as crew, each knowing his life depended on the other, exultant in their control as they challenged wind and sea. Even James's fitness got on Jancie's nerves.

Unlocking a drawer, he took out the envelope and stared, mesmerised, at the letters in the corner: The Prime Minister. After a minute, he slipped out the letter and laid it flat. Chin in hands, he read it for the eighth time since he'd received it the day before. It was written in the Prime Minister's own hand.

My dear James,

I write this with a heavy heart. You will be hearing from the Foreign Secretary tomorrow. For the past two years you have been the most excellent of ambassadors –

everything I had hoped for when I offered you the post. But you will know that Jancie's reluctance to meet the obligations that go with the job has become too great an embarrassment to continue. I have decided to appoint a career diplomat as your successor. The deputy permanent secretary at the Foreign Office has agreed to take over the Washington post six weeks from today.

There will be no official announcement until you and I have agreed on one. I would like you to draft the wording, as I have been proud of your own achievements in Washington, and I want your departure to be a proud one.

As ever, Martin

The tears running down his face reached his hands still cupped beneath his chin. James sat back and took the neatly folded white handkerchief from the breast pocket of his jacket. It wouldn't do for his cuffs to get damp: Miles Brewster was due in half an hour. Opening the handkerchief wide, he held it against his face. His entire body shuddered and a single sob broke from his lips, but otherwise he was silent as the square of linen soaked up the tears.

When he removed the sodden handkerchief from his face to glance at his watch it was 11.20. Putting the letter back in the drawer, he turned the lock. In the small room behind panelled doors, he took care to keep his cuffs dry as he rinsed his face. Rapidly he patted his skin with a towel, and when he looked in the mirror, only his mouth showed the hurt. He lifted his chin. Then he took a clean handkerchief from the Queen Anne dwarf chest of drawers, folded its points, put it in his breast pocket and gave a final glance in the mirror. There he saw a boyish-looking clever man, impeccably turned out, a perfect British Ambassador to Washington.

*

Born and bred in Colorado, Jancie Wharton was a spunky television newscaster just starting to get ahead when she first met James. He was at Princeton for a term, lecturing on defence.

When they married, she moved to London and carved out a niche for herself as the BBC's only American anchor-woman. The Whartons' careers sat well together. Though she realised her love for James lacked the fire she read about, they had a good partnership. Then she got pregnant and gave up her career to be at home with the twins for their first five years. Just when she was to return to the BBC, James got the ambassadorship.

At first Jancie embraced the role of ambassadress with enthusiasm and grit and charm. But she had no previous experience of the constrictions of diplomatic life. After the first three hundred and sixty-five days of keeping to a rigid timetable of x, y, z, she woke one morning to the realisation that however glamorous her life might seem, being British Ambassadress meant no more than being James's appendage.

Her rebellion was fairly responsible at the start: she would get 'a migraine' (from which she had never suffered before) and would ask the wife of the number two at the Embassy to act as guide to the latest batch of Brits expecting a tour of Washington while their MP spouses engaged in weighty matters.

But then she fell in love with Simon Fleet, and her small rebellion turned into full-scale revolt. For the first time Jancie rode the rollercoaster of passionate love. Simon was spontaneous, outrageous, unconcerned about duty for its own sake, everything James was not. And Simon introduced her to sexuality she'd not experienced before. Her passion for him became adoration.

At charity balls she took the dance floor with Simon, oblivious to flash-bulbs and the tabloid photographs that followed. If he phoned at noon to ask her to meet him in half an hour, she had her secretary call her hostess and say the Ambassadress's migraine meant that sadly she could not attend that day's luncheon. When he appeared at a government reception, she at once abandoned her obligation to look after the visiting dignitary's wife, hanging on Simon's arm instead. Not only did her flagrant affair wound her husband's heart and mock his pride: he couldn't understand it.

Miles's Lincoln turned into the crescent of the front drive less than twelve hours after he and Marigold had left it. Having to break up his morning like this was a pain. Within the yawning hall the Ambassador's private secretary waited to escort him up one of the twin staircases beneath the flying arch. Entering the library, they found the Ambassador standing with his back to them, looking out the window at trees whose green was beginning to parch. When he turned, the sadness stamped on his face took Miles aback.

'I don't wish to be disturbed while Mr Brewster is here,' James said to the secretary.

They took facing sofas, and James looked away in silence. When his eyes at last met Miles's, James gave a horribly twisted smile. Quickly looking away again, he gazed half-seeing at the dark wood panelling with its carvings symbolising power, knowledge, wealth. As so often during the last two years, his eyes moved to the circular niches which held nothing – no objects of any kind. The architect had evidently liked emptiness, but the vacant niches had always given James an uneasy feeling, a sense of foreboding, he realised in retrospect.

He began to speak in a jerky monotone, very different from his usual fluency. 'I've been recalled. I got the Prime Minister's letter yesterday morning. In the overnight bag,' he added, as if every detail mattered. He handed the letter to Miles.

After he'd read it, Miles put it on the table between them.

'I can't sit on it for ever,' James went on. He looked desperate. 'It's bound to leak out. I find it hard to think of any form of words that will do. Obviously it will be seen as a great humiliation.'

Again he broke off, his eyes returning to the empty niches.

'If you have any ideas, Miles, for a form of words to lessen the humiliation, I'd be glad to hear them.' Even though his hair was neatly brushed, his suit impeccable, he seemed dishevelled.

'Does Jancie know?' Miles asked.

'I told her last night – after everyone left. She began to cry.' He talked in the same monotone. 'She couldn't speak. She sobbed as if her heart was breaking. For what her actions have cost me? Probably. But mostly, I imagine, because my being recalled to London means she will be separated from her darling.'

He gave a short low laugh like a dry sob.

'Look, James,' Miles said, 'give me a little time to think about it. I'll draft something in the car on my way back to the *Express*. I'll call you, and we'll sharpen it up together. As soon as you and the Prime Minister have settled on the final form of the announcement, the *Express* will run the story. It will make crystal clear that when you depart, Washington and Britain will be the losers.'

He got up to go. As they walked to the library door Miles said: 'When you've just been mugged, you don't feel much like looking ahead. Even so, have you thought what you might do next?'

'Going back to journalism is an obvious possibility –

but it seems rather mundane after this job. That's the trouble.'

'Well, think of a few options. I'll see they're worked into the piece the *Express* runs once the official announcement is ready.'

Miles didn't need to spell out that every word of this particular story would be scrutinised by him before it went to press.

The Jaguar used by the British Ambassadress pulled over to the kerb of Pennsylvania Avenue, coming to a stop at the glass canopy of the Willard Hotel. The doorman stepped forward smartly to open the car door, and Jancie hurried into the grandiose lobby. Her curls bobbed on the shoulders of her pink linen jacket, nipped in at the waist to emphasise her hour-glass figure.

But her expression betrayed her anxiety as she looked around the marble-columned lobby with its big red rugs spread luxuriously on a mosaic floor. A few of the English oak chairs and red leather sofas were occupied, but the person she sought wasn't there. She went over to the concierge behind a marble desk so long it made Jancie think of an ocean liner.

'Has anyone asked for Mrs Wharton? I was to meet Mr Simon Fleet here at three. I'm a few minutes late.'

'No, madam, Mr Fleet has not been in this afternoon. Would you care to sit down and wait?'

'I'll have a look in the bar,' she replied.

A quick glance into the perpetual semi-darkness of the Round Robin Bar revealed that the politicians' favourite meeting place was empty apart from a barman polishing glasses. At this hour, journalists and lobbyists had to go to Capitol Hill if they wanted to see a politician.

Returning to the lobby, Jancie settled herself on the circular velvet buttoned settee encircling a gargantuan flower arrangement at the room's centre. Facing the front door where Simon could not possibly miss her, she crossed her legs prettily and composed her face. God knows she had enough to think about. She would never forgive herself for what she'd done to James. How could she make up for it? In six weeks she would have to say goodbye to Simon. For ever? No. Again no. Perhaps she could stay in Washington for a little while after James went back. He might actually like to be on his own while he sorted out his future. But where could she stay? With Simon? Her heart leapt: he was here.

The man who strolled through the Willard's front door was of middle height, slightly overweight and looking younger than his thirty-five years, with a mass of butter-yellow curls cut short. His face was full and the plump lips gave him a puckish appearance which a number of women found intriguing.

'Sorry I'm late, my love,' he said. His English accent had been slightly modified by his six years as a journalist in Washington. 'My lunch with the bloody Energy Secretary went on longer than I expected. Where shall we go? I've got to get back to the paper soon, alas, but you said it was urgent.'

'I need to talk with you where we can't be overheard,' Jancie said. She had already got to her feet and was standing so near him as to be almost touching him.

'Let's have a look in the Nest,' he said, taking her arm proprietorially. 'If no one's there we can treat it as our own nest for two.'

No one else was in the pretty room, and they sat at a table in the corner by the carved Victorian fireplace. Mirrored walls made it easy to see if anyone else arrived, but only a waiter came in to take their order. Simon had a brandy, Jancie nothing.

'Something horrible has happened. James got a letter yesterday from the Prime Minister. We've got to go back.'

'For how long?' asked Simon.

'For ever,' she said, her mouth trembling.

'What's happened, my lovely?' he asked, putting a hand under the table to pat her thigh.

She spoke haltingly as she tried to keep herself under control. 'The Prime Minister said I've failed to meet the obligations that go with the job. He said I'm an embarrassment.' Tears started down her face. Simon fished in his pocket for a handkerchief, but she found one first.

'Poor, poor darling,' he said, meaning it, yet at the same time he could almost feel his nose twitch at the excitement of having a Washington scoop. 'Silly Prime Minister,' he said, tenderly stroking her thigh. 'I don't suppose you brought his letter with you?'

'James showed it to me and then locked it away again. But I can remember it. Every word of it. How can I ever forget?' Her mouth trembled again.

'Tell me what that jerk of a prime minister said.' Simon brought his hand up to stroke Jancie's cheek. 'God, I hate politicians,' he added, the last remark half true, half false. 'Is James upset?'

'Devastated. We had a dinner party last night. Zoë was there. Things were strained enough by the hostility between Miles Brewster and Gerald Scrope. I thought they'd come to blows. I didn't yet know about the letter, but James had to get through the evening knowing he'd been dumped. He said it was the worst evening he's ever had in his entire life.'

'When will it be announced?'

'Not till James and the Prime Minister agree what should be said. The deputy permanent secretary at the

Foreign Office has already been told to take over in six weeks. You can imagine how much the wording of the announcement means to James. Poor guy.'

'What does he want it to say?'

'He's so shattered he can't think straight. He asked Miles to come and see him this afternoon and give some advice.'

'Fuck it.'

'Fuck what?'

'I must get back to the paper.'

'But what am I going to do?' asked Jancie. 'Am I meant to leave you for ever – just like that?'

'Listen, sweet darling,' Simon said, bending over her. 'There's nothing I want more this minute than to take you to bed and hold you in my arms for ever. But I've got to get back to the *Express*. It won't help matters if we all get fired.'

Jancie saw a chink of light. 'If you got fired you could come back to England too. Any London editor would give his eyes to get you on his staff.'

'I've got to go, my sweet. You stay here until you feel better. I'll phone you later.'

'When?'

'As soon as I can.'

He leant over and wiped away a fresh tear with the fingers of one hand. At the door of the Nest he turned back and blew her a long kiss.

As he crossed the lobby, his expression hardened into concentration. Could he write the story in such a way that it would not be spiked by the boss? Up until now, the Whartons' friendship with Miles Brewster had produced nothing but jewels for Simon Fleet, jewels of inside information which Jancie gladly offered to her lover. But now the Brewster–Wharton friendship could cost him his scoop. Yet you never knew. As he often said, usually to excuse a lapse of his own: 'We live in an uncertain world.'

When his taxi pulled away from the Willard, he'd already taken out his notebook to scribble down everything Jancie had told him about the Whartons' fall from grace. Here and there Simon added phrases of his own.

It didn't occur to him that he was betraying his lover. He saw the story purely in terms of a Washington–London exclusive, though as the taxi turned into M Street and drew up in front of the ten-storey building which housed the *Express*, a poetic thought brought a smile to his lips. There was something romantic, almost fated, about his being the one to break the news that the British Ambassador had been sacked because of his wife's dereliction of duty.

SIX

Simon was entitled to a glassed-off room, visible from the newsroom yet apart from it. In charge of the paper's foreign correspondents, he also wrote articles of his own. Passing his overworked secretary at the desk outside his door, he blew her a kiss. 'Has Downing Street been on the line?'

'Not yet,' she replied, uncertain whether Simon was teasing her or really was expecting a call from the British Prime Minister.

'Unless it's Downing Street or Baghdad or the Quai d'Orsay, I don't want to be disturbed until I finish my piece,' he said, and closed his door behind him, slinging his jacket on the sofa.

Like the man, his environment appeared more disorderly than it was. The sofa was strewn with half a dozen international editions of Europe's English-language press. When it came to European news, the time difference worked in favour of Washington journalists, though it was a bastard when events unfolded on the west coast just when Washington was thinking of going to bed.

Reading through his notes, Simon underlined passages with a red pen. For a few minutes he sat with his elbows on his desk, his round chin with its dimple cupped in his hands, gazing unseeing at the blank screen before him. It was when he put his fingers on the keyboard that his adrenalin surged. The piece almost wrote itself.

'Washington will be shocked to learn that the British Ambassador, Mr James Wharton, has received a letter from Prime Minister Martin Mather abruptly recalling him from the most prestigious post in Embassy Row. His successor will be the present deputy permanent secretary at the Foreign Office. The Ambassador is understood to be devastated.

'After ten years as the distinguished defence correspondent of the London *Times*, James Wharton was hand-picked for the Washington job by the Prime Minister. Not only has he been a popular figure in the capital during his two years here, as a defence expert he has had much closer links with the Pentagon than are usual for a diplomat.

'It is understood that the Prime Minister wrote his letter with a heavy heart. For he has the highest admiration for Mr Wharton. But it appears that the Prime Minister believes Mrs Jancie Wharton is spending too much time on her own affairs instead of playing the role of British Ambassadress in the manner that tradition requires.

'This verdict will sadden many of the Colorado-born Ambassadress's friends in the capital. Before the birth of her twin children, she was a successful television newscaster, first in America, then Britain. Like her husband, she is a popular figure in Washington.

'Unlike him, she has an unconventional style and outlook, and it is this unconventionality that has led to the humiliating termination of the Whartons' posting here. She has unusually close contacts with key journalists in the capital, and the Whartons' departure will mean a two-way loss for the important relationship between the British Embassy and the Washington press.'

He flicked the screen back to the top of the piece and read down it, smiling at his tact in speaking of Jancie's 'own affairs' and her 'close contacts with key journalists'. Using the plural should keep him from being accused of slyly trumpeting her affair with him. That should do the trick with the big white chief upstairs.

Waiting for the piece to print out – the editor liked to read a story in hard copy first – he opened the bottom drawer of his desk and took out a file marked '*Amigas*'. Simon had picked up a smattering of Spanish from Washington's ever-growing Hispanic population – chicanos who came east to work in service jobs, Puerto Ricans and Cubans and Peruvians who came north, some of them illegal immigrants, the luckier ones qualifying for government employment. From his '*Amigas*' file he took out a snapshot of Jancie.

She was wearing a bikini and was perched on the seat of his motorcycle. Simon sometimes used it to show off to his weekend hosts – so long as they lived within seventy miles of the capital, anything further being too wearing however much Simon enjoyed the effect created when he zoomed up to their front door. In the picture Jancie was laughing, one hand held high in a thumbs-up gesture. He scribbled her name on the back, along with the approximate date when they'd gone on his bike to the Eastern Shore of Maryland. He would slip it in the picture desk's file on the Whartons once his piece was OK'd by the editor. Only those in the know would guess it was Simon's bike. He loved presenting a story at two levels – one for the general public, the other for politicians and journalists and society hostesses already in the know.

'I'll be with the editor,' he said to his secretary. Through the glass wall of the editor's office, he saw Bob Short was alone. Simon held one hand aloft with his copy. Short looked up and nodded him in.

'I've got a great scoop for you,' said Simon.

Automatically Short glanced at the clock on the wall: 5.15. Plenty of time for the first edition. He began reading the copy as Simon settled himself on the sofa.

'Holy cow!' Short exclaimed when he'd read the first

sentence. 'How the hell did you get hold of this?' he asked admiringly. As soon as he put the question, he knew the answer. Everyone on the capital's network knew about Jancie Wharton's affair with Simon Fleet. Short's eyes glinted as he read on. Yet gradually his brows pulled together and his mouth set in a thin line. Finishing the piece he put it on his desk and looked at Simon.

'There are difficulties,' he said.

'What do you mean?' demanded Simon.

'There are difficulties,' Short repeated. 'I'll have to think about it. Are you going to be around the office?'

'Oh for Chrissake, Bob. You've got on your desk a story that will make every other newspaper editor puke with envy. And you say there are difficulties. What difficulties?'

Short said nothing. They both knew what difficulties: Miles Brewster's personal friendship with James Wharton and Jancie. Anyone who mattered could read between the lines of Simon's story. Miles would never sanction it. But what editor would admit he censored a news story because the paper's owner didn't want to see it printed? Short drew in his lips again. And most journalists, goddammit, had the tact – cunning, if you wish – not to try and force an admission from their editor, Short thought sullenly.

While Simon had more than his share of cunning, he also had the cockiness of a journalist whose skill in nosing out a story guaranteed a job with any newspaper he wanted. And you never knew: if he pushed the editor hard enough, Short might – just might – not clear the story with the big white chief. Or the big white chief might have other things on his mind, or get stuck in an elevator and no one know where he was until the first edition had come out. Simon could bear it if his scoop was pulled by Miles after the first edition, for other newspapers would treat that as a further story in itself, and the more Simon's name was spread around, the better it suited him.

'Listen, Bob,' he said airily. 'I know that you know about my, um, friendship with Jancie Wharton. Did I let that friendship gag me? No. I've given you what you prize: an exclusive. And this particular exclusive will bring the *Express* another hundred thousand readers. Why should you sit on it?'

A deep flush had spread up Short's face. 'I told you. I'll think about it. But for now will you just fuck off and let me get on with my goddam editorial on Arabi and the goddam arms embargo.'

A quarter of an hour later, Short put on his jacket, folded Simon's story and put it in his pocket, then stepped into his secretaries' office to say he would be upstairs in Corporate.

On both sides of M Street, office buildings rose to the maximum height permitted. Breaking their ranks in calm defiance of the developers' lust stood an early-nineteenth-century frame house, painted Williamsburg blue, three storeys beneath a slate roof, its dark-green shutters kept open to the world hurrying past. What had a century and a quarter earlier been acres of garden with a paddock and orchard was now reduced to a fringe of grass and azaleas and an ancient magnolia whose waxy leaves shaded the front steps.

From his windows on the top floor Miles often looked down on this serene relic from another era. It was the kind of house one of his forebears might have lived in. Occasionally he toyed with the idea of asking the owners if they would sell it to him. At the end of his day, he'd be able to leave the *Express*, cross the street and at once be in that peaceful clapboard house. Not that Miles left his work behind at the end of any day: it was as much a part of him as his lungs. Nor did he imagine Marigold would be overjoyed by his fantasy of stepping out of the limelight for an evening into the calm that lingered from a bygone world.

When Bob Short arrived, the sun had dipped behind the tall buildings opposite, but at that moment it reappeared where the phalanx of cement was broken by the clapboard house, a blood orange flooding the walls of Miles's room with ruddy light. The furniture – bleached mahogany, leather soft as kid – was handsome, comfortable, expensive. Yet the general effect was curiously spartan. Above all, it was impersonal – until you saw the two paintings on otherwise bare walls: a winter landscape by Winslow Homer, and a sensual self-portrait by the icon of Mexican women, Frida Kahlo. It was as if Miles had decided to allow nothing, except the pictures, to reveal anything of his inner self.

He left his desk to sit on one of the sofas either side of a marble coffee table. Bob Short took the other. He came straight to the point.

'Fleet has turned in a first-class exclusive. Every other editor would give his mother to have it.' He paused for only a moment. 'The British Ambassador has been fired.'

Short had the impression that a flicker of red flashed for an instant across Miles's eyes, but it was gone so fast that he put it down to a trick of the setting sun.

'Have you brought it with you?'

Miles read through the story twice. Then he handed it back. His expression revealed nothing.

'We can't print that.' He said 'we' as if his decision was a joint one with his editor.

Short was silent.

'Look, we both know Fleet's source for his story,'

Miles said. 'I'm not going to use the confidences of a love-struck woman to jump the gun on the announcement of Wharton's dismissal and further screw up his life.'

That's when Short realised Miles already knew the Ambassador had been fired. What he couldn't guess was that Miles had already phoned James with a form of words which would minimise the humiliation and maximise his job prospects. Nor did Miles tell his editor – he didn't need to – that when the *Express* did run the story, it would be Miles Brewster, not Simon Fleet, who would determine its tone.

Short picked up the piece and put it back in his pocket. 'I don't think Fleet will take it well.'

Miles got to his feet. 'That's Fleet's problem.'

By the time the editor got back to the humming animation of the newsroom, he had almost convinced himself that it was *his* decision not to run Simon Fleet's story.

Apart from the initial flash of rage at Fleet's exploitation of Jancie, Miles felt no emotion at gagging the story. Even had Fleet obtained it by less contemptible means, Miles wouldn't have run it. The British Ambassador had been fired for personal reasons. No great issue was at stake. What the hell was the point of the risk and stress of owning these papers if he couldn't tell his editors how to handle a personal matter?

Before Short had reached the newsroom, Miles was already absorbed in his survey of the newspaper market in Britain. Highlighted in red was the *London Dispatch*.

Zoë printed out her story and switched off her computer. Those coming up to their own deadlines stayed concentrated on their screens. Others, waiting for the sub-editors to tell them how many lines had to be cut to fit the new layout or how many lines must be added, watched Zoë as she sauntered towards the features editor's office, her dark hair pulled back in a ponytail. She was wearing a narrow black suit, its long jacket unbuttoned over a white shirt whose severity made others think about what it covered.

Simon was standing amidst the news desks when she passed, his face petulant when he said to her: 'The man upstairs has forgotten how to run a newspaper. You'll have to use your cutest female wiles if you want to get your story into tomorrow's paper.' Political correctness was not Simon's scene.

'Bye, bye, Simon,' she replied without lingering. He was harmless enough generally, but she resented his hold over Jancie: everyone except Jancie knew he was only using her, and even she must sometimes have a glimmering, Zoë suspected. She stopped to chat for a moment with the features editor's secretary and then took her copy into his office.

He read it while she waited. 'Good stuff. Put it into the system. You'll stick around, won't you, in case the lawyers burst into tears.'

Back at her desk, Zoë was keying her story into the system when she felt someone's presence behind her. She turned to find Simon grinning. 'Just having a little read over your shoulder,' he said. 'You have a nice way with words, Miss Hare.' He gave a teasing little bow. 'Or do you prefer Ms? I never can remember.'

Zoë finished her keying in and switched off the screen. Simon's archness annoyed her.

'I'm going out for an hour to get a drink and a sandwich,' he said. 'Will you do me the honour of joining me?'

'I can't, Simon. I have to wait for the lawyers to pick over my piece.'

'Shall I tell you, lovely one, which piece of you I would adore to pick over?'

Zoë turned back to her desk.

'Listen, Zoë. We need to talk. I know something about Jancie and James that you should know.'

She faced him again. 'I don't want to talk about Jancie.'

As she said it, her face was expressionless. It made Simon think of one of those paintings by Marie Laurencin – the almond eyes and lips and tendrils at the temples carefully delineated, with the rest of the oval not drawn in at all.

'OK. Don't talk about her,' he said. 'Don't say a word. But I'm telling you now, something most unfortunate has happened to your chums the Whartons. I'll wait until you get the green light from the lawyers. We ought to have a drink.' He ambled back to his office.

Soon after seven they left the *Express* together. Even when irritated by Simon she loved early evening in Washington, rush-hour traffic over, sidewalks nearly empty. As they made for a bar around the corner in 14th Street, she glanced across the street at the clapboard house and smiled.

They took their drinks to a booth. The tinted wall light made Simon's lips redder than usual.

'James Wharton has been recalled to London,' he said.

'*What?*'

'Because of Jancie's behaviour.'

She put her elbows on the table, looking down at her drink in silence. Simon couldn't help being pleased at the effect he'd created.

At last she asked: 'Did Jancie tell you?'

'Who else? And the editor has been told not to run the story.'

'You mean to say you wrote it up?'

'What am I hired for? To get the Washington scoop of the year and put it in a lace handkerchief under my pillow?'

'Did she know you were going to write it up?'

'What did she think a journalist would do with that information?'

Zoë didn't answer. Debating ethics with Simon was a waste of energy. There were other points to think about.

'Here's an exclusive that Washington would lap up,' he went on, 'and the fucking editor spikes it.' He gave a harsh laugh. 'Or rather, that tawny-eyed bastard I have never learned to love ordered the editor to spike it.'

He gave her a furious look.

'Have you ever noticed, Zoë, that when it comes to the crunch, the true American gent will always protect his fellow gent – even though he owns the *Express* and should put its independence first?' Simon was a great believer in trotting out the ethical argument when it was in his interest to do so.

'How's Jancie taking it?' asked Zoë.

'Tearfully. She'll be telling you soon enough, I expect.'

He paused for a fraction of a moment before going on:

'By the way, I hear you were at the British Embassy dinner party last night. Jancie mentioned that our boss nearly came to fisticuffs with Lord Scrope. What the hell went on between them?'

Zoë told him. Whatever her distaste for Simon's treatment of Jancie, she had the journalist's pleasure in chatter with another journalist. Also, she didn't mind showing off a little that she was invited to the dinner.

'Ostensibly it sprang from Miles Brewster learning that before he'd even made a bid for the *London Dispatch*, Lord Scrope decided to block him by putting in a bid himself. But if it hadn't been that, they would have found something else to go to war over.' She shrugged. 'People meet somebody and take a like or dislike. It's chemical. Then they rationalize it. The chemistry between those two could have blown the lab sky-high.'

Simon ordered another whisky. Zoë sipped the one she had.

'Lord Scrope didn't say where he was staying, did he?' he asked.

'Not to me.' She looked at her watch. She was meeting a girlfriend for dinner at a fish restaurant across the Potomac. 'Look, I've got to go, Simon.'

'I'm going back to the paper,' he said, drinking off the rest of his whisky.

On the sidewalk they went their separate ways. Brooding about what had befallen the Whartons, Zoë never gave another thought to Simon or his interests.

SEVEN

Lord Scrope was hunched at his desk on the top floor of his famous British newspaper, the *Javelin*. The enormous room was deep wine-red throughout, three walls lined with burgundy flock, the fourth made of glass. He sat in a heavily carved Jacobean chair. He was engrossed in the file spread before him.

When Gerald Scrope took over the *Javelin*, the balance of power in the British media lunged further to the right. Self-made, he never questioned that it's every man for himself. From day one, he saw the *Javelin* as his private arsenal to assault the enemy – be it American trade restrictions on electronics imports, or Britain's left-wing opposition party, or some hapless individual who incurred his wrath. The aggressive support he gave the Tory government had been rewarded by a previous prime minister with a life peerage.

In America his flagship was the *New York Mail*. Just when Americans thought they had him pegged – thuggish lord pushing me-first values – he bought *The Monocle*, the most celebrated glossy literary weekly in America and one of the nation's cherished institutions. To astonishment and wide relief, he didn't tamper with it. You could never be absolutely certain what Gerald Scrope would do.

The keystone of Scrope Opportunities Ltd was his electronics empire. A multimillion conglomerate, it began as a garage business. His media chain came later. For years he ran the whole of his empire from a flashy office building, Scrope Tower, on the north bank of the River Thames.

Then it took his fancy to move his headquarters across the river to the *Javelin* building on the south bank. He'd been born and bred south of the river, in Wandsworth. Scrope Tower continued to house the myriad offices of his empire, but Gerald now ran it all from his suite atop the *Javelin*.

'Your guest, Chairman.'

An open-faced, loose-gaited American was shown in. This was Speers Jackson's first visit to Gerald's London office. Normally they met at Scrope Southwestern's plant in Texas, not far from the Mexican border.

Gerald gave a curt nod of welcome and got up to come round his desk and shake hands.

'I've left orders I don't want any calls,' he said, swivelling on the balls of his feet and marching ahead without further effort at conviviality.

The dining-room was the same wine-red. Silver trophies gleamed on an outsize dark oak sideboard. The Jacobean period suited Gerald: Georgian furniture would have been too elegant, too delicate for the electric force that charged the room as soon as he entered it.

He stopped by the sideboard, pointing to a trophy shaped like a silver whippet. 'That was the start – before all them.' He swept his arm proprietorially over the array of honours garnered from government and various bodies in return for services rendered. Had some other services been publicly acknowledged on the Jacobean sideboard or anywhere else, it would have caused international scandal.

Swivelling again, Gerald strode to a dining-table long enough to seat fourteen people. Only the chair at the head had arms, and behind it stood the Chairman's butler. Gerald flung himself down, Jackson taking the place at his right.

Without preliminaries Gerald said: 'I'm about to step

up my campaign to replace the Prime Minister with a man who sees the world like it is, not like some prissy schoolboy's pipe dream. The Defence Secretary. Once we get rid of that limp sausage at 10 Downing Street and put Alan Rawlston in his place, you'll see Britain's arms embargo on Arabi lifted within the month. Do you know how much bloody money my British electronics lose because of this fucking embargo?'

Speers Jackson said nothing.

'If Britain had a guy with balls running the show, you'd hear no more sanctimonious claptrap, Mr Jackson, about how' – and here Gerald mimicked the Prime Minister's recent statement from the steps of Number Ten – '"history will judge us harshly if we allow nuclear components to fall into the hands of the dictator of Arabi". The Right Honourable Martin Mather's own Sermon from the Mount. Jesus.'

Jackson gave an amiable chuckle.

'I've been talking to people in Washington, Mr Jackson. So've you. Do you get the feeling the President's going to lift the arms embargo on Arabi, whatever the British Prime Minister thinks?'

'No.'

Gerald swore.

'Look, Lord Scrope. Everybody knows Arabi's dictator is still our best bulwark against Islamic fundamentalists, but we can't send him sophisticated weapons openly. Congress wouldn't buy it. The American people would be outraged. Each night they see Arabi soldiers herding families into barbed-wire compounds while the dictator thumbs his nose at the Great Satan of the West. Hell, we're teetering on the edge of war with Arabi. How could the President possibly justify lifting the arms embargo?'

'Easy. Do what the Frogs do. The French don't go in

for this bogus sentimentality. They know if they don't trade with their enemies, someone else will. Every French soldier knows he may face enemy fire from weapons made in France. The British used to be like that – practical. It's only lately they've come down with this morality bug. They must have caught it from America. Americans have always had this goo-goo thing about morality – even when they were sticking bayonets in Vietnamese nuns.'

Abruptly he threw one hand in the air and snapped his fingers. Two waiters appeared with dishes of thick-sliced roast lamb and a harvest of fresh vegetables. The butler stepped to the sideboard where a bottle of Bordeaux had been decanted, and offered it to the Chairman to taste. Rejecting the ritual with an impatient shake of the head, Gerald said magisterially: 'I take few things on trust, Mr Jackson, but I make an exception when it's Cos d'Estournel 1961 – a gift from the French foreign minister.'

He waved a hand, and his butler poured out the wine.

'Drink up, Mr Jackson. Enjoy it. When a foreign minister sends wine to Gerald Scrope, he never sends less than a case.' He paused to indicate his next words were to be studied: 'Fruits of the vineyard go to them that reach up and grab.'

Jackson chuckled and helped himself to redcurrant sauce.

Gerald ate steadily until his plate was empty, then pushed it away.

'You want anything else?' he asked.

'I wouldn't mind a cup of coffee,' replied Jackson.

They moved back to Gerald's office to have their coffee, sitting in armchairs as they went over problems Jackson was facing at Scrope Southwestern near Austin, Texas.

A nervous personal assistant appeared at the door: 'I

felt I'd better disturb you, Chairman. The foreign editor of the *Washington Express* is on the phone. He says it's urgent he speak to you. He says to tell you it concerns Miles Brewster.'

'I'll talk to him now. What's his fucking name?'

'Simon Fleet.'

A red light flashed on one of the platoon of phones. Gerald picked it up.

'Yeah?'

'It's Simon Fleet. I'm foreign editor of the *Washington Express*.'

'So?'

At the line's other end Simon tensed at the arrogant monosyllable.

'I'm sorry not to have met you when you were in Washington earlier this week, Lord Scrope. I've got a deal to propose to you.'

Gerald didn't answer. He was lighting a cigar.

'Lord Scrope? Are you there?'

'Lots of people propose deals, Mr Fleet. Very few of them appeal to me. What are you selling?'

'Is this conversation private?'

'I've got where I've got by keeping conversations private, Mr Fleet.'

Jackson's blue eyes crinkled at the corners.

'You might say I'm selling Miles Brewster,' said Simon.

Exhaling slowly, Gerald watched the smoke thin until it disappeared.

'Lord Scrope? Are you there?'

'Where do you think I am, for Chrissake? What you got on Miles Brewster that might interest me?'

'I've got hold of a story that will be hot in Washington and London. Miles Brewster has gagged it because the story involves a friend.'

'So what you got in mind, Mr Fleet?'

'If I sell you the story – and believe me, Lord Scrope, you will want to buy it – everyone will know it came from me. There's nobody else it could come from. I'd have to clear my desk at the *Express* within the hour. And I'm one of their highest paid journalists.'

Gerald reached over to tap his ash against the side of a Lalique crystal bowl.

'Lord Scrope?'

'Yeah?'

'The story I'm selling has two parts. The story itself. And how Miles Brewster suppressed it.'

'I got the picture, Mr Fleet. In exchange, you want a job on the *Javelin*. If I like the story enough – both parts of the story – I can give you a job with ten per cent over the salary you're getting at present. We don't need to fuss about the details now. But don't take it into your nut to try and up the ante. Only an asshole would try to con me into thinking his pay at the *Washington Express* was higher than it actually is. I'm sure you are not an asshole, Mr Fleet.'

'You had dinner at the British Embassy two nights ago, Lord Scrope. Nobody there knew, except the Ambassador, that he's been sacked by his friend the Prime Minister. A government announcement will be made any day now, and we need to get in there first.'

'I'm going to bring my personal assistant into this conversation, Mr Fleet.'

Gerald jabbed a button and his PA came on the line.

Gerald said to Simon: 'I have got my assistant on the line and when I finish, you will dictate to him the story that Miles Brewster has gagged. You will then write a second story – maybe three hundred words – about why Brewster gagged it. You will then dictate your second story to my PA. After that you and I will talk again. I'll hand you over now to my PA.'

He put down the phone.

For a minute or two he lay back in the armchair, his eyes fixed on the column of smoke rising from his cigar. Then he hunched forward again.

'You were saying,' he said to Speers Jackson.

EIGHT

The first item on the morning news was the President's careful statement about the dictator of Arabi's latest threat. Zoë was leaning over, brushing her hair upside down before pulling it into a ponytail, when the second item began:

'It has been reported in the London *Javelin* that the British Ambassador to Washington, Mr James Wharton, has been recalled by Prime Minister Martin Mather and will return to London in six weeks' time when he will be succeeded by the present deputy permanent secretary at the Foreign Office.'

Zoë didn't move, the brush poised in mid-air.

'According to the *Javelin*, the reason for Mr Wharton's dismissal from the number one diplomatic post is the unconventional conduct of his wife, Mrs Jancie Wharton. The Prime Minister's office in Downing Street, as well as the Foreign Office and the British Embassy in Washington, have declined to comment on the report.'

'The *Javelin* also alleges that Mr Miles Brewster, chairman of Brewster Media Corporation and owner of the *Washington Express*, personally intervened to stop Mr Wharton's dismissal being revealed in the *Express*. Mr Brewster has declined to comment on the report.'

When the third news item started, Zoë stood upright, throwing her hair back, and caught a glimpse of her angry face in the mirror, the hair standing out from it like some exotic wild animal's.

Half an hour later she strode into the *Express* newsroom and headed for the foreign editor's office. Through the glass wall she saw the soles of Simon's shoes propped on his desk and the top of his head over the newspaper he was reading as he lounged in his chair. Marching in, she spotted the *Javelin* atop European papers strewn on the sofa. She snatched it up and shook the pages furiously into place.

The story and pictures covered half the front page. One photo was of the Whartons in evening dress with the President and First Lady. The other showed Jancie in a bikini on a motorcycle, and its caption read: 'The British Ambassador's American wife on an unofficial weekend.'

Simon watched Zoë over his newspaper as she read, her face tight. The bones of the story were the same as his original piece – much expanded with anecdotes about James's schooldays at Eton and Jancie's earlier career as a newscaster. But someone at the *Javelin* had put an altogether new gloss on the story. It was being used as a stick to beat the British Prime Minister.

'This petulant and wholly unjustified action by the Prime Minister will deepen concern already felt by those close to him. One colleague said: "The sacking of the Whartons is another instance of increasing swings of mood in a Prime Minister who has lost his way. The sooner Martin Mather resigns, the better for Britain."'

Zoë gave a wry smile. Respected journalists often quoted an unnamed source so accurately that sophisticated readers could guess who it was. Shameless journalists used the 'unnamed source' to invent a quote to suit the editor's and owner's purpose (and they usually found their jobs short-lived, for once no one would trust them their usefulness came to an end). Everyone knew the *Javelin* went in for both practices.

She read on:

'Another source close to the Prime Minister said: "Martin Mather's appointment of James Wharton to the all-important Washington post was widely hailed as an imaginative and shrewd decision. Wharton's defence expertise made him the right person at the right time to argue Britain's defence policy with the world's only superpower. Now he has been abruptly recalled – on the shoddy excuse that Mrs Jancie Wharton spent insufficient afternoons serving tea and buttered toast to politicians' spouses. This capricious decision on Mr Mather's part can only raise further doubts about the Prime Minister's state of mind."'

Then came the attack on Miles:

'A further strange factor was the role played by the chairman of Brewster Media Corporation, Mr Miles Brewster, who owns the *Washington Express*. When the foreign editor of the *Express* learned of Mr Wharton's dismissal, due to take effect in six weeks' time, he wrote an exclusive account of it for the paper. Mr Brewster ordered this report to be suppressed. He has refused to give an explanation for his conduct.'

Simon had laid down his paper and sat with arms folded, eyes amused as he watched Zoë's expression of cynicism deepen.

Immediately after the story, a single paragraph was printed in bold type, a device the *Javelin* sometimes used to juxtapose editorial comment with a supposedly factual report.

'Miles Brewster is given to drawing veils over his past. But this time his cover-up stands revealed. Britons will want to know whether this blatant example of a proprietor interfering with the freedom of the press will militate against Mr Brewster should he try to exercise his unhealthy influence on the British press. It is believed he wants to take over the *London Dispatch*.'

Zoë grimaced when she read 'his unhealthy influence'. How much of the gloss put on Simon's piece had been directed by Gerald Scrope? And what was this about drawing veils over the past and cover-ups? Was that a reference to the car accident in Mexico? She resented the attack on Miles.

When Simon saw she'd finished, he grinned and said: 'Oh ye of little faith. There's nothing in that story that could damage Jancie. And it's a positive paean of praise for James. I wonder how the *Javelin* got hold of it.'

'I didn't realise you were acquainted with faith, Simon. And your handprints are all over the basic story.'

Zoë was standing with one hand on her hip.

'But I agree, Jancie comes out of it pretty well – apart from the innuendo under that picture of the bike. The Prime Minister and Miles Brewster have been made the culprits. Quite effective, in its fashion.'

Turning to go, she added acidly:

'I wonder where the *Javelin* got that cute picture of Jancie on your bike. Any ideas, Simon?'

By noon the newsroom was filling up and Zoë was standing at the file – the long raised shelf where newspapers were clamped in separate files. As she skimmed through them, another journalist at the file dug her in the ribs. She looked around. Half the newsroom was watching Simon stroll nonchalantly towards the editor's office. By then most of them had read one of the increasingly battered copies of the *Javelin*.

Ten minutes later, Simon sauntered back to his own office and began to clear his desk. From time to time he came out to chat with colleagues, smiling as if he hadn't a care in the world. When he stopped at Zoë's desk he said:

'They can't prove that story came from me. And I can't be bothered to go through a long legal song and dance about unfair dismissal. So we've settled for a year's pay for my contract being terminated without notice.'

Suddenly his expression was surly.

'Miles Brewster will regret getting rid of the best foreign editor this paper ever had,' he said. 'Everyone knows I can unearth whatever it is that people want to conceal. If I put my mind to it, I could throw light on Miles Brewster's past – just like that!' He gave an imperious snap of the fingers. 'I'll phone you next week. We ought to have dinner. *Hasta mañana, amiga.*'

Back in his office, he continued collecting the files he wanted to take with him.

Where the sierras march south above Saltillo, skinny goats – *cabrito* – grazed on sparse hard grass on the upper slopes. Further down mesquite grew thick and cattle fed on it. A rough turning led into a red dirt road which wound across a butte. A quarter of a mile along it stood two adobe buildings, long, with corrugated tin roofs. Beyond was the house, painted white, its roof made of red clay tiles. Clustered around the doorway, gushing up to the window above, were the vivid purplish-red bracts of bougainvillaea.

The Lopez house was built traditionally around an open courtyard where the shadow of a mountain rising above kept the afternoon sun at bay. A woman in a bleached linen dress lay on a swinging settee. Cushions along the back were the colour of burnt sienna. More cushions, stitched with bright colours, were piled against one end, and these propped up the woman as she read. Her hair was braided and twisted atop her head like a coronet of polished jet, and the delicate face suggested the innocence of a Mexican convent girl rather than a woman in her late thirties. It could have been the absence of the marks of time which gave the impression that she lived an internal life. She reached down to the courtyard's packed clay floor and gave a shove to make the settee begin its rhythmic swing again.

From within the house a woman appeared carrying a wooden tray of hot chocolate and *bizcochos* made with sugar-cane and shaped into small pyramids. Putting the tray alongside the settee, she helped the woman lying there to sit higher against the cushions.

Next a neat-limbed monkey danced up, small and brown, with honey-coloured eyes and a snowy muzzle below a perky mantle of ginger hair that swept back from the brows. With an elegant little leap it joined the woman on the settee. Laying aside her book, she divided a *bizcocho* into pieces which the monkey took daintily from the plate, eating one bit at a time, unhurriedly, before helping itself to another while the woman resumed her reading.

Not long afterwards, a heavily built man entered the courtyard. The leather chaps pulled over his trousers were smooth from wear, and he walked with the rolling gait of a man who has lived much of his life astride a horse. The swarthy face clamped into an angry scowl as it did each day when first he saw his daughter lying helpless.

Not once had Pedro Lopez ever acknowledged – least of all to himself – that if her crippling had never happened, they would not be living in a house more agreeable than any he'd known before or was known to most of the *señoras* who'd been at the convent school with his daughter. He saw the money deposited each month in a bank in Monterrey as his due, and his hatred for the gringo who provided it was as implacable now as when they had met in that hospital fifteen years before.

NINE

At least twenty times she'd tried to reach him.

'The goddam answer-machine is always on.' Jancie's voice was taut as she tried to check panic. She couldn't stand people who got hysterical. 'I leave messages for him to phone me. Nothing happens. I've been around to his apartment house. He's not there.'

The afternoon sun streaming through the window laid bare the havoc on her face, her usually fresh skin mottled from stress and weeping, eyes shrunk in puffy folds.

'He must be so upset about everything,' Jancie went on.

She took a quick look at Zoë, whose face was troubled but otherwise hard to read.

'I know. You've always been sceptical, Zoë, about Simon's reliability when it comes to women. But he said I was *different*. He said I made *him* want to be different.'

Zoë pushed the coffee pot towards Jancie. Jancie ignored it.

'I stare at the phone and try to will it to ring,' she said, her voice breaking. 'When it does, I hate whoever it is for not being Simon. Do you suppose he doesn't call because he thinks I'm upset that he gave what I told him to the *Javelin*?'

Zoë didn't reply. Bleakly she eyed the pretty chintzes and frilled cushions of the Embassy's morning-room. Other times she loved them, but today they seemed to mock the cheerless conversation.

'Anyhow, the story may not have come from him,' Jancie continued, tugging hard at one of her curls. 'He may have told somebody else in confidence and that person gave it to the *Javelin*.'

'Is there any more coffee in that pot?' said Zoë.

Jancie shoved it towards her. 'And anyhow, the piece was very polite about James and me. It was the Prime Minister that the *Javelin* slated for firing James. I hate Martin Mather. Why should he get rid of James because of my faults?'

She snatched up her handkerchief and scrubbed at her face. Zoë put a hand on Jancie's knee. In the silence the sweet, slightly cinnamon smell from a vase of roses seemed stronger.

'I don't suppose there's such a thing as a drink in this place,' Zoë said gently.

A weak nod from Jancie as she indicated a cupboard.

'When the English are in mourning, do you suppose they still like all these stupid flowered chintzes?' muttered Zoë crabbily as she opened a cupboard and peered within. 'Bourbon or brandy?'

'Brandy.'

Zoë poured a large dollop into a tumbler and took it to Jancie.

'Don't you want one too?'

'You're darn right I want one,' said Zoë. 'But I'm going straight from here to interview our dear Vice-President's wife, and I don't want to breathe fumes all over her as soon as I walk in the door. How is James?'

'Oh God, Zoë. It's awful. I've never felt worse about anything in my life. It never occurred to me this could happen. I keep telling James that somehow I would have done things differently had I imagined the consequences. But he doesn't say anything in response. I put my arms around him, and he remains stiff. You know how James is. It'd be better if he berated me for causing his downfall. If he cursed me. Hated me. Anything rather than this. Watching him bottle up all his suffering is unbearable.'

She gave a small sad smile.

'You know, he only really lets himself go when he's at the wheel of his boat on the high seas. His "schoolboy thing" is what I called it. I wish I hadn't teased him about it. I should have been thankful it gave him satisfaction without taking anything from me.'

She blew her nose. Suddenly she was angry again.

'God I hate Martin Mather,' she exclaimed. 'And I think it's disgusting of Miles to fire Simon just like that,' she added.

'The editor did the actual firing,' Zoë muttered, which of course was irrelevant. She only said it to keep from blurting out things that wouldn't help.

'Everyone knows the editor is Miles's puppet,' Jancie replied furiously. 'I hate him.'

'Who?'

'Miles.'

Zoë reached over again and put her hand on Jancie's arm.

Not long afterwards she made her way back down the stairs, glancing up gloomily at the portrait of the young Queen Victoria. Outside she looked at her watch. The Vice-President's house was only minutes away. Maybe the security check would be fast. She was about to jump in the waiting taxi when a car drew up. Miles Brewster got out.

'We can't go on meeting like this at the British Embassy,' he said, amused by her surprise.

'What are you doing here?' she asked, wishing her face didn't flush when she got excited.

He looked at his watch pointedly and pulled down his brows in a mock frown.

'I could put the question to you, young lady,' he replied. It was his first light-hearted moment in a morning that had been generally grim.

Zoë gave a big smile. 'Actually, if you want to know, I'm on my way to interview the Vice-President's wife. I wanted to see Jancie first.' Her face grew sombre. 'It's a pretty unhappy household in there.'

'It's a goddam mess. Someone better sort something out. I'm about to see James.'

They stood on the kerb, each hesitant.

'I've got to go,' said Zoë. 'I can't have the boss thinking I don't take my job seriously,' she added, smiling again.

She hopped in the taxi and he watched it pull away before he turned and nodded to the footman.

This time the Ambassador's private secretary revealed a trace of impatience when he opened the library door and saw the Ambassador standing with his back to them, looking out of the window to the garden, exactly as he'd been when Miles went to see him the day before. It was Miles who had proposed today's meeting.

'Look, James,' he said when they were seated, 'you really ought to start thinking about what you're going to do next.'

James made no reply. His face, normally ruddy from sailing, was putty coloured, mouth set – like a schoolboy who has had the stuffing knocked out of him.

'You'll have plenty of people vying to get you, no fear of that,' Miles continued. 'Your defence expertise and having been British Ambassador in Washington give you an edge on everyone else. You can call your own shots. Journalism. Television. A chairmanship of a major corporation. You name it. But don't leave it too long. People's memories are short.'

Without looking up, James said in a toneless voice: 'I'm forty years old. I've never been sacked from anything in my life. Until now.'

For a few moments Miles said nothing. There'd been bad times in his own life, but he'd never been fired. He could only guess how demoralising that must be.

'James, I know you didn't want the news to come out yet, but the truth is you and Jancie fared pretty well in the *Javelin* piece. It as much as said the Prime Minister was behaving like some kind of manic depressive in recalling you – that *he* should be the one to go. All the other papers will now follow suit. So don't worry about the piece coming out sooner than you wanted. Hey, are you hearing me?'

'Jancie.' James spoke his wife's name listlessly. 'When her passion for Simon Fleet first became obvious, I asked myself if I would have minded less if she had been discreet about it.'

A dreadful smile, a rictus of pain, broke his face in two.

'I don't know the answer to that,' he went on in the same monotone. 'What I do know is that I dread returning to London. We left there so full of confidence in our new venture – it *was* a partnership, whatever she claims about the Ambassadress's role being peripheral. And to go back with my tail between my legs – whatever gloss the *Javelin* has put on the story – I dread it. This sounds wimpish. I apologise.'

'Come on, you don't sound wimpish. You sound like someone who's been kicked in the balls. As soon as you get your breath and pick yourself up, you'll see opportunities just waiting to be taken.' Miles paused. 'I've got an offer of my own in mind.'

Slowly James looked up.

'You know, something odd happened to me at your dinner party,' Miles went on, settling back in the sofa. 'I've been looking over the newspaper market in Europe – Britain, in particular – with two thoughts in mind:

market and message. The market is impersonal. The message is my own.'

He stretched out his legs.

'So far my President and your Prime Minister have kept the special relationship between our countries alive – barely. But no one knows better than you that it's been touch and go this past year whether our joint foreign policy on the Middle East would blow up. Lord Scrope's papers in both our countries endlessly exhort a divorce – each of us to go all out for our own interests. There's no escaping the fact that this touches a chord in a helluva lot of Americans and Brits.'

For the first time James's expression was alert.

'My American papers,' Miles went on, 'trumpet the need for the special relationship. I want to deliver the same message in Britain. But there are market reasons against my going for the *London Dispatch* now.'

Miles chuckled.

'But then at your dinner party I discovered there was another factor in the equation. His Lordship. The fact that Gerald Scrope wants to stop me from breaking into the British media makes me hell-bent to assert my so-called "unhealthy influence". Childish, of course. Who isn't? I'm bidding for the *Dispatch* on Monday.'

He smiled to himself.

'If I land it,' he went on, 'I'm going to move my base to London. I'll be a more overtly hands-on publisher than I've been here.'

A wry smile appeared on James's face. 'I like the "more overtly". Everyone knows your hands are fastened on the *Express* every day – not least when you gagged Simon Fleet's piece.'

Miles shrugged.

'If I get the *Dispatch*,' he continued 'you could be invaluable as an executive, James. If you like the idea, we could work out details later on. I want someone at my right hand who has first-class experience on both sides of the Atlantic. What do you say?'

Ordinarily James's training held him in good stead, but the last couple of days had eroded his defences. First relief flooded over his face. Then the slumped figure on the sofa disappeared before Miles's eyes, and the fit, athletic James leant forward intently.

'Obviously Lord Scrope will pull whatever strings he can to block me,' Miles went on. 'So until it's certain I've got the *Dispatch*, I can't make you a definite offer. If you decide on something else in the meantime, that's my tough luck.'

'Is my wife here?' James asked his secretary.

As soon as he walked into the morning-room where Jancie was writing a letter, she saw the difference in him.

'Things have taken a turn for the better,' he said. His face was boyish again. 'Miles has made me a provisional offer.' He told her what it was. 'Of course he may not win his bid for the *Dispatch*. But he is confident I'll have a good choice of other offers.'

She stood and rested her hands on his shoulders. Tears of relief filled her eyes. She drew his face down and laid her cheek against his. 'There. There.' Her voice was like a mother's croon when she comforts a child.

After a few moments they drew apart. She recognised the embarrassment in his expression. He always looked like that when he felt his emotions had got the upper hand. He gave a crooked little smile and left the room.

Returning to her desk, she tore up the letter she'd been writing and started it again.

TEN

However much homework you did before an interview, you never felt easy until it was over. Peter had told her where the general-turned-politician would be most vulnerable, and this morning Zoë began by playing up to his achievements. Then when he thought everything was going his way and relaxed, she asked why he had shouldered none of the responsibility for American troops being pulled out of Arabi without toppling the dictator first. He blew his top. That's when she got the meat she wanted.

On her way to the paper afterwards, she felt the relief of a journalist who knows the tape and notebook in her bag contain what she needs to produce a good piece. Minutes later, of course, came the annoyance of realising that if she'd put a further question to him, the piece would be better still.

She went straight to her desk to transcribe her notes. The message was waiting beside her keyboard. 'Zoë: Phone Ambassador Wharton. Urgent.'

She grabbed the phone.

'She's with that shit.'

His voice sounded terrible.

'She wrote me a letter. She arranged for it to be given to me yesterday afternoon, after she'd left.'

He spoke in jerks.

'She said she would always regret the damage she had done me. She would try to be a better wife. But now things were looking up for me, she was sure it was right for her to take a day or two to clear her own mind.'

Zoë pressed the phone against her ear, trying to follow what he was saying.

'The letter was delivered just two hours before we were due at a reception in our honour.'

The thought crossed Zoë's mind that he minded the social embarrassment as much as his wife's disappearance.

'She'd added a postscript. It was written with a different pen. She said she would be back in two days. I rang Fleet's number. The answer-machine was on. I even drove round to his bloody apartment house. I had my driver go in to discover whether Mr Simon Fleet was at home. How abject can one be?'

The question didn't expect an answer.

'The receptionist said Fleet had left the building earlier and no one knew when he'd be back. God knows where they've gone.'

'What makes you so sure Jancie's with him?'

'Where else would she be? And there's a dinner for us tonight. People go to enormous trouble planning these things. Jancie didn't use to be irresponsible like this. If you hear from her, Zoë, for God's sake tell me.'

'All right, James. But at least you know she's OK.'

He made a sound like a single bark.

'If ever I find myself in a position of power over Simon Fleet,' he said, 'I shall be a happy man.'

He could do it in his sleep, Simon said to himself. He couldn't remember when he first realised his tantalising techniques as a lover had something in common with a torturer's skills. And he genuinely did think she ought to be punished for spoiling his weekend. Not that he had anything great planned, but he certainly wouldn't have chosen at this juncture in his life to be holed up for two nights at the Crabshell Inn on the Eastern Shore of

Maryland. That was fine in their early days, but she ought to realise things couldn't go on like that.

When his bell had rung the previous day, he'd opened the door because he was expecting the janitor to fix a loose wire in his kitchen. Instead, Jancie stood there.

Trapped like a rat, he'd thought ruefully. In the end, she had appealed to his good nature. He liked to please, and he would say whatever was wanted at the time: 'I love you deeply.' 'Of course I'll phone you tomorrow.' 'Wild horses couldn't keep me away.' Usually he meant it at the moment the words came out of his mouth. That none of it turned out that way didn't seem to him to be a sin. You had to *intend* to hurt the person to be a shit. That's how Simon saw it.

So here they were at the Crabshell Inn for a final weekend in that little harbour. She said she would remember it for the rest of her life. It seemed eternity to him. True, he picked up bits of information which could come in useful – like Miles Brewster offering James a top job if Brewster won his bid for the *London Dispatch*. When he got back to Washington he'd pass that on to Lord Scrope. *If* he ever got back to Washington.

'All that weeping over lunch,' he grumbled teasingly. 'What have you done to deserve a reward?' He left the bed.

At the window he looked down at the sailboat that had just left its mooring to skip across choppy waves sparkling in the afternoon sun. A young woman loosened the jib ropes while another unfurled the mainsail. A bronzed youth stood at the rudder post like a god.

'He's got 'em trained right,' Simon muttered.

The wind caught the mainsail and it billowed big and gleaming white until the youth turned the tiller and the sail flung the other way, slate blue in its own shadow. Above it gulls mewed as they wheeled, wings white until they tilted and became the same slate blue as the sails below. At heart he was a poet, Simon told himself.

He turned from the window and looked back into the room. The sigh he gave was a mixture of boredom and relish. He walked to the bed to resume his attentions to the woman lying there.

Sunday afternoon traffic had not yet built up when they started the return journey across the Chesapeake Bay Bridge, several miles of gentle ascent before them. When the car reached the low crest and the long decline to the mainland began, tears filled Jancie's eyes. Her curls added to the impression of a sad child being returned to a hated boarding school. Simon took one hand off the steering-wheel and patted her thigh.

'When will you decide what you're going to do next?' she asked for the sixth time.

'There's no hurry,' he replied easily. 'Your friend Mr Brewster had to cough up a year's salary to see me off.'

'I wish you'd come to England.'

He moved his hand higher up her thigh. Until that final cheque was banked and cleared, he had no intention of telling anyone he'd already lined up his next job. She'd find out soon enough when she got to London and opened the *Javelin*. But he could say he'd wanted to surprise her – or he'd wanted to give her time to settle down in England again – or whatever. Funny old business, life. Simon moistened his lips. If Brewster got the *London Dispatch*, it could be useful to have an adorer in the enemy camp. No one could deny that Jancie was an attractive woman. When he felt her responding now to the pressure from his palm, he put his hand back on the steering-wheel. But it was just a game: of course he'd finish it for her before they got to Washington.

The capital's streets were nearly empty. He drew the

car to the kerb where Massachusetts Avenue crosses Columbus Circle and taxis approach Union Station. 'I'll say goodbye here, Jancie. You'll be back at the Embassy in ten minutes.'

'It doesn't matter any longer if you drive me there,' she said. Her eyes made him think of a stray dog's. He unsnapped her seatbelt and reached into the back seat for her overnight bag.

'It's more dramatic this way,' he said, 'and I want you to remember it as the drama of your life – and mine. You have given me the greatest happiness I have ever known. Goodbye, *bellissima*.'

He lifted the hand he had pressed between her thighs and put its palm against his lips. Then he turned the palm outward, extending his arm – like a benediction – to where Jancie now stood on the kerb, her bag beside her. She hailed a taxi.

Eager to call Lord Scrope with his news, Simon drove off before she'd climbed into the taxi.

ELEVEN

Gerald nudged his cigar tip into an ashtray embossed with the House of Commons seal. 'Did the Prime Minister refer to the *Javelin*'s latest attack on him?' he said.

The British Defence Secretary, the Right Honourable Alan Rawlston MP, rocked himself in his armchair, beaming with satisfaction.

'At this morning's Cabinet,' he replied, 'the PM gave us one of his little lectures: "My colleagues will have read that some of those close to me are increasingly concerned about my emotional equilibrium. It would be a pity – would it not? – if someone close to me here was responsible for that quote in the *Javelin*." Ha hah!'

'Did he mean a minister sitting near him at the Cabinet table?' said Gerald.

'You know the PM. He likes his little word games. He could have meant any one of us.' Alan Rawlston beamed again. 'You will be glad to know, Gerald, that the Foreign Secretary beetled his brows so ferociously at any hint he might be conspiring against the PM, that at once the thought came into everyone's mind. As for myself, I looked as innocent as the proverbial lamb.'

He slapped his thigh.

They were sitting in leather armchairs, bottle-green like all coverings and fabrics in the Defence Secretary's room at the Commons. The minister had just returned from casting his ten-o'clock vote when Gerald arrived in the ante-room manned by a Special Branch detective. 'Good evening, m'lord.' Gerald went through.

Alan Rawlston always held his most private conversations in this room where, unlike the Ministry of Defence, no civil servant hovered.

On the coffee table stood two whiskies and soda, produced from an oak cupboard designed to blend with Pugin's panelling. The great architect helped rebuild the House of Commons following the fire of 1834, and when the Second World War destroyed much of it again, Pugin's rich carving was lovingly restored. Tonight the Defence Secretary's curtains were open to London's rosy sky, neo-Gothic *flèches* in silhouette against it. Big Ben struck the quarter hour.

The Defence Secretary looked rumpled, but then he always did. He was a stout man, physically awkward, genial, but anyone who mistook him for a teddy bear dropped that notion fast if they crossed him in any way. Thick round spectacles magnified his eyes, and though they still remained so small their colour was indeterminate, they gleamed with cunning. Alan Rawlston was a formidable politician. Seldom an hour in any day passed without his considering how he could undermine Martin Mather in order to grasp the premiership for himself.

'What do you make my chances of getting the *Dispatch*, Alan?'

Alan sighed. 'From the moment you said you wanted to buy the *Dispatch*, Gerald, I told you I thought the Monopolies Commission wouldn't wear it. It'd be a walkover if you had only your provincial newspaper chain in this country. But unless you sell the *Javelin* – and you're not about to do that – it's almost certain you can't have the *Dispatch* as well.'

'Says who?'

'My colleague at Industry told me today. And he's the one who appointed the Monopolies Commission.'

'Tell him to get rid of the bloody vicars he appointed.'

Wedged in the armchair, Alan's body shook with merriment.

'I don't see the joke,' said Gerald coldly.

Alan readopted a serious manner. 'You must realise, Gerald, he can't remove his own appointees without any good reason.'

'Then give him a good reason to make them change their minds,' said Gerald. 'Like me being a Brit and Miles Brewster being a fucking American. What's happened to patriotism?'

Alan shifted his bulk as if it confined him unduly. 'I'll have another word with him. But I'm not optimistic about this one, Gerald.'

Without a bridge in the conversation, Gerald said: 'What have you got to tell me about the Cheetah deal, Alan?'

Alan shifted in his armchair again. 'I can't give you an answer yet. As you know, my advisers on defence contracts are against the Cheetah contract going to Scrope Electronics.'

'I could have sworn you were the Defence Secretary,' Gerald said evenly. 'If the Defence Secretary can't run his own show, maybe he wouldn't make such a hot prime minister after all. Maybe I should think about backing another horse.'

Alan's face flushed. 'You may disapprove of the democratic principle, Gerald, but as it happens this country runs on that principle. If I ride roughshod over my own civil servant advisers, I'll have to answer for it in the House of Commons.'

'Where'd you get the idea I'm against the democratic principle, Alan?' said Gerald in the same even voice. 'Find me a better product of democracy than a boy from nowhere building a garage business into an empire, and ending up a peer in the House of Lords. You get Scrope Electronics the Cheetah deal with the MoD, and the *Javelin* will come up with any hymns to democracy you need.'

The flat vowels acted like a file on the minister's nerves. He took a swallow of his whisky. 'You'll have to be patient, Gerald.'

'I don't like being patient, Alan.' Gerald's eyes made the Defence Secretary think of the deep coldness of a subterranean tunnel. 'Maybe I should remind you of some of the things we done together not so long ago.'

'We have each helped the other,' Alan said stiffly.

'Yeah. Well, I want that Cheetah contract and I want it soon. The boy who came from nowhere sure as hell didn't get here by being bleeding patient, and I ain't going to start being patient now.'

Other life peers in the House of Lords regretted that their titles, received as personal rewards, could not be handed down to their children like the hereditary titles of the old nobility. Gerald Scrope couldn't have cared less. He knew that many men cared passionately about fathering children to carry on their name, their genes, a kind of immortality. So far as Gerald was concerned, when his mortality was up, the story ended. No sequels.

He had married when he was twenty-four, his bride the daughter of a Wandsworth motor mechanic who had built up a chain of garages in south London. However seedy and rough much of south London, among its hoodlums there was less warring between families than in the East End, where if you messed with one of the family you had four brothers and sisters after you. Wandsworth included streets of neat terrace houses occupied by bank clerks or teachers as well as skilled labourers who had turned plumbing or construction or garages into a going concern, and whose wives resented the prostitutes plying their trade around Wandsworth Common. Gerald's parents-in-law lived in one of these neat houses.

He had already started a garage business of his own

before he married. His father-in-law, a generous man, was particularly fond of his daughter, and the bridal dowry was three garages for Gerald to add to his embryonic chain. Within five years he had the biggest chain in south London, and his wife's father was left with only three garages.

'You gave me three as a dowry. You better have three for your old age,' Gerald told him. Someone on television had once said human beings differed from other animals in their capacity to trade with each other, but Gerald thought this crazy. For him, human beings were there to be raided.

Then he scooped up a company which supplied electronics for garages. The firm's owner hadn't wanted to sell. His light aircraft came down one night within minutes of take-off, killing him and his pilot. ('Too bad about his accident,' Gerald said later to Alan Rawlston.) Examination of the aircraft revealed two wires had got inexplicably crossed, reversing the ascendancy levers. An open verdict was returned on the deaths. Shortly afterwards Gerald Scrope bought the electronics firm from the widow at a mark-down price.

Not long after that, he 'pensioned off the missus'. She received a handsome divorce settlement and the assurance of cash to be delivered once a month. He'd never shown the slightest interest in discovering whether it was her infertility or his which accounted for there being no children. So far as he was concerned, his cock was there to give him pleasure.

When he got his title, far from wanting to emulate the old English nobility, Gerald flaunted being self-made, parading himself as the robber baron he was. What he didn't flaunt were details of his early years. The state school he'd attended had long been shut down, its management so incompetent that records of one-time pupils were non-existent. When Gerald became a national figure and the media tried to discover something about his childhood and youth, no one knew where to look. Searches of birth records failed to find a Gerald Scrope. Hearing he had once been married, a newspaper sent three reporters to scour south London, and eventually they tracked down Gerald's former wife.

She stood inside her doorway, blocking it, eyes expressionless as she said flatly: 'He never said anything about any family.' She wasn't going to jeopardise her monthly money by talking to the press. And it was true: so far as she knew, he didn't have a family.

Journalists bold enough to press Lord Scrope about his background got nothing for their pains. He laughed in their faces: 'I'm just a boy from nowhere.'

Someone else might have brooded after learning his rival was likely to beat him in their bid for the *London Dispatch*. But Gerald had hardly left the Defence Secretary's room before he was planning what he could seize instead. He knew from Simon of Miles Brewster's interest in James Wharton, reason enough for Gerald to want to grab James.

But there were hard, practical reasons as well. Having the ex-Ambassador to Washington on board would lend Scrope Opportunities Ltd a respectability it still lacked in many people's eyes. Given some of his unpublicised activities, Gerald reckoned he might one day need an esteemed Establishment figure in tow. Meanwhile, Wharton's entrée to the Pentagon would help get contracts with the American military.

And there was the other thing. Having this honourable Old Etonian at his mercy would provide some sport. Gerald liked to have his sport.

TWELVE

Bright water rushed pell-mell over a bed of giant rocks, some worn smooth, others craggy as if just hurled into the canyon from the heights. Zoë always loved it when her taxi turned into Rock Creek Park, with its poplars and pines and people bicycling on the towpath with their office clothes strapped behind the saddle.

They came out at the exit for Georgetown. Leila Sherman's house, an early-nineteenth-century mansion, was set back in a garden dominated by a horse chestnut tree. Ahead a limousine pulled away, and Zoë recognised the couple going in through the gate.

Arriving on her own at a party like this was a strain. As she paid the driver, she kept an eye out to see if the President's national security adviser and his wife had reached the top of the steep flight of steps. If she took long strides – she didn't want to appear to be sprinting after them – she might overtake them by the front door, where it would be normal to introduce herself, and she could go in knowing someone. But they'd disappeared inside by the time she got there.

The cocktail party was bound to be big; otherwise she wouldn't have been asked. Leila Sherman had praised her work when they'd met, but Zoë didn't kid herself this made them friends. The rich widow of a distinguished Southern senator, Leila Sherman had made her home the place where power-wielders liked to meet and be seen. She'd entertained widely for Frank Lambert when he was still presidential candidate, financing his advertising campaigns, holding fund-raising events in her opulent home.

You never knew if the President or First Lady might drop by at one of Leila's parties.

Zoë rang the big brass bell.

The first thing she took in was the serenity of the centre hall, despite the hubbub not far away. On a mahogany table, turned gold by sun and age, stood a pair of art nouveau vases, amber glass with cream-coloured palm trees and elephants. Above them hung one of Monet's paintings of lush water lilies on a pond. For a wild moment Zoë thought she might simply perch on a chair in this tranquil hall rather than dive into the mêlée.

'This way, miss,' said the butler.

Sixty or seventy people were already there, even though it was not long after 6.30 – politicians and media whose faces looked out at Zoë from the newspapers every day. Well, here I go, she thought.

A fine-boned woman of indeterminate age left a group to come and greet her.

'Zoë Hare. How nice that you could come,' said Leila, as if nothing could have given her greater joy. 'Do you know Senator O'Connell? No? Let me introduce you.'

She led the way to a small group clustered around the senator, a senior member of the Armed Services Committee. 'Patrick, this is Zoë Hare of the *Express*. I'm sure you know her work. She does some of the best interviews in Washington,' whereupon Leila dissolved into the crowd.

At once the senator separated himself from those around him. 'You don't have a drink, young lady,' he said kindly, gin and tonic in one hand as with the other he beckoned to a waiter with a tray of drinks.

The senator delighted in the company of young women, and when they were as attractive as Zoë, he didn't always succeed in keeping his hands to himself. But he did his best, especially when his wife was in the same room. Essentially he was a nice, dull man, and Zoë listened to him respectfully, just as others always did. In any case, she was relieved to have someone to talk to. He had launched into an account of going to the Oval Office to discuss the latest threat from Arabi.

'And then the President looked at me with those honest eyes,' he went on, at which point a woman strode up briskly and planted herself at his side. When the senator introduced his wife, she gave a summary nod to Zoë. 'Patrick, I promised the Secretary of State I would find you. He wants to talk with you about Arabi.'

The senator gave Zoë a rueful smile. 'It was a pleasure to meet you,' he said. His wife, without another word to Zoë, linked her arm proprietorially through his, leading him away.

Zoë sipped her drink. The close-out treatment was one she'd encountered a couple of times before. Yet she had to talk to someone at a party, for God's sake.

'Zoë. How are you?' A self-possessed woman swept up. She was an attorney, married to a congressman, and Zoë had interviewed her a few months earlier. She was half of a couple in the way Zoë admired – having her own pursuits as well as being a wife. The two women were deep in conversation when a stirring at the door made them look around. Leila Sherman was escorting the First Lady into the room.

'Oh,' said Zoë. Despite Nona Lambert's reputation for informality, her air of authority was intimidating.

Instinctively guests nearby stepped back to make an opening around her. Then a few who already knew her began getting in position to have a turn at exchanging a few words with her. Leila slipped into the crowd to select others to introduce to the First Lady.

'Do you know her?' Zoë asked the attorney.

'We were at law school together,' she replied. 'Do you want to meet her?'

'I'd love to.'

They moved nearer the focal point, and when an opportunity presented itself, the attorney went up, Zoë in tow.

'Nona. You hit the nail on the head in your speech the other night. This is Zoë Hare. I'm sure you've seen her interviews in the *Express*.'

When they shook hands the First Lady was simultaneously friendly and distant. But then this was pretty common with politicians, Zoë reminded herself. At least when Nona Lambert greeted you, her eyes hadn't already moved on to the next person. A moment later, Leila reappeared to present a distinguished professor of ethnic studies.

Feeling much more confident than when she had arrived, and buttressed by a second drink, Zoë spent the next hour thoroughly enjoying herself, going up to people she was acquainted with, introducing herself to several famous faces, storing away new knowledge she had picked up. It was when the party was thinning out that she saw Peter.

He was standing near the door, surveying the room, and she wondered if he had just arrived. When their eyes met he gave a brief knowing smile.

Zoë looked for Leila to say goodbye, and she passed near Peter. He was talking with the bureau chief of the *New York Times*.

'Hullo, Zoë.'

'Good evening, Senator,' she replied, inclining her head in a little bow. More naturally she said to the bureau chief: 'Hullo, Johnny,' and continued on her way.

'Where were we?' she asked when for the second time that evening they sat down at the gateleg table overlooking the Potomac. A bottle of Sauvignon in a wine cooler was half-empty. Beside it was a wooden bowl of salad, still untouched.

Earlier they had finished the crab cakes she'd picked up on her way home from the cocktail party. She'd been about to help herself to salad when Peter proposed they have a short recess in her bedroom. On their return to the living-room, Zoë's dark hair swung loose to below her shoulders and she was wearing only a silk kimono. Peter had put on some of his clothes, his shirt unbuttoned at the throat.

'That's one of my favourite bits,' she said, reaching across the table to lay a finger for a moment on the soft skin which would be locked away when he did up the top buttons later.

'We were talking about Senator and Mrs O'Connell,' he replied to her question.

'Oh yes. What I find annoying about a wife who beelines across the room and seizes her husband's arm in that assertive way is her presumption that I want him for myself.'

'It's called the coupledom disease,' Peter said, 'often found in a couple who don't terribly like each other.'

Zoë laughed. 'I couldn't stand that kind of marriage,' she said. 'My compartments system is much better. I invented it soon after I came to Washington, when I was sitting on a bench in Lafayette Square. Shall I tell you how it goes?'

He put a hand over hers.

'As no one was at the centre of my life,' said Zoë, 'obviously I couldn't have all things integrated in one relationship. And most men I meet in Washington are already married – assuming they're interested in women in the first place.'

Peter poured out more wine.

'So instead of looking for Mr Right Forever and being

constantly disappointed,' Zoë went on, 'I thought maybe I could have the whole shebang of emotions by compartmentalising myself. Different kinds of friendship with different people.'

He put his hand on hers again for a moment.

'Career, weekends on the Eastern Shore, all went into their own compartment, my grandparents and the farm in a special one. And think of not having to answer to anyone,' she said brightly. She looked a little dubious before bursting into laughter. 'Except my editor, of course.'

'What compartment am I in?' he asked.

'That's harder to define,' she replied, reaching again to touch what she called 'the tender place' where his collar was open. After a minute she said: 'But whatever it's called, having you there is not only happiness itself. It's also like a bonus that makes all the other compartments better.'

Not long afterwards he went back to the bedroom to collect his tie and jacket.

'Your armour,' she said, smiling. At the same time she felt wistfulness. She'd had it before when he was getting ready to leave for his own home.

THIRTEEN

Often Scrope executives acted as Gerald's bag carriers. But on this quick trip to Washington, the lone hunter was by himself on Concorde.

When his driver drew to the kerb in Pennsylvania Avenue, Gerald glanced impassively across the street to the White House. 'Nice to have you back, milord,' said the doorman beneath the Willard's ornate canopy.

Inside the soaring lobby the manager said solemnly: 'You have your usual suite, milord. I'm sorry your time with us will be so short.'

'Yeah.'

The elevator door was almost shut when Gerald reached across the bellboy and put a thumb on stop. The door opened again and he stepped out. 'Miss Hare,' he called.

He had seen her as she crossed the lobby.

Almost at the front door, she turned and saw him. As they walked towards each other, she felt a burst of curiosity.

'What are you doing here?' she asked.

'I've just arrived,' he replied. 'I'm too much the gentleman,' he went on, deadpan, 'to ask you, Miss Hare, what you are doing here at four-thirty in the afternoon.'

Zoë burst into laughter. She hadn't expected the intimidating Lord Scrope to be almost flirtatious.

'Nothing very wicked,' she replied. 'I've been doing an interview over tea. In the Nest,' she added. 'What could be more conservative?'

'I'm flying out tonight,' he said. 'Have a drink with me before I go. I'll be back here by seven at the latest.'

'I'd like that.'

'I could invite you to have a drink in my suite. What could be more conservative?' He smiled. 'But something tells me you might prefer to meet in the bar. I'll see you there at 7.15, Miss Hare.'

He turned back to the elevator.

The suite was at the corner of Pennsylvania Avenue and 14th Street, and from it he looked down on the Mall, where sprinklers fought their losing battle with the searing sun, the Capitol gleaming at the far end. After a cursory glance at the ponderous dome, Gerald threw himself into an armchair. One of the phones beside him was unmarked by any number. The Willard catered for clients whose privacy had to be guaranteed.

For an hour he was engrossed in his calls. Several times he phoned the same number in Austin, Texas.

The British were second only to the Japanese in owning property in America. Six Scrope electronics factories were scattered across the United States. The Southwestern Plant stood twenty miles south of Austin, near Mendoza, four hours' drive from the Mexican border, not much more than an hour by plane. Lots of electronics companies were based at Austin, and it was unusual for a plant to be that far outside the city, out where the big ranches began, some so big their owners didn't even know when strangers used their landing strip. There were few signs of human life on these anonymous, hostile stretches beneath an empty sky.

Most of Southwestern's twenty-acre site was scrub brush, mesquite trees, cactus with beautiful yellow blooms in the early summer, all enclosed by a high electric cyclone fence. Of all the factories owned by Gerald, this one alone did not proclaim his name. Even when you were close to the sign on the electronic gates you were likely only to read 'Southwestern Plant', so small was the print at the bottom which said 'Scrope Opportunities Ltd'.

Bisecting the site was a narrow landing strip. On one side a hangar. On the other side stood a cluster of two-storey industrial buildings. The closed doors of a loading bay made a big metal square on a wall. Immense satellite dishes crowned each flat roof. From within came an unsettling sound like the hum of a power cable.

It was still early afternoon in Texas when a Cessna 337 made a quick descent from the cloudless sky. It had left a small ranch in northern Mexico less than two hours before, refuelling at Nuevo Laredo before crossing the border. Taxiing to the hangar, the pilot and his companion waited patiently until the overhead door folded up. The plane disappeared inside. The metal door dropped to enclose the entire entrance.

Minutes later a side door opened: Speers Jackson and his passenger reappeared. Both were wearing leather chaps over their jeans, and as they crossed the oven-hot tarmac to the industrial complex, Pedro Lopez pulled his sombrero low on his forehead, frowning.

The two men were friends in the way an American and a Mexican can be in business. Pedro Lopez had focused his resentment of gringos on the one who had crippled his daughter – and then thought sending money each month would buy his forgiveness. When Speers Jackson first approached him, the Mexican thought he'd make enough money, maybe, so he could tell the bank to send back Miles Brewster's money. Quite often he had the image of flinging it on the floor of the bank in Monterrey. It hadn't yet happened. Pedro Lopez was greedy.

His frown deepened as they neared the first building and the humming got louder. He always disliked the hum. It made him feel uneasy. He suspected an unknown god was lurking.

When the unmarked phone on the table began to ring, Gerald cut short his other call. Five minutes later he ended the conversation: he had learned what he needed to know from Speers Jackson. At once he switched his mind to the meeting ahead.

James was more than a little curious to discover the reason for this visit in his final weeks as British Ambassador.

'I want to say, Lord Scrope, that while I wish my impending departure from this post' – that was how James now described being sacked – 'had not come out so soon, my wife and I appreciated the tone the *Javelin* adopted as far as we were concerned.'

'Only what you both deserve,' Gerald said, one hand waving away James's thanks, as if assisting the Whartons in their misfortune was what the *Javelin* would have done whether it suited the owner's purposes or not. 'I'll come straight to the reason I'm here, Ambassador. What are you going to do when you return to London?'

James would have preferred a slower approach, so he could test the waters a bit. 'I have one or two things in mind,' he replied. 'Why do you ask?'

'You and I could be useful to each other,' Gerald said, leaning forward. 'OK, you've already got attractive offers from various quarters. Let's consider a few possibilities. You could go back to being a defence correspondent.'

He sat back and drew on his cigar.

James felt distinctly uncomfortable at this avuncular approach from a notoriously tough operator he knew only slightly. But after a moment he gave an entirely truthful reply: 'The trouble with that scenario is I've already done it. It would feel like my career was going backwards.'

Gerald hunched forward, his eyes fixed on James. 'You could become chairman of some finance house. They're always looking for big names like yours.'

James said nothing. He'd already discovered top directorships were not lying around just waiting to be picked up. The two offers he'd received were far from inspiring.

'I'll tell you what's wrong with you settling for that option, Ambassador. You'd make a big salary, sure.'

Never let the other party know *you* know he hasn't been offered the salary he's seeking – unless you wish to offend him – was one of Gerald's tactics.

'But you'd be bored stiff. These City chairmen and directors have a great aura of being men of the world – contacts with statesmen, all that crap. Most of it's sham. You want to be where the action is, Ambassador.'

James's unease at this interrogation began to change into the pleasure of a man flattered.

'Where better to find the action than on the most influential British newspaper?' Gerald said. 'You wouldn't think your career was going backwards if you returned to journalism at the sharp end. I'm talking about the top of the pyramid, Ambassador. And believe me, there's all the difference in life between working for a firm and running it.'

As a boy Gerald had liked fishing. He thought of it now, of playing out the line so the fish was hardly aware its lips were already around the hook.

'I've thought of that,' James replied. 'Actually, I've had such an offer – been sounded out – but I'm not making up my mind on anything until I get back to London.'

Gerald hunched further forward.

'This is what I propose,' he said. 'The main staff of Scrope Opportunities are at Scrope Tower. I run the show from the other side of the Thames – at the *Javelin*. It suits me having only a couple of key members of my staff there with me. I can cross the river any time I feel like it and drop in on my other executives, unexpected, unannounced' – a glimmer of a smile flickered – 'or I can summon them to the *Javelin*.'

He paused to let the line play out a little further.

'I've got two hands,' he went on, glancing down at the wide hands, half-clenched, resting on his thighs. 'What I need, Ambassador, is a third hand.'

Even at the time, the phrase struck James as unusual. Others would have said they needed someone at their right hand. Indeed, Miles had said just that.

Gerald continued. 'I'm away a lot. I need someone I can trust to decide what decisions can be taken in my absence, what can be put on hold, what has to be put to me that minute wherever I am.' He paused. 'And that's just the start.'

James waited, intrigued.

'I need someone with your expertise to oversee the defence team on the *Javelin*. But I want a lot more than that, Ambassador. Scrope Electronics makes a helluva lot of parts for smart weapons. I want a defence expert who also has big international contacts. I want you to be my personal defence adviser, Ambassador.'

He sat back.

After a moment James said: 'Let's get this clear. You want me to be second to you on your personal staff. Does that mean that once I have worked myself into the job, I would be number two on decision-making that affected all parts of Scrope Opportunities – media, electronics, the lot?'

'You would be number two, full stop,' Gerald replied. 'All my other executives would be ranked below you. The media would be informed that you were my *chef de cabinet.*' His face gave no indication of the disdain he felt as he added this grand title to the bait. It was the kind of thing bleeding toffs valued.

'I see,' James said in the manner of an English gent who is interested but not committing himself. 'And I would direct the *Javelin*'s defence coverage?'

'You would of course be above the defence editor,' Gerald said carefully.

James had been badly bashed and now, thinking about the rank on offer, he didn't register the ambiguity of the answer to his question.

'And you would want me to use my connections to help you get defence contracts for Scrope Electronics.'

'That is putting it at its crudest, no bad thing. Despite our different backgrounds, Ambassador, you and I can get on well.' For the first time Gerald gave a big smile. 'What you want, Ambassador, is a job that will do justice to your talents and experience. I'm offering you influence, action, prestige and money to match.'

After a pause James asked: 'What sort of money are we talking about?'

'That's the easy part,' Gerald said truthfully, the big smile reappearing. 'Twice your ambassador's pay. First shot at buying Scrope Opportunities shares at a discount. Plus the usual extras – car and driver et cetera – to match your rank as *chef de cabinet*.'

James was a little ashamed to find the 'extras' mattered so much. Once you had them, he realised, you acquired a taste for them.

And there was something dynamic, he found, about the image of being Gerald Scrope's trusted second-in-command: two ends of the social spectrum, the crude self-made south Londoner, the polished gentleman. A perfect duo in its way.

'It's a very attractive offer,' he said. 'I'll need a few

days to think about it. I have a particular difficulty. I mentioned earlier an offer from another newspaper. For reasons I can't go into, that offer cannot be firmed up yet. But I have already expressed an interest in it.'

Gerald's eyelids dropped just enough to eclipse all light in his eyes, their deep blue appearing black.

'That is for you, Ambassador. I have flown from London for the purpose of making this offer to you. My offer is firm. You can take it or leave it. By all means, think about it as long as you like – just so I have your answer before I leave this room.'

After a moment James jumped to his feet and began to pace the floor.

Zoë came straight from work. It was well after 7.15 when she jumped out of her taxi. Several people watching her cross the lobby smiled as this young woman in a business suit slightly at odds with her ponytail took long steps in her high heels so she could go faster without breaking into a trot.

The half-dark of the Round Robin Bar always took a minute to get used to. Then she saw him on a banquette in the corner. When she reached his table, Gerald made not even a perfunctory gesture of getting to his feet.

'Do you make it a practice to be late, Miss Hare?' he asked.

'I'll answer you as soon as I've caught my breath,' Zoë replied. 'I couldn't get away earlier from work. I'm sorry you've had to wait.'

With one hand he brushed the subject aside.

'What'll you drink?'

'I'd love a Scotch.'

'A large Famous Grouse for the young lady,' he said to the hovering waiter, who then took it upon himself to ask if she might prefer a brand of Scotch currently voguish in America.

In an even voice Gerald stated: 'The acoustics in this bar are as bad as in the slammer, mate. I said I want a large Famous Grouse for the young lady.'

The waiter stiffened and hurried away.

'How long have you worked on the *Express*, Miss Hare?' asked Gerald.

'Five years. Right after college I got a job on the *Philadelphia Enquirer*. Then I came to the *Express* as a reporter. Quite soon I started writing features.'

The waiter returned with her Scotch. Gerald watched her take a sip.

'Where'd you go to college?'

'Vassar.'

'Is your family rich, Miss Hare?'

Zoë began to laugh. 'You don't have to be rich to go to Vassar. I won a scholarship.' She decided to take a large swallow of her drink.

'Where'd you go to school before that?'

'I should've brought my c.v.,' she answered, disconcerted and animated by Lord Scrope's form of conversation. 'I went to a public school in Vermont. Public in the American sense. If you care to know my means of transport, I can tell you that too. I lived on a farm, so a bus picked me up.'

Gerald smiled.

'Have you ever been married, Miss Hare?'

This was too much for Zoë. She gave a peal of laughter.

'No. Shall I tell you why, Lord Scrope? Because I'm one of about ten Americans who actually had a happy childhood. Half the people I know are convinced they were blighted for ever by their childhood.'

She took another swallow of her whisky.

'Their parents split,' she went on. 'Or they were non-communicado. Or something horrific for a family took place. So there was no role model for the children, the theory goes. Ergo' – she was putting away the Scotch faster than usual and on an empty stomach – 'their own marriages were doomed from the start. My situation is just the opposite, Lord Scrope.'

It was contagious, she decided, this constant use of the other's surname.

'My grandparents, who brought me up, have an exceptional marriage. If I can't have a marriage like that – and in Washington I've seen a bare handful of what I regard as good marriages – then I'd rather hoe my own row. Lord Scrope,' she tacked on belatedly. 'What a long monologue.' She stopped speaking.

'It interested me, Miss Hare. I've never read a c.v. in my life. It tells you nothing about the person.'

He beckoned to the waiter to bring two more drinks.

'Would it be impertinent if I asked a question too?' asked Zoë.

'It's a free country, Miss Hare. Or so they say.'

'What are you doing in Washington?'

'Business. More business. Calling on one or two editors while I'm here. Keeping my eyes open for talent, Miss Hare.'

There was a fractional pause.

Then he asked: 'What's it like working for Miles Brewster?'

'If you're a journalist, you hardly ever see him,' she said. 'When he comes down to the newsroom, it's to see the editor. But you're certainly conscious of his being up there on the top floor. Even though he's out of sight, everyone knows he's running the show.'

'Like God,' said Gerald.

Something in his voice made Zoë hesitate. She'd better

tread cautiously in anything she said to Gerald about Miles.

'What happened to his leg?' he asked.

'I don't know,' Zoë answered, 'except that it was a car crash.'

'Don't you find it unusual, Miss Hare, that when a man is as well-known as Miles Brewster, there should be this secret about something most people would treat straightforwardly?'

She shifted in her chair.

'I can think of things in my life that I don't want to discuss,' she said. 'Can't you?'

'We are not talking about me, Miss Hare.' He looked at his watch and called for the bill. As he got to his feet he said: 'We shall meet again, Miss Hare.'

Even as they walked out of the bar together, she knew contact had already been terminated. In the lobby he nodded goodbye, his face without expression.

FOURTEEN

It was to be just the four of them, a private farewell at the end of the ambassadorship. The Wharton family was returning to London the following week. Marigold looked at the carriage clock on the bedroom mantelpiece. Miles was cutting the time close. Then she recognised the heavy swish of tyres as his car drew up outside. As soon as he walked in the room he told her.

'Guess what – I've got the *Dispatch*! The Monopolies Commission turned down that son of a bitch's bid. It'll be announced in a couple of days.'

'Oh, Miles. Does it mean we'll be moving to London?'

'Yup.'

She jumped up from her dressing-table stool and crossed the room to stand close to him, her eyes sparkling with happiness. She hadn't yet put on her dress, and his eyes dropped to her breasts swelling above the lace of her bra.

'I love that perfume you're wearing,' he said.

With an index finger he traced the upper curve of one breast, then the other.

She leant across his hand to lay her cheek against his, tilting her face so her hair wasn't mussed up. Then she drew back and lifted his hand, holding it in front of her as if to examine it before taking his finger and returning it to continue tracing the curve of her breasts. What she felt when confronted with the coarse aggression of Gerald Scrope was locked away. It had nothing to do with her love for Miles and her pride in him.

He laughed softly at the little hissing sound she sometimes made through her teeth, like a cat teasing.

'Unless you want to start your make-up and hair from scratch,' he said, his voice thick, 'you'd better put your dress on damn fast.'

Miles was touched by the contrast between Marigold's public assurance, even hauteur, and the insecurity she let him see. Beneath the outer seductiveness was a need to hold a high position in society – and be seen by all to hold it, which could occasionally irk him. But as soon as she saw his irritation, she dispelled it with a show of appreciation that had utter charm, like an excited girl who has just been given the present she yearned for.

He had met her father twice and had no desire to know him better. A successful solicitor in Surrey, he seemed almost to relish humiliating his own wife, flaunting his philandering. Marigold said he'd treated his mistresses just as crudely, courting them and then dumping them with self-serving bluster as soon as he fancied the next one.

From an early age she had absorbed the lesson learned from him: if men were not to be trusted, and a woman depended on them, she must dissemble to survive, though that part of her formation she never mentioned to Miles.

Using her instinctive skills to make her way became so much second nature to Marigold that she couldn't always distinguish which of her responses was genuine, which feigned. But her physical attraction to Miles wasn't feigned. And her gratitude for the life he provided was equally genuine.

On those few evenings when they dined quietly at home, his presence gave a meaning to hours which had a vacuum at their centre if she was by herself. She needed him there to give a point to her physical beauty, wasted if she was alone. Similarly, her quick-wittedness called for a feedback. On her own she was uneasy.

When their car turned into Massachusetts Avenue, her mind's eye was already surveying London. Her first choice would be one of those grand apartments in St James's Place, in that celebrated modernist block designed by Denys Lasdun, overlooking Green Park. If Miles paid over the top he might persuade someone to sell.

Marigold had so little occasion to think of her dead first husband that it required an effort to recall him at all. But she retained vivid memories of people and places he'd introduced her to. A friend of his, who was heir to one of the great dukedoms, lived in the Lasdun block, and whenever the old earl and Marigold had dined there, she had said to herself that one day she would entertain there in a stunning flat of her own. True, the Georgetown house had delightful rooms for entertaining, and the brownstone on New York's Upper East Side was envied by all, but the Lasdun block was in a different category. From it the guests would look down admiringly on the plane trees of Green Park.

Miles's voice broke into her day-dream. 'We're here. I'm really looking forward to telling James about the *Dispatch*.'

'Will you make him a firm offer tonight?'

'Of course. It should make a big difference to his state of mind.'

James greeted him in the fulsome way people adopt when embarrassed. 'Marigold, do you mind if Miles and I join you and Janeie in ten minutes? I need to talk to Miles about something.'

Good, Miles thought. He would tell James now.

'I thought we could step out to the garden for our drink. It should be cool enough in the shade,' James said.

The humid summer heat had settled upon Washington with a vengeance.

'I've noticed it before. You English have some weird immunity to heat. You take vacations in the gates of hell,' Miles remarked as they went down stone steps into air like a turkish bath. 'I've something to tell you too,' he added. 'I think you'll be pleased.'

Clumps of English roses surrounded them. Elisabeth Frink's bronze horse slept on a spreading lawn.

As soon as they were seated on a square-backed bench in the shade of a maple, James said:

'Before you tell me what you want to say, I want to tell you something. When you said you hoped to be able to offer me an important job, it was like a lifeline. I'll never forget it.'

He hesitated.

'You also said if I got something else in the meanwhile, you'd understand.'

For a moment he longed to shift the blame on to Miles for leaving him in a position where he could accept another offer. But that would be too dishonourable. He ploughed on.

'Another offer was put to me a couple of days ago. It has two distinct attractions. One is that it is a wider ranging job: I would be second-in-command not only of an influential newspaper, but second-in-command of an entire conglomerate.'

A curious light flickered for a moment in Miles's eyes.

'The other reason . . .' James had carefully considered every word that would lessen his embarrassment – how it would be 'healthier' to take a job from a relative stranger who could not be supposed to have acted out of sympathy. But Miles cut him short.

'Have you accepted this other offer?'

'Yes.'

'In that case, I can ask you: who made you this offer you find so attractive?'

'Lord Scrope,' James replied, hoping his discomfort was not evident. If he could conceal any sense of having let Miles down, perhaps Miles would regard it as a straight business decision – which it was – rather than some kind of defection to the enemy. 'Do you want to know the other reason for my decision, Miles?'

'No.'

Miles stood up.

'It will be announced in two days' time that I've won the *Dispatch*. I was going to make you a firm offer this evening,' he said impersonally. He might have been discussing the weather. 'I've never had a real look at the Frink horse. I'll take a walk before we all meet.'

He had no doubt whatsoever that Scrope had been motivated largely by the desire to snatch James away from him. That was for sure. But how the hell did the bastard know of Miles's intention? Suddenly he knew the answer: Jancie had told that fucking Fleet.

He put a hand out to stroke the neck of the bronze horse lying placidly on the grass. It was ridiculous to regard James accepting Scrope's no doubt compelling offer as some sort of personal betrayal. Why the hell shouldn't he have taken it? Miles gave a quick shake of his head at the goddam timing. With an effort of will, he shrugged inwardly: sulking was a waste of energy. None the less, the thing rankled.

Inside the house, a corridor of marble and slate squares stretched ahead to the reception rooms. Like walking on a goddam chessboard, he thought. He found them sipping champagne. Jancie jumped up to greet him. Her bright smile couldn't conceal the swollenness from weeping. No one seemed at ease.

As soon as they got up from the dinner table, Miles said: 'We've all got a heavy day tomorrow.'

'What was going on tonight?' Marigold asked as soon

as they were in the car. 'We all know Jancie is having a nervous breakdown. But what was wrong with you and James? I thought you were going to tell him the good news.'

Miles was looking at the embassies they passed, each country showing off its own culture. The domes and minaret of the Islamic Center looked misleadingly toylike.

'Miles?'

Without turning from the window he answered her question: 'We were a little tense because James has already gone and accepted an offer from Lord Scrope. The world is run by carpetbaggers and astrologers, and now Lord Scrope. James is to be second-in-command of the entire Scrope conglomerate – or so he has been seduced into believing. And he will be second-in-command of the very newspaper which is the *Dispatch*'s principal rival. Can you beat that? Wonderful news. Just great. Fuck it.'

Neither spoke further until Marigold said quietly: 'I don't think Lord Scrope is going to let anyone be his second-in-command.'

'You know, that is just breathtakingly perceptive of you, my dear.'

He put out a hand for a moment on hers, affectionately, in apology for being so irritable.

'Did he know you wanted James?' she continued.

'We can assume so.'

'That would be sufficent reason in itself,' she said. They both understood rivals' mentalities.

As the car crossed the bridge over Rock Creek Park, she saw the sky was navy-blue, and she thought of Gerald Scrope. He held the fascination of the enemy.

FIFTEEN

Zoë had never been summoned to Miles's office before. Just as she was shown in, his phone went, and he waved a hand towards a sofa. She walked instead to the windows and looked down.

'Each time I leave the *Express* and walk up M Street, I look at that blue clapboard house,' she said when he finished his call and crossed the room to stand beside her.

'I have fantasies about living in that house,' he said.

Abruptly they moved from the window.

Her clothes satirised a man's pin-stripe suit, skirt cut narrow, jacket unbuttoned over white T-shirt. This time the gleaming braid was threaded through with thick black cord – her business guise, he supposed. She sat back in the sofa, body erect, one leg crossed casually over the other. He took in the body language – assured, alert, female. He sat opposite, relaxed, legs stretched out.

'I asked you to come here because I want to make a proposition. How wedded are you to Washington?'

'I love working in Washington. It's quite a contrast to where I was brought up. I love that in a different way.'

'Vermont,' he said. 'I know.'

Her upbringing on her grandparents' farm on Lake Champlain was no secret, but she was surprised he knew of it.

'More than you might have guessed,' he added.

What did he mean? More about Vermont or more about her?

He saw the faint flush colour her cheeks.

She answered his original question. 'I'm not wedded to Washington for its own sake. It's the job I love.'

No reference to her personal life, he noted.

She looked away for a moment at the painting behind him. There was something poignant and sexy about the way each hair of Frida Kahlo's black brows was delineated. She returned her gaze to Miles, the complement to the Mexican woman he had chosen for his walls. Had the paralysed girl looked like Kahlo? Strange man.

'Have you ever considered working on the other side of the Atlantic?' he asked. 'In London?'

She sat quiet, now really tense inside, wanting him to spell out his proposal before she made any response.

He waited, wanting to see how she handled herself.

'Are we discussing the *Express*'s London bureau?' she asked.

'We might be,' he replied.

There was no concealing the animation that broke over her face. 'I've always wanted to work in London,' she said.

'Good.'

Again she waited. Was it conceivable he was going to ask her to be the *Express*'s London bureau chief? That post usually went to a more senior journalist. More likely, he was expanding the bureau's staff.

'I'm about to move my base to London,' Miles said.

'*What?*'

'I've bought the *London Dispatch*. It'll be announced soon.'

She was so surprised that her determined composure vanished: her face looked as open as a child's.

'Sure, I've enjoyed being owner of the *Express*,' he went on, 'but it's a bit remote control up here in Corporate. I want – something more intimate.'

She was struck by the intensity of his eyes.

'I intend being editor-in-chief of the *London Dispatch* – a visible editor with an office alongside the newsroom.'

'How on earth can you run your corporation at the same time as being a full-time editor?' asked Zoë. Her astonished tone made plain she thought the idea harebrained.

Miles chuckled. 'You think I've succumbed to megalomania. You may be right, of course, but it's not quite so far over the top as you think. The *Dispatch* will be a campaigning newspaper. Instead of directing the campaigns from behind the scenes, I'm going to come up front. It's not the first time, you know, that a newspaper owner has made himself editor-in-chief.'

Zoë's expression – dubious, intrigued – entertained him.

'Look. I think a helluva lot about the television side of Brewster Media Corporation, and cable is where the future lies. But it's mostly either entertainment or soundbites. Print journalism is what gets to me. Newspapers influence.'

He saw she was still dubious about something.

'I didn't say I'd be hobnobbing in the newsroom every breath of air day and night,' he said, finding he wanted to convince her his plan wasn't at all insane. 'I'd have a strong, tight team running each section of the paper. But the point is: I wouldn't be invisible. Journalists would be able to answer to me directly. I'd have contact with them.'

'Is that what you want? More contact with journalists? Most people would run a mile to avoid us,' said Zoë.

He smiled faintly. 'It depends, I suppose, which journalist we're speaking of.'

A new tension was triggered inside her. For a moment neither spoke.

He went on: 'In fact, it isn't the London bureau of the *Express* that I want to discuss with you. What I'm proposing is your coming to work on the *London Dispatch*.'

She gave an odd little laugh, no more than a short exhalation of breath.

'Most staff decisions will have to wait until I'm actually in place at the *Dispatch*,' Miles continued. 'But the features section is so mind-numbingly inertial that I've already decided to replace the head of that section. So I thought of you. You have a great feel for what makes a feature story compulsive reading.'

She didn't move.

'But my second thought was that it might be better to exploit your talents as an interviewer. Better for the *Dispatch*. Better for you. If you became a successful feature writer in London, it would give you a helluva strong position on both sides of the Atlantic.' A flicker of anxiety passed across his eyes. 'Well?'

Without hesitation she said: 'I prefer your second thought. I suppose I could do the administrative stuff that goes with running a section. But I like writing better.'

'Living in London is pricey,' he said. The costs of moving his home to London were being born in on him daily: his agent was doing a fancy deal to get Marigold the apartment she'd set her heart on. 'I'd be offering you a big jump in your salary.'

He offered a figure she'd be unlikely to refuse unless she didn't want to go to London anyway. For all he knew she might have a private life she wouldn't want to give up.

'It's a very attractive offer,' she said. 'Could I think about it?'

He looked at his watch. 'It's now just past high noon.'

She laughed. 'OK. I'll let you know by the end of the day.'

As soon as she got back to her desk she phoned Peter's

office. He wasn't there. She'd get a sandwich and go to Lafayette Square. It was only a ten-minute walk. The blanket of heat pressing on the city had lifted during the storm the night before, and today it was just cool enough to be comfortable in the capital's most entrancing park.

Only a few benches were occupied. A skinny little girl sucked on a straw stuck in a Pepsi while the bundled woman beside her, probably younger than she seemed, delved in a black plastic bag. A shaggy-bearded man, who must have spent the night on his bench, was absorbed in tying together the broken lace of one of his sneakers. Two neat youths in lightweight suits – they might have been bank clerks – talked animatedly as they unwrapped their pizzas. Police kept such a close eye on Lafayette Square, lying as it did in Washington's most prestigious area, that there was little inducement for even the most insolent crack-dealer to ply his trade here. A bench facing the White House was empty, but Zoë chose one facing Decatur House.

Uncountable times as a child she had implored her grandfather: 'Tell me again about Stephen Decatur.'

Each time the terrible ending.

He had seemed to Zoë the most glamorous of heroes, turning back the Barbary pirates, vanquishing the British in the War of 1812: *'Our country! In her intercourse with foreign nations, may she always be in the right; but our country, right or wrong.'*

Even when the story reached the peaceful part, when Decatur and his wife lived in this house designed for him by Washington's most prominent architect, entertaining with lavish hospitality, Zoë had always sat tensely, waiting for the duel when he would die.

Now she drew two columns on a memo pad – one for the *Washington Express*, the other for the *London*

Dispatch. Her grandfather had taught her this method as a way to make a difficult decision by herself. Alongside the columns you listed the various considerations, each valued from one to ten. (Even morality – 'A grand word for what you think is right and wrong,' he said – was listed occasionally.)

Then you added up the points in each column. (One time she had burst into tears when the result made her realise that was not what she wanted *at all*. But then her grandfather told her she could cheat a little, as the system wasn't foolproof. Immediately she downgraded the practicality column, thus shifting the balance to what she now knew she wanted.)

Sitting here on her bench she was about to write 'Peter' at the top of her considerations, but decided she'd better start with her career.

So. She was carving out a name for herself in Washington. It was far easier now to get a VIP to agree to an interview. The job security was pretty good for journalism, which wasn't saying much. (10 points in the *Express* column.)

In Britain no one had ever heard of her. It would mean starting all over again to build up a reputation. And the competition in the British media was known to be horrendous, with all the big papers produced in one city and vying with each other. (2 points in the *Dispatch* column.)

Peter. In six months they had grown far more attached than either had expected. He was her only confidant. He gave a focal point to her emotional life. They knew 'it wasn't going anywhere'. So far that suited them both. It gave a special excitement to each meeting. Maybe if Peter weren't married she would want him to be more central to her life. Maybe he was already more central than she would acknowledge. That would be disastrous. Maybe he was the real reason she held back from the leap to London. In which case, maybe she should leap. (7 points in both columns.)

Grandaddy's farm. In Washington it was easy – well, fairly easy – to get back to Lake Champlain. (10 points.) London was across an ocean. (1.)

The *Express* column was winning hands down.

Then she added challenge. If her boss thought she could succeed in London, why should she be afraid to try? And no one had ever heard of her in Washington a few years ago. If she stayed on the same track all her life, it had to come to its end. If she hopped on to a different train, it was a new adventure. (*Express* 3. *Dispatch* 10.)

What about adventure? She had been to Europe only a couple of times, as a tourist. Now she was twenty-eight and independent. (*Express* 1. *Dispatch* 10.)

Suddenly an old image surfaced – the photograph in the music room of the two-year-old girl walking hand in hand with her parents.

It's strange, Zoë thought; if she went to London she'd be making the move which fate denied her father. She could cross that threshold in his place. She added a final consideration to her list. Fate.

As soon as she entered his office, Miles left his desk and gestured to the sofas. Instead, she walked to the windows and looked down. She suddenly knew her decision would change her life. She thought of that white sliced bread, good to eat but you can compress the whole loaf like a concertina till it's only an inch wide. Had her life up to now – all the compartmentalising – been a bit like that? She turned and went to the sofa.

'You told me the pay you're offering. What are the other terms?' she asked.

He told her. At the end he said the contract, renewable, would run for a year.

'OK,' she said. 'I accept.'

His face broke into an enormous smile of unconcealed delight. Zoë had never seen him look like that before, like a schoolboy who has just hit the jackpot. Miles was astounded by his relief. He hadn't realised he'd tightened his stomach muscles as if to receive a blow. He relaxed them and stretched out his legs.

Flattered and excited as she watched his reaction, Zoë gave a soft laugh. Miles was the person who had made her take the leap.

Abruptly his manner changed. Matter-of-factly he outlined the timetable he had in mind.

Almost immediately she got up from the sofa. It was not just his switch of manner that made her want to leave now the details were settled. There was also something like shyness, but not shyness, that she felt unexpectedly. She had just made the decision to set out on the path that her father had intended to take.

Miles too got up, and when she put out her hand formally, he smiled once more (not so broadly, he made certain), as much to himself as at Zoë.

When she closed the door behind her, she was acutely aware of the man standing on its other side.

PART II

SIXTEEN

When the clouds parted, the land was vivid green and she was looking down at a toy castle, round tower, crenellated ramparts, flag flying. Zoë realised it was Windsor Castle. She'd read somewhere that the flag flew over whichever castle or palace the Queen was in. A square tower and wing were still blackened from the fire, but the rest looked too perfect to be true. She pressed her forehead against the glass until the castle disappeared beneath the plane.

She emerged from airport limbo into soft drizzle. 'Raining,' said the porter redundantly.

It added to her excitement: England as you expected it. A Californian had told her that when she first stepped out of Heathrow into England's air, her skin sighed and went *thrruppp*, sucking in the moisture, and it wasn't even raining that day.

'Maybe that's why the English don't need normal-size pores,' Zoë said, thinking of Marigold Brewster.

The porter gave her an odd look: another nutty American.

'We keep going in a straight line to your hotel,' said the cab driver. 'Long holiday?' He'd had to rearrange her suitcases and boxes twice to get everything in.

'No. I've come to work here. I've got to find an apartment.'

'They're called flats here,' he said, looking at her in the mirror, gearing up to do his stuff. 'You'll like your hotel. Got style.'

It was a present from Peter – for her first two nights in London. 'Something to remember me by,' he'd said when he learned the travel agent had booked her into a place in Earls Court. 'It's just off Piccadilly, secluded, elegant. You'll feel you're really in London. You can go to Earls Court on day three. The one proviso is you think of your lonely friend in Washington at least once each night you're at Dukes,' Peter said.

When the Hammersmith flyover was behind them, the road flattened out between tall nineteenth-century houses, with glimpses of trees, serene in the drizzle, lining side streets. Exhilaration mounted as she half-remembered where she was from her previous visit to Britain. The traffic was like New York instead of Washington, but there wasn't New York's din. When her driver pulled out from behind a doubledecker red bus, cars in the next lane let him in without everyone leaning on their horn.

'Natural History Museum on your left,' continued the driver. She definitely remembered how aloof it looked in its blue and terracotta slabs. 'Victoria and Albert next.' A moment later: 'Know what that red dome is up ahead?' She did, but it seemed churlish not to let her self-appointed guide continue. 'Harrods,' he announced, as if he himself had pulled it out of a hat.

Into an underpass and out the other side. 'Green Park on your right. In winter you can see across to Buckingham Palace.'

The plane trees were taller than anything in Lafayette Square, and even in July the leaves were emerald green, grass unparched.

'Ritz Hotel. Yours is almost behind it, but we have to go around.'

He turned off Piccadilly into a steep side street, then more turns.

'St James's Palace. That's where Prince Charles hangs his hat when he's in London. Princess Di's at Kensington Palace sometimes.'

The little street they entered was so pinched she wondered if the driver might have got lost. Its eighteenth-century houses seemed jarred by a concrete and glass building up ahead.

'What's that big hunk?' she asked.

'Ugly, innit? Most famous block of flats in the West End. 26 St James's Place. Brainchild of Sir Somebody Something.'

Before she could see more, he turned into a courtyard so tiny he had to inch the cab around a Bentley trying to get out.

'Here we are.'

Dukes Hotel was everything Peter had said – like stepping into another world where no one seemed in a hurry; dark mahogany, brass rails, beckoning doors. She peeped into a secluded sitting-room, then looked more boldly into a magnificent bar which made her think of a man's club. Upstairs in her bedroom with its chintzes and four-poster, a ceiling fan with wooden blades waited calmly. She did a little pirouette of pleasure at how good the real air felt after the plane. It was the first time she'd been entirely alone since starting her journey the day before.

Ignoring jet lag, she spent the afternoon walking around sightseeing, keyed up, responses heightened. Sitting on a bench in St James's Park, she smiled at the ducks' ridiculous waddle as they plodded down the grassy slope and plopped into the lake. Two pin-striped young men hurrying past smiled when this dark haired girl, by herself, burst out laughing as she watched the ducks.

That evening, after a long bath, she left the hotel to look for somewhere to eat. She liked looking through strange restaurant windows, examining the menu displayed in a brass frame outside. What she wanted was a glass of wine and one course that came from England.

Leaving the hotel courtyard, she went further up the pinched street to where it opened into a bigger space commanded by the modernist block of flats the cab driver thought so ugly. Well, it certainly was formidable. She retraced her steps.

Ten minutes later, in yet another dark narrow street – though she glimpsed the bright lights of Piccadilly only a few minutes away – a green awning bore the words: Green's Restaurant and Oyster Bar. Zoë loved oysters. Too bad you're only meant to eat them when the month has an R in it. She read the menu: plenty else. And she liked the name.

Inside it was dead-chic. She sauntered past dark booths where people chatted, one or two watching to see who this self-possessed, striking young woman, hair in a pony-tail, had come to meet.

'Have you a table for one?' she asked the head waiter.

'The tables are booked, madam. You can sit at the bar if you wish.'

It curved across one corner of the dining-room, and she climbed happily on to a tall stool. The lighting was soft. Conversation was a murmur at tables now out of sight. In the mirrored wall behind the bar she saw her face smiling above the lined-up bottles.

It was funny: in a place like Washington where you were known, you felt odd going to a smart restaurant for dinner by yourself. Maybe it was because you realised other diners, in couples or groups, would imagine you were lonely. Zoë couldn't stand the idea of anyone thinking she was lonely, especially when she was not. But when you were in a city where you were anonymous, it was different. You had the confidence peculiar to strangers.

While she re-examined the menu, she ordered a glass of house champagne, and thought of Peter, giving him a little toast when she saw herself lift the glass in the mirrored wall.

'Where do the giant prawns come from?' she asked one of the men behind the bar, slim and quick in his white shirt and bow tie and narrow black trousers, pleasant in a deadpan way.

'Dublin Bay. Caught this morning.'

Not quite England but close enough. She swivelled to look for a moment at the tables. All the men were pin-striped, the women coiffed by a hairdresser. She turned back just as her plate of prawns – they were enormous – was put before her.

'Fancy seeing you here.'

She turned and looked straight into Miles's eyes. He burst out laughing at her expression of amazement. The blood rushed to her face.

'But I only just arrived,' she said. 'In England, I mean,' wildly flustered by finding him at her shoulder. Then she looked over his. Red-gold hair, poreless skin, green eyes. God she was beautiful.

'You remember Zoë Hare,' Miles said to his wife. 'She's joining our happy band at the *Dispatch*.'

'How nice to see you,' Marigold replied.

'Where are you staying?' asked Miles.

'I'm starting off at Dukes,' replied Zoë.

Marigold lifted an eyebrow.

'Then I'm moving to something less grand while I look for an apartment. Flat,' she mocked herself.

'We're staying nearby,' said Miles, 'while Marigold tears our own new place to pieces. You'll see it at the end of that narrow street when you return to Dukes. Most people hate its outside, but once you're in and looking out, it's good.'

'Designed by Britain's most famous living architect,' said Marigold gaily. 'Staying at the Ritz makes it convenient to oversee the redecoration. I'll go ahead to our table, Miles. Nice to see you,' she said again to Zoë.

A bundle of fun, Zoë muttered to herself. 'I'll be at the *Dispatch* in two weeks,' she said brightly to Miles.

Miles hesitated. 'You're not having second thoughts, are you?' he asked.

'About coming to the *Dispatch*? Oh no.'

Another hesitation. 'I'm very happy you came.'

The limp was pronounced when he turned away, but then it seemed no more than a stiffness as he started across the room. She turned back to her plate of prawns, watching in the mirror until he disappeared from it. She sipped her champagne. Her face still felt hot. She took another swallow.

'Would you like some more champagne?' asked a barman.

'That would be nice.' Nice? I could drink the whole bottle, mac.

Soon after finishing her prawns she climbed off her stool, hoping she looked delighted to be by herself as she strolled to the door without looking around.

During Zoë's two remaining days at Dukes, she was glad not to collide with Marigold in St James's Place. As for Marigold, she had no reason to give Zoë Hare a second thought.

It wasn't homesickness, she was sure. Anyway, at the moment home was this dump in Earls Court, where west London began, and single-dwelling houses were pressed between endless bed-sitters, and rain came down like bullets from a leaden sky. The British summer was undergoing a bad patch.

Actually, Zoë's hotel wasn't a dump, but she called it that when she was tired after another fruitless day of looking for a flat – not a 'spacious flat', for God's sake, just one that didn't face north or look out on a high brick wall. When she was shown one which allowed the sun to peep in before being swallowed by the leaden sky again, the windows shook from trucks lurching past. Washington's broad calm streets were a world away. Meanwhile she was camping in this clean, rambling, bed-and-breakfast hotel near Earls Court Underground station.

But where the hell *was* the bathroom had been an initial problem. Even though the place was still in the throes of being modernised, there must be a bathroom somewhere on the fourth floor. She prowled corridors until she spotted gleaming avocado-green at the end of a passage. This country must have a fixation on avocado-green bathrooms, she thought: half the flats she'd been shown had them, usually with a bidet completing the set. But there were no floorboards yet to reach the bathroom. As probably no one else would teeter along the scaffold board, at least she'd have it to herself.

She was no nearer finding a decent place to live than when she'd started, though she was getting the hang of the various neighbourhoods in this vast metropolis, each a bit like a village, some smart, some seedy, with their own food shops and newsagent and quite often a betting shop (everyone in England seemed to like 'a flutter'). Once she started at the *Dispatch* there'd be no time to flat-hunt, and she saw an unbroken future of walking the plank to the avocado bathroom. Her money was disappearing at a helluva rate.

Each day as she set forth she was conscious of being on a new adventure. Yet it wasn't only her sharpened awareness that gave objects a startling clarity: colours really were more intense than in the States. Perhaps the moist air made them like that. Geraniums in window-boxes were brighter than the same species at home. There was something touching, she found, about the English passion for window-boxes, beautifully kept, no passers-by helping themselves to your petunias. Hibiscus was a more vivid blue than in Washington.

'I've never seen so many blue flowers and shrubs,' she wrote to her grandparents, 'which is a good sign.' Blue was her favourite colour.

The sense of being alive was acute when she took the Underground to the Royal Opera House to hear *Tristan und Isolde*, still her favourite Wagner. Walking to the station afterwards, she hummed the surging, swooping light–dark, love–death oppositions. Why did people feel the thrill of the familiar when it came to music, she wondered, yet they didn't seem to find this in real-life sexuality? Why shouldn't that stay thrilling too, if it was enmeshed with real love?

Outside Earls Court station a newspaper kiosk brandished placards about the rise in crime – encouraging, she thought, how many people in this country bought papers day and night – but she had no sense of fear walking alone after dark. London felt safe in a way New York did not. It added to this new sense – hard to describe to herself – of feeling more whole.

Most of her evenings were spent in her hotel room, and then the exhilaration of being in a strange city went distinctly flat. In Washington she'd never wanted to spend every evening with friends. Yet without the option, Quiet Night was not the same treat. If Peter could be here for just one night it would make all the difference. Then she would have enjoyed going to bed early and reading on the other nights.

She discovered it was one thing to choose to have solitude. It was different when no one offered you a choice. The patches of what she called wistfulness recurred.

Twice she phoned her grandparents to hear their voices.

And she was overjoyed whenever Peter called her from his office 'just to check you haven't picked up a Limey accent'.

And then she found the place in World's End, two sunny rooms and a kitchen and bath (and if the tub was sort of worn, it was also white and enormous – one of those English bathtubs that made American ones look as if they were meant for washing the dog).

The name added to the charm of this fringe of Chelsea where the King's Road bent and a few streets later became Fulham. Each time she passed the Victorian pub standing on the corner, its scrolled letters proclaiming 'The World's End', she tried to imagine how once it had marked the western edge of London. Two streets away from the pub was her flat, at the top of a nineteenth-century terrace house with no lorries grinding past. She took it for a year, lease renewable.

Jubilant, she moved in the day before she was to start at the *Dispatch*. Her wistfulness evaporated.

SEVENTEEN

'For God's sake remember to call him Chairman.'

'How'd he know I just walked in?' asked Simon. It was his first day as the *Javelin*'s new foreign editor. He hadn't yet got to his own cramped office and was just checking in with the editor when the summons came.

'He's like Argos. Wherever you are, one of his eyes sees you.'

When the lift opened at the top floor he found a secretary waiting to lead the way. They walked through two rooms of secretaries, then down a short corridor which led past a largeroom. Simon glanced through the glass dividing wall. The room showed no sign of being occupied. It appeared newly furnished, its handsome desk and leather sofa and armchairs indicating high executive rank.

'Whose room is that?' he asked.

'It's for the *chef de cabinet*,' the secretary replied before opening the door into Lord Scrope's suite.

Gerald was at the big Jacobean desk. Not until they were alone did he look up and nod curtly to an armchair nearby. It was so low-slung that Simon felt like a supplicant looking up at his master. Any mad hope that Gerald might say a word of welcome at their first meeting went up the spout.

'Tell me what you know about Miles Brewster's accident, Mr Fleet.'

'It was in Mexico and very messy. Something like fifteen years ago. He was driving.'

'I can read, Mr Fleet.'

Simon flushed. Was every summons to Lord Scrope's office the overture to an ulcer?

'None of the articles about him give any details. Why is that, Mr Fleet?'

'Mexico may be next door on the map, but it's far away. Brewster wasn't newsworthy when it happened. So there wouldn't be anything in the cuttings library. Chairman,' he added. 'But the word around Washington is he was drunk at the time.'

'Does he often get drunk, Mr Fleet?'

Simon had no idea. He gave a short laugh. Gerald remained expressionless.

'Not that I know of, Chairman. People who knew him before it happened say he's changed since then.'

'For instance?'

'Less exuberant. More reticent.'

'Tell me, Mr Fleet. Have you ever met a reticent man who hasn't something to hide?'

Without rising from his chair, Gerald indicated the audience was over.

Just as Simon reached the door the flat-vowelled voice said: 'One other thing, Mr Fleet. Beginning next week, the fine office outside my door will be occupied by my *chef de cabinet*.'

The last three words were spoken with a pomposity that gave them an ambivalence: he could have been speaking of a grandee or a court jester.

'I believe you and he know each other well, Mr Fleet. But you will address him as Ambassador. He will be surprised to discover you are working for me.'

Simon blinked, uneasy.

'You have heard of "creative tension", Mr Fleet. I am a great believer in it. Some employers think staff produce their best work when they feel the confidence of security. I disagree. I believe I get the best out of the buggers when they're kept on edge. Good day, Mr Fleet.'

*

The new owner and editor-in-chief of the *Dispatch* divided his long work hours between his corporate headquarters on the top floor and the newspaper below.

The imposing structure stood south of the Thames, half a mile from the *Javelin* if you were a crow, much longer by road because of the river's bends. It was built after Rupert Murdoch made his midnight flit from Fleet Street – and the other press barons saw how his cheaper premises and new technology soon put his newspapers in the ascendant. After that, it was only a matter of time before they all decamped, leaving Fleet Street a ghost street. But though dispersed all over London, Britain's twenty national newspapers still referred to themselves as 'Fleet Street'. Journalists have a strong sentimental strain.

When Miles was in his editor's role there was only a glass wall between him and the newsroom. During the initial weeks the deputy editor could be seen sitting alongside him.

Zoë sat among the feature writers in the newsroom maze. Her desk and filing cabinet were identical to others in the crowded room, but everyone had heard she'd already done well on the *Washington Express* and that Miles Brewster had hired her personally to come to the *Dispatch*. There were the usual suspicions and resentment.

'You and Zoë Hare will, of course, consult on what she is to write,' Miles told the head of the section. 'She'll need your guidance while she's finding her feet in London. I shall be discussing her work with her fairly regularly.'

The features editor got the message: Zoë was answerable to him only in a formal sense. He expected this to be a pain in the ass, but had to admit he found her very personable. So far she had given no indication that she was not working directly to him.

Though twenty other desks stood between, Zoë's was in a direct line with Miles's office. Several times she had a strong sense of being observed. Once she looked up to find him watching her, and he quickly returned his eyes to his own work. At the start of her second week she asked another journalist to help turn her desk around. That afternoon when Miles came down from Corporate and took his editor's chair, glancing through the glass partition he saw no sign of the oval face: in its place was the ponytail. After a moment's annoyance, he chuckled.

Minutes after Marigold left the Ritz she turned into St James's Place. As she reached Number 26 – her goal – she glanced at an eighteenth-century mansion opposite, Spencer House. She knew it was leased to Lord Rothschild by Princess Diana's family in return for a sixteen-million-pound restoration. The Brewsters had already been to a lavish party there. But for herself and Miles, she preferred the dominating force of Number 26.

Like many people planning the interior of their home, she imagined one particular guest. On arriving to find London's best-known decorator supervising plumbers, joiners, painters, she walked straight through to the main reception area, half again as tall as the rest of the huge flat. Standing alone at the wall of bronze-framed windows that looked over Green Park, she imagined showing off the view to Lord Scrope.

Simultaneously she felt a guilty unease. It was out of the question, she knew, that he actually be their guest. Why should she even want to entertain this man who was her husband's enemy? Yet she did.

'It's not just with my head that I want to start afresh,' Jancie said to James. 'With all my heart I want to try and make up for what I did to you. Can you ever forgive me?'

They were having a drink alone in his study overlooking their garden. He pressed his lips together for a moment. Then he said: 'I already have.'

Jancie's eyes filled with tears. James gave his crooked smile and took another swallow of his whisky.

'Even when things were their worst' – he always avoided referring directly to Simon – 'I never considered a formal separation, let alone a divorce.'

She stared at his honourable schoolboy expression.

'Marriage is a contract. One honours a contract,' he said. Jancie took a large swallow of her own whisky. ('Maybe if you could think of it as touching you wouldn't go bananas when he talks like that,' Zoë had said.)

For Jancie the renewal of their marriage required daily determination and a little dissembling. The pretty Kensington house where she'd been so content before they went to Washington seemed incomplete. She could absorb herself in Danny and Nell, first-graders now, when they got back from the local primary school. But at other times even the most tremendous effort couldn't keep Simon from her thoughts.

'I go to sleep at night thinking about him. I wake in the morning thinking of him,' she told Zoë grimly.

They were having lunch at a pub near the *Dispatch*.

'When I walked in here, I looked around, hoping he might be here. It's like an illness I can't throw off.'

Both were silent.

'Got any ideas up your sleeve as to how one actually stops being in love?' said Jancie.

'Have you thought about going back to work at the BBC? Everyone in London says you were a brilliant news presenter.'

'A helluva lot has changed in the six years since then,' Jancie said.

'So have you,' said Zoë. 'You must have learned something out of all this misery. Turn it into something you can make work for you. And remember it's a big plus that you've got the experience – the connections – of having been ambassadress to Washington. Write to whoever's in charge of television news and ask for an appointment as if you're doing them a favour.'

Jancie's face grew thoughtful.

'Well, it would certainly be a distraction,' she said, 'even though with James's salary we won't need the money. He starts at the *Javelin* on Monday. He's really looking forward to getting buried in work again, poor guy. I know Miles didn't like it when James opted for Lord Scrope's offer. But it has everything James needs to boost his battered ego.'

EIGHTEEN

A sleek Jaguar purred to a halt outside the Whartons' home. Twenty minutes later James strode into the *Javelin*'s foyer and looked round the art-deco palace with the satisfaction of a man who has nearly drowned and then comes out on top again.

'I'm James Wharton,' he said to the commissionaire. 'Lord Scrope is expecting me.'

As he ascended in the glass lift used only by the Chairman and his senior staff, James was taut with the exhilaration of a journalist returning to a newspaper office from a long absence. He looked out at the *Star Wars* atrium: from it a honeycomb of corridors ran to executive offices, newsroom, cuttings library, photo library, accountants. He would be second-in-command of this and Scrope Tower as well. When the top-floor light flashed he felt adrenalin surge as he approached the seat of power.

The door opened. The young man who met him seemed tense, though extremely respectful, as he said: 'Welcome, Ambassador. I'm Roy Matthews. I shall be your personal assistant. Let me show you your office.'

In the first room the staff got to their feet, and on entering the second room – 'This is where I sit,' said Roy Matthews – the staff were introduced. When they came to James's office, he took in its impressive size and furnishings at a glance.

'Before you start making yourself at home,' said Roy, 'I'll take you through to the Chairman.'

Only a few steps along the short corridor, he opened a door that looked much heavier than the other doors. For a second James was taken aback. His own fine office, by its location, could be mistaken as an ante-room to Lord Scrope's suite.

'Ambassador Wharton, Chairman,' Roy announced.

Gerald looked up, unhurried. Then he rose from his chair and came round his desk to shake hands.

'I hope you will enjoy your stay here, Ambassador,' he said.

The phrase 'enjoy your stay' struck James as unexpected. But what he found most unsettling was how Gerald pronounced his courtesy title, giving it an ambiguous emphasis.

'Sit down, Ambassador, for a few minutes before you start your duties.'

Gerald gestured to an armchair as he took another.

While James was gratified when the staff initially used his courtesy title, he was glad that in a place as democratic as a newspaper office they would all quickly be on first-name terms.

'I hope you'll call me James.'

Gerald looked at him steadily before saying: 'I like to keep a distance between myself and my staff. You will want to do the same, Ambassador.'

He paused.

'We all have our roles to play, Ambassador.'

Another pause.

He went on: 'I have informed all staff that you are to be addressed as Ambassador. If you wish to call those under you by their first names, that is for you. You will call me Chairman.'

A cold unease took hold of James.

Gerald switched roles. Menace disappeared. 'No other newspaper office can boast of a former British Ambassador to Washington as *chef de cabinet*. We take pride at the *Javelin* in being able to address you by the title you have earned – and you will see the same pride when you go across the river to Scrope Tower.'

There was a silence.

Then James said: 'I take it we'll go over to Scrope Tower later today.'

'You will find I prefer spontaneous action to excessive scheduling, Ambassador,' Gerald replied. 'You will remember from your own experience in Washington: events outside our control occur around the world twenty-four hours a day. Three-quarters of my life is spent responding to these events. I might cross the river later this morning and drop in at Scrope Tower. I might not.'

Another silence.

'I don't think we should leave it too long before I'm introduced to Corporate executives I'm to oversee,' James said.

'Oversee?' said Gerald, his face impassive. 'You will be my third hand. But "oversee" is not the word I would use, Ambassador. I prefer to think of you as my trusted adviser. In good time I shall introduce my third hand to Corporate. For the present, I want you to concentrate on the *Javelin*'s coverage of defence and foreign affairs. You will want to remind everyone that you are Britain's expert on defence before turning your mind to other matters.'

He picked up one of the phones banked beside him. 'This is the Chairman,' he said, as if any of his staff could possibly mistake the voice. 'Ambassador Wharton is with me. You will give him a tour of the *Javelin*. Later in the day, you will consult with him on the defence coverage planned for tomorrow's paper. You will present yourself to him in ten minutes. He will be in the *chef de cabinet*'s office.'

He put down the phone. 'Duncan McCavvy is the

paper's defence editor. He will be reporting to you, Ambassador.' A pause. 'And to me.'

'At present, who writes the editorials – the leaders – on defence and foreign affairs?' asked James.

'I expect you will be writing them when you feel ready, Ambassador. I particularly value your knowledge and understanding of international defence. Once you feel at home as *chef de cabinet*, you will find I rely on you for many things.'

Gerald stood up, his movement as always more agile than expected in a burly man. 'I must not detain you further, Ambassador.'

James got to his own feet, nonplussed. 'Who are my personal staff?' he asked.

'Did not Roy Matthews inform you that he is your personal assistant?' said Gerald. 'I must tell him to improve his fucking manners.'

'No, no,' said James, 'he told me that. But who will be the rest of my staff?'

Gerald lifted his hands like a pontiff. 'I told you, Ambassador, you are my third hand. In the room where Matthews sits, every person is at your disposal as well as mine.'

'Let's get this straight,' James said. 'Is Roy Matthews my personal assistant or yours?'

'He is yours, Ambassador, just as a cabinet minister's private secretary is his.'

The analogy was only too clear to James. A cabinet minister's private secretary is a civil servant with two masters. One master is his minister, who is transient. The other is the head of the civil service, the aptly named permanent secretary. James was the transient, Gerald the permanent master. While the full implications of this bore in, Gerald pressed a button on his desk. Seconds later the door was opened by Roy Matthews.

'You will show the Ambassador whatever he needs to know on his first day at the *Javelin*,' said Gerald.

After the oppressive weight of the Chairman's room, James found his own office felt strangely insubstantial.

'Let me explain the telephone system, Ambassador,' said Roy.

Several minutes later Duncan McCavvy walked in. 'Glad to meet you, Ambassador. Let me take you downstairs and show you around.'

As the lift descended and James again looked at the corridors fanning from the *Star Wars* atrium, his disquiet was somewhat allayed. None the less he found it necessary to reassure himself that even a *chef de cabinet* is bound to feel a newcomer on his first day.

'Delighted to meet you, Ambassador,' said the editor. 'I'm afraid I am due at a meeting with the Prime Minister's press officer, but you and I will have a chance to talk later.'

'I'll take you to meet the editor's lieutenants,' said McCavvy, leading James to the first of the small offices running along one side of the newsroom. 'This is Ambassador Wharton, the Chairman's *chef de cabinet*,' McCavvy said to the news editor.

When they were moving on to the next office, James said: 'I'd prefer you to introduce me as James Wharton.'

McCavvy stood absolutely still for a moment. Then, in a friendly way, he said: 'The Chairman gave me clear instructions. The staff is to call you Ambassador.' He turned and led the way to the features editor: 'This is Ambassador Wharton.'

As they approached a third office, McCavvy said: 'I think you already know the foreign editor. He was at the *Washington Express* when you were in Washington.'

Through the glass wall James saw the foreign editor's feet propped among newspapers slewed across his desk.

Above the *Herald Tribune* he was reading, only his yellow curls could be seen. James's training as a boy, his practice in diplomacy, his innate pride, all came into play. Without faltering in his stride, he followed McCavvy in.

'I think you know Ambassador Wharton,' said McCavvy.

Simon lowered the paper and jumped to his feet with a smile.

'I heard you were coming,' he said, 'but I hadn't realised it was today.' He stuck out a hand.

After only a moment's hesitation, James shook hands. As he did so, he had actively to suppress an image of the plump fingers palpating Jancie's breasts. As for the other parts of Jancie those fingers had explored, James had never allowed the thoughts to surface in his mind.

Coolly he said: 'I hadn't realised I would have the pleasure of having you work under me.'

The tip of Simon's tongue flicked out to moisten his lips. He glanced at McCavvy, who stood there, deadpan. James turned and left the room.

When they'd completed the rounds, McCavvy said: 'You'll want to have some time upstairs to sort yourself out. After lunch we can talk about things in the pipeline for the next couple of days.'

Alone in the ascending lift, James looked out. Deep indignation burned inside him. That goat. Had Fleet claimed his new job as his reward? If so, what the hell did this say about Lord Scrope?

In his own room he walked straight to the window and looked down on the Thames flowing steadily to the sea. The turmoil inside him was growing unmanageable. He must calm it. He mustn't try to analyse Gerald Scrope's intentions. It was too soon to attempt that. The Chairman. He must remember to call him the Chairman.

With an effort of will, James turned his thoughts from the Chairman to that yellow-haired bastard. He must think constructively. If he was at the helm of his boat in a force 8 gale, he would keep calm and think constructively. He, James Wharton, was second-in-command to Lord Scrope. Simon Fleet was an underling. James remembered something he'd said to Zoë: 'If ever I find myself in a position of power over Simon Fleet, I shall be a happy man.' That was the way to think of it.

He sat down at his handsome desk with its virgin blotter in a tooled-leather holder. He looked at his watch. It was only noon. He opened the first of the right-hand drawers and took a sheet from a neat pile of vellum writing paper. '*Javelin*' was embossed in large red letters, and beneath them: 'From Ambassador James Wharton, *chef de cabinet* to Lord Scrope.'

He gazed, fascinated, at this letterhead. It looked so grand. Yet there was not another piece of paper of any sort on his desk. No files to read and digest before initialling the margins. No list of pressing appointments. Nothing. For the first time since he was a small child, James had nothing to do.

Reaching to his breast pocket, he took out the folded handkerchief and wiped the sweat gathering on the back of his neck even though the day was cool.

NINETEEN

'Push your knees back when you walk through the door,' said Zoë. 'It has this amazing effect on the psyche. It'll make you feel confident and look it.'

'How can I push my knees back and walk at the same time, for heaven's sake?'

'You sound like Gerald Ford, Jancie – well, LBJ describing Ford.'

'Yeah, yeah. "Can't walk and chew gum at the same time," though "chew gum" was a euphemism for what Johnson really said.'

'Are you standing up now?'

They were talking on the phone.

'Push your knees back now – as far as they'll go,' Zoë instructed.

'I just grew an inch.' Jancie gave a wild laugh. 'I could rule the world.'

An hour later a BBC security guard lifted the barrier and she began the surrealist climb up that concrete cube. The last time her car had groaned up its ramps, she was five months pregnant.

The lobby of Television Centre retained its cathedral-like self-importance. The right hand of the right hand of God, she was told, wanted her to stop by before her main appointment. She shoved back her knees.

He came round his desk, an unsettling smile stretching the cramped face. 'We last met at the Embassy when you and James gave the dinner for Prince Charles,' he said.

He couldn't have been more cordial, yet she was filled with foreboding when she left him. In a place like the

BBC, too often affability meant they'd already made up their minds that you wouldn't get the job.

The personnel woman was brisk. 'Six years' absence is a long time in the life of a woman presenter,' she said matter-of-factly.

Buck up, pal, Jancie said to herself.

'I wasn't thinking only of being a news presenter,' she said cheerily, sitting very straight. 'There are other areas where my particular experience in Washington – all the on-going contacts that follow from it – could be of value to the BBC. There aren't that many people who understand how television works and also have connections with people the BBC needs on its side.'

A brief silence.

'Have you considered doing PR work?'

'Yes,' Jancie lied. 'I'd be very good at it.'

A week later she received a letter from the publicity director asking her to telephone his office to arrange an interview.

Two weeks after she went for her interview, knees back, she received a further letter. Assistant in publicity. So-so pay. A year's contract, renewable. A job.

Late that evening when James, ashen-faced, got home from the *Javelin*, Jancie ran downstairs to meet him. 'The BBC have offered me a job. In publicity. It's not brilliant, but it's a foot in the door.'

He put an arm around her and laid his cheek on hers. This was one night he wouldn't tell her what his own day had been like.

Some days there'd be the sudden summons, and they would climb purposefully into Gerald's Rolls and cross the river to Scrope Tower, where Gerald might turn to James for confirmation on some point, or he might wave him away like a fly when James intervened with a view of his own.

Some days he would be summoned to be told portentously: 'In this entire building you and I alone, Ambassador, are able to grasp what is taking place in the Middle East. Write me a leader I'll be proud to read in tomorrow's *Javelin*.'

Another day Gerald would barge through the door shouting: 'You fucking idiot. The *Javelin*'s got two and a half million readers from the Prime Minister to the cab driver. They're not going to run to the bleeding dictionary each time you get the urge to show you can spell twenty-letter words.' On one occasion he crossed the room, flung open the window and threw the pages out.

Only in one area was the Gerald treatment predictable. When he courted a cabinet minister in the wine-red dining-room, or an industrialist or American congressman, invariably he displayed respect for James, turning to him to lead the discussion. Key power-wielders were impressed by Gerald's aggressive force and enterprise, but they trusted James.

Why, he would ask himself after a dreadful day, did he tolerate the good cop–bad cop treatment? The answer he always reached was that Gerald Scrope was a self-made genius, and his brutality had to be overlooked as just one part of an exciting, complex personality. James had the inverted snobbery of many born into the privileged professional classes of England: he condoned grossness in a self-made man which he would never have tolerated in one of his own kind.

Today Gerald had started politely enough when he rang through and said: 'I'm going over to Scrope Tower at twelve-thirty, Ambassador.'

'Right. I can finish my leader on Arabi before then. I'll join you at twelve twenty-five,' James replied.

'I shall be going alone, Ambassador.'

James bridled. 'But we agreed only an hour ago that you and I would go over to Scrope Tower together,' he said. He could hear the tension in his own voice.

'I decided one minute ago that you will stay here. Have you forgotten the terms of our agreement, Ambassador? I said I needed someone I could trust to sift out what decisions can be taken in my absence. Are you saying I can't trust you, Ambassador?'

'For God's sake, Chairman, when we were originally discussing this job we were talking about your being absent on the other side of the world, not just the other side of the Thames.'

'You fucking Eton idiot, *you* may have been dreaming about me being on the other side of the world. I didn't say where I'd be.'

Although Jancie's PR work was a far cry from that gilded period as a TV news presenter, she found she enjoyed it and was good at it. James was invaluable with his advice and contacts. And the job was a distraction from thinking about Simon. When James had first told her Simon was the foreign editor of the *Javelin*, he might have been giving a weather report. He'd not referred to Simon since. One day her longing had got so bad that she rang Simon at the *Javelin*.

After only a moment's hesitation he said: 'ESP. I was just going to call you. It's been much too long.'

She tried to stay calm as joy raced through her. He sounded really glad to hear her.

'I'm snowed under with work,' he said, 'but I'll ring you next week to fix a lunch date. Think where you'd like to go.'

Three weeks passed.

Alone now in her office she clenched her fists and shook them at the phone. 'Ring, God damn you, and be him.' It rang. She seized it. Wrong voice. An hour later her willpower gave way.

'I'm sorry, he's in a meeting. I'll tell him you phoned,' said his secretary. In the second before the phone connection was broken, Jancie heard her snigger.

Television Centre was only ten or fifteen minutes from the Kensington house, and she was usually home by six-thirty. The mother's help had made the twins' supper, and Jancie drank coffee at the kitchen table while Nell and Danny told her their day's news. When they ran out to play in the fading light, she went upstairs to change into something softer that would show off her curvaceous body. If she went through the outer motions it made the whole thing easier. And it wasn't just a charade: the weeks of trying to act like a loving wife had reawakened deep affection.

When James walked into the house he heard the voices piping in the back garden. It was one of those September evenings when the air is warm and motionless, and he looked out the back door to see his children and two small neighbours wielding croquet mallets like golf clubs. The twin blonde heads were differentiated only by the length of their hair.

'Good evening,' he called out, and they looked up and waved before returning to the more important business of hacking at the ball.

He was relieved they were occupied until their bedtime. Even fifteen minutes' conversation with them – his aim on the rare nights he got home before they were in bed – would have been an effort of will after a day as ghastly as the one just ended.

When he reached his upstairs study, Jancie had just put an ice-bucket and glasses beside the drinks tray. She took one look at his face.

'Another wonderful day with Lord Scrope?' she said, putting up her face to kiss her husband.

James poured them each a whisky.

When they were seated in armchairs facing across the hearth he said: 'I'm not sure I can go on with it, Jancie. He's determined to demoralise me.'

'But why does he want to?' she asked. 'What's the point?'

'I don't know.'

He took a large swallow of whisky, and they sat in silence.

Then he went on. 'When we're together with anyone of rank in the world outside Scrope, the Chairman treats me with the greatest respect.'

'Don't call him that when you're home!' she said sharply.

He passed a hand over his brow.

'It's within the walls of his empire,' he went on, 'that Gerald Scrope turns into the cat playing with the mouse. One moment it's "Fine, fine, Ambassador, only a first-class brain could have written that leader on Arabi." The next moment I'm a "fucking twit"' – with a weary voice, he mimicked Gerald's flat vowels – 'to be derided for a "fucking Eton education".'

'But Gerald Scrope is always boasting about how he made his own way to the top.'

'I know,' he said wearily.

James was lying back in his chair, gazing half-seeing at the egg-and-dart cornice of the study ceiling. For a moment his mind's eye saw the richly carved symbols – power, wealth, knowledge – just below the cornice of the British Ambassador's library in Washington. He shook off the memory.

'I don't know what to do, Jancie.'

He didn't whine when he said it: it was a simple statement of despair.

'If you walked out of the *Javelin* tomorrow,' she said, 'we could manage until you got another job. You'd be bound to get a handsome offer from another newspaper, even though it didn't carry a grand title with it.'

James tightened his mouth. The very words '*chef de cabinet*' made him want to retch.

'You're married to a bloody fool, Jancie. You know why I was in such a hurry to accept Gerald Scrope's offer? Hubris.' Despite his melancholy, he smiled. '"Why can't you fucking use words people can fucking understand?"' he said in Gerald's voice. 'Pride. Bloody bullshit pride.'

He gave a dry laugh.

'When Gerald Scrope flew to Washington to woo me, I was flattered. I was flattered by that bloody title he offered and the status I imagined went with it. Being British Ambassador was more seductive than I realised. I got used to all the flim-flammery. I couldn't bear its sudden loss. What Gerald Scrope held out sounded like a substitute for all that. Bloody hubris. Bloody fool.'

Watching him now, she was touched by an innocence in the serious set of his mouth which used to set her teeth on edge when she was behaving her worst in Washington. She had landed him in this shit.

'You've never taxed me,' she said, 'with causing you to lose the job you loved. I'd give anything to be able to reshoot that episode.'

He gave a semblance of a smile.

'The odd thing,' she went on, 'is that what's happened has made me feel closer to you than before. It's as if we now connect in a way we never really used to. You tell me things you never told me before.'

She left her chair and went over to stand behind his, leaning down to lay her cheek alongside his. She liked the feel of his skin, weatherbeaten from all that sailing.

When she'd returned to her chair James said: 'Perhaps if I handled things differently with Gerald Scrope I could still make something out of this job. Part of my problem is I've never known anyone like him before. I don't know what animal I'm dealing with.'

The telephone rang.

They both stared at it. It was one of two phones – the red one – on the table beside James. Everyone who worked for Gerald had to be available twenty-four hours a day.

'Don't answer it,' said Jancie.

After the tenth count, the ringing stopped. Then it started again. James looked at Jancie. She grinned.

She got up and switched on the regular phone's answer-machine. 'The bastard will try that next,' she said, settling down again in her chair. She and James giggled like children when the regular phone started and was cut off mid-ring while the light flashed silently on the answer-machine.

'I'd better go down and throw our supper together,' Jancie said at last. 'Shall I choose the wine?'

'I trust you implicitly,' James replied, smiling. He poured himself another whisky, made himself comfortable, flicked the answer-machine to playback and turned up the volume.

'According to our schedule,' rasped the voice of the resident clerk, 'Ambassador Wharton is at home this evening. We can get no response on the special line. The Chairman wishes Ambassador Wharton to telephone the *Javelin* at once.'

As James smiled to himself, the regular phone rang afresh, the answer-machine's light came on, and he listened to the clenched voice saying: 'The Chairman is in his office at the *Javelin*. It is urgent that Ambassador Wharton return this call at once.'

Minutes later came a third message: 'This is an urgent

call from the Chairman. Will Ambassador Wharton phone the *Javelin* immediately?'

James grunted. Third time round the command had subtly changed into a request of sorts, though the arrogance was still evident enough. He sipped his drink.

Not long afterwards, Jancie went to the foot of the stairs to shout that dinner was ready. She was warm and happy in the knowledge that they had struck their first blow for freedom. The doorbell rang.

'Goddammit,' she muttered, going to the hall table where she kept a purse for getting rid of charity-collectors as fast as possible. When she opened the front door she found a policeman standing there.

'Mrs Wharton? I'm sorry to disturb you. We've had a call at Notting Hill Police Station from Lord Scrope's office. They say there is reason to believe there's been an accident here. Is Mr Wharton at home?'

She began to laugh like a woman demented – peal after peal.

'There's been no accident here,' she managed to say at last to the bemused policeman, 'except for the accident of my husband being employed by a madman.'

Once the policeman was satisfied nothing dire had occurred in the Wharton household, James phoned the resident clerk and was immediately put through to Gerald.

'I regret interrupting your pleasant evening at home, Ambassador. Something has come up with one of our American defence contracts. The time in Washington is now four in the afternoon. It is urgent that we speak with the Pentagon. I need you as my third hand.'

Twenty minutes later, Gerald's driver was standing on the Whartons' doorstep. 'The Chairman has sent me to collect the Ambassador, ma'am.'

Ten minutes after that, James was in the Rolls on his way back to the *Javelin*.

TWENTY

'I'm feeling distinctly iffy,' Zoë said.

She loved it when Peter phoned after she was in bed and could scrunch down in the pillows while they talked.

'Even though parliament hasn't yet reassembled, everyone in the government is back. And I can't get an interview – even a provisional date for one – with a cabinet minister or any other really big gun at Westminster. The pieces I did on Washington politicians don't cut any ice here.'

'It's a pretty big ocean,' said Peter.

She'd found it fairly easy to get interviews with film directors and actors, a junior minister and one or two heads of local government – though a few had regrets when Zoë displayed their vanities.

But the big guns could go on television or radio and speak directly to the public, keeping control – whereas in print a journalist could draw attention to evasions or put a gloss on what they said. Fleet Street tabloids, broadsheets, they were all rough. With eleven competing papers delivered throughout Britain daily, nearly that many on Sundays, editors were ruthless. Leading politicians had good reason not to expose their reputations to a journalist they had no way to assess.

'I'm having lunch tomorrow with Miles Brewster,' she said. 'He's never asked me before, and I have an awful feeling he's going to tell me I'd better improve my act – in the most polite way, of course,' she added gloomily.

'Well, beat him to the draw,' said Peter. 'Bring the problem up yourself.'

*

Miles had told her to meet him at the front door of the building. She was tense as they got in the car together. Neither said much. She either looked out her window or straight ahead. Once or twice she was aware of him looking at her profile. She was relieved that the restaurant wasn't far.

Le Mijanou was popular with the media and politicians. Several people greeted Miles from their tables, then speculated on the brunette with him.

Zoë had planned to bring up her problem as soon as they'd placed their order. But the waiter had hardly turned his back when Miles said: 'Did you ever break your nose?'

Her face was a study in surprise.

'That's not the problem I had in mind,' she said, laughing.

He let that pass. He wanted the answer to his question first.

'I broke it at school,' she said. 'I'd beaten a boy at squash with his friends watching. You know how childish boys are,' she added.

Miles smiled to himself.

'He called me Orphan Annie and said: "What's it like to be dumped with an old geezer and a hag on a farm that's gone to hell?" So I punched him in the mouth.'

'And?'

'He didn't like that. When we were rolling around on the court my nose got broken.'

She watched him taste the wine.

He looked at her again.

'I like the result,' he said. 'How're you getting on with the other journalists?'

'Well, there's less general camaraderie than on the *Washington Express*,' replied Zoë. 'British journalists help each other less.'

'They know they're in a goddam cut-throat business.'

Was that a hint of what was coming?

'But once they become your friends,' she went on, 'it's fine. I don't think the English are all that reserved once you get the hang of them. Quite the opposite sometimes.'

'They aren't all brought up like James Wharton, you mean.'

She took a swallow of her wine.

'There's something I need to talk to you about,' she said. 'I didn't expect it to be this hard getting interviews with political hotshots at Westminster. I feel like I'm back in first grade.'

'Didn't you realise you'd have to carve out a fresh niche in Britain?' Miles asked.

'In theory. But it still comes as a jolt when it happens.' Her hand was gripped tight under the table as she waited for him to give his warning.

'Do you miss people in Washington?' he asked instead.

She flushed. Had he suspected something about Peter?

'I like the way you've got everything in London,' she replied. 'Government, museums, opera, the river. You name it: it's here.'

'I agree – though that's not what I asked you.'

He was watching her over the rim of his glass.

'And the colours are brighter here,' said Zoë. 'I suppose it has to do with the moist air.'

'What colours?' he asked, amused.

'Everything. Haven't you noticed? Didn't you see the buddleias in garden squares? The purple's much sharper than at home. I've never seen anything as vivid as some yellow fields I saw when I took a bus to Oxford last weekend.'

Actually, she was right: he had seen the extraordinary clarity without reflecting on it. For a second he wondered if Marigold ever noticed colours were brighter in England, but then he cut off the thought, slightly ashamed at making a comparison.

'And you can do what you like in your private life in London,' she said. Maybe if she kept chattering, he'd forget to tell her she had damn well better come up with a political hotshot soon. 'In Washington, even though you don't know everyone, you know who everyone is,' she rattled on. 'In London there're so many different worlds you feel anonymous.'

'Some people hate being anonymous,' he said. 'It makes them feel lonely.'

'I know.'

'Do you?'

'Feel lonely?' She hesitated. 'I suppose I do once in a while, though I don't call it that.'

'What do *you* call it?'

She smiled at him, though she was astonished at finding she wanted to cry. She pulled herself together. 'I think of it as wistfulness. It's not a bad feeling. Anyhow, I go out at night with a couple of people on the paper. And I've made some friends in the real world.'

He smiled at the jab: God knows the media world was unreal – frenetic obsession with the latest rumour, then on to the next story without a backward glance.

'Jancie and James have seen to that,' she added. 'And once the British decide they like you, they're very generous: their friends take you on, so to speak. Having the Whartons here has made all the difference.'

'What did you mean "wistfulness"?' he asked.

This guy might be useless at chitchat, but he sure shot the personal question straight into you, she said to herself.

'It's hard to describe,' she said to him. 'Sort of a soft, sad feeling. Sometimes it happens when I'm listening to Wagner or swimming alone far out in the sea. I used to have it where I was brought up in Vermont. I loved the solitude of my grandparents' farm. At the same time I would get this wistful feeling – that something momentous was out there somewhere, and I wanted to know what it was, I wanted to be able to feel it.'

'Feel it like touch it – from the outside? Or feel it inside you?'

Zoë laughed nervously.

'I thought I was the one whose job was to probe other people's feelings,' she said.

She saw the colour move up his face.

'How far have you got in lining up a cabinet minister?' he asked abruptly.

Zoë wished she hadn't said that. She'd hurt his feelings. But she couldn't say so. That would make things worse.

'I had a date fixed with the Transport Secretary, but then it got cancelled,' she said.

'Before or after your piece on the British Airways chairman appeared? Which by the way I greatly enjoyed.'

He seemed OK again, she thought. 'After,' she said.

Miles grunted. 'There's always that danger when you take the mickey out of a big wheel. All the other big slick wheels rejoice at his discomfiture – good old *schadenfreude* – but they don't want the same thing to happen to them. Don't worry. As soon as you've established your name here, they'll come around. They'll see it as a challenge to be interviewed by Zoë Hare. Don't ever underestimate human vanity.'

His attention was caught by a bulky figure filling the doorway, self-importantly surveying the room before entering.

'Even Alan Rawlston, if he put his mind to it, might charm you into presenting him the way he sees himself.'

'Hullo, Miles.'

The Defence Secretary looked down pointedly at Zoë.

'I hope you're more polite to your friend, Miles, than your paper is to me,' he said.

Miles gave a tight smile. 'This is Zoë Hare – one of my best feature writers. Specially imported from America to see the British as they rarely see themselves.'

Alan chortled.

'You and I ought to have lunch one day,' he said to Miles. 'Whoever wrote that leader in yesterday's *Dispatch* got my position on the Arabi arms embargo quite wrong.'

'I wrote it,' Miles said curtly. 'I could have sworn it was spot on.'

Another chortle.

'What about doing an interview with Zoë Hare?' said Miles. 'You could voice your views then.'

Alan looked at her again, appraising her.

'Ring my office, Miss Hare.' He gave a friendly nod to Miles and moved on to his host's table.

'I could get to love him,' said Zoë.

'Try blocking his path and see if you love him then.'

Miles gave her a sharp look and laughed.

'If Alan Rawlston calculates it could improve his relations with the *Dispatch*, you'll get your interview. And presto, you'll have your foot in Westminster's door.'

They were both at ease as they left the restaurant. But as soon as they were in the car Zoë felt the awkwardness return. It must have something to do, she decided, with two people being confined together in the back seat, always more intimate than you'd expect given it was the common form of transportation. Again neither said much. A couple of times she felt him looking at her.

The tension was only relieved when the car pulled up at the *Dispatch* and she returned to the newsroom, he to the editor's office.

TWENTY-ONE

She stood at the wall of windows looking down. Some of the plane trees' leaves were changing colour. The Brewsters had moved in several weeks before. The redecoration was all she'd imagined: dramatic, elegant, perfect for entertaining. Yet Marigold was dissatisfied.

She knew it wasn't the discontent of pure materialists who see their neighbour's grander patio, build one themselves and still feel unfulfilled and irritable. Marigold had a discerning eye and she genuinely enjoyed the beautiful objects that money could provide.

She'd encountered Gerald twice since she and Miles arrived in Britain. The first time was in the Ritz dining-room. The ancient violinist had wandered off from the little orchestra to do his walkabout, and was half-way through his serenade to her when she saw Miles's face stiffen. He nodded coldly. She looked up to see Gerald Scrope nod back as he passed their table without stopping. She saw another man was with him. For all she knew, Gerald had a harem of women, though she suspected he hadn't the time.

The second occasion was a few evenings ago – at the Queen's state banquet for President Lambert and the First Lady. Marigold had wondered if Gerald Scrope would also be at Buckingham Palace. As soon as she and Miles entered a reception room with sumptuous paintings on green silk-covered walls, she looked around for Gerald. Beneath a massively ornate ceiling there must have been fifty people standing – uniforms encrusted with rows of medals, white tie and tails, stiff satin gowns and tiaras (none prettier than Marigold's, a trophy from her marriage to the old earl). She couldn't see him. Perhaps he was in a different room. A courtier had told Miles there were two hundred guests.

As she sipped her champagne and Miles talked with the American Secretary of State, she looked around again, in vain. Then a rustle moved through the room: from a distant door, the Queen and the royal family entered with the Lamberts.

Minutes later a courtier materialised beside Marigold.

'Mrs Brewster. Mr Brewster. I've been asked to present you to the Prince of Wales.'

Her heart leapt. As the courtier led the way, she took in the other members of the royal family – the Queen, Prince Philip, Prince Andrew – positioned several yards from one another so that the maximum number of guests could be individually honoured. No one was more adroit than the royal family in bestowing full attention on whoever they were talking with. And no one was quicker than the courtiers to take umbrage if a guest misunderstood the informal manner and treated a royal informally in return. Marigold, of course, understood all this. If Prince Charles asked her a question, she knew better than to ask him a question about himself.

When she was presented, she sank in a deep curtsy as accomplished as if she met the future king every week. (She had chosen a gown with its skirt cut wide enough to enable her to demonstrate her grace in this not altogether easy ritual.)

'Your Royal Highness,' she murmured as she rose, and he smiled pleasantly, the expression in his eyes matching the smile.

As an American, Miles gave only a token bow of his head when the Prince shook hands. While the three of them chatted, Miles studied the narrow face with the laugh lines at the corners of the eyes. Surprising, Miles thought, that he had them still after all he had been through with Princess Diana.

The Prince opened the conversation in his unexpectedly melodious voice. (Maybe that tight, high voice was contagious only among the female members of the royal family, Miles thought.)

'How are you enjoying living in Sir Denys Lasdun's masterpiece, Mrs Brewster?' asked the Prince, his eyes twinkling.

You had to give them credit: they did their homework, Marigold said to herself.

'More, I believe, than you would, Sir,' she replied to him.

Prince Charles's detestation of modern architecture was notorious.

'I've always wanted to have a flat there,' she said. 'The view over Green Park is really rather lovely.'

She would have been justified in describing it as spectacular, but given the views from the royal palaces, she thought it best to speak of her own more modestly.

'So long as you are inside Sir Denys's masterpiece and looking out, I dare say its design works quite well,' said the Prince.

Miles began to chuckle.

The Prince, his face cracking into a quick broad smile, turned to him. The royal face then grew serious.

'You have taken on much, Mr Brewster, in choosing both to own and edit a British newspaper. If the *Dispatch* makes a mistake in how it handles a story, the owner can't blame the editor, and the editor can't blame the owner.'

As it was Miles who was now the object of the Prince's attention, Marigold could study the heir to the throne. The laugh lines suddenly looked worn when he made his dry remark about the British press. The latest publication of taped phone calls must be a nightmare.

'I enjoy the dual role, Sir. Someone has to take the immediate decisions on what goes in the paper. I prefer it to be me.'

'Yes.' There was a fractional pause.

Hardly the most tactful thing Miles could have said, Marigold thought. Everyone knew how frustrated the Prince was at being middle-aged and still without a real decision-making job.

'I was interested in your editorial on how the Anglo-American relationship needs re-cementing,' the Prince continued. 'Very apt in view of President Lambert's visit.'

He turned away.

This time when a rustle moved through the room it was caused by everyone going in to dinner. From the other drawing-rooms the rest of the guests converged within the state dining-room, where a vast banqueting table waited (each place setting measured by a footman with a ruler to make sure when other footmen laying the one-hundred-and-sixty-foot table reached its ends they'd find space for the last two settings). The Queen had personally inspected the finished ensemble a few hours earlier – damask tablecloth, gold plate, Stourbridge crystal, everything lustrous in the soft light of candelabras and chandeliers.

Marigold sat between the Admiral of the Fleet and the Tate Gallery's director. The admiral turned out to be highly entertaining, but his manner demanded unswerving attention. It wasn't until the fish course when she turned to talk with the gallery director that she saw Gerald sitting further along the other side. In the candle-light the auburn hair gleamed. She wanted to touch it.

He turned and for a full minute they looked at one

another. He gave a slow nod and turned back to his table partner.

For the rest of the evening, whomever she was talking with, her attention was divided. Glancing across the table again as Gerald conversed with someone else. Looking around after dinner as people moved to the door. In vain.

On the short drive back to St James's Place, she said to Miles: 'Did you talk with either of the Lamberts?'

'A couple of words with Frank,' he replied.

'I'd have expected one of them at least to say hello to me,' Marigold said.

'Well, there were a fair number of people present,' said Miles.

She looked out the window and thought of one in particular. The yearning that followed was so intense it frightened her: she wanted to feel Gerald's body all over.

TWENTY-TWO

Biting her lower lip, Zoë stared at her screen, drafting her letter to the First Lady. The Lamberts had returned to Washington the week before. She reminded Nona Lambert that they'd met at Leila Sherman's party in Georgetown. She mentioned some of the Washington VIPs she'd interviewed for the *Express*. There. She printed it out on the *Dispatch*'s best writing paper.

Silence from the White House.

She bombarded the West Wing with phone calls.

'We'll get back to you,' she was told each time.

Nothing happened.

Then came the call at last: the First Lady had agreed. A date was made for the following month. Zoë could hardly wait to tell Miles.

His face opened in a welcoming smile when she walked into his office. Excitedly she told him about her coup. His face closed.

'Congratulations,' he said coldly.

It was the first time Zoë had been on the receiving end of the Miles Brewster freeze-treatment.

'It'll be the only interview she's given to a British newspaper,' she said, hugely disappointed, uneasy. 'She refused to give one to anybody while she was here.'

'I'm aware of that,' Miles replied.

Flabbergasted, her cheeks hot, Zoë turned to go. At the door she stopped. Why the hell should he treat her like that when she had just lined up something any other editor would dance a jig over for Chrissake?

'As you've known them both a long time – I read you

were close friends at college – I'd like to pick your brain before the interview,' she said.

For a few moments neither spoke as they looked at each other, both faces set.

Then Miles said impersonally: 'Ask me nearer the time. There's not a lot I can add to what you'll discover from other sources. It's been years since I've seen much of the Lamberts.'

'I can't make sense of that guy,' she said to Peter. They were having dinner at Green's Restaurant and Oyster Bar. This time she wasn't perched on a bar stool, the month had an R, and they were eating Colchester oysters on the half-shell.

'You're not alone,' he said. 'Miles and the Lamberts used to take their vacations together. Miles's newspapers drew attention to Frank from his earliest days as a congressman. Yet for years Miles has never indicated he used to know both Lamberts well.'

'They sure can't like his newspapers raising hell about the President's so-called foreign policy,' said Zoë.

'Well, nobody appreciates getting flak. But that doesn't mean they pull down the visor when they meet. In any case, Miles's criticisms are those of a man who believes Frank has the potential to bring about the domestic changes Miles wants in America. When you figure out Miles Brewster, let me know. Meantime . . .'

Her hand was resting on the table's edge, and Peter covered it with his.

They walked hand in hand back to his hotel, her shoulderbag, big enough for her overnight things, swinging beside her. There was a day and a half before he had to be back in Washington.

'The freedom of anonymity,' she said, laughing. They weren't going to bump into someone who would recognise Peter in these dark back streets, though they'd have to be careful at Dukes Hotel. When they turned into St James's Place, she let go his hand.

'Did you know the Brewsters live in that big hunk up ahead?' she said just before they turned into Dukes' courtyard.

She had the same feeling as when she stayed there those first two nights in London – stepping into another world where no one seemed in a hurry. But tonight she was keyed up in a different way. It would be the first time Peter hadn't gone home at the end of their evening. When he closed the bedroom door behind them she flung her arms around him.

It was always like this in journalism, she mumbled to herself as she snatched up the notes from her desk, one eye on the clock. Everything always came at the same time. All right, she needn't have stayed with Peter until he left for Heathrow. He hadn't lassoed her to the bed after all. But, for God's sake, it was the first time they'd seen each other in months. She dashed to the rest-room. Look at her hair. A tied-up bunch of electrified Weetabix. My God.

When her taxi pulled away from the *Dispatch*, she took fresh paper from her shoulderbag, dividing it into clumps, folding each in two. On the right side she'd take notes gutting what Alan Rawlston was saying. On the left she'd scrawl his face and body language – give-aways unseen by a tape-recorder. Recorders were useful – not least if there was an argument later about misquotation – but taped conversation was curiously dead when you played it back. It never revealed the tensions. You had to note those at the time.

Thank heaven she'd done her background work before Peter arrived. She must have talked with nearly a dozen people who knew Alan Rawlston. And of course James had been invaluable – with the proviso, naturally, that she not advertise his help.

She checked the recorder for sound. Thank God she had worked out her list of questions in Peter's bedroom that morning, rejigging the order so the diciest came when Rawlston would be feeling confident the thing was going as he wished. Of course, she might scrub half her questions and go for something quite different: you never knew. She didn't see the Houses of Parliament as her taxi crossed Westminster Bridge. She'd been given an hour with him in his room at the Ministry of Defence.

He presented the manner of a man offering her all the time in the world, yet there was an authority that conveyed they'd better get down to work pronto. She didn't doubt that the private secretary would reappear the second her hour was up.

'May we sit where I can set up house and spread out my notes?' she asked.

Alan gave his amiable chortle and led the way to the quarter-mile-long conference table along one side of the room. As they passed a mahogany bookcase, he pointed to the damage where Churchill, when First Lord, had kicked it. The private secretary reappeared to place the MoD's own cassette-recorder near hers on the table before trekking back to the connecting door to his own domain.

It was half-way through the interview, Alan leaning back in his chair, relaxed, that Zoë said: 'The Prime Minister and the Foreign Secretary keep saying we cannot lift the arms embargo on Arabi while the butchery continues.'

Behind their spectacles Alan's eyes grew wary.

'It's said,' Zoë went on, 'that you have mixed feelings about Britain and America continuing the embargo.'

James had not suggested Alan's feelings were at all mixed: privately the Defence Secretary wanted the embargo lifted now. But a little tact was likely to get a more forthcoming response.

'How would you answer the moral argument for keeping the embargo in place?' she asked.

Alan smiled.

'Even if you had acquired an English accent, Miss Hare, one would know you're an American,' he replied. 'Americans have idealistic dreams of a world where good and bad are totally separate and every problem has a solution. Any defence minister worth his salt knows there's no such thing as a solution, let alone a simple moral solution. The most one can do is ameliorate a problem. History is cluttered with horrors caused by people acting in the name of morality.'

'As I *am* an American' – she gave a light laugh – 'let me get this clear. Are you saying morality shouldn't come into the question of lifting – or not lifting – the arms embargo on Arabi?'

'You must not believe everything you hear, Miss Hare. I have expressed no view, moral or otherwise, on lifting the arms embargo on Arabi. Such a decision would be made by the Cabinet. All I am saying is that these decisions are not as black and white as fairy-tales make out.'

It was a skilful politician's response.

He watched her scribbling, the red lights steady on their recorders. These attractive female journalists could not be relied on to be softies.

When she looked up she asked: 'How did you feel about that scandal several years ago when it appeared that a member of the government actually helped British manufacturers evade the arms embargo?'

Alan gave her a look of indignation at her effrontery.

'At the time,' she went on, 'you were still Trade Secretary and he was one of your junior ministers.'

Any amiability disappeared.

'If you had done your homework properly, Miss Hare,' he said pompously, 'you would know I demanded his resignation as soon as I got a whiff of what he'd been up to. He will never again serve in any government I am a part of. No member of *this* government would sanction arms-busting.'

Pointedly, he looked at his watch.

Without transition she said: 'The *Javelin* keeps putting the case for you to replace Martin Mather as Prime Minister. How do you feel about that?'

He stepped through the minefield with care – offering something so he appeared at ease with the question, disclaiming the rest.

'Politicians who claim they never dream of being prime minister are liars, Miss Hare. Any politician worth his salt' – Alan liked that phrase: it smacked of strength and earthiness – 'will want to be in a position to put into practice what he believes is best for the country. That is separate, however, from wanting to overturn one's leader. Loyalty comes first.'

Glancing at the door as it opened and the private secretary entered, Alan got to his feet at once.

'Our hour together has gone too rapidly,' he said, watching Zoë assemble her paraphernalia, ushering her as far as the door. 'I hope you have everything you want. I saw your editor only the other night at Number Ten – at the dinner for President Lambert. Goodbye, Miss Hare.'

TWENTY-THREE

The *Dispatch* was spread on his desk. Gerald circled two passages in Zoë's interview with Alan Rawlston. Then he reached in his pocket for the Stanley knife he always carried – a habit since he was fourteen – and carefully sliced through the page.

It was the day for Prime Minister's Questions. Two places away from Martin Mather sat the stolid figure of his Defence Secretary. Immediately Questions were over and the Prime Minister left, Alan went to his room in the Commons.

Minutes later the Special Branch detective nodded to Gerald: 'Good afternoon, m'lord.'

As soon as he sat down, Gerald reached into his pocket. He unfolded the piece of newspaper.

'I was interested in what you told Miss Hare about how you'd never think of overturning the PM.'

He ran a finger under one of the red-circled quotes and read aloud: '"Loyalty comes first."'

He looked up.

'That brought tears to my eyes, Alan.'

Alan's shoulders heaved.

'Yeah. But it'll be less funny when you find you can't overturn him. And until Scrope Electronics gets that Cheetah contract, Alan, there'll be bugger all in the *Javelin* about how the Right Honourable A. Rawlston would be a better PM than the arsehole who's at Number Ten now.'

Alan's manner altered.

'I am working on it, Gerald, I promise you,' he said gravely. 'Regrettably my MoD advisers remain unchanged in their advice that Cheetah should not go to Scrope. Our last contract with Scrope cost us far more than had been agreed.'

'And I remain unchanged in what I told you before, Alan: I thought you ran the MoD, not some bleeding little civil servant.'

'This advice, Gerald, came from one of the Ministry's top civil servants,' Alan said in a pained voice. 'If it came out I'd overruled his advice, I'd have to be able to defend my decision in the House of Commons.'

He swivelled his head to indicate the expanse of his oak-panelled room with the Commons crest blazoned on anything covered in green leather.

'Stuff the House of Commons,' Gerald said. 'Don't tell me you can't get them to approve a contract with an orang-utan if you put your mind to it. I've seen you operate in the House of Commons – going for the Opposition like some killer dog. One of the great parliamentarians, they say. That's one reason I've been backing you, Alan. But I sure as hell want something in return. I'm not Santa Claus for fuck's sake.'

'You shall have it, you shall have it, Gerald. Once I'm in Number Ten, you'll see what a good friend I am.'

'If you think I'm going to sit on my nuts waiting until the day of Paradise, mate, you got another bleeding thought coming. You won't never be there unless you get me that contract.'

A tremor ran the length of Alan's bulky body. Important as Gerald was to his ambitions, he, the Defence Secretary, was not going to be pushed around by a hoodlum. He got to his feet.

'This conversation is going nowhere, Gerald. I'll phone you tomorrow when we both have had time to cool down.'

'If I felt any cooler, I'd be dead. You better sit down

again and make sure this conversation goes somewhere fast. You see, Alan, I've been thinking about some of your other skills as a politician. Let's speak specifically. You're a right genius, awe-inspiring, at keeping your personal finances private.'

Remaining standing, Alan said stiffly: 'Every sensible person endeavours to keep personal matters private.'

'Yeah. So it'd be a bleeding shame if some things suddenly weren't so private any more – like the school fees I paid for your children when you were in Opposition, and those nice long holidays the Rawlston family still enjoy in the Bahamas and the south of France.'

Gerald gave a smile more chilling than if he'd remained expressionless.

'Don't get the wrong idea, Alan; it makes me very happy to make life more comfortable for you. Everyone knows MPs' pay is a joke compared with American congressmen. Even Cabinet ministers' pay ain't that great. And I appreciate the way you wanted to give me something in return when you got in a position to do so. I never forget a favour, Alan.'

Gerald stopped to light a cigar, taking his time. Then he moved his finger along the second red-circled quote as Alan watched him.

'It wouldn't look too good if some things became public, mate.'

Gerald looked up almost pleasantly.

'I guess you'd have to resign, Alan. That would be too bad. I'll miss our cosy chats in this room. That's life.'

Alan's eyes narrowed with rage.

'You sound as if you're threatening me, Gerald. I hope I'm wrong.'

Gerald drew on his cigar.

Alan sat down. He too was now cool. Not for nothing

did he have the reputation of being a politician at his best when on the defensive. He changed tactics.

'If I have to overrule my procurement officer on Cheetah,' he said expansively, 'so be it.'

At once he switched the subject to more equable matters.

When he got to his feet a little later he said: 'I'll be in touch within the fortnight, Gerald.' His tone was so amiable he could have been talking about a social engagement.

Gerald's mouth pulled up in a brief smile: the Cheetah contract was his. He stubbed out his cigar and stood up to go.

'Sure, sure,' he said in a friendly way. 'You do that, Alan.'

Marigold loved the security rigmarole at the gates of Downing Street, the Special Branch police rolling their search mirrors under the car. This girlish side of his wife always touched Miles.

'Look,' she said, pointing up the short street, 'the Foreign Secretary and his wife are just getting out of their car.' All the most senior Cabinet ministers would be present, she knew, for a dinner in honour of the European Community President.

'Good evening, ma'am. Good evening, sir.' The policeman on the step of Number Ten displayed the friendliness of the self-assured.

Inside the entrance hall more Special Branch police stood in a corner, dispassionate as they watched the arrival of some of London's most notable public figures. With Miles beside her, Marigold gathered her long skirt in one hand to climb the wide stairway, proudly aware of the engravings of prime ministers ascending the wall on her other side, those many men and one woman who had lived here since 1735 when Sir Robert Walpole, effectively Britain's first prime minister, moved in. Miles had told her that in his schooldays he'd been intrigued by Walpole, that Old Etonian who'd used courage, cunning and corruption to transfer power to the House of Commons and himself.

Just inside the White Drawing-room, his wife and the guest of honour beside him, Martin Mather stood greeting his guests. He was less prepossessing than Marigold had expected, but then she reminded herself that politicians were usually smaller in the flesh than they appeared on television.

When a flunkey boomed out their names, she went ahead to shake hands with her host. Although Miles had been with the Prime Minister for various things, this was the first time Marigold had met Martin Mather.

Smiling at her, he used his grip on her hand to propel her firmly forward to the guest of honour. Inwardly Marigold bridled: the Prime Minister might have shown *some* interest in Miles Brewster's beautiful English wife.

With Miles he talked shop for a couple of minutes before Miles of his own accord moved on.

They were sipping champagne in the Pillared Drawing-room, talking with the Foreign Secretary, when Marigold saw the back of Gerald's head and shoulders. At the end of the room, just beyond the white Ionic pillars, a pair of gilded Chippendale mirrors flanked a painting by Zoffany. In one mirror she saw the auburn hair reflected, the shoulders looking confined in the dinner jacket. Her body tensed.

On a private occasion, it wouldn't have happened. A press lord whose newspaper was trying to undermine the Prime Minister would not have been invited to Number Ten. But this was not a private dinner: it was an official one. Other leading newspaper proprietors would be there, and to exclude Lord Scrope would have caused more trouble than it was worth. The *Javelin* would have trumpeted the slight as proof that Martin Mather spent all his time reading the papers searching for any word of criticism, and was too thin-skinned and defensive to lead the country. The Prime Minister had shaken Lord Scrope's hand with the coldest formality.

Marigold moved slightly to one side, trying to see around the group between her and Gerald. It was impossible. She resumed her first position where she could watch the reflection in the mirror.

Moments later people started moving into the State Dining-room, and the Defence Secretary materialised beside Marigold.

'Let me take you in,' Alan said expansively.

Like all members of the British government present, on his way to Downing Street he'd briefed himself from three sheets of paper – potted biographies of the guests along with a table plan. No civil service provided this meticulous detail as well as the British.

'My command of the German language is going to be sorely taxed by one of my table partners,' he said to Marigold. 'Thank God I have the pleasure of you on my other side.'

He might never get the *Dispatch* to come out cheering for him – and Miles was certainly distant whenever they met – but nothing was lost by buttering up Marigold Brewster. And it wasn't that painful: she was a stunning, quick-witted woman. He took her to her place, facing the portrait of the Duke of Wellington standing proudly with a red silk sash across his chest.

'Do you know why the French have been seated on the other side of the table?' he asked, and went straight on: 'Two centuries after the battle of Waterloo they *still* are outraged if they're expected to sit looking at the British victor.'

Marigold burst out laughing. She'd heard this somewhere before.

'And what do the French do when one of *their* national portraits isn't the favourite of visiting statesmen?' she asked.

'They cover it with a curtain. They imagine we are as touchy as they are. Very odd, the French.'

She could see Gerald seated further along beside the French Ambassadress. 'You must know Lord Scrope well,' she said to Alan.

'A remarkable man, Gerald Scrope,' Alan replied, choosing his words delicately as he praised his patron. 'Britain needs more men like him. Strength of purpose. Vitality. Puts it on the line: Britain first and foremost. Do you know him well?'

'No. We sat beside each other at a dinner at the British Embassy in Washington – when James Wharton was still ambassador.'

'A sad business,' Alan said, shaking his head. 'With all credit to the wisdom of our host this evening, that was not one of his finest hours. Wharton was excellent at the job. A pity that such a precipitate action removed an ambassador who had real rapport with the Pentagon.'

He shook his head again.

'Lord Scrope did well to obtain James Wharton's services,' he said.

Marigold rapidly decided it was in no one's interest to allude to Miles's feelings when James chose Lord Scrope's offer.

'I understand James is not frightfully happy at the *Javelin*,' she said.

At this, Alan nearly choked on his wine. When he got his breath he said: 'You put it with great delicacy, Mrs

Brewster. Lord Scrope's undoubted gifts do not include sensitivity in employer–employee relations – or so I'm told. And his *chef de cabinet* is an employee.'

She could see that people had nearly finished their trout mousse and she longed to hear more about Gerald. 'Who are Lord Scrope's personal friends?' she asked.

'I count myself as one of them,' Alan said pompously.

But before she could pursue it, there was a rattle of china and bustling of waiters as fish plates were removed, claret poured out. Reluctantly Marigold turned to the Italian Ambassador on her other side.

At ten o'clock sharp the Prime Minister rose from the table and the doors to the Pillared Drawing-room were thrown open. As Marigold went through, Gerald fell in beside her.

'Mrs Brewster,' he said in his formal manner.

She hesitated, unsure how to proceed.

'Lord Scrope,' she replied, and was at once aware of the flirtatiousness in her own formality.

He gave the smallest nod, like someone acknowledging what is laid out before him.

People were moving into new little groups, networking. Gerald saw the head of the Bundesbank approaching. 'Come sit down,' he said quickly to Marigold, steering her towards a sofa in the corner beyond the Ionic columns.

She sat very upright. With deliberate slowness his eyes moved over her and when they returned to her face they were hard and bright. She was suddenly so suffused with heat she wondered if she was about to faint.

'How'd you get that St James's Place flat without waiting twenty years?' he said.

'Miles offered the owner a price well over the market value.'

'Yeah. Have you ever observed, Mrs Brewster, that

you can buy anything in the world if you pitch the price right?'

'That may be,' she replied. 'But it's different with people. You can only buy some of them.'

'A myth,' he said. 'Everyone has a price tag on them. You just need to know where to look for it.'

He took a brandy from a tray being offered. She took a glass of champagne.

'Some people got no idea they got a price tag dangling. No one is as surprised as them when you lift up the corner of their jacket – maybe their skirt – and pull out this little tag with the price written on it plain as day.'

'You make us all sound like potential prostitutes,' Marigold said irritably.

'Yeah.'

There was a silence.

'Some people make the mistake, Mrs Brewster, of assuming price tags always speak money. If that's all there was to it, life would be a walkover. Anybody can make a buck – or marry it – if they care about it enough. But I bet you didn't marry the old earl just for his money – though that must of been a nice bonus. You wanted all the razzmatazz that goes with a title like that. Why not?'

As he said it, he inclined his head to her so slightly she almost thought she imagined it.

She took a sip of her champagne.

'And Miles Brewster? You got much more than a title and money when you married him. You got the power as well – everything a beautiful, clever' – he paused – 'sexy lady would want. *Almost* everything.'

The needling got its response.

'Is your conversation always so personal, Lord Scrope?' she said haughtily.

'I'm talking about people the way they are. Facts is facts. If you recognise facts, you can't go wrong.'

'Have you always been this sure of yourself?'

For the first time he grinned.

'Always. Let me make a suggestion, Mrs Brewster. You interest me. I interest you. Maybe we could learn something from each other.'

Her indignation gave way to a chaos of doubt. She wanted to see him again. Miles never resented it when she lunched in her favourite restaurants with one or another male friend. He trusted her. But Lord Scrope was in a different category – and it precluded having lunch *à deux* in public with Mrs Miles Brewster.

He read her mind.

'Let me invite you to have lunch with me at my flat,' he said. 'It's on top of that classy block across the river from Parliament. Nice view. I got a good cook. All very proper.'

She fiddled with the rose-cut ruby on her wedding finger. Carefully he pressed his advantage.

'Don't give me an answer now. I'll ask you again. Tell me a good time to phone you. Tell me your number, Mrs Brewster.'

As if spellbound, she told him the unlisted number. For the second time heat poured through her body.

'You think I won't remember it, Mrs Brewster. You're wrong. I never forget a single detail when it's something I want.'

As their car drew away from Downing Street, Miles asked: 'How'd you get on with Alan Rawlston?'

Her mind went blank. She had been thinking about Gerald. With an effort she recalled Alan's conversation.

'He was charming in that way you know is being put on,' she replied. 'We talked a bit about the Whartons. And Alan Rawlston made a subtle jab – well, fairly subtle – at the Prime Minister for his "precipitate action" in sacking James. I wonder how Martin Mather feels about all this speculation that he'll be pushed into resigning.'

'Until the *Javelin* cooked it up, there wasn't any speculation,' Miles said drily. 'Then these things take on their own momentum. The PM looked absolutely washed out this evening.'

They lapsed into their own thoughts. When their car sped past St James's Palace, she looked unseeing at its turrets against the pink night sky.

'Did you enjoy your chat with Lord Scrope?' said Miles.

'It was all right. I'm not sure he takes any great interest in women.' They returned to their thoughts.

TWENTY-FOUR

It wasn't easy for James to go back to Washington so soon after expulsion from his Eden. He thought of what Jancie said just before he left London:

'However hellish it is working for Lord Scrope, he's one of the few British, apart from Margaret Thatcher, whose name actually means something to Americans. And when you go to the Pentagon to sell Scrope to the top brass, you're going in your own right as well. How many other Brits have access at that level? You can be proud, James.'

He squared his shoulders.

It was not as if he were pushing shoddy goods. Scrope Electronics's international reputation for technical skill was impressive. James was confident in the worth of the product.

He felt Concorde shudder as its power switched off. Below stretched the Blue Ridge of Virginia, its colour fading in the distance. The plane swept down to Dulles Airport.

His first meeting was with the chief of Air Force procurement. Then on to the general who dealt with artillery. Both responded to James's assured knowledge of what they needed and what he could offer. When he returned to his room at the Willard, he was certain of their good intentions.

That night when he and Peter Stainsley met for a drink in the Round Robin Bar, James asked Peter to put in a good word at the Senate Armed Services Committee for another Scrope weapons system that the Pentagon had already decided to buy, and which needed Senate approval for the budget required.

'We can offer something in return,' James went on matter-of-factly. 'Lord Scrope has close connections with the British Defence Secretary. An American engine manufacturer like, say, Danvers, could find the door swing open for a big MoD contract if the Armed Services Committee looked favourably on Scrope Electronics for NASA's new radar programme.'

Danvers was an engineering firm in Peter's state. It had been hit hard by the recession. Rapidly Peter calculated the jobs – and the votes – that an MoD contract would engender.

'With you personally backing Scrope,' he said, 'and an assurance that some of the work would actually take place in my state, you can tell Lord Scrope that I'll be happy to push this in the Committee.'

'That's settled then,' James said, reaching for his drink.

'It's just as well Zoë isn't here,' said Peter. 'She still gets shocked when lobbyists and politicians get together. She still has some ideals left.'

James pulled a face. 'Not easy in journalism or politics – and her work combines the two.'

As he was signing the bill James said: 'By the way, do you happen to know a man called Speers Jackson?'

'I've met him a couple of times,' Peter said. 'A Texan. Lives there. Comes to Washington a fair bit. Has a shooting lodge on the Eastern Shore of Maryland. He's a businessman with a finger in various pies. When the gun lobby made a contribution to my election expenses, he signed the covering letter. Why do you ask?'

'I'm making a quick trip to Texas tomorrow. To Austin.'

'Scrope has an electronics plant there, doesn't it?'

'Yes. And I'm to see this Speers Jackson. Organised by Gerald Scrope.'

*

As soon as the passengers stepped from the aircraft, even in late October the air was dry. Twenty minutes later James checked in to Austin's smartest hotel, and as he turned to follow the bellboy, a pleasant-faced man came forward.

'I'm Speers Jackson, Mr Ambassador. Welcome to Texas.'

He had a strong, good handshake. Right from the start James liked Speers Jackson's easygoing charm. It was an American characteristic that had a particular appeal for his own buttoned-up nature.

'When you've put your things in your room, come on down. We could drive to the plant, but I thought you might get bored looking at mesquite and cactus. I'll fly you there.'

The Cessna 337 was one of a dozen or so small planes standing at a private airport on the fringe of Austin, where the sprawl of electronics factories making up the bulk of the city's economy began. By the time the two men had strapped themselves into the cockpit, they were on first-name terms.

Speers flew low, conducting a Cook's tour through the headsets. As Austin dropped away behind them, waist-high cactus and close-growing mesquite the size of pear trees spread as far as the eye could see, interrupted only by an arrow-straight highway and long thin dirt roads criss-crossing the ranches.

'All them horns you see in the mesquite belong to wild steer or white-tail deer. The deer don't get much time to relax late October to December, and buddy you gotta wear your leggings if those rattlesnakes aren't to get you.'

'What happens to the hunters' dogs?' asked James.

'You put laced-up boots on them to protect them. They get so used to it that some dogs won't go in the field unless you put their shoes on.'

'Why is Scrope's plant out this far?' asked James.

'Well, some people will tell you it's cleaner out here. Clean rooms are critical to the production of chips. Any dust can damage them. But if you think about it, you could have your factory in the middle of Austin and still manage to have atmosphere-controlled white rooms. I guess the real reason is you want to make it a little bit harder for people to nose around. There's a lot of competition around here. Scrope Southwestern is producing all kinds of things – next generation of microprocessors for desktop, logic chips for multi-media computers, lotsa things. There it is, all twenty acres of it inside that nice high electric fence. Old daddy six-by-six is sure gonna jump in the air if he decides to scratch his antlers on that hotwire.'

They dropped fast to the runway separating the hangar from the factories where each building was multi-crowned by immense satellite dishes.

'Cost seven hundred million dollars to build this plant here. You pay out money like that, buddy, and you gotta win an awful lot of contracts to keep them guys at the bank off your tail.'

He parked the plane outside the hangar, and they climbed out, James pleased with his fitness. His only dissatisfaction with his visit to Washington was there hadn't been time to drive to Annapolis, where his boat was still in a marina. Few waters could match the east coast of the United States for pleasure and challenge.

In the intense dry air he strode beside Speers towards the industrial complex. A hum like a high-powered cable grew louder as they neared the first building. At the steel door Speers held a card to a metal plate on the jamb. Click. He pushed the door open.

'Hiya,' he said, producing two passes at the manned

barrier. 'This one's for my good friend, the Ambassador. We gotta show him we know how to behave real nice in Texas.'

The security man grunted and pressed a lever. Speers led the way. The hum now was overbearing and curiously unpleasant, James thought. They stopped at a closed door which Speers opened without knocking.

'Nice to know you're expecting us,' he said genially to the khaki-clad man drinking coffee at his desk, collar open and sleeves neatly rolled up. And to James: 'Meet the manager of Southwestern, Mickey Finn.'

Speers and Finn clapped each other on the shoulder.

'That's his name, I swear. This is Ambassador Wharton. You know who he is. Come all the way from London to inspect Southwestern.'

James and Finn shook hands.

The inspection was like any other tour of a factory. 'I've seen it already,' Speers had said, opting to stay behind in the manager's office with the electric coffee-maker. Finn took James into one big dust-free chamber – they didn't feel like rooms – after another, white-clad technicians working silently, the hum hardly discernible in some areas, in others so dominating that James was anxious to get outside and have the airtight door closed again behind him.

'Welcome back,' said Speers, removing himself from the chair he'd been occupying behind the manager's desk. 'Have a cup of coffee. It's on me.'

Finn laughed.

As they drank their coffee, Speers said to Finn: 'You got those documents ready for the Ambassador to sign?'

Finn took a couple of files from the top drawer of his desk.

'Lord Scrope called from London this morning,' Speers explained to James. 'He wanted to check I got everything ready for signature. He said you got power of attorney for this trip. "The Ambassador is the only man I trust to sign for me," the Lord said.'

'What's the hurry on getting the papers signed today?' asked James. He directed his question to Finn.

Speers answered. 'Thirty million dollars of machine-tool parts are already in the trucks, ready for delivery to an urgent order from Mexico. You know what Customs is like – ornery for the sake of being ornery. Keep you waiting until your ass falls asleep. But if Lord Scrope's signature – or yours this time – is on the Customs declaration forms, the stalling stops and you get the green light.'

The consignment forms went on for pages and pages of single-spaced small type. James sat at one side of the desk and began reading, signing each section as he went along.

'Christ, what a lot of jargon,' he said, ploughing on. 'I've never heard of most of these machine parts. Anybody wanting to mislead the Customs boys could blind them silly with this bloody detail.'

'See ya,' Speers said to the security men when he and James went back through the barrier at the front door. Outside, the sun was a white ball in the sky, the air like oven air.

Across the runway, another small plane was disappearing into the hangar. James glimpsed trucks inside the hangar. Then the rolled-up doors dropped.

Speers and James had just reached the Cessna when a side door of the hangar opened and a Mexican appeared alone, pulling his sombrero low on his forehead. As Pedro Lopez walked past them he looked up from under the broad brim and his eyes met Speers's. Neither man gave any sign of recognition.

On the return flight Speers resumed his Cook's tour.

'See that ranch below? Seven thousand acres of mesquite and cactus. Belongs to the chairman of an oil company. Board members rent it for weekend hunting. Bow and arrow in the deer season, or rifles. Weatherby .270 is what I go for. It's only back east that people use shotguns. When you're walking through there looking for them pretty blue quail, you wear leather chaps or the cactus will puncture you to death.' He chuckled. 'We got everything that sticks, stings or bites.'

'What's to keep cross-border cocaine smugglers from dropping their bundles in there for somebody else to pick up?' asked James.

'Nothing. Seven thousand acres is a lot of mesquite and cactus for any ranch owner to keep track of.' He pointed ahead. 'That ranch has eighteen thousand acres. Forty working oil wells. A Mexican bird-dog handler – has to be seventy if he's a day – told me they lately had large holes punched through the runway's cement to discourage night flights using it. He says he often hears small planes flying low without lights. Some ranch managers find envelopes stuffed full of cash in their mail boxes – thousands of bucks – with instructions to keep their main gate unlocked on a specific night or "bad things" could happen to them. One rancher I know found his prize bull and half a dozen Longhorn shot dead when he didn't follow the instructions.'

'How do the smugglers' planes get through the radar network along the border?' asked James.

Speers chuckled. 'The USA spent two billion dollars on that anti-drug network. Its backbone is the aerostats – high-flying balloons loaded with sophisticated radar equipment – a lot of it made by Scrope, by the way. But aerostats can't fly in winds above fifteen m.p.h. Planes can. When Customs spots you flying the border in bad weather, they can send their planes to chase you. But they gotta catch you on the ground with the stuff. This is the USA. We don't shoot airplanes down.'

James turned to glance at the good-humoured face as Speers retailed his lore without relaxing his concentration on the sky around him. In the late afternoon a lot of executives were flying their planes back to base. Outside the hotel, Speers said: 'I'll pick you up at seven-fifteen. You'll have the best beef you've ever eaten in all your life.'

When they parted later that evening, James meant it when he said: 'I hope we meet again.'

TWENTY-FIVE

It was the Defence Secretary's day to answer Questions in the House. At 2.30 sharp, the first woman Speaker in the House of Commons called out: 'Mr Alan Rawlston.' In the Chamber, only the Speaker addressed MPs by name.

Alan heaved himself to his feet and with the awkward gait of the thick-thighed man moved to the dispatch box.

Through his spectacles his eyes glittered with genuine detestation as he looked at the benches opposite. One reason he was such an effective parliamentarian was that bellicosity came naturally to him. When the Prime Minister looked across the gangway, he saw men and women not greatly different in their characters, good or bad, from those behind him. But to Alan they were all the enemy, and he hated them as he hated anyone who tried to balk him.

A tame government back-bencher tabled the question needed about Cheetah, and now he put the supplementary one the minister required.

In his powerful voice Alan replied:

'My Honourable Friend will be glad to know I have today signed letters to two firms telling them I have accepted their applications. Both firms are British. Northwest Metals will produce Cheetah's shell. Cheetah's electronics system will be made by Scrope Electronics.'

A jeering whistle added to the hubbub of shouts and groans that broke loose among MPs opposite. Furious men and women jumped to their feet, waving order papers to catch the Speaker's eye.

'Order, order,' the Speaker bellowed. Bang went her gavel. She called an Opposition MP.

Acidly he asked: 'Will the Right Honourable Gentleman tell the House whether his decision to award a five-hundred-million-pound contract to Scrope Electronics was influenced by the efforts of Lord Scrope's flagship, the *Javelin*, to make the Right Honourable Gentleman the next Prime Minister?'

Ironic 'oooohs' followed on Opposition benches. Government supporters sat silent.

Alan was on his feet again, glaring at the MP as if he were a worm recently wriggled from a rotten apple.

'The Honourable Gentleman's question, Madam Speaker, could only have been asked by a' – he paused – 'person' – his pronunciation of the word invited all to substitute any insult of their choice – 'who himself measures the nation's good in terms of what's in it for him. He makes the mistake of those who live in the gutter: they imagine everyone else has the same low horizons as themselves.'

Alan threw himself back on the front bench. Behind him MPs laughed and shouted: 'Hear, hear.'

The Speaker called on a woman Opposition MP waving her order papers.

'Can the Right Honourable Gentleman tell us the basis on which he gave this contract to an electronics firm owned by a blatant supporter of the Right Honourable Gentleman's party?'

Alan was back on his feet.

'I am happy to tell the Honourable Lady my reasons. Scrope Electronics enjoys the highest reputation, in this land and others, for workmanship. Scrope Electronics can meet our timetable. Scrope Electronics submitted costs as low as any from other British firms. And its proposal was competitive with offers from American firms – with one exception.'

Here Alan paused as if about to make a great confession.

MPs tensed. He pushed his spectacles back on the bridge of his nose.

But what followed simply diverted attention from other British firms' competitive offers:

'One reputable American electronics firm's tender met the timetable and matched costs submitted by Scrope Electronics. The tenders being equal in these respects, I took it upon myself to award the contract to a British firm.'

Wheeling his body in an arc, his glare challenged Opposition benches from one end to the other.

'I will do everything I legitimately can, Madam Speaker, to assist British industry and create British jobs – unlike Members opposite whose interest is in scoring points, no matter the cost to our country's economy.'

Shouts of outrage from the benches opposite as he sat down.

Rollicking 'hear, hear's' from the benches behind Alan – for whatever their private thoughts about his motives, government ministers and back-benchers always enjoyed the Defence Secretary's combativeness.

Bang went the Speaker's gavel.

A brief report of the MoD contracts was carried near the bottom of the *Javelin*'s front page. Two of the tabloids were preoccupied with hounding the royal family. All the other papers splashed with the Cheetah story.

No interest was shown in Northwest Metals winning the contract for the shell of the missiles. It was the electronics contract that was hot – the plum fallen into Lord Scrope's lap.

The killer assault came from the *Dispatch*.

Industrious digging by its defence correspondent had uncovered the MoD advice against accepting Scrope's tender. Miles persuaded a senior official – so long as he wasn't quoted by name – to confirm the story.

The full-width headline read: 'Minister Flouts His Own Advisers'.

A greater disquiet than usual pervaded the two rooms of secretaries as James went through.

'Good morning,' he said, his tone making plain there was nothing good about it.

Seconds after he reached his room, the red buzzer on his desk went like a dentist's drill.

'Your friend will pay for this,' said the flat voice at the other end.

As he opened the door to the Chairman's suite, James steeled himself.

Littered on the floor around Gerald's desk were the morning papers, some rumpled and torn at the edges, others tossed aside intact after a cursory glance. Atop the desk lay the *Dispatch*, opened out so the whole front page was on view.

'I wouldn't have expected Miles Brewster to make it so personal,' James said. 'You must have got under his skin.'

The pair of photographs crossed six columns. One showed Gerald at the Horse Guards entrance of the Ministry of Defence – 'The Minister's Friend'. The other showed Alan Rawlston waving on the steps of Number Ten – 'The Grateful Minister'.

'Our American gent plays rough,' Gerald said.

There was no aggrievement in his voice. He was stating a fact.

'I have been exactly once to the MoD,' he said, 'for a reception when the American Defence Secretary was there on an official visit. And that picture of Alan on the steps of Number Ten could have been taken after any Cabinet meeting. But it makes him look as if he's celebrating becoming PM. Fucking clever layout.'

'When you read the rest of the captions,' said James, 'they make clear the circumstances in which the pictures were taken.'

'Yeah. Master Miles would always make sure the fine print was right so nobody could accuse him of cheating. But he sure as hell knows the tricks to put a message across. Nobody arses around reading small print. And they sure don't miss that special editorial comment stuck in the middle of the front page – with that blockbuster line around it and signed by our smart editor boy, like God handing down the verdict.'

It was the first time Miles had used this device to grab readers who wouldn't get as far as the editorial page. He'd kept it short:

'Not only Caesar's wife must be above suspicion.

'Mr Rawlston has awarded a five-hundred-million-pound contract to a firm owned by the industrialist and media magnate, Lord Scrope. The public – who pick up the tab – are entitled to ask: can it be coincidence that Lord Scrope's flagship, the *Javelin*, is running a dubious campaign for the Defence Secretary to supplant Martin Mather as Prime Minister?

'The suspicion is bound to cross the public's mind that Mr Rawlston has been a servant to the financial interests of his most powerful promoter.'

An angry red scrawl went round and round the offending text.

Yet Gerald appeared calmness itself as he said: 'Even the thickest punter can figure where the lawyers restrained Brewster, and that makes them think even harder about the sub-text.'

He lit a cigar.

'Tell me, Ambassador, when you presided at the Embassy in Washington you would have heard people talking about Miles Brewster. Some of them must know something about that little accident in Mexico.'

'I can't help you there, Chairman.'

Since James's recent trip to Washington, his relations with Gerald, however strained, had been relatively dignified. ('Fine, fine, Ambassador. No one else could have put our case so well.') He gave the answer any of a hundred people in Washington could have given:

'People speculated, but no one pretended to know other than that it happened in Mexico when he was young.'

'Yeah. What's the best place to find old newspaper cuttings in America?'

'The Congressional Library,' replied James. Any American could have told Gerald that.

'You are to contact three investigative reporters on my American papers, Ambassador. Make sure they work for different papers. Tell them to get their fat arses over to the Congressional Library and sit there until their nuts rot or they find what I want. However long it bleeding takes, I want them to find something – even if it's only six lines long – about our young Master Brewster having a car accident.'

Unexpectedly, he grinned.

'Tell each of 'em that two other buggers are working on the same story, and whichever one comes up with it will earn Gerald Scrope's most sincere appreciation.'

James was standing on the same spot in front of the desk where he'd been since he entered the room. Some days Gerald let him stand like that throughout a ten minute confrontation. The prefect's honour now asserted itself.

'I'm sorry, Chairman. You put me in an impossible position when you ask me to play sleuth against an old friend.'

James was aware he was holding himself very erect as

he waited for the diatribe that would follow. He almost hoped for it. Following his highly successful lobbying for Scrope, if he walked out today – to hell with money and status – into the unknown but a free man, Gerald would know he was the loser.

Gerald looked at him steadily.

'Everyone is sentimental about something, Ambassador,' he said. 'I do not want to embarrass you. You will tell the foreign editor to come to my office at once. Mr Fleet will be happy to make the arrangements I require.'

Marigold was restless, and she answered the phone eagerly: 'Hullo?'

In the moments of silence that followed, she heard the beat of her heart. Later, lying awake that night, she asked herself how she'd known in the silence that it was Gerald. And she'd known he knew Miles was not with her.

'Mrs Brewster,' he said at last.

'Lord Scrope,' she replied.

'I told you I would remember the number. I wish to invite you to have lunch with me. At my flat. Do you have your appointments book there?'

It was that conventional question, she realised when reconstructing the dialogue later, which made it certain they would meet. He didn't leave her time to consider. It was the only question he posed.

The rest was assumed.

Zoë got back to the *Dispatch* just after one. She'd been to see the American Ambassador – an unusually candid ambassador – as part of her homework for her coming interview with the First Lady.

The newsroom was nearly empty, most people at lunch. She'd have a sandwich at her desk, she thought, while she transcribed her notes.

She glanced towards Miles's office. No one there. Maybe she'd see him later. She wanted to tell him how much she liked his front-page editorial. Funny, she thought. He could be infuriating. Yet increasingly his reactions were uppermost in her mind. She didn't need him to agree with what she wrote, but she wanted to impress him.

The message was lying on her desk.

'Ring Peter Stainsley at his Washington home. Urgent.'

She looked at her watch. Just past eight in the morning in Washington. At his home. She always rang him at his Senate office. Urgent.

Her stomach tightened.

'Senator and Mrs Stainsley's home,' said a butler, his tone subdued.

'It's Zoë Hare. I'm calling from London. Is it convenient for Senator Stainsley to come to the phone?'

Moments later, Peter picked up an extension.

'Zoë. Thank you for calling back.'

There was something odd about Peter's voice.

'Is everything all right?' she asked uncertainly.

'No.'

The back of her neck felt stiff.

'My wife was driving home from Baltimore yesterday afternoon. A truck coming the other way crashed through the barrier. She's dead.'

'Oh.'

Her voice was small.

'Oh dear God.'

'She was killed instantly.'

Both were silent.

She tried to visualise him. Was he lying down holding the phone at the other end, trying to ease the weight of news unwanted, irreversible? Was he sitting in a chair with his hand over his eyes?

They talked a little.

His voice was jerky. He broke down once and got hold of himself again.

'You know I loved her deeply,' he said.

'I know that. I've always known that, Peter.'

They talked a little more.

'It doesn't seem right being here,' she said. 'I can fly to Washington tonight.'

'It's better, I think, if you stay where you are,' he said.

When they'd hung up, she sat motionless, chin in hands.

She had never thought it was anything other than a good, strong marriage. He would be shattered by her death. He already was.

Even when the most terrible tragedy strikes, a trivial thought intrudes. What would the butler decide was the right time to stop saying 'Senator and Mrs Stainsley's home'? After the funeral?

Then the return to non-triviality.

How had the children learned their mother was dead? Did Peter tell them? Did they hear it from someone else before he could? A TV report? Radio? They could have heard before they got home from school.

Zoë stared blankly across the newsroom.

PART III

TWENTY-SIX

She turned over, flipping her hair the other way, in that restless sleep where you think you're not asleep as misgivings trudge across the mind. The alarm woke her, so she must have slept. Her closed curtains wore the dead look when everything is grey outside.

Awake, the images continued their anxious march. Funerals are also for the bereaved. For the bereaved most of all? She wanted to be near him in his pain. Maybe she could go and sit at the back of the church. Yet the funeral was for his wife. It didn't seem right for her to be sitting there at his wife's funeral.

And now he didn't have a wife any more. As soon as Zoë thought what this could mean for her, a tumult of guilt followed. His wife was dead. Peter was shattered. And she was wondering how it would affect her future. How revolting could you be? She flung back the covers and yanked the curtains open. A dull sky lay heavy on the houses opposite. Even the trees along the pavement were leaden.

She must get going. Feature writers seldom had to be at the paper in the evening, but her section head made plain she should get there on time in the morning. She wished to God that stupid interview with some stupid lawyer hadn't been fixed for today. Whoever invented coffee should have got the Nobel prize, she muttered as she headed for her narrow kitchen. Before she got there the images of the Stainsley family started again.

'O death, where is thy sting?' she said aloud coldly.

She'd always hated that line. How could anyone ask such a question?

*

'Long time no see, *amiga*. Except in newsprint.'

Oh, go away.

'I cannot open the *Dispatch* these days without beholding Zoë Hare in big letters. Where're you going?'

She was poised on the kerb at Lambeth Bridge roundabout, looking for the moment to get across Millbank. Simon had been lunching a Foreign Office minister at a nearby restaurant, and he'd glimpsed Zoë in the back room with a well-known Australian barrister. She hadn't looked very chirpy. A lover's quarrel? he wondered. But then Simon saw her scribbling alongside her plate.

They hadn't seen each other since arriving in London.

'As the Victoria Tower Gardens is just there, I want to have a look at the Rodin before going back to the office,' she replied, stepping back smartly as the upper half of a bus heaved over the pavement's edge.

'Much too dour a sculpture for a grey day,' Simon clucked, 'all those city elders roped together on their way to a grizzly death. Had it been me, I would have skipped away from Calais and gone to live somewhere else, and let the English king get on with destroying the city if that's what he had a mind to do. I never liked Calais anyway.'

Zoë gave a smile of sorts.

'So we could do two things,' said Simon. 'You could go and look at the bronze elders, and I could go with you and offer my handkerchief. Or. We could meet for a drink at a place of your choice at the end of our hard day's work – even have a meal if you're free. There's lots to talk about.'

'That's three choices,' said Zoë.

Actually she hadn't been looking forward to this evening on her own.

'I'll take the second. What about a drink at a pub halfway between the *Dispatch* and the *Javelin*?'

'You have such a fine sense of what's appropriate, Zoë. One of the many things I admire about you.'

They fixed on a pub, and Zoë finally got across Millbank.

Despite Simon's reservations about the burghers of Calais who six hundred years earlier surrendered to Edward III to save their city, she found the monument as moving as it was sombre. Slowly she walked round it. There was a bench nearby, and she put down her shoulder-bag and sat looking at the bronze figures. She thought of her grandfather. He would have done what they did.

She went close again to look into their faces, trying to imagine what they had felt as they went to their doom. Walking to the river side of the garden, where the damp grass was scattered with a few yellow and russet leaves, she gazed at the Thames glinting dully like pewter, shifting before the drag of the tide began. 'Time like an ever-rolling stream bears all its sons away . . .' She glanced at her watch. She'd better get back to the paper.

Had she been less drawn in on herself, she would have glanced across the river at the gleaming tower block that broke a placid skyline of low rooftops, its top floor like a belt of glass.

Marigold woke early that morning, soon after six, Miles asleep beside her. Lying on her back, eyes wide, she stretched her body, rubbing her back sensuously against the sheet. Slowly she opened her legs until one foot suddenly touched Miles. A shudder went through her. She closed her legs and lay still.

Soon after one she got out of a taxi and disappeared into the ostentatious lobby.

'Lord Scrope is expecting me.'

Her imperiousness or Gerald's instructions led the receptionist not to ask her name. As soon as he replaced his phone he said: 'Take the lift to Penthouse A, madam. You'll be met when you get out.'

She was alone in the mirrored lift. It rose in virtual silence. Each tiny hair on her arms felt aware, alert.

The doors slid apart. She stepped out directly into an entrance hall. In one of a pair of Sheraton mirrors flanking the archway ahead she saw the smooth brass of the lift door seal the exit.

Like a beautiful insect drawn into some carnivorous orchid, she moved through the archway and found herself in an enormous room, its far side made of glass. In an armchair by the wall of windows, Gerald was on the phone.

Continuing his call, he watched her as she walked to the middle of the room and stopped, standing before him, uncertain. When he put down the phone, his eyes still on her, he reached to a switch.

'There will be no more telephone calls while we are enjoying our lunch,' he said. 'Welcome, Mrs Brewster.'

He made no effort to get up from his chair.

She stood where she was, tempted to start chattering out of nervousness, yet so tense from the concentration of his surveying that she stayed silent. She felt the blood rush to her face.

Just when the tension grew unbearable for her was the moment he chose to get out of his chair. He turned to the windows.

'Come look at my view.'

For the first time she took in her surroundings. Some designer had made the drawing-room a fantasy of a rich man's lair: outsize sofas and armchairs of mohair and supple black leather, steel-limbed marble-topped tables, a deep carpet as inviting as a bed.

As if in a dream she moved across the room and stood next to him. 'Not bad for a south London garage owner,' he said, looking out on the sweep of the river with the Houses of Parliament opposite, beyond them St James's Park and Buckingham Palace. His eyes on Victoria Tower he said, pleased with himself: 'If that House of Lords tower wasn't in the way, you could even see where you live.'

Garagiste, she thought, keyed up by the associations that the English attach to that word. Coarse, insolent, boastful, everything Miles was not.

Abruptly she turned and walked back to the centre of the room.

Gerald swivelled but remained at the window.

'I shall not lay a hand on you, Mrs Brewster.'

He paused.

'Until you are ready for me to do so.'

He gestured to an adjacent room.

'I told the housekeeper I didn't want a lot of people running about,' he said, leading the way. 'The cook has done her best. It's all on the sideboard. Help yourself.'

Marigold looked around at the Jacobean furniture. Everything in the room was heavy and pretentious and suited Gerald's brashness, even an immense carved gilt mirror on the wall opposite the windows. It had once hung above a fireplace in an eighteenth-century mansion. The low ceiling of a modern penthouse meant the mirror reached nearly to the floor.

On a silver dish was an entire Scotch salmon adorned with a platoon of lemons halved and cut like crowns. On another was cold roast beef, rare in the middle, sliced thick enough to maximise its taste – 'Just the way I like it,' said Gerald, piling up his plate.

She picked at her food. It was, in fact, extremely well cooked, but she was too wound up to swallow more than a few mouthfuls.

When he'd pushed his plate away, he looked calmly at her.

'Tell me the reasons I want you, Mrs Brewster,' he said.

For a minute or more, Marigold didn't answer. Then, speaking very clearly, like a girl before an interrogator, she said: 'I am beautiful. Men are attracted to me. I have style.' She stopped.

'And?'

He watched her as impassively as if he were considering what grade to give her.

She waited some time before saying in the same clear voice: 'I am Miles Brewster's wife.'

Gerald grinned.

Marigold looked down. Her hands were in her lap. She fiddled with the rings on her wedding finger.

'What do you usually do this time of day?' he asked.

She must have forgotten to inhale, she thought, as she took a big breath in relief that he was asking her something normal.

'For the first month we were here I concentrated on the redecoration of our flat. But now I lunch quite a lot with friends. After all, until five years ago I lived here. I know a fair number of people in London.'

She gave a warm smile.

'I had a letter this morning from 10 Downing Street telling me there's a vacancy on the board of trustees of the National Portrait Gallery. They've asked me to be a trustee.'

'What do you want to bet they think if you're on the board they might get a big donation from your husband?'

'That's as may be,' said Marigold, pique producing hauteur, 'but as it happens I would make a good trustee. The arts are one of the few things I really know about.'

'I'll remember that,' Gerald replied.

'Meaning?'

He smiled.

'We'll see, Mrs Brewster.'

He looked at his watch. He surveyed her again.

'The elegant English lady, impeccably dressed,' he said. 'We would make an interesting couple, Mrs Brewster.'

He watched her recross her legs.

Abruptly he pushed back his chair.

'My driver will drop me off at the *Javelin* and then take you where you like,' he said.

'I'll get a taxi,' she replied, as he guessed she would.

In the lift neither spoke. When they crossed the lobby, the receptionist made a production of not seeing them.

While his driver flagged down a taxi for her Gerald said: 'I'll phone you,' and started to get in the Rolls.

Then he stopped and came back a few steps to where she stood.

'I am not a patient man, Mrs Brewster,' he said.

At once he turned and got in the car.

TWENTY-SEVEN

Half an hour before he and Zoë were to meet, Simon strolled from the *Javelin*. There were bound to be other journalists at the pub, some having a few drinks before going home, others throwing back a quick one before returning to their offices. Someone else might have supposed that after a day in the newsroom they would have chosen different company to relax with. But gossip with each other remained their central recreation, swaggering when they'd had a scoop in that day's paper, sullenly needling when things were flat for them, exchanging the latest anecdotes about their editors.

And you never know, Simon said to himself. If he threw Miles Brewster's name into the conversation, a clue might emerge. He'd been his most grandiose when he got through to three reporters on Scrope papers in America and told them to sit in the Congressional Library 'until your nuts rot, as the Chairman so delicately puts it, or you find something about that accident in Mexico.'

Zoë liked this time of day south of the river, people walking home to nineteenth-century terrace houses, some still occupied by working families that had lived there for generations; Hawksmoor steeples pricking the evening sky; the sober battlements of Lambeth Palace asserting the presence of God.

Her evening plans had changed since she and Simon arranged to have a drink. Jancie had phoned to say James was working late. Zoë was especially glad to be able to see her tonight. So now instead of going home from the pub, she'd be off to the Whartons' house.

Simon was standing at the bar with two political

columnists, and when he saw her in the mirror he called a noisy welcome:

'Beautiful one, you bring light into darkness.'

All four chatted for a bit before Simon and Zoë took their drinks to a table.

'I just heard about Peter Stainsley's wife,' said Simon.

He lifted his brows questioningly.

'I used to see you lunching with him,' he said.

'Which means you saw me having lunch with him once,' Zoë replied easily. No one was better at throwing up smoke-screens. She switched the conversation to some mutual friends in Washington.

Simon drained his glass.

'Are you ready for another, *amiga*?' he asked out of courtesy, as she'd barely tasted her whisky. Returning with his drink trembling at the brim, he took a sip before resuming his seat.

'Bad luck to lose a drop,' he said. 'You gotta have enterprise and you gotta have luck. Neither's enough without the other. How's your love life?'

'Nothing to make you swoon,' replied Zoë.

There was a pause.

Then Simon asked: 'How's Jancie? I hear she's doing a good job for the BBC.'

'We're having supper together tonight. She's doing all right generally. Great example of a woman whose marriage is better when she has a job outside the home. She and James are very much back on course.'

'I thought they'd get things together again,' said Simon. 'The past is the past, and I always thought the sooner Jancie recognised that, the better. Her problem was she didn't understand the difference between marriage and an affair.'

He grinned.

'Nobody knows that better than you, eh, Zoë?'

'It's a good thing I'm so well brought up, Simon. Sometimes you make me want to punch you in the mouth.'

'I surrender,' he said, raising his hands. 'I have only the highest respect for you, *amiga*. And for Jancie. She's a sweet girl. None nicer. Will do anything for a chap.'

A fleeting memory of Jancie on the bed at the Crabshell Inn led him to moisten his lips.

'You thought I took advantage of Jancie, Zoë, but these things are two-sided, you know. Every girl needs a breakout from time to time. It's healthy. Would you want to be married to James? True, he's got a string of accomplishments. But he's still a prefect, for God's sake – boy's honour and all that.'

She glanced at her watch. She might have guessed a drink with Simon would not be unalloyed pleasure.

'Do you and James run into each other at the *Javelin*?' she asked.

'Not a lot. I dare say he can't be having the time of his life as *chef de cabinet*' – Simon laughed as he used the title – 'sitting in that room outside the Chairman's office, constantly at the mercy of the Chairman's inconstant moods.'

He bobbed his head to acknowledge applause for his play on words.

'That's what everyone in the organisation has to call Gerald Scrope,' he went on. 'Chairman. Even when he's not around.'

'Are you afraid of him?' asked Zoë.

'You're damn right I'm afraid of him.'

'Were you afraid of Miles Brewster when you worked for him?'

Simon emptied his glass.

'Back in a sec. You're OK?'

She nodded.

When he returned he took a long swallow of his drink before answering her question.

'Gerald Scrope is frightening all the time because he's capricious – plus a big streak of sadism. You never know from one minute to the next whether you're in or out.'

He took another swallow.

'With Miles Brewster you know when you cross the line of what he deems acceptable – and if he finds out, you've bloody well had it. In that ultra-courteous way he'll hand down an order that consigns you to Siberia.'

He gave her a quick look.

'Do you ever have lunch with him?' he asked.

'Miles?' she said. 'Maybe once?'

'What's he talk about?'

Zoë laughed, her guard up. 'I can't remember, Simon – except it was shop talk.'

'If a chap has a personal secret,' said Simon, 'he keeps talk on the shop – especially an absolute man.'

The same word Peter had used, Zoë remembered.

'They cannot bear to think,' said Simon, 'that they let down their own standards.'

He was used to drinking heavily, and his words were only slightly slurred.

'Shall I tell you something, Zoë? I'm going to blow that bastard sky high. He thinks he's got away with whatever he did in Mexico fifteen years ago – when he wrecked his leg. "A crooked leg betokes a crooked soul." You didn't know I was a poet, did you, beautiful one? Poetic justice is what I seek. The quest has begun. And when it is completed, Miles Brewster's secret will belong to the world.'

He had tipped into maudlinism, but the venom was real.

'What do you mean "the quest has begun", Simon?'

Leaning towards her, he wagged a finger from side to side, slowly, teasing, significant.

'A secret,' he said with a broad loose smile. 'But before too long you shall know more.'

Zoë finished her drink. 'I've got to go, Simon.'

Nell opened the door.

'Me and Danny have been arguing about the colour of your eyes. I say they're the same grey as Mummy's velvet jacket but he says they're more bluish. He wants you to come upstairs. He's got chickenpox.'

'Oooh, Nell,' said Zoë, taking off her coat, 'that means you'll be next I suppose. Still, it's best to get it now and out of the way. You can only get it once you know.'

Not long after she returned downstairs, she and Jancie were into a bottle of Chardonnay.

'By the way,' said Zoë, 'I ran into Simon this afternoon. First time since I've been in London.'

Yearning spread over Jancie's face.

'We had a drink after work this evening. Almost at once he asked after you.'

'What did he say?' Jancie asked in a strained voice.

'He'd heard you were doing really well at the BBC. I said your job had helped get your marriage back on course.'

'Did he talk about anyone else – any other woman, I mean?'

'Nope. It was mostly chat about the difference between working for Gerald Scrope and Miles. Simon's looking for dirt on Miles. If you ask me, playing bloodhound means more to Simon than anything else.'

They sipped their wine.

'He's trying to discover what exactly happened in Mexico all those years ago,' said Zoë.

'Are you going to tell Miles?' asked Jancie.

'I don't know. I don't want him to think I'm pushing my nose into his affairs. Yet since we know each other pretty well, it seems unnatural not to warn the guy to watch out.'

They talked for a long time about Peter's wife. Jancie already knew about her death, but she didn't know any details.

Zoë had intended only to describe what happened on the Baltimore–Washington freeway. She had never confided in anyone, even Jancie, about Peter.

'How did he seem when he told you?' Jancie asked.

'A wreck.'

A moment's hesitation. Then Jancie said: 'Once or twice it crossed my mind there might be something going between you and Peter.'

Zoë flushed.

'It was never something that was going anywhere,' she said, looking away. 'He has a good marriage. Had,' she corrected herself uncomfortably.

Jancie's round blue eyes were watching her.

Zoë's face was a mixture of guilt, relief at telling Jancie, and something else Jancie couldn't read.

'Has her death put you on the spot?' she asked.

'Maybe. I don't like to think about that yet,' she said, her gaze meeting Jancie's.

'Because it can go somewhere now?' said Jancie in a quiet voice.

Zoë gave a sad little smile.

'I thought of that when I woke up this morning,' she said, 'and for the first time since I've known Peter I'm ashamed of my thoughts.'

'Join the club,' said Jancie.

Miles called her into his office the next day. He wanted a

piece on President Lambert's latest threat of imposing a trade barrier.

His face lit up when she walked in. Running a hand through his hair as he got to his feet, he came round his desk to sit near her while he went through what he was looking for. Did British businessmen and women realise what was at stake if America and Britain, the West's only instinctive allies, erected a trade barrier between themselves?

When they'd finished talking about the assignment, they both got up.

Zoë lingered, ill at ease.

'By the way,' she said, 'I understand Simon Fleet is working overtime to learn what happened in Mexico fifteen years ago.'

Beneath his freckles all warmth drained. He stood so still it frightened her.

After a rigid silence she turned to leave.

'Who told you this?' he asked.

'Simon Fleet. He was drunk.'

Another strained silence.

In a scrupulously polite voice Miles said: 'In future I would be glad if you didn't concern yourself in my private life.'

Her face stung as if it had been hit with the flat of his hand. Striding from his office, she jerked the door shut behind her.

TWENTY-EIGHT

Next day Miles stopped by her desk.

'That goddam egg I had for breakfast yesterday must have been rotten,' he said with a lopsided smile.

For a second Zoë intended to be stiff-mannered, but she was so relieved to be back on good terms that she returned his smile.

A few days later he stopped at her desk again. It was the eve of her trip to Washington.

'You wanted to talk to me about Nona Lambert,' he said. 'How about now?'

Notepad in hand, she followed him to his office. They sat either side of the coffee table.

'This won't add a lot to what your Washington sources can tell you,' he began.

'You know the problem with other sources,' Zoë replied. 'Those in the loop pretend they're being frank when in fact they're not about to put a foot wrong with the Lamberts. And those no longer rubbing shoulders with power can afford candour, but personal grievance distorts their memory.'

'Personal grievance,' said Miles with a shake of the head. 'It has blighted the entire course of mankind's history. It's a curse on all and sundry.'

She waited, head tilted, hoping he would expand.

'Right,' he said instead in a let's-get-down-to-business voice. 'Nona always had a high opinion – rightly – of her own intelligence. Even in college days she knew exactly where she was going. The difference between her and Frank Lambert was that he was ambitious, she was *certain*. Even then he aspired to become president. What

American politician doesn't? But Nona *knew* they would get to the White House. Not by luck – though you need that too. But by determination, organisation, thinking about it day in and day out.'

As he watched her scribble, his expression softened, but it became impersonal again when he went on.

'Frank threw himself into every step of his journey. It was not theatre: he took seriously the opportunities he had as a senator to make people's lives less hopeless. He genuinely felt for them.'

He waited while Zoë caught up.

They were sitting only three feet apart and there was the faintest scent, yet he couldn't be sure it was perfume. Maybe that's how she smelled. Was it true that someone's particular smell is what attracts you?

'With Nona it was different. Sure, she was not some everyday hypocrite, pretending emotions she didn't feel. But she didn't respond to things spontaneously, because for her they were always judged in terms of what was useful, what was not, to reach the goal.'

He looked at her dark head bent over her notepad, at the sooty lashes. He could see the lower lip caught in her teeth as she concentrated. She looked up.

'Would you describe her as cold, even when she was young?' she asked.

'In the sense that the goal was all – yes. But it wasn't a forbidding coldness. She was fired by her conviction that they *should* be in the White House – that Frank would be better for the country than any of his contemporaries. This conviction gave her a warmth, as fervour always does. It made you want to help them reach the goal if, like me, you shared their values and imagined they'd put these values into action when in a position to do so.'

'How does she take your criticism of the President now that he's there?' asked Zoë.

'Well, no one loves being criticised,' said Miles.

Zoë looked up at him, her eyes twinkling.

'You've noticed,' she said.

He pulled a face.

'But despite some of the cowboys Frank has brought with him as advisers, I still think he is far the best man for the job. He has the guts to try fresh ways of resolving old problems, and the modesty to accept tested wisdoms in resolving new ones.'

He gave her a couple of seconds for that.

'A helluva lot that's crucial – nationally, internationally – would be jeopardised if he wasn't in the Oval Office. I have no regrets' – he paused, and it occurred to Zoë that he was uncertain how to phrase what would follow – 'about the help he has had from my newspapers.'

She was certain that's not what he'd wanted to say.

When he saw she'd caught up, he got to his feet.

'When you get back, let me know how things went,' he said, friendly but no more than he'd be to any staff about to go off on an important foreign assignment.

Zoë must have been to the Hay-Adams a dozen times when she'd been writing for the *Washington Express*. 'An island of civility in a sea of power', someone had called it.

It stood where those nineteenth-century luminaries, John Hay and Henry Adams, had lived side by side, a door cut between the connecting wall of their homes. Unlike most political stars, they remained intimate friends to the end. Then in 1927 their famous houses were replaced by the Hay-Adams Hotel with its marble baths and accommodation for personal servants, the lofty lobby intended to make visitors feel they were entering a grand English country house.

But Zoë had only been here before when interviewing

a congressman or other hotshot in the Adams Room – which remained the power-brokers' favourite for breakfast or lunch (always put down on someone's expense account).

This time she was actually staying at the hotel. Like other newspapers, the *Dispatch* begrudged expenses incurred by staff based in the main office, but journalists were expected to live in style when representing the paper abroad. When her taxi drew up at the hotel's portico, she felt a wild burst of elation. Only a hundred yards away she could see Decatur House, home of her childhood hero.

As soon as she'd got settled in her room, she went back to the lobby. Outside she stepped across the road into a late-afternoon fog over Lafayette Square, the White House blurred on the far side. Beneath the maples the ground was carpeted in red, while more leaves, glowing through the mist, still clung to the branches. The colours must be fantastic in Vermont. She went to the bench facing Decatur House, the one where she'd sat that day in June, making her columns when deciding whether or not to accept Miles's offer.

She was more nervous than she'd ever been before meeting Peter, not counting the beginning. Would he look different in his widowhood? Would he behave differently? Would she?

Back in her room she had just finished changing when the telephone rang.

'Zoë. I'm downstairs in the lobby. Shall I wait for you here?'

She spotted his back at once, the broad shoulders and straight brown hair. He was looking at the Medici tapestry which took up most of one wall. She stopped before she reached him, afraid she might startle him if she touched him without warning.

'Hullo, Peter.'

When he turned, his face looked younger. She remembered the mother of a friend who'd died in an accident at Vassar: she had an almost childlike look, dazed, normal adult tensions replaced by something so much deeper that the taut muscles of her face had softened. Peter looked like that now.

His face creased into a warm smile. They embraced – like close friends or members of a family coming together in a shared sorrow. Not that she could share his sorrow. Who could? Except his children perhaps.

'Are you sure you wouldn't rather go out?' he asked. 'It just seemed uncomplicated if we ate here.'

'I think it would be peaceful to stay in one place,' Zoë answered, putting her arm through his. 'Let's find a quiet alcove before we have dinner. I'm dying for a drink.' She could have cut off her tongue for her choice of verb.

Once they'd placed their order he said: 'We can talk about me later. It's been dreadful.'

The exact word, she thought.

'Let's start with you,' he said. 'Do you mind?'

She laid her hand for a moment on his.

'Right,' she said, unconsciously imitating Miles. 'Me. Well, here I am back again – and very uncertain, too, I can tell you, about the prospect of interviewing Nona Lambert.'

'I'm not surprised,' said Peter. 'She's one formidable lady. And she will be determined to keep control from start to finish. How long do you have?'

'One hour.'

'Well, it's a challenge anyway.'

Their drinks arrived. Before taking her first sip, she made a little salute with her glass. He tipped his own to her.

'How are the children taking it?' she asked.

He pondered before saying: 'It hasn't sunk in. For them.'

They fell into silence.

Then he started speaking rapidly.

'I keep wondering what she felt when the truck burst through the barrier. Is it true that your life passes before your eyes? A lingering death is terrible. But at least it gives people a chance to say things to each other – to make a proper farewell.'

Zoë was struck again by how boyish his face was in its lost expression.

'We never talked about the other part of my life,' he went on in the same staccato. 'When we first married and we'd be having a nice time in bed, she sometimes said: "I couldn't bear it if you ever wanted to do this with someone else as well." But later, when I was having a discreet affair – oh God, that sounds as if I think because it was discreet it didn't count – she didn't say that any more. So I thought she guessed, but didn't want to discuss it.'

She saw his hand tremble from tension. He threw back the rest of his whisky. Zoë finished hers. They both got up.

The Adams Room was exactly as she remembered it – old Washington's blend of formal and informal, gold tapestry-covered walls and crystal chandeliers, starched white tablecloths over full-length floral skirts, voile curtains gathered at the windows. The tables were far enough apart to keep conversation private, and tonight instead of the politicians and lobbyists who were there earlier in the day, networking on the way to their tables, there were couples, even a family of four. She thought of Peter's family, smashed.

When they'd placed their dinner order he started again in the same jerky sentences.

'Seventeen years is a long time together. The shared experience and memories. The shared relation with other people – children, friends.'

He hesitated, then probed the awful doubt which could never be resolved.

'In her heart, would she have preferred me to discuss it – the infidelities – with her? *You* know I wasn't rushing from one woman's bed to another. There are not that many women I want to spend time with.'

His expression was one she hadn't seen before: sheepish, tormented.

'I'll tell you what she said to me the first time I gave her jewellery as a penance. It was an aquamarine ring. I'd picked out the stone myself. It was unusually large, and when she opened the box she said: "My mother used to say you can always tell a couple have a hundred-per-cent faithful marriage when the husband gives his wife careful-good-taste jewellery, the stone so discreet you hardly see it. When our friends see the size of this rock, they'll start to talk." She laughed when she said it.'

'What was the last special piece of jewellery you gave her?' asked Zoë.

He gave a short wild laugh.

'A sapphire and moonstone brooch. She never wears any other jewellery with it.'

He didn't notice he'd switched to the present tense.

A shiver went over Zoë, as if from a cold draught. She remembered the brooch vividly. She'd noticed it when Peter's wife sat across from her at the British Embassy dinner. She took a large swallow of her wine.

'I gave it to her soon after you and I . . .'

He broke off and emptied his wine glass.

They talked about other things as well. Life in London. What it was like to work for Miles. The Whartons.

On their way out of the Adams Room she thought:

separate elevators still seem right, even if it's not necessary like before. 'I'll go ahead. It's room three hundred and ten,' she said.

'See you shortly.'

When he knocked on her door a quarter of an hour later, she was wearing a simple silk kimono. He knew she didn't want him to undress her. They hadn't discussed it, but there was an unspoken agreement that they wouldn't make love tonight. He stood inside the closed door, looking at her. He loved it when her hair hung loose on her shoulders.

He took her in his arms, and she was the comforter, her lips pressed against his neck, her hand resting on his other cheek. The room was so quiet she heard his heart beat.

When they drew apart so he could undress, both still intended, they were sure, to sleep together chastely. She slipped out of her kimono and drew him down beside her, one arm around his shoulders, small kisses as if he were a child. When he began returning her kisses they grew longer. He moved his hand from her face to her breast.

Afterwards he fell asleep still lying on her, her arms around him. She stayed like that for some time before slipping out from under him. He turned in his sleep and put an arm around her. And in the night when he rolled to his other side, she rolled too, putting her arm around him.

He woke soon after six when the pale sober light of early morning stood in the room. She watched him dress to return to his home, and lifted her arms when he bent over her once more. Then he left.

TWENTY-NINE

The message was waiting when Simon got back from a long lunch. 'Urgent.' It was from one of the reporters he'd assigned to comb the Congressional Library in Washington.

The reporter had come on it in the *Boston Globe*. Fifteen years ago. Two paragraphs.

'Mr Miles Brewster, owner of the *Massachusetts Gazette* and the *New Brunswick Echo*, has been seriously injured in a car crash in Mexico. He was flown home from Monterrey, and is now in Massachusetts General Hospital where he is expected to remain for some time. He was nearing the end of a two-week vacation when the accident occurred.

'Mr Brewster, 27, is a graduate of Harvard University. Four years ago he embarked on a career in publishing. His father, Mr Harvey Brewster II, is a senior partner at the law firm of Whitney, Brewster & Dunn.'

Simon gave a shout of delight. Nothing else in life held quite the bliss of tracking down a story that someone wanted kept hidden.

He buzzed his secretary.

'Get me total information on flights to Mexico. I want to be based at Monterrey. I don't know how long I'll need to be there. To rest between my endeavours for the Chairman, I will require the best hotel you can unearth – like the one where I stayed in Guatemala. A peon scattered a thousand fresh gardenias in the pool each morning. Inhaling their perfume while doing the daily breaststroke does wonders in restoring a chap's strength. Get me the information today.'

*

In the White House library the press secretary lingered, nervous, fiddling with a government cassette-recorder on a table near the fireplace.

Zoë put her own alongside. Trying to look unhurried she strolled around the room taking in fast as much as she could, scribbling notes.

The library was less formal than rooms on the State Floor above – debonair curtains, painted panelling, coral-coloured cushions enlivening the Federal furniture. On a bookcase stood a lighthouse clock, its hands at 2.25.

She got closer to see whose portrait was in the clock's medallion, and was pleased to find it was Lafayette – one of her grandfather's heroes.

A Gilbert Stuart painting of George Washington hung above the carved wooden mantelpiece. On the facing wall were portraits of American Indians.

Zoë smiled as she looked at the prototypes of youths she saw in London street markets sporting out-of-fashion Mohican haircuts, ears impaled with jewels just like those of one chief on the wall – only the chief's jewels were more feminine, Zoë thought, pearls lining the entire edge of his ear and then cascading below it like tears.

Only the two elbow chairs placed either side of the fireplace, five feet apart, were forbidding – and that, she realised, was because they'd been placed like adversaries.

A rustle made her turn. A secret service man was settling himself in a corner. Nona Lambert and an aide were in the doorway, appraising her. Nona stood quite still for several moments, imparting the message: I am the First Lady and don't forget it.

Then she came forward, one hand out, conveying an opposite message: she, Nona Lambert, was on equal terms with Zoë Hare. With a big smile, not quite matched by the rather guarded look in her eyes, the First Lady said:

'We met at Leila Sherman's.'

'Yes,' said Zoë. 'I've been looking at those paintings of the American Indians. Who are they?'

'You mean the Native Americans,' said Nona briskly. Like a ruler's quick rap over the knuckles. 'They were invited to the White House in 1821 – to meet their "Great Father".'

She spoke the last two words drily, wrinkling her nose. She had an interesting face – good-looking, strong rather than pretty.

'President Monroe was worried that westward expansion would be slowed down by militant tribes of the Great Plains. So the chiefs were invited to visit the nation's most formidable forts, and the White House was the *pièce de résistance*.'

Nona's brows drew together in disapproval.

Zoë made a mental note: direct, tough, tactless.

'The administration's idea was to overawe them,' Nona went on, pointing to the imperious bare-chested Indian with fiery feathers and the enchanting pearl teardrops arraying his ear. 'Does he look overawed to you?'

The question clearly being rhetorical, Zoë said nothing. She began taking notes on her sheaf of paper folded in two.

The press secretary twitched and cast a yearning eye at her recorder standing across the room.

But Nona made no comment. She was a confident professional who preferred her words to be written down accurately rather than half-remembered. And she knew Zoë Hare had good credentials.

'And that wonderful woman,' she went on, emotion in her voice as she pointed to the portrait of beautiful, calm Eagle of Delight. 'She caught measles during her visit. She died soon after she returned home to the Great Plains.'

'Did she catch the measles in the White House?' asked

Zoë, trying to remember whether President Monroe had young children at the time.

'Not literally,' Nona replied impatiently. 'But it symbolises the shameful fate that our forefathers visited on Native Americans. Let's sit down.'

The straight-backed brocaded chairs required both women to sit even more upright than they might have done naturally. The press secretary dissolved into the furniture across the room, her duties done now that the conversation was taking place within range of the recorder. A butler appeared with a silver salver. On it stood three glasses of water, two with ice. Nona was a perfectionist.

'We didn't know whether your months in England had turned you against ice,' she said.

Zoë smiled politely as she took a glass with ice. She didn't care one way or the other, but she felt slightly annoyed by the implication she might have abandoned her normal American habits.

'Everyone knows you're the President's most important adviser,' she said. 'How do you make your judgements of other people?'

The First Lady's face grew stern.

'On moral grounds primarily. And that doesn't mean merely an individualistic morality – but a societal morality as represented by the individual.'

'For example?' asked Zoë.

'For example the recent change made in the cabinet. The new education secretary not only is of the highest calibre herself – she is also a representative of two cultures that have been suppressed since society was first determined by Anglo-Saxon males. She is a woman. She is African-American.'

'And she is open about her lesbianism,' Zoë added.

'Ms Hare.'

Nona pursed her lips in distaste.

'I would have you note that we remain the only superpower in a world that is daily threatened with annihilation by famine, disease and Muslim fundamentalists. Personal sexual preoccupations are, therefore, only of marginal interest.'

As she scribbled, Zoë gave a little smile acknowledging Nona's ballsiness.

Looking up from her notes, she asked: 'Now that the socialist camp no longer exists, do you feel that Muslim fundamentalism has taken over the role of antagonist?'

'Ms Hare. Let me make myself well understood. We have nothing whatsoever against our Arab brethren. What we object to is the opportunistic mingling of politics and religion – whatever that religion may be. As you will recollect, one of my husband's recent predecessors largely funded his political campaign under the flag of religious zealotry.'

The toe of one of Nona's shoes tapped the floor silently.

'This, need I remind you, is at direct odds with our Constitution. I dare say it is also against God's.'

'May I ask you, First Lady, if you personally believe that there is a God?'

'I have just answered that.'

Nona waited while Zoë caught up her notes.

'People who knew you in college,' said Zoë, 'say you were certain even then that Frank Lambert would be President one day.'

A fleeting image of Miles's face, expressionless, crossed her mind's eye as she paraphrased what he'd told her.

'It's also said that this determination meant you couldn't always respond to situations spontaneously – that you were more detached than your husband in your relations with other people.'

Zoë had wanted to say 'colder', but she had to tread carefully.

'There is an element of truth in that,' Nona replied. 'Members of a team are only effective when they complement each other.'

'You're talking about a team of two?' said Zoë.

'Yes. My husband is an outgoing person, eager to communicate with a wide variety of people.'

An expression crossed the First Lady's face and then vanished. Zoë realised it was vulnerability.

'There are circumstances,' Nona continued, 'where moral assessment is not easy. Black can appear white, and vice versa, so it is necessary always to look very hard before you act.'

Morality was a recurrent theme throughout the interview.

When Zoë asked how she'd found her trip to Britain, Nona replied: 'There was much that I admired in Britain, but I was disturbed by the moral frivolity that showed itself.'

'Such as?' asked Zoë.

'Such as the fact that the *Queen* allows smoking at Buckingham Palace. It is well known that her son concerns himself in ecological matters. There appears to be a philosophical discrepancy amongst the British royals.'

Up to then Nona's hands, capable, well-kept, had been clasped in her lap. Now she unfolded them long enough to make a fierce fist when she added: 'Leaders of a nation must at all times lead by example.'

She folded her hands again.

'Supposing a situation arose,' said Zoë, 'where you had to choose between leading by example and compromising for the sake of a greater good for the nation.'

The First Lady's stillness was not serene: it was intense. She considered her answer before she said:

'It would cause me deep personal pain to compromise with what I know is decent human behaviour. If, however, circumstances forced me to recognise that a compromise was required if the nation was to prosper, then I would have to master my deep regret. I hope never to be faced with such circumstances.'

She tilted one of her wrists so she could see her watch.

Across the room the press secretary cleared her throat.

The secret service man shifted on his chair in the corner.

Zoë looked at the lighthouse clock ticking on the bookcase. Two minutes left of the hour agreed.

Putting down her pen and gathering up her papers to show the on-the-record interview was over, she raised a final subject, simply to satisfy her own curiosity.

'I gather you and the President were close friends of my editor when you all were younger. Do you still see a lot of each other?'

Nona smiled, but her eyes were wary.

'We have great admiration for Miles Brewster,' she said evenly. 'But our paths diverged, as paths do.'

'Yet your political aims are intertwined,' said Zoë. 'His newspapers, despite their criticisms, are among your husband's strongest supporters.'

'Yes,' Nona replied stiffly. After a hesitation she added: 'Mr Brewster is a distinguished man of great influence. But my husband's responsibilities have steadily increased, you know. Sadly there isn't time for all the personal friendships of youth.'

It was the only moment she sounded defensive, Zoë remarked to herself.

The First Lady's hands had been clamped so tight she seemed to have to wrench them apart. She stood up.

'It has been a pleasure to meet you again,' she said, her smile bright.

The library door opened. An aide waited.

The First Lady left, the secret service man padding two paces behind. The press secretary picked up her recorder, and Zoë dropped her own into her shoulderbag. She saw the hands of the lighthouse clock were at 3.31.

Outside she took a big breath, the blue dome of Washington's sky stretching above her. There was something about Nona Lambert that she couldn't put her finger on.

THIRTY

Soon after daybreak Peter slipped out from under the sheets. She watched him dress, and when he sat at the edge of the bed to put on his shoes, she reached up. He leant over her and her arms enfolded him one more time.

Yet when the wheels of the plane began spinning hard in the never certain moment before lift-off, she felt an excitement. Abruptly the plane was airborne. In the roaring steadiness which followed, she found herself thinking about walking into the newsroom of the *London Dispatch* and seeing Miles on the other side of the glass wall.

There wasn't time to think about jet lag. She checked in with the features editor by phone. Then she stayed at home all day to work on the article.

Weaving together her source material with her own impressions and Nona Lambert's quotes proved even more subtle a task than usual – not least because of Zoë's own ambivalent feelings about the First Lady.

Her driving ambition and moral certitude made her chilly. More than once her confidence had spilled over into arrogance. The self-righteousness of her puritanism was maddening.

Yet the President wouldn't have got within sniffing distance of the White House without his wife's single-mindedness. And you knew where you were with Nona Lambert, she thought.

Or did you?

For she had also glimpsed chinks in the armour. There was that fleeting vulnerable expression before the visor dropped again. And the unexpected defensiveness when she explained why the Lamberts and Miles were no longer close friends.

Miles was sprawled loosely in an armchair, his legs stretched out.

'Hey, what's up? What's bugging you?' he asked.

'Nothing really,' Marigold replied.

They were having a nightcap together after a dinner at the French Embassy. They dined out most evenings during the week, social gatherings which were part of a web of contacts with senior politicians, editors, television moguls, writers, international bankers. These occasions had nothing in common with cosy dinners among friends who've known each other half their lives and get together simply for relaxed companionship. Nor were they Hollywood tycoon-style affairs where conversation dries up before the end of the meal and everyone troops into a private theatre to watch a movie.

At the London gatherings attended by the Brewsters, people remained poised and alert throughout the evening: the unacknowledged agenda was exchange of inside information. And if the theatre director who'd cornered Marigold hoped to build a bridge to Miles, he'd also had genuine pleasure in Marigold's company.

'I don't believe you,' Miles said, his voice kind.

He was not chastising her. He was concerned.

'We know each other pretty well, kiddo. Something is bothering you.'

She played with her rings.

'You're sleeping badly,' he said. 'And sometimes when you think no one is noticing, you look unhappy. I don't like to think of you being unhappy.'

She left her chair and crossed to his. Taking the glass from his hand she slid on to his lap.

He liked her perfume – clean yet musky. It suited her.

She moved the flat of her hand slowly over his shirt, not yet unbuttoning it, feeling the heat of his body through it.

'You have made me happier than I have any right to be,' she said.

'Come on,' he said, taking her hand and pressing its palm against his face by his mouth. 'You have every right to all the happiness in the world.'

Almost as soon as she took her arms from around him Miles fell asleep beside her. She drowsed, yet in minutes was wide awake.

Why was she risking all this? When she'd gone back a second time to that extraordinary penthouse, the conversation was as tense as before. Next time, she knew, something would have to happen. 'I am not a patient man, Mrs Brewster.' They were to meet the following day.

How could she feel as she did about her husband and still want to go to Gerald? She'd asked herself that question a hundred times. She felt she'd passed through aeons of introspection. Yes, she had discovered in her teens that corruption held an attraction for her. But she'd never let it get out of hand, never let it jeopardise her ambition or security. Since she met Miles, it had been safely buried. What she felt for Gerald was something far beyond that.

It was an obsession.

'The elegant English lady,' Gerald said when he'd put down the phone.

She stood just inside the archway.

He remained in his armchair by the wall of windows, inspecting her from the moleskin high collar of her buttoned-up jacket to her court shoes. She felt the flooding of desire begin.

He pressed the switch beside his phones and then got up from his chair.

She stood where she was.

He walked past her into the entrance hall. She heard the lift's locking bolt slide home. He passed her again. At the door to the dining-room he stopped.

She felt her outer self would fly apart.

'Come have some lunch, Mrs Brewster. I wouldn't like you to think I got no manners.' He smiled.

Conversation was not so much awkward as tense. For her the tension was almost excruciating.

She went through the motions of eating some of her smoked trout, but soon sat with her hands in her lap, watching the concentrated relish with which he devoured his food. It didn't repel her – this intent gluttony. It fascinated her.

When he finished, he returned his attention to her.

'I said I wouldn't lay a hand on you, Mrs Brewster – until you are ready.'

The room had become unbearably hot. She slipped off her jacket. Her mouth was dry, her body wet.

His eyes were the way she'd seen them in those moments they'd had alone at the Number Ten dinner.

'I think you are ready now, Mrs Brewster.'

Turning her back on him, Marigold rose slowly from her chair. When at last she faced him, he was still seated, watching her.

He got to his feet. He put out a hand to the neck of her blouse. With a quick downward thrust he ripped the silk apart and with both hands pulled it aside, leaving it hanging, tattered, over her skirt.

Her bra had a front fastening. 'You do it,' he said.

He watched the slender hands with their coral nail varnish as she undid the clip, her eyes still on his, as if mesmerised.

'Nice hands,' he said. 'Just right.'

He pushed the bra aside. For a few moments he said nothing. He gave a slow nod of the head. Marigold could hear her short breaths.

'Miles Brewster is a lucky man,' he said.

He took her to the ornate mirror that hung nearly from ceiling to floor beyond the far end of the table. He stood behind her, looking over her bare shoulder, her cloud of hair brushing his cheek.

'It wouldn't be nice,' he said, 'for the elegant Mrs Brewster to leave here with her skirt in shreds. You better do that too.'

They both watched the beautifully groomed woman, make-up immaculate, step out of her skirt.

The navy-blue of his eyes was so dark that the iris and pupil appeared as one in the mirror. She thought of a satyr.

'I'll do the rest,' he said.

THIRTY-ONE

Standing in the north-east corner of Mexico, not far from the border formed by the Rio Grande, Monterrey was the port of entry for air traffic. New businesses still enjoyed tax exemptions granted the town back in 1888, and it was now the second largest industrial city in Mexico.

Bureaucracy remained as susceptible to the bribe as a century before. Duty-free Jack Daniels was sufficient for most purposes, but customs officials required something more to cast a blind eye at illegal goods – or even to ease the passage of the legitimate which officialdom loved to delay.

Simon's suitcases contained nothing drastic this time, and the bribe he proffered was routine, pocketed by an acne-scarred official as his due.

The hotel was the best the city could boast, Spanish colonial updated, fax machine available in reception. From his room Simon saw the sierras, smoky blue, ranged along the western horizon against an azure sky. The poet inside him looked forward to sunset.

Meanwhile he went downstairs for a quick swim to try and banish jet lag. On his way back he faxed his secretary in London: 'No fresh gardenias floating in hotel pool. Inform Mexican ambassador soonest.'

Then the grind began.

'The newspaper library has to be seen to be believed,' Simon said to two English girls he'd picked up in the hotel bar. 'You'd think they were guarding the crown jewels instead of performing a service.'

He had said to the librarian: 'Miles Brewster killed someone in a car crash near Monterrey fifteen years ago.

There must have been a court case. What do you have on it?'

Forty minutes later the chap had returned from some hinterland, beaming.

'"Nothing on *Señor* Miles Brewster," he announced proudly, glad to disappoint. Jesus,' Simon said to the girls as he retailed the story.

Then he'd handed the guy some moolah. 'I know this is taking a lot of your time, *amigo*, but could you check it out again? Maybe it would be under fatal accidents.'

This time he thought he had lost the geek for ever.

'But when he returns, he has the grace to adopt a doleful air when he says: "Nothing on *Señor* Miles Brewster." And not a peep about returning the bucks I'd paid out for *nada*.'

The two girls giggled, and Simon bought them another drink, courtesy of Lord Scrope, though he didn't mention that.

Examining the courthouse records was a nightmare of obstruction, idleness, incompetence. Opaque eyes and shrugs of blamelessness. In some years were gaps of weeks, months, as if no judgements whatsoever had been delivered by Monterrey's judiciary throughout that time.

'If you want to commit a crime,' Simon said to the girls, 'do it in Monterrey. No one will ever know.'

Police records were even vaguer. Sheaves of Simon's banknotes produced nothing in return.

'You'd think my sole function in this world was to make up for the rotten pay they get,' Simon said to his latest friends at the hotel bar, the English girls having moved on to Mexico City.

The main hospital's fifteen-year-old records were virtually nonexistent after a bureaucratic attempt to go on disc, chaos resulting. No record of a Miles Brewster anywhere, the administrator told him flatly.

The American consul, bored and marking time before a better posting, was happy to have evenings enlivened by dinner with the worldly foreign editor of the *Javelin*.

'We're preparing a profile of Miles Brewster,' Simon explained, as if objectivity was his main concern, 'and the big gap in Brewster's life story is that accident. What's the great mystery about it? So he was driving with a few drinks inside him. Not an unknown occurrence in many a young man's days of joy. Your predecessor fifteen years back would have known about the accident. See if you can come up with some information, *amigo*,' he said to the American consul, and ordered them another bottle of the excellent Burgundy he'd discovered on the wine list.

But there was nothing in the consulate's files on Miles Brewster.

'Maybe it wasn't important enough even though someone got killed,' said the consul, genuinely sorry to disappoint his host. 'Life in Mexico has never had the same value it has in Boston.'

Simon swore under his breath.

Miles was concentrated on writing a leader on Arabi's latest use of chemical weapons to eliminate dissidents. Something made him look up.

Zoë had just walked into the newsroom. He watched her chatting with a journalist before taking her copy into the features editor's office. Her hair was in a ponytail. He'd never worked out whether it was significant when she braided her hair in that club or allowed some of it to fall free in the ponytail. Maybe it was no more than whim on her part. She must wear it loose in bed. He finished his leader. Moments later he went to the newsroom.

'How did it go?'

She looked up with a broad smile. 'You'll have to ask the features editor.'

She already knew what he'd tell Miles. ('Great,' he'd told her 'Let me take you to lunch at the Savoy to celebrate.')

'I'll ask him now,' said Miles. He paused. 'It's nice to see you back.'

From the corner of her eye she saw him come out of the features editor's office, someone's copy in his hand. She was sure it was hers. In that long-limbed gait he went another route back to his office, stopping to speak to one or two other journalists on the way.

Her phone went.

'It's Miles. Can you come in?'

She wound her way through the desks. A door opened directly into his office, but she went through instead to where his personal assistant sat. The PA was one of the few people who were completely natural with other staff, for she kept clear of office politics.

'Was Nona terrifying?' she asked before pressing a button.

Zoë rolled her eyes to the ceiling.

'Zoë Hare is here.'

Miles was at his desk.

'Brilliant,' he said. He gestured to a nearby chair.

'Perceptive, clever, witty. The lot. You got some whammo quotes out of her.'

She could feel the grin stretching her face.

'There's just one problem,' he said, sitting forward.

She groaned inwardly.

'The bit at the end. It would be fine in a novel,' he said, 'but this is reportage. You say "We all have something hidden." So there's no point in then saying you wonder what is hidden inside Nona. You could say the same thing about anyone under the sun. The piece is stronger without those two sentences.'

'Let me look at it again,' said Zoë.

He handed the article across his desk.

As he watched her reread the whole of the last page, he thought of a college student totally engrossed in her exam paper.

She looked up.

'I take your point. But I still think it's better as it is. It's not just reportage, after all: my own responses to her are interwoven. In so much of the piece she comes over as strong and controlled that I want to plant a doubt in the reader's mind.'

Before her eyes, Miles's face hardened.

'It adds nothing,' he said. 'Take it away and see if you can find a different ending that would be stronger.'

She got up to go.

'Bring it back to me when you have it ready,' he added.

'Fine,' she replied, her face closed.

She made a genuine effort to find a better ending. He might, after all, be right.

An hour later she was back in his office. Handing him her copy, she resumed her seat across from him.

Before he could start reading she said: 'I tried various other endings, but I think the way I wrote it before is best. So I put it back as it was.'

Their eyes met, his face unreadable, hers challenging.

'Perhaps it would be wiser if I look at it later,' he said.

There was not exactly a threat in his voice, but she found the meaning implicit enough. He was going to put his red pencil through those two sentences. Even if he was right, and she was sure now he was wrong, she felt he was carping unnecessarily – and just after he'd praised her so highly.

As she got up to go she said in a controlled voice:

'Given the odd way you and Nona Lambert talk about each other, is it possible that the editor is not the best judge of this particular article?'

'Meaning?'

'Meaning how when I first asked to pick your brain about Nona Lambert, you said you couldn't add much. Yet obviously you've known her very well indeed.'

Once she'd started speaking her mind, her anger took on a momentum of its own. Her voice remained low, but they both heard its hard edge as she went on:

'And she goes all weird when I mention your close friendship in the past. Yet lots of people grow apart from earlier friends, for heaven's sake, and they don't treat it as some great mystery one can only mention on pain of death.'

She heard herself mimicking Nona: '"My husband's responsibilities have steadily increased, you know. Sadly there isn't time for all the personal friendships of youth."'

Miles glanced at the copy lying on his desk.

'No, I haven't added that,' she said. 'It wouldn't occur to me to refer to the editor in his own paper. Anyhow, we were talking off the record when she said that.'

There was a lull before he said: 'When you were talking off the record, was she the one who brought up the subject of our friendship?'

Zoë felt her cheeks flush. Why the hell couldn't her face stay inscrutable like his?

'I brought it up,' she said defiantly.

This time the lull was ominous. His stillness was far more frightening than if he had raged. She resented the way he made her feel she'd done something terrible.

'God!' she burst out angrily. 'Anyone would think you

and Nona Lambert had some wild secret love affair the way you carry on!'

In a tight voice Miles said: 'I'm sorry I failed to make myself clear before. Let me try a second time. Why don't you mind your own goddam business?'

She looked at him in disbelief. Then she spun on her heel and left.

THIRTY-TWO

A box on the front page alerted readers to Zoë Hare's interview with the First Lady. It was given a special page to itself, stunning photographs, not a word cut.

Zoë's pride was simple enough. But her relief was complex. Happy that the piece remained as she wrote it, she found what she cared about most was Miles's decision not to override her. She shouldn't have said that stupid thing about him having a love affair with Nona. Even so – his words still stung. Maybe he regretted them and his way of showing her was to leave her article as she wanted it.

He hadn't come down from Corporate when she called in on his PA to say: 'I need to have a quick word with the editor. Could you tell him, please?'

She'd just got back to her desk when her phone went.

'That's neat,' said Jancie. 'A real triumph. Every other journalist in Fleet Street will be eating their hearts out. Time for a celebration. Are you free tonight? James has to be somewhere or other with you-know-who, so it would be just you and me. Home would suit me best.'

'Done.'

Her phone rang again. She grabbed it.

'Miss Hare.'

All her antennae came out. She was sure she'd heard that flat accent before.

'Yes,' she said, a question in her voice.

'It's Gerald Scrope. I want to congratulate you on your article this morning.'

'I'm glad you liked it,' Zoë said, her eyes darting unseeing about the room as she tried to think why he might have rung. 'It was a difficult piece from start to finish.'

'Yeah. When can you have lunch with me?'

She was taken aback by the directness – as if she and Lord Scrope often discussed meeting for lunch. They hadn't met since their drink in Washington.

'Are you free today?'

She didn't have time to think about the rights and wrongs of having lunch with her editor's rival.

'Well, yes I am.'

'We will meet at the Ivy. One o'clock. Goodbye, Miss Hare.'

'Goodbye,' she said, but he can't have heard because in the same moment she heard the click as he hung up.

Her phone went again.

'The editor's in his office, Zoë, if you want to see him now,' said the PA.

Miles stayed seated at his desk. Zoë remained standing.

'I just wanted to thank you for how you handled the piece on Nona Lambert,' she said.

'You made your case, Zoë,' he replied.

It was the first time he'd used her name since their fraught conversations about the Lamberts had begun. Studying his expression, it occurred to her he looked relieved, almost as though he was glad she'd won that round.

'That's really all I came to say,' she added. She gave a tentative smile.

'Thank you, Zoë,' he replied, with an odd little ducking of his head, like someone suddenly shy.

'Lord Scrope has just arrived,' said the head waiter and led the way.

She saw his slicked-back hair; he was reading the menu

spread on the table. She noticed a man nudge his companion when he saw where Zoë was headed.

'Miss Hare.'

Gerald swivelled his wrist to look at his watch.

'Much better than last time.'

She laughed uneasily.

As soon as their order was taken – 'Make it quick,' said Gerald – he got down to business.

'How'd you get that interview?' he asked.

'It may have helped that I'd met Nona Lambert when I was still on the *Express*.'

'Yeah.'

He took a slow swallow of his whisky. Gerald seldom drank much. Zoë was waiting until the wine came.

'Do you ever miss living in America?' he asked.

'Not in the way I thought I might,' she replied. 'Maybe I live more in the present than some people.'

'You mean you don't look back, Miss Hare? Do you look ahead?' he asked.

Zoë smiled. Here we go again with one of Lord Scrope's catechisms.

He read her thought. 'I prefer my own way of finding out what I want to know, Miss Hare.'

Abruptly he moved his gaze to the lamb cutlets just presented, and when a waiter offered the vegetable dish Gerald scooped the air with one hand to show he wanted everything. Zoë was half-way through her first cutlet when his knife and fork clattered on to his empty plate.

He took up where he'd left off: 'I need to know if your present life is bound by restrictions so you can't move where you like.'

'How do you mean?' she asked.

'If you were offered a job in the States – a job, Miss Hare, that other journalists would betray their mothers for – are you free to take it? Maybe you've fallen madly in love with some Limey.'

Zoë abandoned the rest of her meal. Her stomach had gone tight.

She didn't answer.

'You do not like strangers to pry, Miss Hare. I am sorry you regard me as a stranger.'

This time he got his response.

'There is no operatic mystery to pry into, Lord Scrope,' she replied sharply. 'I haven't fallen madly in love with some Limey. Maybe I should have done,' she added.

'Love,' he said. 'The grand illusion. When we catch it, it disappears into its opposite – death. Buddha said the cause of all human suffering is expectation.'

Zoë looked at him in astonishment. His eyes were weird.

'Buddha?' she said.

He gave a low, amused laugh.

'Yes, Miss Hare. Never make assumptions. Just because I skipped school don't mean I can't read. You must try not to see the world in stereotypes, Miss Hare.'

Zoë gaped. His face had transformed, its contours softened, his eyes so dark she couldn't see their expression.

'Death is not the great betrayer. Death is the reality – pure and simple. But we can't understand the pure and simple, can we, Miss Hare? That's the problem. You feel guilt over Senator Stainsley's wife because she is dead – but this is wrong. Perhaps you should have felt guilt over Senator Stainsley's wife when she was alive – but that's another matter.'

Zoë paled.

'Your parents died very young, Miss Hare. You lived in a world of fantasy more developed than you would have known otherwise – listening to your records and imagining heroic ventures more dramatic than you would otherwise have been capable of imagining.'

'How did you know that? No one knows that!'

'Don't be frightened, Miss Hare. We are all made of the same clay. I speak to you directly because you are modest enough to hear it.'

'What do you mean? I don't understand you!'

He gave a small smile that had no sarcasm in it.

'I mean most people are deaf and blind because they have no modesty. They are too busy thinking they are superior or inferior, villains or martyrs. Christ was the perfection of modesty. Do you understand what I'm saying, Miss Hare?'

Zoë didn't answer. She felt suddenly deeply sad.

They sat for a minute or more without speaking.

Then she said almost humbly: 'Did you ever love someone a lot?'

'Me? A long time ago. Once was tough enough.'

She said nothing.

'You were two. If you'd been fourteen,' he said, 'it would have been too late to escape into the world of fantasy.'

'Is that how old you were when . . . something happened?'

'It was my mother I loved.'

'How did she die?'

'My mother? The old man hurt her bad.'

There was another silence.

'What became of him?'

Gerald was slow to answer. 'He got written out of the story.'

'You mean he went away?'

'We could put it like that.'

He had slipped a hand into his pocket to grip the wedge of his Stanley knife, its blade retracted, that he'd carried ever since. After a minute or so he withdrew his hand and took a long swallow from his glass.

'There's plenty of pleasures without love like you're talking about. Food. Sex. Playing the game rough – and winning. It don't mean you make the world worse than it is. It's already a bear pit. It just means you don't screw things up with an emotion that's guaranteed to confuse things more.'

The hard outline of the wide mouth re-emerged as if drawn by a sharp pencil. Any trace of softness there – had she imagined it? – was erased. She was still shaken.

He lit a cigar.

'As you know, the gem of my American magazines is *The Monocle*,' he said. 'I treat it differently from my other interests.'

It was as if the business discussion had not been interrupted. She felt as if she was going crazy.

'I don't interfere with its policies,' he went on. 'But.'

He paused.

'That don't mean, as the present editor seems to think, that I'm made of bleeding money and can pour it out for ever while he does fuck all. Sixty-five thousand subscribers disappeared in the last year alone. This week's issue has eight fewer full-page ads than the week before. I ain't about to let that continue.'

He hunched forward.

'You got a real touch for the American scene, Miss Hare. Don't get me wrong. I been reading your stuff on Britain, and it's good too. But that piece on Nona Lambert is in a different class.'

'Well, she's in a class of her own,' muttered Zoë, wondering what else Lord Scrope could see about her life.

'So are you, Miss Hare.'

He tipped the ash off his cigar.

The waiter put down their coffee.

Zoë tried to relax the back of her neck.

'You got a feel for what interests readers, Miss Hare.'

Almost the same phrase, she realised, that Miles had used when he proposed she move to the *Dispatch*.

'I'm going to ask you again: how far ahead do you plan your life?'

'Not very,' she replied guardedly, rashly adding, 'though if I decide to get off one train on to another, I usually do it pretty damn fast.'

'I'll tell you something,' he said. 'It's time you put all your talents in a suitcase and jumped a new train. I'm offering you the editorship of *The Monocle*, Miss Hare.'

She was too astounded to speak. First the total change of personality. Now this – America's most prestigious weekly magazine for the culture vultures and those who want to know what the culture vultures think, a must on the coffee table in every hotshot's office.

He waited.

'I've never been an editor,' she said. 'I mean, I've never even been head of a section of a paper. It's been offered to me – to head a section, I mean – but I preferred to be at the writing end of journalism.'

She could hear herself jabbering as she tried to collect her wits.

'Rabbits are timid, Miss Hare. I always thought hares were bold.'

She flushed.

'This is what I propose,' he said. 'Ten days from now you take Concorde to New York.' He paused. 'When you cross the Atlantic, do you normally fly Concorde?'

'I've never flown Concorde.'

'You shall do so from now on.'

Her jaw set.

'You misunderstand me, Miss Hare. I do not offer you

a vulgar bribe. I use Concorde as a symbol of the level you'll move on when you're editor of *The Monocle*.'

'But I haven't said I will be editor, Lord Scrope,' she said, her voice almost a wail. 'I'd have to think about it. Anyhow, I have a contract with the *Dispatch*. I can't just break that.'

Gerald jabbed the air with the back of his hand, as if swatting a fly.

'No serious editor holds a writer to a contract once she tells him she's been offered the big break.'

He went straight on.

'When we had that drink at the Willard, you spoke about your grandparents. I am told their farm is on Lake Champlain.'

'Who told you that?' she asked.

'Mr Fleet. You would fly to New York in ten days' time. You would have three days to acquaint yourself with *The Monocle* staff. You might even make the first changes any new editor wants to make to show who's in charge. That is for you to decide, Miss Hare. You would then have two weeks to go back to Lake Champlain – or fly to the moon if you prefer.'

He gave one of his rare real humorous smiles.

'At the end of that fortnight you would take over at *The Monocle*.'

He allowed her time to absorb the glistening prospect.

Her face remained unhappy.

'Of course,' he went on, 'you would need to find somewhere to live in New York. When you first get there, I would expect the editor of *The Monocle* to stay at the Waldorf. But you'd have to find an apartment soon. We can discuss later what *The Monocle* will pay to your rent and expenses, as you will need to do considerable business entertaining.'

Any trace of his smile vanished. His expression was intent.

'That is enough about practical details, Miss Hare,' he said without taking his eyes off her. 'I want you to be editor of *The Monocle* because you know how to grab the reader. And we sure as hell aren't going to get the advertisers back if we don't get the readers first. Do you accept the challenge?'

Her neck really hurt.

'Let me ask you something,' she said. 'You use the *Javelin* to push for whatever you want.'

He interrupted her. 'And Miles Brewster? What do you think he's doing? You must not mistake style for substance, Miss Hare.'

That caught Zoë off balance. She shifted in her chair.

'You think he's motivated by ideals,' Gerald went on. 'You think I'm motivated by what's in it for me. But if our actions are similar, what does it matter what our reason is? It sure as hell don't matter to the punter. He's the bloke who has to take the consequences. That's what matters to him.'

She was silent, uncomfortable.

'Go on with what you wanted to ask,' he said.

'You said how you treat *The Monocle* differently from your other interests. And certainly when I read it after you bought it I never got the impression you were using it the way you use other papers. Even so you might require its editor to use writers who see things as you do.'

'Horses for courses,' he replied. 'Do you like racing, Miss Hare?'

He didn't wait for an answer.

'*The Monocle* is my lithe filly in the Derby, the sharp, elegant runner who shows the world an unexpected side of Gerald Scrope' – he smiled – 'the civilised side, some would say, Miss Hare. I never flogged any editor of *The Monocle* to follow a line dictated by me. My quarrel with the present guy ain't a policy one.'

Zoë looked miserable.

'Well, I'm very flattered at your offer,' she said. 'Obviously it's something I can't turn down out of hand . . . but there are difficulties.' She paused awkwardly. 'I'll need time to think about it.'

'Of course.'

He signalled for the bill.

'You say you don't plan your life too far ahead,' he said, the smile reappearing. 'Can you think as far ahead as lunch tomorrow?'

The tension broke. She smiled too. But she stalled.

'Can you phone me in the morning?' she said.

'Of course. Perhaps you will be hungrier than today, Miss Hare.'

Outside he told the doorman: 'Get a taxi for Miss Hare. At once.'

He stepped into the waiting Rolls.

She watched it pull away from the kerb, and through the rear window she saw the back of his head.

THIRTY-THREE

'This won't be unalloyed celebration,' said Zoë. 'In fact I may start crying.'

'What's happened?'

'I don't know. That's just it.'

Jancie topped up their glasses. They were sitting at the kitchen table, the twins put to bed.

'I had lunch with Gerald Scrope. Why is it that just when I thought I could feel secure in my new job I'm put in a dilemma.'

'Don't tell me. He's offered you a job. No doubt the greatest job in the world,' said Jancie, tilting her chair on to its back legs as she waited for it.

'Actually, lots of people would think it is,' Zoë said in a quiet voice. 'He wants me to be editor of *The Monocle*.'

'*What?*'

The front legs of Jancie's chair came down with a clunk.

'That's what he said,' said Zoë bleakly.

'What did you say?'

'I can't even remember. I think I went into shock. Two shocks, one on top of the other.'

'What was the other one? Did he propose marriage as well?'

This made Zoë laugh so wildly she began to cough. When she'd settled down again she said:

'Right in the middle of telling me about *The Monocle* – "a job, Miss Hare, that other journalists would betray their mothers for" – without the slightest warning he began talking in a really weird, spooky way about Buddha and Christ and my whole history. Like some kind of holy man.'

She emptied her glass.

Jancie glanced at her with an eyebrow raised. 'Rasputin maybe?'

'Goddam it, Jancie, you don't understand. He's got ESP or something, like X-ray eyes boring into God knows how many areas of my soul. It was scary as hell. He referred to Peter's wife's death. But what he said about himself was even more unsettling. You know Peter's daughter is fourteen. Gerald – as I suppose I can refer to him now – told me he was fourteen when his mother died.'

'Did you bring up Peter?'

'Of course not.'

They sipped their wine.

'I think Gerald's mother may have died after his father beat her up. He didn't spell it out. He doesn't want that kind of pain again. He's never loved anyone since.'

'What became of his father?'

'Someone wrote him out of the story, he said. He didn't say who. I don't know, maybe Gerald killed him.'

Jancie pushed the wine bottle towards her. For a few minutes the only sound was a glass being replaced on the polished table and the ticking of the moon-faced clock on the wall.

'Do you think Miles and Gerald Scrope are the same kind of guy?' Zoë asked suddenly.

'Now I've heard everything,' said Jancie.

'I know,' said Zoë unhappily. 'Yet when he puts the thought in your mind, it makes you wonder if there's as much difference as you'd believed. Miles is honourable, Gerald a thousand per cent ruthless. Yet if they are both using their paper for propaganda, what's the great difference?'

She fumbled behind her in a pocket of the jacket hanging over her chair and found a Kleenex. 'This is ridiculous,' she said, blowing her nose.

Jancie got up to uncork another bottle of wine.

'Help yourself,' she said, sitting down again. 'As my mother would say, "You're all strung up, dear." Now look, let's go through it in sections. I hate Gerald Scrope because of the way he's browbeaten James. I wish to God James had sat tight and waited to see if Miles would get the *Dispatch* – though I suppose even then Lord Scrope might have offered James irresistible inducements.'

'Is everything OK now between James and Miles?'

'Yes, though not like before. Miles is the same with me. There's no reason,' she went on, 'to think Gerald Scrope would try to browbeat you. Everyone knows he keeps his hands off *The Monocle*. The worst that would happen is he'd decide to appoint another editor to replace you just when you thought everything was hunky-dory. How much do you want to edit *The Monocle*? He's right, of course, in saying most journalists would jump at the chance.'

'I would too, probably,' Zoë said uncertainly, 'if I didn't have a contract with the *Dispatch*. Even if Miles was willing to waive it, I'd still feel I had a commitment to stay.'

'Why don't you talk to Miles about it?'

'It doesn't seem right,' Zoë continued. 'His great enemy. It would seem disloyal. It *is* disloyal.'

'Come on, Zoë. Miles didn't offer you your job out of the goodness of his heart. He thought you were the best person for it. You talk about commitment as if he were your lover or something.'

Jancie looked at Zoë sharply.

'He's not, is he?'

'Don't be crazy,' Zoë said, her face getting hot. 'I don't make a regular practice of having affairs with a million married men,' she added defensively.

She took a gulp of wine.

'Do you think Miles and Nona Lambert could have had a love affair at some time?' Zoë asked.

'What on earth put that in your mind?'

'They are both so odd when the other's name comes up.'

Jancie waited, enquiringly.

'Yesterday when I thought Miles was going to cut out my ending to the Nona piece, I flipped and said he was acting like someone who's had an affair and wants to keep it secret.'

'Christ. What did he do?'

'Told me to get lost – in that really horrible way I've heard about but never seen before. This morning we made it up after I saw he'd left the piece uncut. When I thanked him, he said I'd made my point.'

The pendulum was slightly offbeat. Tick-*tock* . . . tick-*tock*.

'Have you talked to Peter about *The Monocle*?' said Jancie.

'No.'

'Why don't you phone him – just to clear your mind?'

'But my mind *is* clear. I want to stay on the *Dispatch*.'

'Just out of loyalty?'

'No. That's where I want to be.'

She'd barely sat down at her desk the next day when her phone rang.

'It's Gerald Scrope.'

'I regret that I am unable to accept your kind invitation to lunch today,' Zoë said, mocking a formal reply to keep things light, her voice friendly.

'That means you ain't going to give me the answer I want.'

Each of those words made her feel worse.

'If you'd asked me nearer the end of my contract it might be different,' she said, wanting to make some amends. 'But I knew there was no point in my thinking about that.'

'I don't want to hear your thought process, Miss Hare. I wish you well.'

Click.

She put her own phone down slowly, relief tempered with a regret. Until yesterday she hadn't imagined another side to him. She didn't like the thought of hurting that side.

Returning to his room from his daily swim – the only thing that kept him sane in this ridiculous city, he was sure – Simon tensed when he heard his phone ring. He'd given up expecting anyone in Monterrey to return a call.

'I find it hard to believe, Mr Fleet,' the south London voice said without preamble, 'that after more than a week at the most expensive hotel in Monterrey you have discovered bugger all. Perhaps I had better consider appointing a new foreign editor for the *Javelin*.'

'I'll come up with what you want if anyone can, Chairman. You've got to trust me.'

'Why? I don't trust anyone else.'

In truth, Simon was near despair.

When he got back from his swim the next morning his phone was ringing as he unlocked the door. He looked at his watch. It was the very time the Chairman phoned the previous day. Simon flung himself backwards on to the bed before picking up the receiver. Might as well be lying down when you receive the blow.

'*Señor* Fleet?'

'*Si.*'

'I am Luis. At the courthouse.'

Simon held his breath.

'*Señor* Fleet?'

'Yes, yes, Luis, of course I know who you are.'

'I have find something I believe will interest you, *Señor* Fleet.'

'I'll be with you in twenty minutes, Luis.'

Grabbing his jacket, wallet, passport, notebook, Simon rushed from his room. Ignoring the closed elevator he raced down the stairs.

Luis's face was stolid as he led the way through the courthouse maze to a room not much larger than a cupboard. They sat down on folding chairs either side of a wooden table. Simon found the legs of his chair needed tightening.

'You are near despair, I think, *Señor* Fleet. Yes?'

'Yes.'

'I shall tell you, *Señor* Fleet, why we are unable to find courthouse records on *Señor* Miles Brewster.'

Simon braced himself.

'You believed, *Señor* Fleet, that the records were mislaid. Maybe by carelessness. Maybe by intent. Who is to say about such matters?' He lifted his hands, palms up. 'But sometimes there is another explanation for why we cannot find a courthouse record. Shall I tell you what it is?'

Simon sat absolutely still.

'There was no court case.'

Simon's face crumpled.

'I think you do not understand this country, *Señor* Fleet,' Luis went on calmly. 'We are more patient than maybe you know. We do not hurry to bring a charge against a man, because then there are many complications, many difficulties, *Señor* Fleet. It is better for everyone when accommodations are made before the charge is placed.'

'You mean bribes,' said Simon.

'You put these things too simply, *señor*. Everything in this world it costs money. For the Mexican. For the American. Everyone.' Luis made a small spreading gesture with his neat hands. 'I believe you have make enquiries at the bank.'

'No fear, Luis, I offered a bloody fortune for information. The manager looked as if I'd offered him an adder.'

A trace of a smile lightened Luis's sombre expression.

'I have make my own enquiries, *Señor* Fleet.'

Luis allowed a significant pause.

'For fifteen years the bank receives a payment every month from a law firm in Boston.'

Luis took a small notebook from his breast pocket and turned the lined pages until he came to what he sought. 'Whitney, Brewster & Dunn.'

Simon felt the cold clarity of mind of the hunter when he knows his quarry is close.

'Who collects the money at this end?' he asked in a controlled voice.

'Pedro Lopez. Father of Teresa Lopez. They live near Saltillo.'

Simon leapt to his feet.

'Where in the hell is Saltillo, Luis?'

'Not so far away, *Señor* Fleet. Maybe two hours by the road. You havc scc thc cordillcras rising wcst of Monter rcy. Saltillo is on thc other side. I can arrange a driver if you like.'

An embarrassed small smile flitted across the doleful face, as if he felt shy at bestowing so much pleasure.

'There is another thing, *señor*. I have discover that *Señorita* Lopez speaks excellent English.'

Reaching inside his jacket, Simon produced an envelope. He counted out a heap of banknotes.

'I shall always do what I can to help you, *Señor* Fleet,' said Luis, leaving the money to lie on the table for a few moments to show he was not a common grasping man. Then he picked it up.

THIRTY-FOUR

When they reached the other side of Huasteca Canyon, the real climb into the foothills began. The sierras stretched ahead as far as Simon could see. He disliked heights. The grinding of the gears began to get on his nerves.

'I say, *amigo*, are we going all the way in second?' he asked, and at once regretted it when the driver turned to him, grinning, stained teeth interrupted by a single gleaming gold one, while the car made steadily for the outside shoulder and the drop from it. Simon snatched at the wheel.

'Señor, señor,' said the driver laughing, 'I know the road to Saltillo like I know my own wife.'

Twenty minutes later they turned on to a narrow dirt road, so hard it might have been petrified. The Lopez ranch was on a butte scarred by erosion from flash floods. Mesquite scattered the land and was thick along the escarpment, acting as a barrier to keep in the grazing cattle. A small landing strip came into view.

It had been slow work for Pedro Lopez to clear that runway. With one of his ranch-hands he had dragged a heavy length of chain between two tractors, uprooting mesquite, cutting a path through no more than fifteen acres a day even going full-bore.

'Do many small ranchers have runways?' asked Simon.

The driver shrugged. 'Maybe he has visitors.'

Two long adobe buildings with tin roofs stood in a clearing. Beyond them was the house.

Simon glanced at the shrubs climbing either side of its front door. He knew what they were, and he took it as a good sign that they weren't in flower. He didn't share others' admiration of bougainvillaea in blossom, when it made him think of gushing globules of blood. He knocked on the heavy wooden door.

He knocked again.

'Maybe siesta, *señor*,' the driver called from the car. It was two-thirty in the afternoon.

'*Hola!*' Simon shouted.

Minutes later the door opened, a woman keeping her hand on it, her face stony.

'*Buenas tardes,*' said Simon. '*Está Señorita Teresa Lopez aquí? Es importante.*'

He handed the woman his card. Foreign Editor of the *Javelin* was engraved below his name.

Leaving the door ajar, she disappeared.

When she returned, still expressionless, she swung the door wide and led the way. Simon's eyes were adjusting to the blue shade within when he was dazzled by light from a courtyard around which the house was built.

Shielded from the sun's direct glare by a mountain rising above, each object in the courtyard stood out. On a swinging settee lay a woman, propped against heaped up woven cushions, her black hair worn like a coronet. She was dressed in white, a woven blanket the colour of red ochre thrown across her legs. A small brown monkey perched on the back of the settee. Both watched Simon approach, their eyes alert and curious.

'*Señorita* Lopez,' he said, stopping a few feet away, inclining his head in a small bow.

It was not one of Simon's self-mocking little bows. Something about the woman's stillness and her face unsigned by the years made him ill at ease in her presence.

'I have come to talk about Miles Brewster,' he said.

He saw her grace when she gestured to a cane chair near the swing.

'You know Miles?' asked Teresa Lopez.

'I was foreign editor of the *Washington Express* when he bought it,' Simon replied. 'I have the highest admiration for Mr Brewster. But I am English, and last summer I felt it was time for me to return to my own country. That's when I became foreign editor of the London *Javelin*. Had I known Miles Brewster intended buying the *Dispatch* and moving to London, I would be writing for him now.'

'It is cool in the courtyard this late in the year,' Teresa said. 'Would you care for hot chocolate?'

She spoke in Spanish to the hovering woman, who disappeared.

'I am preparing a profile of Miles Brewster for my newspaper,' Simon went on. 'He is, of course, a man of great influence, and much has been written about him. But accounts of the car accident are contradictory. The *Javelin* prides itself on accuracy. I hoped you would help me, as I want my portrait of Mr Brewster to do him justice.'

It was a familiar enough technique, perfected by years of practice. Volunteer enough to appear frank. Suggest more has already appeared in newsprint than is the case. (There had never been contradictory reports on the car crash. Only vague references.) Where necessary for your purpose, lie.

Glancing at her legs lying motionless beneath the blanket, he said: 'I'm sorry about . . . You must have moments of bitterness.'

'Regrets, yes. Of course,' she replied. 'But not bitterness. No one intended it to happen.'

The woman returned and put down a tray on a low table close to the swing.

Teresa motioned to a plate of *bizcochos* alongside cups brimming with chocolate. 'Please,' she said to Simon.

Again he watched the grace of the movement. She must have been a stunner when she could walk.

'How long were you in hospital?' he asked before sipping his chocolate cautiously lest he burn his tongue.

'I cannot recall,' she replied. 'Once it was clear that all efforts at rehabilitation were in vain, I returned to my father's home.'

'Here?'

'It was here.'

'You say "was", as if it was different from today.'

'That is true. My father's ranch is not large, but it is more prosperous than it used to be,' she replied. 'He has more pastureland now. Our house has grown larger and more comfortable.'

'Both you and Mr Brewster were in the Saltillo hospital?' Simon ventured.

'We were moved from there to the main hospital in Monterrey. Then, of course, it made more sense for Miles to be moved to a hospital near his own home.'

'In Boston,' Simon said. 'The efforts at your own rehabilitation that you speak of. Was this done in Monterrey? Or did you too go to the United States for treatment? Boston is famous for its medical service.'

'Yes.'

She broke a bit off a *bizcocho* and watched the monkey take it daintily between thumb and middle finger.

'I'm sorry, I don't understand,' said Simon. 'Yes you went to the United States for treatment?'

'For a time,' she replied.

She sipped her chocolate.

He itched to take out his notebook and proceed more systematically, but he didn't dare lest she go completely clam. He had imagined that once he established himself as on the side of right, she would have the volubility of the resentful. Instead, he was confronted by this dignity and reserve, making him unsure how to proceed.

'Do you ever hear from Mr Brewster?' he asked.

'Oh yes.'

'You mean he writes to you?' asked Simon.

'We were friends at the time of the accident,' Teresa replied. 'There is nothing unusual, Mr Fleet, in friends keeping in touch.'

She reached to the hard clay ground and gave a little push. The settee resumed its quiet swinging, back and forth.

'I did not realise you were writing the story of my life, Mr Fleet.' She said it pleasantly, but he felt the wall go up.

The monkey resettled itself at her feet. The spiky ginger hair sweeping back from its brows made Simon's lips twitch into a smile, but he wished to God it would stop looking at him with those honey-coloured eyes. The *zikky-zikky* of a cicada startled him by its loudness in the quiet.

He took another swallow of his chocolate. There was no hurry. He was the only hunter after this fox. Next time he'd come wired up beneath his jacket.

'I see you're reading that new biography of Cortés,' he said, looking at the book lying open, face down, on her lap.

'Yes. His was a remarkable achievement. Cruel and remarkable – so few men able to terrorise a warrior race and subjugate it.'

'But then the Aztecs had never seen horses before, or guns,' said Simon, glad to be on neutral territory where he could show he was not the single-minded bloodhound she might have imagined. Also, he was intrigued by her calm detachment when speaking of a history which inflamed other Mexicans.

'True,' said Teresa.

She smiled.

'Can you imagine the alarm at seeing those armoured men on armoured horses and believing they were a single alien creature? Where are you staying?' she asked without transition.

'In Monterrey,' he answered.

'For long?'

'Perhaps a few days,' he replied. Two could play this game, he said to himself.

He finished his chocolate and stood up.

'It has been an honour to meet you, *señorita*,' he said. 'A great honour. I hope our paths cross again before too long.'

As he turned to leave, the woman reappeared to lead the way. Just when they reached the front door, it swung open. Framed against the light was a thickset man, sombrero pulled forward.

Simon stepped back.

The woman said something in Spanish. The man replied in a hard angry voice. Simon heard the word 'gringo', uttered like an oath. The man took off his hat as he entered, and now Simon could see his face. The scowl was more than bad temper: enduring resentment was stamped on the mouth and chin.

'*Señor* Lopez?'

'*Si.*'

'My name is Simon Fleet. I am English.' Speaking with slow precision, he dug in his pocket for his business card. 'I am foreign editor of the famous London newspaper, the *Javelin*.'

With a little bow he presented his card.

'*No hablo inglés,*' Pedro Lopez replied curtly.

He had been standing full frontal to Simon, blocking the open door. He moved aside to make plain that Simon was to depart at once.

Smiling, Simon started afresh in his phrase-book Spanish. '*Soy editor extranjero de Londres Javelin.*' His smile became diffident. '*Excuse mi pobre español, señor. Señorita Teresa habla inglés. Ella ayuda . . .*'

With a thrust of one arm, fist clenched – like delivering a side blow to an opponent – Pedro gestured to the open door.

Simon walked towards it unhurriedly, as if unware of any threat, and just before stepping into the sunlight he turned around to make another formal little bow to Pedro. Next time they met, there would be a bloody interpreter in tow. Not that Simon believed for a minute that Pedro Lopez spoke no English, but if that was how the game was to be played, so be it.

'*Señor* Lopez, *adiós. Adiós, señor.*' A further bow.

The moment his feet touched the baked earth outside, he heard the door slam behind him. The driver, still sitting behind the wheel, grinned.

When he heard the drone of engines, Pedro Lopez returned outside to squint into the vapid brightness. He watched the Cessna give a wide berth to the mountain as it drew closer to the butte where the Lopez ranch stood. He walked fast through the pasture and reached the runway as the wheels touched down.

For security reasons, he and Speers Jackson never wrote or phoned each other. Without their business interests their paths would not have crossed at all. As things stood, they were friends of a sort. When Speers climbed out of the cockpit, Pedro strode forward to greet him.

THIRTY-FIVE

The *Dispatch* was spread on Gerald's desk. Everyone who mattered would recognise the incisive, stinging style of the leader. Miles's attack was three-pronged:

'We have a Defence Secretary who piously professes loyalty to the Prime Minister while furtively plotting to overthrow him.

'We have self-interested back-benchers who wrap their personal motives in the British flag.

'We have the deep cynicism of Lord Scrope, who trumpets patriotism while directing the *Javelin*'s vicious pursuit of anyone who does not serve the business interests of Scrope Opportunities Inc.'

It would need to be answered. Gerald had too much at stake to be vilified now. Reading Miles's leader again, he nodded slowly.

He and Marigold were sitting in armchairs by the wall of glass. A buzzer went on his table. Normally Gerald had calls blocked while she was with him. He looked at his watch and picked up the phone.

'Yeah? . . . Put him through. Get me a cigar,' he said to Marigold. 'On a desk through that door.'

When she opened the door the smell of tobacco was stronger than in Gerald's other rooms. She'd never been in here before. It must have been meant for the maid, she thought as she walked into a cramped narrow room. The desk and chair looked like something you'd glimpse in the manager's office at the back of an upmarket shop. A battered armchair in some sort of printed felt was worn almost through in places. The walls were stained by nicotine. Her father had been a heavy smoker too, and she knew that golden brown well.

She went to the window. South London stretched below as far as she could see, rows of terrace houses, Wandsworth Common off to the right.

Against the wall at the other end of the room stood a cheap wooden bookcase, all its shelves the same height. Some of the books were faded to nondescript grey, with spines split at the seams. Others wore jackets. Quite a few were piled on their sides because the shelves weren't tall enough to take them upright.

It was a moment before she realised what was before her eyes: Gerald must have kept these mundane sticks of furniture all this time. Had he got them when he bought his first garage? The bookcase might have come from earlier. The cigar smell and colour of the walls indicated he still came to this room to read. She felt a rush of an entirely new emotion – compassion, even awe. She was looking into a secret part of Gerald, which he cherished.

'Hurry up, will you?' came the shout.

Taking the box of cigars from the desk, she closed the door quietly behind her. He was still on the phone. As she crossed the deep-pile carpet to where he sat, he saw the stunned look on her face, and he smiled to himself.

'Take a look at that empty mansion in Berkeley Square,' he said a few days later, lighting a cigar and leaning back in his chair. 'You could tear down as many walls as you like, redecorate the whole bleeding thing from top to toe.'

Each time now that Marigold walked through the archway, she had the unconstrained joy of knowing she no longer had to resist carnal abandonment. But she felt much more as well. The ritual meal at that ponderous table had ceased to be achingly tense for her, he sitting at the end away from the mirror, she on his right. They often sat talking after he'd pushed his plate away, until her words faltered when his gaze changed.

'Put the gallery where you like – ground floor, first floor, wherever.' He waved a hand. 'The collection would be entirely your doing. It'd make the Saatchis look like pebble-collectors.'

Of course it couldn't happen. She smiled inwardly at the thought of saying to Miles: 'Oh, by the way, Gerald Scrope wants to back me in building up an art collection.' But she enjoyed the fantasy for its own sake.

'What would I do with the other rooms?' she asked. 'It's a big place.'

'Live in 'em.'

A cloud passed over her face.

'Gerald, I'm not going to leave Miles.'

'Why not?'

'I love him. He has given me everything I ever wanted.'

'No he hasn't.' A pause. 'I got what you want.'

She shifted in her chair.

He looked at her thoughtfully.

'I got the power he's got – and I'll have more. I can buy you everything he can – and more. I'm not a gent like him but I got a title and people have to respect me because they fear me. So far that makes him and me near enough even.'

'And?'

'And.' Gerald grinned. 'I'm a thug.'

As soon as Luis led him into that cupboard of a room, Simon saw the yellowed document on the table. Once more they sat in the facing folding chairs.

'*Sí*, *Señor* Fleet. It is here. I make arrangements. Expensive arrangements, *Señor* Fleet. The police report must be return to Saltillo *comisaría* tomorrow. You understand it is the formal police report.'

Simon stared at the discoloured document lying in conspicuous solitude. Reaching for it he saw his hand trembling with tension.

'I don't trust my Spanish, Luis. Translate it for me. *Por favor*,' he added.

Luis gave a shy smile as he dug in his jacket pocket for his spectacles and hooked the metal arms over his ears. He sat a little taller in his chair. Then he began to read out slowly:

'On eleventh August, where the road to Saltillo crosses the cordillera, the car driven by *Señor* Miles Brewster, age twenty-seven, of Boston, Massachusetts, USA, hit and killed Perdita Orozco, age seven, daughter of Roberto Orozco, where she was standing beside the road.'

Luis looked up.

'You will excuse the stiff manner in which *policía* write the report, *señor*,' he said apologetically.

'Yes, yes,' snapped Simon.

'The car then went over the escarpment and hit mesquite. *Señor* Brewster and a passenger, *Señorita* Teresa Lopez, age twenty-two, daughter of Pedro Lopez, were badly injured. The two American passengers had only *poco*,' he corrected himself, 'were only slightly injured and –'

'What?'

Pedantically, Luis went back a little to start again:

'*Señor* Brewster and a passenger, *Señorita* Teresa Lopez, age twenty-two, daughter of Pedro Lopez, were badly injured. The two American passengers were only slightly injured and they climbed back on to the road and stopped a truck. *Señor* Brewster and *Señorita* Lopez were laid on the flatbed of the truck and all four were driven to Saltillo hospital, along with the body of the child Perdita Orozco.'

'Read the last two sentences again,' said Simon.

Luis did so. He waited.

Simon nodded thoughtfully.

'Shall I go on, *señor*?'

'Yes.'

'*Señor* Brewster accepted full responsibility for the accident. Blood tests showed alcohol in his blood.'

Simon sat back on the wobbly chair. After a moment he leant forward.

'Is it normal, Luis, for Mexican police records not to name all passengers in a fatal car accident?' he asked.

'Nothing is normal in Mexican police records, *señor*,' Luis replied gloomily.

'Read it all again, slowly,' Simon directed, his notebook ready. When he'd finished writing it down he said: 'I'll need a photocopy of the document.'

Luis's face became a study in sorrow.

'This may not be possible, *Señor* Fleet.'

'For Christ's sake,' said Simon, 'even in Mexico it must be possible to photocopy two pieces of paper.'

Luis shrugged, spreading his hands sadly.

Simon reached inside his breast pocket.

'Of course I had intended to cover the expenses you must be incurring, Luis.'

He clapped a wad of banknotes on the document.

'Isn't it possible, Luis, that an earlier police report was made? What happened to the car, for instance? Did it just go up in smoke? Do you know anyone at Saltillo police station who could do some more digging?'

'Many things go up in smoke, *Señor* Fleet. But I shall speak again to Lieutenant Marquez when he returns to Saltillo police station. I believe he has just gone away sick for eight days.'

Simon made no comment on how Luis could foretell the exact duration of the policeman's ill health.

'Is there anywhere I can see Lieutenant Marquez before then?' he asked.

'No, *señor*. And it would be better, you will find, if I speak to him first.'

'For Christ's sake, Luis, tell me if he gets back sooner.'

Luis appeared at a loss.

Reaching again for the envelope, Simon counted out the remaining notes.

THIRTY-SIX

'Where's your imagination?' said Gerald. 'Think what an interesting couple we'd make. Talk of the town.'

Marigold smiled and ate another bit of her chicken.

'You and Miles Brewster make the kind of classy couple people expect. So he's American and you're English, but that ain't earth-shaking. With me, you'd have the power, the money – plus the nudge-nudge from everyone when we walk in a room together.'

He drew on his cigar.

'"Lord Scrope took her away from Miles Brewster, you know,"' he said, mimicking a clackety English county accent.

'If I wasn't Miles's wife,' she said, 'I wonder how much you'd want me then.'

'That kind of spec is stupid. Nothing to do with nothing. Would you give a toss about Diana if she wasn't Princess of Wales? But she *is* Princess of Wales. Would all those women tickle themselves when they think of Frank Lambert if he weren't President? But he *is* President. You might as well say would I feel the same if you were bald.'

His eyes moved to the wonderful hair.

'It's a package deal. Being Mrs Miles Brewster is part of the deal. Ditto being the ex Mrs Miles Brewster.'

Marigold put her hand on his arm.

'Try to understand, Gerald,' she said, 'I can't make the decision you want. It must stay like this. I'll come to you in private as often as you want. But I'll never tell Miles.'

He threw off her hand.

'Look at it this way,' she persevered. 'If it were open and respectable' – using that word for them, her eyes laughed, but she was serious when she said 'we wouldn't have what we have now. Coming to you secretly is the most pure excitement I've ever known.'

'Pure!' he said. He stubbed out his cigar in the ashtray. He nodded.

She rose from her chair. This time she had a fleeting image of the Bernini statue of Saint Theresa in ecstasy, even before he began.

Behind his desk Lieutenant Marquez sat like an Aztec idol in khaki shirt-sleeves. Slowly he closed and opened his eyes. Then he gestured to the metal chair across from him in his sparse office.

He was a handsome man, well-made, nails neatly trimmed. He hadn't the pinched look that Simon expected in someone whose absence was caused by illness.

'I know this will take up your time, Lieutenant. But it is important, very important, that I find . . .'

'I know what you want, *Señor* Fleet. Luis told me.'

'If there *was* an earlier police report about Miles Brewster, what are the various things that might have happened to it?' asked Simon. 'Could it be buried in a pile of shit somewhere else in Saltillo?'

A smile appeared briefly on the policeman's face.

'Impossible to say, *señor*.' Lieutenant Marquez took on the expression of a man who has seen the whole of life parade before him. 'All that is certain in this world is its uncertainty.'

Simon shifted irritably on his chair. A bloody philosopher.

'Look, Lieutenant,' he said, adopting the hearty manner of two men of the world who understand each other. 'I know from Luis that you have just returned from sick leave. I hope you are entirely recovered.'

The idol inclined his head to show appreciation of Simon's concern.

'Would it be better, Lieutenant, if I came back to see you tomorrow morning, so you would have a little more time?'

Simon reached in his breast pocket for the envelope he'd filled with cash.

'I know searching for papers that go back fifteen years will involve expenses.' He laid the envelope on the desk.

Lieutenant Marquez gave no sign of interest in it.

'If you find what I want,' Simon went on, 'my employer will be as grateful as myself. He would be offended if you did not accept something further for yourself.'

The acrid smell of ammonia that hit you inside the entrance was stronger today. What was it meant to conceal? he wondered, as he always did when he entered a police station. Normal lavatory odours? Or ones induced by fear and pain? Three Mexican men sat on a bench, apart from each other, looking down between their feet. The plaster wall at their backs was stained and chipped, half-erased graffiti scrawled low down.

'*Buenos días.* Lieutenant Marquez is expecting me,' Simon said to one of the two policemen regarding him dispassionately from behind the tall counter. He'd explained his purpose in Spanish the previous day and been cut short, one of the policemen stating coldly: 'I speak English.'

Ten minutes later he was led through the narrow corridor.

'Sit down, *Señor* Fleet.'

Once more he took his place on the uncomfortable chair facing the desk.

'It has not been easy, *señor*. Not easy at all.' Lieutenant Marquez was wearing his unfathomable mask.

Instinctively Simon put a hand flat against his chest. He could have been measuring his heartbeat, or about to burst into song. In fact he wanted the reassurance of feeling the fat envelope inside his jacket.

The policeman's opaque eyes followed the movement. Like an actor in a melodrama, he took his time.

'You find patience it is difficult, I think, *señor*.'

'Yes.'

The mahogany face split into a dazzling smile. Lieutenant Marquez pulled open a drawer.

'Está aquí,' he said triumphantly, plonking a small sheaf of lined paper, its top edge ragged, fastened with a rusty paperclip, on to his desk. The pages looked as if they'd been torn from a pad long ago.

'It was written at the hospital in Saltillo where the injured were taken along with the body of Perdita Orozco. She was well-named, I think.' His face had become inscrutable again. 'The Mexican has more need than you in the north for names of sadness, I think.'

Simon dipped his head in deference to the Mexican's greater sorrow. Then he said: 'My Spanish is not reliable, Lieutenant. Please translate the report for me.'

Lieutenant Marquez read slowly and without inflection, in the same spirit as the report was written fifteen years before. The description of the accident matched the formal report already in Simon's possession. As the lieutenant went on to another page he looked up.

'This is not an exact translation I make you, *Señor* Fleet. The policeman who wrote the report did not have a good command of language.'

Simon indicated appreciation of the lieutenant's superior Spanish and English.

Lieutenant Marquez continued: 'The two American passengers in the car whose injuries were slight, *Señor* F. R. Lambert and *Señora* N. T. Lambert, said they would make arrangements for . . .'

'Jesus Christ. What did you say?'

'The two American passengers in the car whose . . .'

'Their *names*,' Simon shouted.

He snatched at the page, running his finger down the spidery writing. He looked at the two names, thunderstruck, his heart pounding.

'My God,' he said.

After a moment he handed the page back, carefully, as if it might break.

'Go on, Lieutenant.'

'. . . said they would make arrangements for the car to be removed. The car, a Chevrolet sedan, Maine licence plate CLN 821, was registered in the name of N.T. Lambert.'

He checked the order of the pages before shaking them back into place and replacing the rusty paperclip.

'They were lucky, I think, *señor*, that they were able to climb back to the road and flag down a truck. Saltillo hospital is well equipped. Not so good, maybe, as Monterrey. But good enough for most things.'

He allowed a significant pause, and Simon guessed that a sardonic remark would follow.

'Of course even the best equipment, *señor*, could not bring the Mexican child back to life.'

After a moment's show of respect, Simon said: '*Por favor*, Lieutenant, read it again. Slowly.' He took out his notebook and pen.

When the policeman had completed his translation, Simon reached inside his jacket and placed the envelope unopened on the desk.

'I will need a photocopy of the report, Lieutenant.'

The idol, neck straight, inclined himself in a grave bow.

'You will return to this room at this same time tomorrow, *Señor* Fleet.'

He had written the letter on hotel stationery. It had to be

worded so he could not be charged with deception should she ever show it to other press.

> Dear *Señorita* Lopez
>
> On the eve of my intended departure from your country, something has arisen which it is essential I tell you. If I do not see you, there is danger of a grave misunderstanding occurring.
>
> Yours very sincerely
>
> Simon Fleet

As he crossed the courtyard, his driver watched him from behind the wheel. Simon knocked.

When the door was opened, he handed his letter in.

The second time, the door was swung wide.

His letter was lying in her lap as she watched him approach, her expression non-committally pleasant. With a bow, he took the chair near the swing. This time she didn't offer him hot chocolate.

'I am glad you could see me, *señorita*,' he began.

She dipped her head in acknowledgement, keeping her eyes on his.

'When we spoke before,' he said, 'you mentioned it was normal for friends to keep in touch. The other two passengers in the car – have they also kept in touch with you?'

Unhurriedly Teresa lowered her lashes over her eyes, like a curtain. She reached to the ground and gave a shove. The monkey rearranged itself.

When she looked up she said. 'What is the grave misunderstanding you speak of, *Señor* Fleet?'

He was uncomfortable under her gaze.

'I know who the passengers were, *señorita*.'

'Oh yes?'

A shrewd one, he thought. She was taking no chances. He might be bluffing.

'I know it was President Lambert – Congressman as he then was – and his wife,' he said.

After only a fractional pause Teresa said: 'What is the problem, *Señor* Fleet?'

He was flummoxed.

'Why didn't you mention them to me before, *señorita*?'

'You didn't ask me,' she replied. She kept her expression untroubled, but the eyes revealed defiance.

Leaving the house, Simon adopted a jaunty gait, as though unburdened by discomfort at her wrong-footing him.

Descending through the foothills was as hazardous as the climb, but his bursts of irritation at the grinding of the gears were few. Most of the time he was absorbed in writing in his notebook. When they reached Huasteca Canyon he put aside his pen while he brooded.

THIRTY-SEVEN

Sitting at her dressing-table, Marigold was fastening the perky front buttons of her *décolleté* dress. She always took trouble to look enticing for their dinners at home together. When she heard the door open and saw him standing there in the mirror, one hand on the knob, something in Miles's stillness made her heart thump with fear. He knew. Impossible. Somehow he knew. She turned from the mirror.

His face was ashen and drawn.

'We'd better have a talk,' he said.

She followed him to his study. He poured them each a drink. When she was seated in one of the armchairs flanking the fireplace – he could smell the perfume he liked – he handed her a folded sheet of cream-coloured vellum, and sat down opposite. She hoped he didn't see her hands tremble as she unfolded the page.

It was embossed with the House of Lords seal and signed by Gerald. She had never seen his handwriting before – neat, slightly crabbed script.

> Dear Mr Brewster
>
> I write to inform you that I intend to marry your wife. I have no wish to announce this publicly while she remains under your roof.
>
> I look forward to learning from you or your wife how soon she will be leaving your home.
>
> Yours sincerely
>
> Gerald Scrope

Her face white she exclaimed furiously: 'What an extraordinary letter!' She flung it to the floor dismissively. How could he have done this to her?

'How long has it been going on?' asked Miles wearily. Did the length of time matter? he asked himself. If his wife had been deceiving him for a month, would the taste of ashes in his mouth be less than if she'd been deceiving him for a year, five years, a decade? Did he ask the question only because that's what people seemed to do in this situation? Just to give themselves time to absorb the blow?

'Oh, Miles. This is the last thing I wanted.'

The room felt cold, she realised, as if the temperature had dropped sharply. Starting to shiver, she made a concerted effort to keep her body still.

'Where do you meet him?'

A long pause.

'At his flat.'

She was as aware of her floundering as he was. His questioning made her sullen like a resentful schoolgirl, and at the same time achingly aware he was the one who needed comfort and support.

A solid silence filled the room.

After a time Miles said: 'How is it that your' – he sought an impersonal word to describe their bedroom intimacy – 'behaviour with me has not altered?'

'I could answer that you are a wonderful lover,' she replied, 'which is true. But the main reason is I love you.'

She said it with a young girl's simplicity. Miles took a sip of his drink, all expression withdrawn from his face.

'And Lord Scrope? Would you make those same statements about him? Does he reproduce in another model what you experience with me – so you know it twice over?'

She sat stiff with tension as she sought the answer that would allow salvation.

'It is something else, Miles,' she said. 'It is the dark side of me. It is completely different from the feelings I have for you.'

'I must be very insensitive,' he said sardonically, 'not to have realised this dark side.'

'It was buried a long time,' she replied. 'Since I met you.'

Both sat quiet. She saw a hint of expression return to his face. Was it the beginning of doubt in his own hard judgement of her? She pressed against the crack she'd made in the wall he had put around himself.

'But it must always have been there,' she went on. 'I would give anything to have kept it buried. I do not even like it.' As she spoke, she had almost forgotten how much bigger than that was her compulsion to go to Gerald.

Watching his wife explain herself, Miles took another swallow of his whisky. It tasted flat.

'Can you find it in your heart to understand me?' she asked. 'I do not know why the dark side is there. It has no effect on everything I feel for you. None at all. I promise you.'

'Am I to understand you want to have me and Lord Scrope in tandem?'

'That is putting it too simply,' she replied.

'Simple or not, was that your programme?'

She leapt out of her chair and stood before him.

'Miles, I'll give him up. Just give me time.'

He looked away. The drawn look was still there, but it had also softened. Marigold had once been to see a friend in hospital who had just been critically injured. His face looked like that.

But Miles's face now became a mask.

'You ask too much,' he said.

She gave a cry almost like a howl and threw herself in his lap, her arms around him. He felt her tears soaking through his shirt. His own inner conflict was almost intolerable.

His face remained set.

After a time she drew away from him. The tear-stained face, usually so perfect, pulled at his heart. He dug in his pocket for a handkerchief and handed it to her.

Still clutching it, she stood up and walked from the room, slowly, leaving the door ajar.

The hands on her bedside clock seemed suspended. After an eternity, she saw ten minutes had passed. Then more. When half an hour went by, reality settled itself upon her. He was not going to come to her. Gerald had seen to that. She was his possession now.

PART IV

THIRTY-EIGHT

Time spent together was like a grotesque parody of a movie where a couple have just agreed to part. Sleeping in separate bedrooms formalised withdrawal from intimacy. But neither knew how to proceed from there.

He had not communicated with Gerald Scrope. It had been agreed that Marigold tell him she and Miles would officially separate as soon as was feasible if the thing was to be handled with a vestige of dignity. Miles had mentioned it to no one. He knew he must soon inform his lawyer, but he couldn't face it yet.

The evenings they went together to other people's dinners were less painful than tonight when they were dining in their grand flat alone. Any attempt to talk about what they'd done during the day quickly petered out, and the only sound was the clink of cutlery against china. The swinging door to the pantry must have developed a stiff hinge: usually hushed when the maid pushed it open, tonight it broke the silence with a sigh each time she came and went.

Afterwards, as they left the room, Marigold could no longer endure the absence of normal responses. She put out a hand to touch him. They stood looking at each other. His face was so immeasurably sad that she thought there might still be hope she could somehow keep him too. He gave a lopsided smile. Then he turned away and went to his study.

Two hours after arriving to take Miles to the office, his driver still waited outside. Within the flat Miles and Marigold sat with two lawyers, locked into one of the most painful conversations Miles could recall in nearly fifteen years. No announcement would yet be made, but physical and financial arrangements had to be faced.

Soon after his lawyer departed, Miles left too. The day was heavy, pressed by a low grey sky, not unlike his inner landscape. His driver greeted him and said no more as he got back behind the wheel. He'd seen the strain and exhaustion stamped on Miles's face.

When he came down to the newsroom that afternoon, Zoë was shocked by his appearance. What the hell had happened? He looked as if somebody had died. He passed near her desk without taking any notice of her.

She was scrunched down in the bedclothes that night, reading, when her buzzer went. She looked at the clock. Nearly ten. Each flat had a bell by the front door, but there was no entryphone system. Maybe someone had pressed the wrong button.

This time the buzz was longer. Goddammit. She threw back the covers and padded to the hall window above the street. The balcony over the front steps made it impossible to see a fucking thing except a man's shoes and trouser-legs.

She flung open the window and leant out. The cold nipped her cheeks and went straight through her thin nightdress.

'Hullo?' she bellowed.

The shoes went down the steps and from the pavement Miles looked up at her.

'Am I disturbing you?' he said.

While her body shivered from the wintry air, heat flooded her too.

'What are you doing out there?' she called down, laughing.

'Do you feel like offering me a drink? I happened to be passing by.'

'This was meant to be Quiet Night.' She was still laughing.

'I'll drink it very quietly,' he said.

'I'll be down in a sec.'

Closing the window with a bang, she ran to the bedroom and grabbed a fairly warm kimono from the cupboard. She looked in the mirror. God. Hope he likes the well-scrubbed look. The pup-pup-pup of her bare feet went down the half flight to her own entrance door. Leaving it open she ran the rest of the way.

'Good evening,' he said.

There was something vaguely different about his speech. She realised what it was when he closed the front door behind him and the smell of Bourbon whisky was rich and warm on his breath.

'I hope you like mountain-climbing,' she said, leading the way.

Inside her own door she watched him shut it. Then she continued up the half flight, intensely aware of him following a few stairs below her, his face on a level with her hips.

Once in a while Zoë gave a drink to a date before they went out to dinner, but she avoided having someone come up for a coffee or nightcap later. The intimacy of her flat made her feel slightly exposed alone with a man if he was interested – and she always knew when he was.

The sitting-room was comfortable, uncluttered, cosy.

'Was it like this when you took it?' Miles asked.

'Pretty much. I pushed things around and added bits.' She pulled a face at her coyness – she'd spent untold evenings and weekends making the flat personal.

'I like it,' he said.

He crossed to the sofa and made himself comfortable.

The precise ping-ping of a Victorian carriage clock struck ten.

'That came with me from Vermont,' she said uncertainly.

'I like that too.'

'Do you want a drink?' she asked, still standing. This was her home, for heaven's sake. Why should she be the one to feel ill at ease?

'Is there such a thing as a highball?' he said, looking around the room, loosening his tie.

'I don't have any Bourbon. But there's some Scotch.'

'Perfect.'

She burst out laughing. She was extraordinarily happy, whatever had brought him here.

'I'll be back,' she said, leaving quickly before he decided to get up and follow her.

She returned from the kitchen with a bottle and two glasses, a soda siphon tucked under an arm.

'Say when,' she said as she began pouring whisky.

Glug glug glug.

She stopped and looked up questioningly, the bottle held in mid-air.

'Sorry, I was looking at you,' he said. 'When. And lots of soda, please. I've never seen your hair loose.'

When she'd poured a drink for herself, she took the armchair at the other side of the coffee table.

'Why do you suppose it's called a coffee table?' he asked. He took a small swallow from his glass and put it down. He stretched out his legs. 'I forgot to say thank you.'

Then he lapsed into silence.

She stared at him, puzzled, and sipped her drink. He didn't look shattered the way he had at the office earlier. He didn't look anything. What on earth were they both doing sitting here? She tried to appear casual while her excitement was so sharp her skin felt taut.

'Do you mind my being here?' he asked.

'No,' she said cautiously. 'I just wondered why you didn't phone first.'

'Maybe I didn't plan to come.'

He had settled with his head against the back cushions so that his eyes were slightly hooded and she couldn't read his expression as he watched her.

'Consciously,' he added.

'Is your driver outside?'

'No. I gave him the night off.'

She re-crossed her legs.

'It gives you an odd feeling,' he said, 'to work closely in the office with someone you admire, and have this recurrent feeling of desire. Do you ever have anything like that?'

Every inch of her became tense.

He waited.

'I know what you mean,' she said.

'A half answer.'

More silence. After a minute or more had passed she took another sip of her highball. He hadn't touched his much darker one again.

'Had I been available, as they say,' he said, 'I expect I would have flung myself at your feet long ago.'

The self-mocking Victorian image was oddly touching. In the quiet she heard the busy little ticking of the carriage clock.

'Things change in new and unexpected ways,' he said, 'and are never the same again. Like a kaleidoscope. You get any number of intricate patterns, some very beautiful, but you can never get the old one back.'

It was as if he were talking in shorthand and she didn't know what all the symbols meant.

'Would you mind if I touched you?' he asked. 'I shan't throw you on the floor. I just want to touch you.'

She drew in her breath, slow, deep.

He got up and came around the coffee table. Standing above her, he put out a hand and laid the pads of his fingers on her mouth.

After a moment he said: 'I love your face entirely bare like that.' He moved his hand slowly over it, like someone who wants to feel the contours and texture of each part of a valued object.

He drew her to her feet.

They stood in the centre of the room, both with their arms at their sides. He kissed her face, her hair, her mouth, light kisses that didn't force a response. Not until her body swayed against him did he put his arms around her, and then his kisses changed. After a moment she did what she had yearned to do all these months: she lifted her arms and put them around him, tightening them as their kisses grew deeper.

Abruptly she pulled away and turned her back, her breaths quick and shallow like a dog she once tended when it was dying. Dying of desire, she thought, almost at the point of no return.

'I *hate* not being able to do what I want to do,' she said in a strangled voice as she almost stamped to a far corner.

When she turned to face him again, her hair tumbled in disarray, she made an attempt to sound light-hearted.

'I think I'd better keep a piece of furniture between us,' she said. Her smile was soft again.

He gave a faint smile in return, staying where he was.

'Things aren't the way they seem,' he said. 'We better have a long talk soon. I'll let myself out. Thanks for the drink.'

They went on looking at one another.

'I wonder if you have any idea how beautiful you are,' he said at last. He turned and left.

She heard the uneven footsteps going down the half flight. The bolt clicked. She listened. Maybe he'd changed his mind and was still inside her door. She ached to hear his footsteps returning up the stairs.

Far below she heard the front door slam.

As if in a dream, she moved to her hall window. The steps beneath the balcony were empty. He must already have reached the pavement. She went back to her sitting-room and switched off the lights, and in the darkness a street lamp made a penumbra around the closed curtains. She pulled one edge aside. Her heart filled when she saw the rangy gait as he neared the King's Road. Then he turned the corner and was gone.

THIRTY-NINE

She couldn't sleep. She didn't want to sleep. She wanted to remember each second since that buzzer had gone the first time.

Throwing back the covers she returned to the sitting-room and opened the curtains. The pavement was empty where last she had seen him. Night fog made each street lamp a blurry full moon. Beams from a car's headlamps moved like ghosts along the short stretch of the King's Road she could see. Back in her bedroom, she opened the curtains there. The mist stood at her window.

She lay watching it.

She didn't try to combat her overwhelming desire for him. He'd felt the same for her – physically at least. What else had he felt? *She* now knew the rapt wonder of love. Recognising it brought a flood of relief.

The mist remained absolutely still, even where the window was open at the bottom.

He was married. She couldn't do that again. It couldn't go anywhere. She must stop it. Now. She must stop herself now. Maybe he had regrets even before he left her. Anyhow, he was bombed – certainly when he first arrived. Did he fall asleep as soon as he got home to bed? Had his wife been awake? That red-gold hair on the pillow. How would he feel when he woke in the morning and remembered what happened in the sitting-room in World's End? Well, it hadn't really happened. Yet it had.

She started again with the buzzer at the beginning and went through each detail with utter longing for him.

*

In his dressing-room at 26 St James's Place, Miles lay alone, awake.

As soon as he walked in to the newsroom, he looked to see if Zoë was at her desk. No sign of her. From his own desk he glanced up frequently.

When he saw her come in, he waited until she was settled. Then he left his office to go to her.

'Hullo, again,' he said, pulling up a chair.

She looked up.

He couldn't read her smile.

'I hope I didn't create too much disturbance in the middle of the night,' he said.

Too overwhelmed by joy at seeing him and fear for what might happen next, she couldn't think what to say. After a moment she replied, still smiling: 'I enjoyed it – even if we were both a little out of it.'

There was an awkward silence.

He leant back in the chair, looking into her face intently.

Even to Zoë her smile began to feel false. It was false: she yearned to leap up and jump on to his lap.

'You've got your hair in that ponytail today,' he said.

She put her hand tentatively to the coil that bound it, and then dropped her hand slowly to her lap, uncertain what to do in the middle of the newsroom when all she wanted to do was throw her arms around him.

He gave a small smile before he got up abruptly and went back to his office.

In the House of Commons that evening, three more government backbench MPs went to the Defence Secretary's room. Here Alan made it implicit, as he did to each small group that went to see him at the House, that they'd have a role in any government he would form once

Martin Mather could be pushed into resigning. Tonight it was decided these various disaffected MPs would band together to launch a more cohesive group. It would call itself: 'Britain First'.

Its declared object was to persuade the government to lift the arms embargo on Arabi, whatever the Americans thought. Its undeclared aim was to get the Right Honourable Alan Rawlston into Number Ten.

'Fine, fine, Ambassador. Only a trained mind could put the case so effectively.'

Whenever the anti-embargo ground swell showed any sign of subsiding, the *Javelin* turned up the pressure, its compliant editor distorting wherever necessary to meet the Chairman's demands. As James refused to knuckle under intellectually, he had to be muzzled most of the time.

But occasional objectivity confuses the enemy was one of Gerald's axioms.

It was a balanced argument James made in the leader he'd finished writing an hour earlier. First the moral case for continuing the embargo. Next the price paid by British industry in loss of profits and workers' jobs. He was able to write it with integrity. Both sides of a genuine argument commanded a growing amount of air time and newsprint each week.

'But I didn't have the guts to come down on either side,' he said bleakly to Jancie that night, 'and of course I want the arms embargo to stay in place.'

'Listen,' she said, 'the second you decide to write exactly what you want in that goddam paper and you're shown the door, I'll send my own personalised spitball, gift-wrapped, to Lord Scrope.'

He gave a grateful smile.

She would never know wild passion with James. But

deep love for him never had to be striven for now, as in those faltering early days of restoring their marriage. Sometimes weeks at a time could go by without her having to sit on her hands to keep from snatching up the phone and dialling Simon's number.

James looked up from his desk. Simon gave a cheery smile and flapped a hand, his other gripping a folder as he continued to the Chairman's door.

'You have deigned to return, Mr Fleet,' said Gerald. 'I trust you have brought information that will justify your expenses.'

'May I sit down?'

Gerald waved to the low-slung chair across from his desk. Simon hated that supplicant's chair.

'I've got what you want, Chairman.'

He stretched up to put the folder on the desk.

Gerald took his time opening it. He had waited for this moment.

He scanned the photocopies – there were not many – and then went through them slowly. Bank statements selected over a fifteen-year period showing monthly cheques drawn on a Boston bank. The formal police report copied by Luis. The earlier one Lieutenant Marquez had come up with.

'Tell me the rest, Mr Fleet.'

Simon retailed everything that had happened in Monterrey and Saltillo. He described each detail of his visits to the Lopez ranch.

'She won't play ball, Chairman. And her father would polish his machete on me if left to his own devices. But we've got enough already.'

Gerald leaned back in his chair.

'You have done well, Mr Fleet.'

They sat in silence, Gerald's face reflective, Simon waiting.

'Write it, Mr Fleet. Then bring it to me. I shall run it when the moment is right. That will be soon.'

A flicker of a smile crossed Gerald's face, but it had no warmth.

'Tell me, have you had the pleasure of Mrs Wharton's company lately?'

'Jancie?' Simon was taken aback.

'She is a very attractive woman, Mr Fleet. I understand she has taken to public relations at the BBC like the proverbial duck to water. It occurs to me it could be both useful and agreeable if you and I entertained Mrs Wharton to lunch. At my flat. This week. Offer her two dates. I have no doubt I can manage one of them. Good day, Mr Fleet.'

FORTY

The phone in her office was ringing when she returned from lunch.

'Buenos días, bella señora,' Simon said jauntily, as if they chatted with one another habitually.

She heard the blood pumping in her ears. She must play things cool.

'I heard you were in Mexico,' she said brightly.

Simon broke into song. *'South of the border, down Mexico way, that's where I fell in love and stars above came out to play . . .'*

He laughed good-naturedly.

'Actually, it wasn't like that at all. I hate Mexico. And I haven't fallen in love since Jancie Wharton swept me off my feet. How are you?'

'No thanks to you, I'm fine,' she said, laughing, for the thousandth time realising that when Simon set out to please, it was impossible not to forgive his neglect.

'Now that your husband and I have the same boss, it seemed altogether suitable to invite you to lunch at the Chairman's flat.'

'If one more person says "the Chairman" I shall scream,' said Jancie.

'Call him what you will, he's a fan of yours. Wants to play footsie, I gather, with the BBC. It would be just the three of us. He detests planning weeks in advance. If I prostrate myself at this end of the phone, will you chuck whoever you've already lined up for tomorrow or the next day? Hang on while I lower my body to the floor. There. Ouch. What's your verdict?'

With another burst of laughter Jancie said: 'I'm sorry

you've developed rheumatism. But you can climb to your feet. I can make it on Thursday. See that I keep my mind on the BBC's interests. I don't want to forget myself and tell Lord Scrope he's a thug.'

'You remain my favourite woman. Do you know where his flat is?'

'In that glitzy tower across the river from Parliament?'

'The same. One o'clock. I look forward to it more than you know, *mi amor*.'

James was home that evening at a relatively civilised hour. He and Jancie were sitting in his study catching up with each other's news.

'I saw Peter Stainsley when I was in Washington,' he said.

'How is he?' she asked.

'Not too good. I told him how distressed you are about his wife – how you keep thinking what it must be like to have the person you have loved and lived with for seventeen years suddenly disappear just like that.'

Jancie smiled affectionately. She could imagine the scene exactly – James finding it easier to express his own feelings by talking about *her* sadness for Peter.

Just when they were thinking of getting ready for bed, she said: 'You'll never guess where I'm having lunch on Thursday. At your great Chairman's flat. He wants to talk about the BBC. Do you know what's in his mind?'

James suppressed acute irritation. He was the one, after all, not his wife, who worked for Gerald Scrope. Why shouldn't Jancie have lunch at his employer's home?

'Haven't a clue,' he replied. 'I'll try to find out before you see him. Who else is going to be there, do you know?'

After only a fractional hesitation Jancie said: 'Simon Fleet.'

James tightened his lips and went into the bathroom without a word.

From her taxi window Jancie glanced at the flag flying over Buckingham Palace. When James was ambassador they were summoned back for everything that involved America's president and top policy-makers. Since he was recalled they'd been to the palace only once. Occasionally she thought of the glamour but forgot it as soon as she remembered the tedious protocol of official life. Anxiously she peered ahead to the traffic waiting to get across Parliament Square to the bridge beyond.

'I'm lunching with Lord Scrope.'

'Who shall I say is here?'

'Mrs Wharton.'

In the lift's mirrored wall she studied her reflection. It was not Lord Scrope's reactions that mattered to her. Would she look different to Simon? She'd worn her most flattering suit, the skirt cinched with a wide belt beneath the open jacket, legs sleek in high heels, curls bobbing on her shoulders. Despite nervousness, her face was radiant with anticipation.

When the doors slid open, Simon was waiting in the hall. He threw his arms wide, and when she broke into an ecstatic smile he kissed her on both cheeks. In one of the mirrors she saw the doors close behind her.

'You're even more ravishing to behold than I remembered,' he said, standing back to admire her. He took her arm proprietorially. 'Come in and see what you think.'

Like an established couple, arms linked, they strolled into the spectacular drawing-room, the deep-pile carpet giving way beneath their step. He led her to the windows overlooking the Thames.

'You may find the décor a little, shall we say, *outré*, but you've got to admire the view,' Simon said.

She looked up at him, laughing. 'The whole thing's extraordinary. People are always talking about the aphrodisia of power. This place reeks of it.'

'You break my heart,' said Simon. 'Why could you not have said it's my presence that has this effect?'

She gave him a teasing look.

'Where is he, by the way?' she asked.

'A last-minute hiccup,' said Simon. 'He asked me to convey his deepest apologies. He insisted you and I go ahead with our lunch. His housekeeper had already prepared it. May I offer you a drink?'

Watching him cross the room to the ornate commode where decanters and glasses stood like a regiment, she had the heady exhilaration she hadn't known since those days in his Washington apartment. The feeling was so electrifying that she would let herself revel in it for a few minutes before cutting it short.

He handed her a glass of Puligny Montrachet, and his eyes met hers. 'You still have the same effect on me, Jancie,' he said, his voice serious.

They sat on separate sofas. Conversation was as ebullient as if the rupture had never occurred. Rippling gossip that appealed to them both. Abundance of shared interests. His arch humour evoking her wit. No reference to James.

'I always like being in someone's home without that person being there,' Jancie said, looking around in wonder. 'It's like stepping through a door and finding yourself on a stage set.'

'I know. You become an actor in a drama that has nothing to do with you.'

When he led her to the dining-room she'd had only half a glass of wine, yet she was on a high of intoxication.

He gestured to the dishes on the sideboard. 'The form

is we help ourselves. The housekeeper puts out everything and then goes away. That's how the Chairman likes it.'

It wasn't 'the Chairman' that struck her now. It was the implication of what Simon said: not even the housekeeper was in the flat with them.

Jancie said nothing. If she didn't comment on it, it need never have been said, it needn't have consequences. James did not specifically enter her mind – only the instinctive sense that she had to guard against doing something she would deeply regret.

He uncorked the wine standing in a cooler, while she helped herself to salmon. Three places were laid at one end of the long table. There was something forbidding about the elbow chair at its head. She took a seat beside it. Simon sat down facing her and poured them out some wine.

'To the woman I have loved more than any other,' he said, lifting his glass.

'To the man who has an odd way of showing it,' she replied gaily as she lifted her own glass.

Throughout their lunch they chattered animatedly. The feeling grew that this was not real life at all – that they had stepped through the looking-glass. Her face glowed.

With her second glass of wine she was drunk on joy. Once Simon reached across the table and put his forefinger delicately on her blouse where a nipple pressed against it. Jancie stopped speaking and, keeping her body very still, looked down at this hand she had adored. He withdrew it and gave a quick shake to his head, as if trying to banish an unholy thought.

When they walked to the sideboard to get coffee, his arm brushed hers. She took a slow, deep breath as the sweet flow of longing filled her. She would bask in it for one more moment before making the massive effort to control it.

They lingered at the sideboard, and he examined her face with the intensity of a warrior returned from afar to his beloved. The cup and saucer in her hand trembled. He couldn't see her throbbing, but he sensed it. Suddenly Simon felt the same urgent desire for her that he'd known when he first seduced her. Only a saint, he told himself, would resist the opportunity.

'For old-times' sake?' he said.

He placed a finger carefully between her lips so she could taste it. He took the cup and saucer from her hand and put them on the sideboard. As he lifted his finger again she saw the tip of his tongue. She parted her lips and when he touched the tip of her own tongue she moaned.

'You are my darling,' he said.

Neither spoke when he took her back to the drawing-room. An open door beckoned. Through it she saw the foot of an enormous bed with a wine-red cover reaching to the floor.

FORTY-ONE

'I got a funny feeling about that Austin plant, Mr Jackson,' Gerald said.

They were in his office. Documents and photocopies lay on the low table between their armchairs. Speers had flown into London that morning.

'And I'm sitting in this room, running an empire,' Gerald went on, and Speers gazed around as if to acknowledge the handsome furniture, 'because I pay attention when I got a funny feeling.'

Speers smiled sympathetically.

'What's the alternative, Lord Scrope? Well, sir, you can quit trading and let another electronics manufacturer who isn't too fussy move in.'

Gerald clenched a fist.

'Since you got that funny feeling – and I know what you mean, Lord Scrope – I'd sure like to tell you what you want to hear. But there's no way the President of the United States can lift that embargo while the dictator thumbs his nose and lobs another chemical shell on to the dissidents.'

Gerald's face was sullen.

'It's not for me,' said Speers, 'to remind you of another reason you're sitting on top of an empire.'

'Such as?'

'Such as your liking for risk-taking. The mark of the real empire-builder.'

He might have added a further reason – greed – but Speers was too amiable a Texan to be so tactless.

After Speers left, Gerald went over to the Defence Secretary's room in the House of Commons.

'We better get you into Number Ten bleeding quick, Alan,' he said.

'Miss Hare.'

At once she knew the voice at the other end of the line.

'I want to talk to you about something. When can we have lunch?'

'I'm not sure,' she said tentatively.

'What has happened to that clear brain of yours, Miss Hare?'

Zoë bridled. Then she half-smiled. He had a way with him all right, this Lord Scrope.

Stepping out the *Dispatch* front door to hail a taxi, she looked to see if Miles's car was waiting at the kerb. He was the one she wanted to talk to. Each of the last few days he'd stopped by her desk. Each time there was no allusion to what was centre of her thoughts. He'd looked strained. And she was too proud to say: I need to talk with you.

Before he came to World's End that night they'd lunched together three times – she could recall every detail of their meetings – and each time she had felt they understood one another better. Could she ask him straight out if they could have lunch again now?

She looked down at the Thames flowing remorselessly. Over and over she had thought what she would say. She would ask him if it was better if she returned to the *Washington Express*.

But better for which of them? For him, because she had become an embarrassment? He was too nice a guy to tell her just like that. He had to have guessed from the other night how she felt about him. Better for her? – not to see him every day, yearning for him to stop at her desk, even if he didn't really say anything when he stood there talking about her work.

Since that night he'd not once been critical of her work, even though two of her pieces had been less than terrific. It was as if he wanted to show her he cared about her feelings. The way she cared about Peter's feelings and didn't want to tell him she was in love with someone else in a way she had never understood before?

Her taxi came to a complete halt. She saw they were outside the Ivy. For once she must have arrived early. But when she glanced at her watch the hand was already past one.

Gerald was at the same table. When he looked up, he gave a slow nod as if to say: you're late but you're forgiven.

As soon as their order was taken he said: 'I want to talk about the offer I made you. Who'd you discuss it with?'

After a hesitation Zoë replied: 'Jancie Wharton.'

'I thought you would,' he said. 'The world is one big web.'

'With you at the middle of it?'

He ignored her remark. 'Did Mrs Wharton give you any advice?'

'Not really. I told you, Lord Scrope, I have a contract with the *Dispatch*.'

'You mean you have a contract with Miles Brewster,' he said.

She flushed.

'Or do you? Maybe you should discuss it with him.'

The hairs on her arm moved.

'Unless he's got his own private agenda, he won't hold you to a contract as a feature writer when you've been offered the editorship of *The Monocle*. What sort of man would do that?'

She looked down.

'Are you in love with him?' Gerald asked.

'No,' she replied shortly, meeting his eyes.

'You should give him the opportunity to make his own judgement,' Gerald said.

When she got back to the *Dispatch* she phoned Peter's office. Two minutes later he came on the line.

'Can I talk to you,' she asked, 'or is this a bad time?'

'Shoot.'

She poured out Gerald's offer from the beginning, wondering why she hadn't discussed it with Peter before.

'He says I should at least give Miles the chance to know about it. Maybe it would actually suit Miles,' she added uneasily – which wouldn't make much sense to Peter unless she also told him what had happened between her and Miles.

But she didn't want to tell him about that. Not yet, anyhow.

'Do you think I should discuss it with Miles or just forget the whole *Monocle* thing?'

There was a long pause.

'Let's take it in stages,' he said. 'First of all, congratulations. That's one helluva fine offer.'

'I know.' Her voice was subdued.

'And I think Lord Scrope is right. We both know examples of writer-turned-editor with enormous success.'

Silence. Then another 'I know.'

Peter went on. 'How much does it worry you that you'd be working for a highly unpredictable man? At any time, for God knows what personal reason, he could suddenly take against you. You'd have better job security with Miles.'

She flinched.

'I don't even know if I want to work for someone like Gerald Scrope,' she said. 'Each time I see him I understand him less.'

'Come on, Zoë. Do you have to understand everyone you work for? What matters is that *The Monocle* is known for being free from proprietorial interference. You could hardly say the same of the *Dispatch*, by the way. Miles uses it all the time to assert what he cares about.'

'But he doesn't care what he personally gets out of it,' she replied hotly. 'Anyhow, he's editor. He has a right to express his opinions.'

'Anyone would think you were in love with Miles,' Peter said. 'You're not, are you?'

'Don't be ridiculous.'

'Look, Miles and Gerald Scrope have very different values. But what's that got to do with deciding whether or not you want to edit *The Monocle*? Any more than it's relevant that Gerald Scrope has the raider's mentality and will get a kick from taking you away from his rival. He's too shrewd a cookie to bother with a raid just for its own sake: clearly he believes you can pump some life back in *The Monocle*.'

Zoë chewed her lip.

'The more I think about it,' he went on, 'the more I think it's an inspired idea. You'd be editing a magazine which is essentially first-class feature-writing – the thing you've got such a nose for – not day-to-day news and editorials about the whole goddam globe. The editor of *The Monocle* isn't expected to have an instant opinion on everything under the sun.'

Elbows on desk, her free hand screening her face from the newsroom around her, Zoë was close to tears.

'Why the hell can't you discuss it with Miles?' Peter asked. 'He's not some china statue that will crack if someone slams a door. Anyhow, you're not slamming any door. You're just discussing the thing with him.'

'Well, I guess that's about it then,' she said bleakly. 'Unless you have something to add.'

'I suppose I ought to declare an interest,' he replied. 'If you moved back to these shores, it would gladden my heart, as *my* grandmother used to say. I've got something too that I want to talk to you about.'

As soon as she entered his room Miles looked up from the copy he was reading. The strain on his face lightened.

'Come sit down, Zoë.'

He gestured to the sofa and walked around his desk to take an armchair near her.

'I need your advice, Miles,' she said.

Watching her face – its openness, the uncertainty he'd glimpsed before but never seen so evident – he experienced an ease within himself that he had begun to think he would never know again. Was she going to raise the other night and everything it signified? He didn't want to bring it up until Marigold had actually moved out. But Zoë knew nothing about his home life. And if she chose to talk about herself and him – at least allude to the thing – God, what a relief it would be.

Studying his warm and welcoming look, she felt her blood race. Maybe her fears that he wanted an out were wrong.

'Gerald Scrope has made me a job offer,' she said tentatively.

For a second she thought he winced, but she might have imagined it.

The emotion he saw in her eyes made him think of a maiden speaking of the person she loved. Had Zoë too fallen for Gerald Scrope?

She saw his expression alter. This was the moment, the test.

'He wants me to become editor of *The Monocle*,' she said.

The colour drained from his face.

'Of course I can see the advantages of it,' she went on rapidly.

Her eyes were almost pleading with him.

Jesus Christ, he thought. His wife had pleaded for him to understand why she went over to the enemy. Now Zoë was doing the same.

'But I' – she hesitated – 'I love working for the *Dispatch*.'

She stopped, confused by the withdrawal of emotion from his face, desperate for him to persuade her to stay.

Nervously she went on: 'You showed confidence in me when you asked me to move to London. I've been really happy on the *Dispatch*. So some people would think it crazy to turn down being editor of *The Monocle*. But I want to know what you think.'

There. The test was before him. She sat taut with tension.

His eyes were fixed on hers. Then he blinked as if trying to clear his vision. Abruptly he got to his feet, twisting awkwardly as he did so.

'Do what you like,' he said.

He returned to his seat behind his desk and picked up the copy lying there. He resumed reading it as if Zoë were not in the room.

She stared at him, agape. After a few moments she stood up. Her feet were wooden blocks, separate from her, walking to the door on their own.

As she opened it, he said: 'Of course you are free to terminate your contract with the *Dispatch* any time you want.'

She turned to look at him, but he had resumed his reading.

She closed the door quietly, as if a death had just occurred.

'Are you all right, Zoë?' asked one of the journalists.

Zoë nodded, unseeing.

She started emptying her filing cabinet. By the time she got to the second drawer the crushing disappointment had turned into anger. She was shaking all over.

Journalists nearby exchanged glances of puzzlement, some with real concern. Several got up to come to her desk: 'What's happening?'

'I'm leaving,' she said in a cold, tight voice. She was furious.

'But why?'

Zoë shrugged and went on clearing her desk.

Two of them helped her carry her things to the lift, and together they went down to the lobby.

'Thank you for helping me,' she said as she climbed into the taxi, tears suddenly in her eyes. 'I'll miss you.'

As her taxi pulled away from the *Dispatch*, mechanically she looked at her watch. Its black hands were like meaningless insect tracks.

A minute or two after Miles saw her walk out of the newsroom with all her things, he left the editor's office and went up to Corporate where the connecting wall to his room was not made of glass. He told his secretary he didn't want to be disturbed, and when he closed his door she heard the bolt snap shut.

He walked to the drinks cupboard and poured out a whisky, drinking off half of it at once. Crossing to the windows, he looked down on the street below. A taxi was pulling away from the front door.

He sat down at his desk, but almost at once got up, restless, and paced the room. He went back to the drinks cupboard and topped up his glass. Then he sat down again and opened the first of the files waiting for his attention. He took another swallow of whisky. Elbows on desk, he got down to work, his hands cupped either side of his face.

FORTY-TWO

Zoë had dreamt in colour before. In this dream Miles was standing across the room, pale, drawn, very tall, like a figure come back from the dead. Then he moved towards her, and she saw colour tinge his face and she knew he was returning to life, he was coming to her. At that moment she woke, the vestiges of the dream still there, and she tried to return to it. But it eluded her, and she lay numb inside a body which didn't feel like hers, a shell around a cavity.

Watery light filtered through the curtains. She turned her head to see the clock. The day ahead was a conveyor belt of phone calls. She had no energy. She stirred the memory of when she arrived in London. With her head she recalled the quickened sense of being alive in another country, her elation when she moved into this flat where now she lay with the curtains closed. But she couldn't recreate the emotions she'd felt then. All hope was lost. She turned on her side, her face to the wall.

The jangle of the phone made her jump. She reached for it and stopped. If it mattered they'd try again. Anyhow, it would be the way Jancie described it: 'When it rings and it's someone else, I hate the person for not being Simon.' She listened to the rings, like someone hearing a phone next door. Then they stopped.

Half a minute later they started again. This time Zoë picked up the receiver.

'For Christ's sake, what's going on?' It was Jancie.

'Not much,' Zoë replied. She heard the flatness of her voice.

'James just rang me from the *Javelin*. The first thing he

heard when he got there was that you've left the *Dispatch* to become editor of *The Monocle*. It's to be announced this afternoon. Oh yes: congratulations. But isn't this all rather sudden?'

'I suppose.'

'What did Miles say, for God's sake?'

'He said to do what I like.' She could hear the fine anger come into her voice.

Silence.

'Then he went back to whatever he was reading.'

'Oh, Zoë.'

More silence until Zoë said: 'Yeah, well . . .'

'When are you leaving?'

'As soon as I can make arrangements. Gerald, as I now think of him' – she spoke his name with precision, as if in quotes – 'expects me to descend on *The Monocle* in ten days' time.'

She had a surge of anger against him.

'Ten days from yesterday, to be exact.'

After a moment Jancie said: 'Well, at least you've taken my mind off my own problems. Can you come round? I mean soon. I'm in trouble too.'

'What's the matter?'

'I saw Simon two days ago. If I sound all brisk and efficient on this goddam phone, don't believe it. When you walk in the room you better be wearing a raincoat.'

Zoë made herself get out of bed and open the curtains. The sun shone weakly in an impersonal sky. The slate roofs of the terrace houses were impervious: they'd seen it all before. She turned from the window.

She made phone calls – travel agent, landlord, banker, unceasing – as if she were a robot. Even the call to her grandparents was conducted at one remove. But by the end of the morning she was coldly furious again. Goddam him. What a disgusting way to talk to her – as if she were some errant schoolgirl.

Her renewed rage was interrupted by a phone call from the London *Evening Standard*: 'Lord Scrope has just announced you're to be editor of *The Monocle*. We're carrying the story in our late editions.'

Twenty minutes later a reporter and photographer turned up at Zoë's flat.

'How does Miles Brewster feel about you being taken over and elevated by his rival?' the reporter asked.

'You'll have to ask him,' Zoë replied.

(Mr Brewster declined to comment, said the story when it appeared on the news-stands an hour later.)

The rest of the day disappeared in calls from papers on both sides of the Atlantic, interspersed with congratulations from friends. Talking into the mouthpiece, her lips smiled in accord with upbeat messages she was sending out to everyone except Jancie. Her eyes had the dazed look of someone just mugged.

'Mind if I uncork that other bottle?' said Zoë without waiting for an answer. She knew the kitchen nearly as well as the Whartons. From a cupboard she took a box of Kleenex.

She had set off from World's End filled with anger again. But by the time she reached Kensington Park Road, confusion had returned as well. Then Jancie opened the door and Zoë saw *her* face.

'Take your choice,' Zoë said, plonking bottle and box on the table between them.

Jancie blew her nose. 'We make a great pair, you and I.'

'Has he phoned since?'

'Simon? What do you think? If he phoned he might have to express some sort of regret for what took place. And he's never in his life suggested he was remiss in any way. I don't think it occurs to him he might have been. Not that that makes my own actions any better,' she added.

Yet she hadn't cajoled those declarations out of him as they lay on Lord Scrope's bed: 'I went through all those months without seeing you because I didn't trust my own feelings,' he'd said. 'I thought it was better for you if we didn't meet,' he'd said. 'Let's draw a line under all that. Let's start again,' he'd said. And at the moment the words came out of his mouth, Simon meant them.

'I'd give anything to undo it,' said Jancie. 'Yet if he asked me, I'd go to him again. It's like an addiction. I think I'll never be free of him until one of us is dead.'

The noisy beat echoed in the stillness.

'That clock makes one helluva racket,' said Zoë.

After a time she asked: 'Are you going to tell James what happened?'

'I don't know what to do. I feel so guilty.'

'It might make you feel better to confess to James, but it sure as hell would be tough on him,' said Zoë. 'If you don't tell him, he could remain in happy ignorance. Maybe you better feel guilty instead of making him more miserable.'

Unlike the English, wearied by recurrent rain, Zoë loved the sound of it and the look of it. At the farm, she used to go to the music room's bay window and kneel on the rickety sofa to watch slate-coloured sheets of rain froth the slate-coloured surface of the lake.

Now she lay in bed on her last morning in World's End, listless, as water pelted on the glass, quietening into a steady downpour on the street below before gusts sent it beating at the window again. She got up to open her curtains, and went back to bed to lie there, watching pellets bounce off the panes while glistening streams flowed down. She wished it would pour for ever. A car's tyres slapped against wet paving. She must get up.

Half-way through a cup of coffee she was in a sudden cold rage again. None of this had to happen. She wouldn't be leaving this place where she'd been so happy if Miles hadn't behaved like such a pig. God, he was a heartless bastard.

Her taxi went first to the estate agent where she dropped off the keys, then on to the Great West Road, where she looked at grey buildings standing forlornly in grey drizzle. When countryside began, it too was grey. Miles once told her, she remembered, that colours are drained by your state of mind.

The pampering in flying Concorde somewhat raised her spirits. Yet when the plane lifted off, she had only the memory of exhilaration – of being keyed up on take-off when flying back after her Nona interview, back to where Miles would be.

She longed for even a spark of anger to return and relieve the awful heaviness of sorrow and regret.

It was one of the worst rows with the Chairman that James could recall. It stemmed from Gerald demanding he write a leader eulogising Alan Rawlston and calling for the Prime Minister to resign.

Like most journalists, James could stomach proprietorial policies he disliked so long as he himself didn't have to endorse them. He disagreed strongly with Gerald's campaign to lift the embargo on Arabi. He was deeply suspicious of Alan Rawlston's character. And though he regretted Martin Mather's lack of charisma, he respected Mather's sincerity and workmanlike competence, and regarded him as the Prime Minister best for Britain at this time.

'Anyone else would welcome the chance to stick the knife in the man who'd kicked him in the gut,' Gerald said.

He was sitting at his desk, James standing before him.

'It gave Martin Mather no pleasure to recall me from Washington,' said James doggedly. 'Get someone else to write that leader.'

'No one is in your class, Ambassador. That is one reason I am glad to employ you.'

James flushed.

'I do not need your employment, Chairman.'

Gerald rocked himself slowly in his chair.

'You think yourself too noble to write what Gerald Scrope requires. You deceive only yourself, Ambassador. The world is not like the playing fields of fucking Eton. Honour. Loyalty. They are myths, Ambassador.'

'Not to me, Chairman. Not to lots of people. Don't judge others by yourself.'

Gerald stopped his rocking. Until that moment he had not decided what would follow. He reached into a drawer.

'I shall judge by the standards of Mrs Wharton,' he said, taking out four photographs and handing them to James.

They were stills from a video film. Even before James could make out the faces, he recognised Simon's curls and Jancie's legs.

'Reminders of the real world,' Gerald said. 'Keep them. Good day, Ambassador.'

That night James gave the photographs to Jancie.

'I didn't want it to happen,' she told him. 'It doesn't have anything to do with us. It doesn't have anything to do with anything. I can't explain it. I wish I could. I thought I was free of him for ever. I wish he was dead.'

She got up from the chair opposite her husband and left the room. She didn't want to see his reactions.

At St James's Place, Marigold lay awake in the bedroom no longer shared by her husband.

He was in his study, a whisky in one hand. Books lining indigo walls made rows of vivid colours. Gazing at them from his chair, Miles saw only ranks of grey, like an old photograph faded by time.

FORTY-THREE

'God, I'm nervous. You'd never guess I was supposed to be boss,' Zoë said.

She was on the phone to Peter. She'd arrived at Kennedy the previous afternoon, and an hour later checked into the Waldorf-Astoria.

A forbiddingly splendid flower arrangement was waiting in her room. ('From the staff of *The Monocle*.') It made her think of one of those royal courtiers Miles had told her about, whose presence was a firm reminder to the Queen that ceremony and protocol were required. Zoë was sure if the Queen had been staying in this bedroom she would have much preferred a posy.

'You'll be fine once you're there,' said Peter. 'Just remember that everyone at *The Monocle* is terrified of what you could do to them.'

Her car was to pick her up at nine.

She ran about the bedroom making sure she looked the way an editor should. 'Idiot braid,' she muttered, yanking her hair savagely. 'Her Car,' she said wryly, visualising each word with a capital letter. Absurd. Hollow like everything now.

When she stepped from the art-deco elevator, the manager in his funereal clothes glided towards her.

'The car is just outside, Miss Hare,' he murmured, escorting her to the front door. She'd been told it was a Buick. In front of the crenellated silver canopy a Cadillac waited. The doorman tipped his cap and opened the rear door. As she went to climb in she realised the moulded seat on the other side was occupied. She stopped, one foot still outside and turned back to the doorman.

'Good morning, Miss Hare.'

She whipped around and peered into the car.

'You must not imagine, Miss Hare, that I shall escort you to your office every morning. It happened to fit my other plans,' said Gerald, enjoying himself. He'd arrived on Concorde's evening flight.

The car turned into 52nd Street and he nodded towards a building that loomed ahead.

'When I take you through that door, your life will never be the same again,' he said.

She went ahead of him through the revolving door. From across a marble lobby a man and woman came forward, clearly the reception committee. Two rows of perfect teeth stretched the deputy editor's face as he introduced himself. But before he could present his colleague, the smile collapsed. Lord Scrope had emerged from the revolving door.

Gerald was charm itself, greeting the deputy and the woman who was number three in the magazine's hierarchy as if they were old friends. In the elevator Gerald alone was not tense.

'You lead the way,' he said politely to the deputy, 'unless it makes you nervous having someone at your back.'

The deputy held open a door and they went through.

'Good morning,' said Gerald to the personal assistant who had risen to his feet. 'I'm sure you agree.'

Zoë shook hands.

'Please,' said Gerald, one arm extended, ushering her first, and they all trooped into a big, expensively furnished office, its walls adorned with framed caricatures of previous editors and celebrated contributors. Zoë crossed to the wall of windows and looked down at the traffic jam. The ritual blare of horns seemed in a distant world.

'You will be so kind as to summon the rest of the senior staff to come to the editor's office,' Gerald said to the PA. 'At once.'

Within minutes half a dozen men and women had assembled and were standing with their backs to the wall. Zoë stood with her back to the windows. Gerald stood beside the editor's desk.

'I have come here from London to present the new editor of *The Monocle*,' he said.

His pleasantries had vanished, but his manner stayed unaggressive.

'I hold *The Monocle* in great respect,' he went on. 'I shall continue to stand apart from editorial policy. You will be answerable to Miss Hare alone.'

His eyes scanned the intent faces before him, as if photographing each to store in his head.

'I have every confidence your new editor will reward talent' – he paused – 'if it exists in a form comprehensible to readers.'

Zoë felt her face go hot. One or two staff shifted slightly. Beneath the carpet a board creaked.

'I urge your editor here and now,' he continued, 'to show fuck all patience with those who employ their talents merely to impress one another.' He gave a fractional bow to the staff. 'I leave you in good hands.'

He pulled back the chair and waved Zoë into place. Her face was tight with embarrassment. Without another word Gerald strode past the staff and was gone.

Her introductory days tore by in a rush of adrenalin. What Peter had foretold became apparent rapidly. The fact that she was being taught the ropes at *The Monocle* in no way lessened her authority in the eyes of others. Her mounting self-confidence was a daily astonishment when she woke in the morning.

Not that she had been timid before. But neither had she belonged to that élite band of journalists who were subject to no one, for if the editor – or owner – didn't like their work they simply took it to another newspaper which snatched it up. In her seven years in journalism, Zoë had never been in doubt that each piece she submitted was on trial. Now she was sitting in the editor's chair. But where was the sense of well-being? She'd rather be working for Miles.

On her second day she learned a staff member had been assigned to scour Manhattan for a selection of suitable apartments. The changes Her Car made were equally wondrous – not just convenience and saving of time, but the unconcern when rain poured from the sky. But where was the pleasure of ducking into doorways and then dashing for the *Dispatch* when the rain bucketed down in London?

Each afternoon her PA came in with the big appointments book. Months ahead engagements were already filled in, originally intended for her predecessor.

'We haven't discussed the details of your two-week break before you take over full-time,' the PA said.

'I'll be at the farm. On Lake Champlain,' replied Zoë.

'How do you want to get to Washington? There's a new commuter service that goes from Burlington airport to Dulles.'

'Why should I want to go to Washington in the middle of my time in Vermont?' said Zoë.

'That's when the White House dinner is. On the twelfth.'

'What White House dinner?'

The PA looked dumbfounded.

'Hasn't anybody told you? The editor of *The Monocle* goes to various White House functions. This one should be fun. A lot of the media will be there. The original invitation had the previous editor's name on it. A replacement should arrive any day now.'

'You mean my predecessor is disinvited?' Zoë asked, appalled.

'It's a rough world,' said the PA. 'Shall I book you into the Willard?'

Early that evening, Peter caught the shuttle from Washington National Airport. They had agreed he wait until she'd had a couple of days to get her bearings.

'Come up and see my view,' she said when he rang from the lobby.

She flung her arms around him.

'The guided tour,' she said. 'Look at this! Look at that!' She gave a slight jig in a parody of excitement. Below them stretched Park Avenue, street lamps twinkling either side of the broad and verdant ribbon between twin roadways, traffic moving quietly at a stately pace.

'Let's cancel our reservation at Le Cirque,' she went on gaily. 'Room service at the Waldorf is out of this world!' Then she burst into tears.

He put his arms around her.

In the night when she half-woke to find the warmth of him pressing against her, the sense of safety and comfort seemed an era away from the illicit passion she first had known with Peter.

They both woke early. While Peter dressed she rang for breakfast for one. When it arrived he had already left to catch the shuttle back to Washington.

She dawdled over her coffee. Before another crazy day got going, she wanted to think about the night just passed.

What had happened with Miles meant Peter wasn't exciting in the same way as before. But the change was not unpleasant. Far from it. She could count on Peter. He was an extremely attractive man. He loved her. And he needed her now as he hadn't done before. In a funny way, she almost loved him more – and maybe needed him more than she wanted to acknowledge.

'I'll think about it when I come back,' Zoë said to the deputy editor.

Even in those three days it was evident she'd have to make one or two changes among her immediate staff. Some new editors did a complete clear-out, knowing staff already in place would go around grumbling that the previous editor did everything better. Yet it was one thing to be firm, Zoë said to herself; it was something else to get rid of people you'd only just met.

But her antennae were out. On her last day she made calls to the *Washington Express* to sound out two people she'd worked with there. She'd already heard morale on the *Express* had plummeted since Miles moved his base to London. Miles. Thinking about him made her feel almost overwhelmed with wistfulness.

She knew she needed to get to Lake Champlain and calm down, have an inner overhaul, before wading into this job in earnest.

The thing about puddle-jumpers was you had a sense of actually flying. Zoë's forehead was pressed against the window so she could watch the wheel gather speed, as if it had a will of its own, spinning faster and faster until it was a rim with nothing in the middle, and then lift-off and the rest of the wheel reappearing gradually and hanging motionless until it was retracted, which always gave her a moment of regret. Miles.

The Green Mountains appeared, snow on higher peaks, red barns and silver silos in the valleys, each toy village with its white clapboard church and steeple like the garden under the Christmas trees of her childhood. Then the lake was there, its colour bleaching out where it wound into the distance, the Adirondacks like humps on its far side.

Only two passengers got off at Burlington. As Zoë crossed the tarmac, she looked up at the viewing windows and saw her grandfather.

An hour later they turned through the opening in the picket fence, and on the left of the pebble drive was the rough grass with the giant cottonwood standing over it and the lake extending enormous to mountains silhouetted against the sky, everything still except a single gull wheeling over the red buoy.

They stopped at the granite stepping-stone once used to mount horses. On this side of the drive the grass was short and stuck up bristly in the cold. The untenanted barns and sheds hadn't changed since she last saw them. The house looked a little smaller but otherwise just the same with its duck-egg blue clapboard, shutters of Federal green, white-trimmed veranda, cupola jaunty. The front door swung open, and her grandmother ran down the steps.

It was dark by four. When dinner time came, Zoë sat facing the shades of black outside – cottonwood, lake, mountain ridge, sky – and the only colours were lights dotted near the mountains' base and a yellow patch reflecting itself in a wobbly paler version as a barge moved north across inky water. Her hair was loose upon her shoulders. She could have been a schoolgirl, Mrs Hare thought, not the composed journalist that Zoë liked to appear.

They took their coffee into the old music room, where the television stood under a portrait of her great-great-grandfather, one hand resting on his silver-topped walking-stick, his proud gaze under ferocious eyebrows fixed on you. Zoë's grandparents liked to watch the evening news. Only half-paying attention as the theme music came on, Zoë could feel her whole body unwinding as she looked around the high-ceilinged room. The ancient Victrola was still on its stand, framed family photographs still clustered on the worn leather-topped table.

'Good evening. The White House has declined to comment on the story in the London *Javelin* linking President and Mrs Lambert to a fatal car crash in Mexico fifteen years ago. The story appears in the first edition of tomorrow morning's *Javelin*, which has already been distributed throughout Britain.'

Picture of the *Javelin*'s front page. Photo of its owner, Lord Scrope.

'When the accident occurred, Mr Miles Brewster, the newspaper magnate, was allegedly driving too fast through the northern sierras between Monterrey and Saltillo. The car struck a seven-year-old Mexican girl standing beside the highway, and in the crash that followed Mr Brewster's twenty-two-year-old companion, Teresa Lopez, was paralysed for life. Mr Brewster suffered permanent injuries to one leg.'

Picture of Miles stepping from his car, one foot still inside it. Graduation photograph taken at a convent school in Saltillo, camera homing in on a girl in the centre of the front row.

'The *Javelin* alleges that President Lambert, then in the House of Representatives, and his wife were passengers in the car when the fatal accident took place. They were uninjured and able to summon help. All four had allegedly been drinking.'

Recent photo of the President and First Lady.

'According to the *Javelin*, the formal police report at Saltillo contained no reference to Congressman Lambert and Mrs Lambert also being in the car. But the *Javelin*'s foreign editor discovered an earlier police report made at the hospital, and it named the uninjured passengers as F. R. Lambert and N. T. Lambert. The *Javelin* states that the car was registered in the name of N. T. Lambert.'

Picture of Nona, laughing, leaning against an out-of-date Chevrolet.

'The *Javelin* accuses Miles Brewster of conspiring to cover up the presence of the President and his wife in what was potentially a politically damaging incident. The White House has so far refused to comment.'

As the newscaster moved on to events in Arabi, Mr Hare said: 'All hell will break loose now.'

Zoë sat speechless.

FORTY-FOUR

Obsessively she searched other channels. A snapshot of Frank Lambert and Miles when they were at college, both on skis, goofing around. The President with his arm around Nona at a picnic, taken at least fifteen years ago. Miles and Marigold in evening dress as they arrived at the White House last summer.

Awake early, Zoë was back in the music room, scarcely breathing, her chair pulled so close she was almost inside the television. At eight-thirty she phoned her deputy at *The Monocle*, acting editor until she took over properly.

'I need to see everything on the Lamberts and Miles Brewster. The *Javelin*. International editions of other English papers. All the main American papers. Everything. You'll have to get them here each day by courier. As soon as I've seen today's batch, I'll phone you. And I'll need a fax machine. Get my secretary to organise it. No later than tomorrow.'

She forced herself to leave the house, climbing down the rough path that led to the stone slabs sloping to the water's edge, hardly seeing the old rowboat tied to a silver birch. The force of the waves was strong this morning, but not like the pull of the Thames which could drag you under. Restless, like an addict needing a fix, she made her way up to the house where she went straight to the music room to flick on the television again.

When she heard wheels scrunch the pebble drive, she ran to the window. From the back of his van the courier took out a large parcel and put it on the stepping-stone, then he stuck his head back and reached for another. Zoë rushed down the veranda steps to meet him.

The story that broke in the *Javelin* was about as bad as it could be. Simon interwove facts he'd uncovered with his own interpretation. So solid was his feat of investigation that his speculation carried weight as well.

Why had the names of Frank and Nona Lambert not appeared in the formal police record? What became of Nona's car after the crash? Why had Miles Brewster always refused to answer press questions on the episode? Was he only covering up the presence of the Lamberts at an unsavoury tragedy? Or was he also covering up something in his own conduct that had not yet come out?

Why had Mr Brewster never been charged in a Mexican court with causing death and disablement through reckless driving when drinking? Simon didn't actually say the police had been bribed, but the implication was clear enough.

Had Teresa Lopez been bought off so she would never tell what really happened after the accident?

Zoë's upper lip was beaded with sweat.

Having tracked down the father of the dead child, Simon was able to report: 'During the weeks following Perdita Orozco's death, money was paid to her parents by a person acting for Miles Brewster. "It was meant to be a pay-off," Roberto Orozco told me. "The gringo thinks the Mexican has no feelings. No amount of money brings back my child," Mr Orozco went on.'

The Boston law firm where Miles's father was a senior partner continued to deposit money each month in a bank in Monterrey – 'even though a bank in Saltillo would be easier for Pedro Lopez to reach. But then the transaction would also be more conspicuous in a not very large town,' Simon had added.

His contact in Boston had come up with hospital records from fifteen years ago. Miles Brewster had been brought from Boston airport by ambulance.

'Soon after that,' the story went on, 'he began his long stay in the best rehabilitation unit in Massachusetts. Only then was Teresa Lopez brought from the hospital in Monterrey. When Mr Brewster left the unit two months later, he was able to walk with only a slight impairment. But Teresa Lopez was not so fortunate. Her time there was cut short, and she was dispatched back to Mexico. Her legs remain paralysed. A distinguished neurologist at the unit today declined to comment when asked if Miss Lopez might have recovered the use of her legs if her treatment had not been curtailed.'

Zoë jumped up from her chair and strode to the bay window, but even before she could look out blindly she turned and went back to her torment. The story spilled on to an inside page.

Simon wrote so vividly that she could visualise his third visit to the Lopez ranch when – even with a Mexican interpreter in tow – he had failed to extract any information from a surly Pedro Lopez. As before, Teresa had gracefully skirted further questions. Simon reported their lack of co-operation thus:

'Pedro Lopez has the silent anger of the Mexican who sees his daughter as the victim of a rich American. Teresa Lopez, still beautiful at thirty-seven, has the stoicism of the Mexican woman resigned to being used by a rich American holidaying in her country. Maimed for life by his actions, she may decline to voice the word "abandoned" – but it springs readily to others' lips.'

The story ended there.

Zoë's eyes became blank as she looked at the newspaper spread before her. Total depression filled her.

After a time she sighed deeply. However anyone looked

at the story, it was plain that Miles was a conniving cad. And he had lied by omission – made worse because he not only owned a newspaper empire: he had made himself editor of his Fleet Street paper.

But he was not president of the United States. What most shook other Americans was the concealment of the Lamberts' presence at a drunken driving episode that ended with the death and disablement of two innocents. By mid-morning every major newspaper and television company had teams of reporters and cameramen booking into any available hotel room in Monterrey and Saltillo.

When the first of them reached the turning they sought, they found the narrow dirt road blocked by a barrier of mesquite. Beside it stood security men whose identity badges bore only a number. They could have been Mexican or half-caste. All spoke Spanish and English. '*Nadie puede entrar.*' 'No one can enter here.'

The security men had appeared a few hours earlier, not long after a Cessna skirted the mountains and dropped fast on to the rough runway of the Lopez ranch. Speers Jackson spent only a short time with Pedro, and when he was shown in to see Teresa, he apologised for disturbing her. The courtyard was too chilly this late in the year, and the swinging settee had been moved indoors.

After the plane took off again, Pedro and two ranch-hands hacked down mesquite and dragged them on to the runway. Then they got in a jeep and bumped along the road to where it joined the highway. They chopped more mesquite for the roadblock.

At noon the security men arrived by road. Several took up positions at the barrier, but it was pulled aside long enough to allow two cars of other security men through.

When they reached the clearing they stopped, and some fanned out around the long adobe barn and sheds. Two positioned themselves in front of the house.

In London a policeman walked up and down St James's Place.

'You can't stop there,' he directed as another van tried to unload television equipment. But there was nothing to prevent the media assembling on foot, and with the besiegers at the walls of Number 26, its modernist structure looked more than ever like a stronghold. To pass the time, a few photographers wandered across the paved square to examine the front of Spencer House, standing in palatial calm above the mob.

Finally the bronze and glass door of Number 26 opened and Miles came out. His face was taut.

'When will you answer the charges against you, Mr Brewster?'

'I have nothing to say at this time,' Miles replied dispassionately as he twisted into the front seat alongside his driver.

Outside the *Dispatch*, another pack waited.

Eager hopes of glimpsing the wife of the accused man were thwarted, for Marigold remained inside Number 26, a prisoner of circumstance. Both Miles and Gerald had reason to hold back on public disclosure of their private drama.

At the best of times Miles hated the prospect of his dirty linen being hung out. And this was the worst of times.

Gerald knew the *Javelin*'s daily assaults on Miles's character would carry greatest impact if it was not yet known that Lord Scrope had a spectacular personal interest in blackening his rival's name.

Without a word passing between them, both men

colluded in concealing that Marigold now belonged to Gerald.

Incarcerated in the open spaces she had furnished with such care, she kept back from the wall of windows overlooking Green Park. She was outraged that the rabble, skulking among the plane trees with long-lens cameras, should compel her to keep the blinds of her own home closed during the day. Defiantly she left the Japanese linen shades up most of the way. She detested net curtains, but none the less she had fine voile hung to screen the glass. Sometimes she stood motionless alongside the window, peeping through the net.

Standing in the bay window, Zoë watched the red buoy rocking, a seagull perched on top, enjoying the ride, Zoë supposed. A north wind had blown up and the waves were high. There must be some good reason for Miles's behaviour, she said to herself, no longer seeing the buoy or anything else beyond the window. If he was the hypocrite now displayed, how could she feel about him as she did? Why didn't he say something that would clear everything up? Surely there would be a statement by tonight.

She yearned to defend him. Even though *The Monocle* was not a news magazine, she could write whatever she wanted in its important Comment page at the front. She could remind people of the kind of man Miles really was, whatever happened all those years ago. She could choose a cover picture that would present his dilemma sympathetically.

And yet. An editor's job is to disclose the truth. And Miles had not.

The telephone rang in the next room. If only he would phone, she was sure he could explain everything.

It was Peter.

'How're you doing?' he asked in a tone which conveyed he knew she was having a rough time.

'I can't understand what's happening.' Her voice was frantic.

'You're not alone,' he replied. 'But at least you needn't voice an opinion. You haven't even taken over the reins properly yet. And anyhow you should rule yourself out when it comes to commenting on Miles: you should positively *not* voice an opinion about him.'

'But I *want* to,' she said emphatically. 'There has to be some misunderstanding. I don't believe Miles is the fraud that's being portrayed.'

'I hope you're not suggesting you are going to use *The Monocle* to say that, Zoë,' Peter said. 'The fact that the Lamberts were passengers was bound to damage Frank. And Miles's decision to try and conceal it damages him just as much. If you decide to whitewash him in *The Monocle*, you'll be falling into the same trap he did. If for personal reasons you want to whitewash Miles Brewster, do it privately – not as editor of *The Monocle*.'

When she put down the phone, she looked through the papers again and then sat back on the sofa, wretched, gazing at the framed photograph of the two-year-old girl walking hand in hand with a laughing young woman on one side and a debonair young man, in striped shirt-sleeves and seersucker trousers, on the other.

After a time she went to the room next door and dialled her deputy at *The Monocle* again. Was it only two days ago they'd agreed she needn't be kept informed of the magazine's production before she took up the reins?

Never complain and never explain. She always forgot which British Prime Minister had said that. 'Obviously our cover cartoon must reflect the Lambert–Brewster story,' she told her deputy without preamble, her voice brisk. 'I want you to choose the three cartoons you like best and get them to me tomorrow. I'll phone you with my choice.'

She went straight on.

'As for Comment, we've got a couple of days before that goes to the printers. Write it as it strikes you. Fax me what you propose. I'll phone you back with any changes.'

That evening's news opened with the words: 'There has still been no statement from the White House or from media magnate Miles Brewster.'

As the television flickered in the music room, all three Hares sat silent.

FORTY-FIVE

Each member of the public and every pundit had a theory.

'It was crazy for the Lamberts to try and hide the fact that they were in that car. What the hell does that say about their good sense?'

'What does it say about their morality? If they weren't already in the White House, they sure wouldn't get there now.'

'What does it say about the morality of a newspaper magnate who organised a cover-up for the sake of Frank Lambert's political advancement? How can you respect the *Dispatch* after that?'

Since Senator Edward Kennedy's presidential schemes became part of the wreckage at Chappaquiddick bridge, all politicians dreaded an incident that could be compared, however unjustly, to Kennedy's behaviour that night.

'It isn't as if the Lamberts were responsible for what happened. It's the cover-up of being present at all that makes you wonder if you want such a man as President.'

'You forget how vulnerable Chappaquiddick has left politicians. And you forget the climate of the last twenty years – the white American male is the aggressor, the ethnic is the victim. Being within sniffing distance of that crash in Mexico would have been used against the Lamberts.'

From the start, the *Javelin* set the tone for public perception of Miles. On the day it broke the story, its main leader read like a mockery of the one Miles wrote in the

Dispatch castigating Lord Scrope only a few weeks before.

'The rich American media magnate comes to our shores to proclaim sentiments that Americans love to preach – justice for the common man, apple pie on every table, freedom of the press.

'Now we discover Miles Brewster covertly deals out his own brand of justice. Apple pies are stuffed with dollar notes for those he wants silenced. Newspapers are taken over, only to be gagged.

'For fifteen years this American mogul succeeded in concealing that Frank and Nona Lambert were passengers in a car that wiped out a child standing beside the road and smashed for ever the expectations of a twenty-two-year-old woman.

'President Lambert must now come forward and tell us why he and his wife agreed to a cover-up which has backfired disastrously for them. Their friend Miles Brewster has ended in pulling them into the mire with himself.'

Overnight Miles became the knave.

Some of the President's advisers counselled him to say nothing. If he said his and Nona's names were left off the formal police report by chance, he'd sound defensive. Nor could he be seen to disown a friend in trouble. Better to maintain a dignified silence until the storm subsided.

But by the third day this hope was in tatters. Something had to be said. The White House issued a statement:

'The President does not regard it as appropriate to comment on a car crash in Mexico fifteen years ago, for which Mr Miles Brewster has always taken full responsibility. This is a matter for Mr Brewster alone.'

Two hours later a statement was issued in London. 'Mr Miles Brewster wishes to confirm that he is responsible for the car crash in Mexico and the events surrounding it fifteen years ago. At no time did Congressman Lambert or Mrs Lambert deny their presence as passengers in the car. As it was irrelevant to the tragic events that occurred, there was no reason for the formal police report to include their names. Mr Brewster also wishes to state that he deeply regrets, and will always regret, the death of Perdita Orozco and the terrible permanent injury to Teresa Lopez.'

Wherever she was in the house, Zoë listened out for the scrunch on the drive and quick rev of an engine. The courier with his parcel of daily papers – her lifeline – always revved his engine before turning it off.

For a day the story hung fire. Then the clamour began again. The President and Miles Brewster had lied by omission when the crash occurred. They were lying by omission now.

Even in the first report made at the hospital, Frank Lambert had not been identified as an American congressman. Why had he and Nona wanted only their initials used instead of their full names?

The President's defenders pointed out that Mexican police reports were fairly casual.

'Oh, sure,' said his attackers and put the word in quotes: 'casual' became code for easy-to-bribe.

That inflamed other Americans even more. 'Are you suggesting,' they demanded, 'that Mexicans have lower morals than us if one of them accepts a bribe? What about us assuming we can buy anybody?'

'They're in a cleft stick,' Mr Hare said as he turned off the television. 'As things look, the Lamberts walked away from a terrible accident. If they try to explain their action now, it makes things worse. If they didn't realise at the time the risks of concealment, it says something about their judgement. And in the case of the President, judgement is crucial.'

'But nothing was concealed that actually mattered,' Zoë said. 'For all we know the policeman may simply have found it easier to use their initials on that first report. Are you saying they ought to have solemnly volunteered to get the whole record complete? He was a bureaucratic policeman, for God's sake, not a confessional priest. Anyhow, it wouldn't have affected anything.'

'That's what people always say when they walk away from a responsibility,' Mr Hare replied.

'That's one sure thing Miles can't be accused of,' Zoë said hotly.

There was a long silence before Mrs Hare said: 'It's too bad he didn't make a statement until there was no choice.'

'But that's the way Miles is!' Zoë exclaimed. 'He's a reticent man. He hates talking about his private life.'

Even as she spoke the words, she knew his reticence was tainted by the charge of what lay behind it.

'What's so sad for him,' her grandmother said at last, 'is that if he were not editor of such an influential newspaper, it would seem different.'

Zoë jumped up and stalked from the room and out of the house.

The stiff grass shone ghostly blue in the cold light of the moon. The cottonwood's arms were stark. She stood at the edge of the drop to the shore, looking at the steely lake with the moon-white path across it, and she heard the words of the *Javelin*, like reading aloud black letters printed at the front of her mind:

'And now we learn that the preacher is as morally

corrupt as the cheapest conman. Today he stands exposed as manipulator of a cover-up for the most powerful couple in the world.'

When she went to her bedroom later, someone had already turned on her bedside lamp. Beside it she saw Jean Rhys's *Wide Sargasso Sea*, its cover slightly rumpled at the edges. Zoë opened it where a sheet of Mrs Hare's blue writing paper marked a page near the end.

'Zoë dear' – her grandmother's writing was always sprawly – 'While you were outside, I found myself thinking about these lines. They've always haunted me.' A small squiggle in pencil, half-way down the page, marked two lines of the text.

> . . . I said, 'It isn't like it seems to be.' – 'I know. It never is,' he said.

Zoë pressed the piece of paper to her.

FORTY-SIX

The siege of the Lopez ranch remained at stalemate. Aerial shots made the world familiar with the red roof of the whitewashed house turned in on itself. Cameramen stayed clustered at the barrier, and one of them in a notable clip captured the robotic detachment of security guards as they scanned the crowd of journalists facing them.

'Who is paying those guards to keep Teresa Lopez and Pedro Lopez under wraps?' the media demanded. 'The President declines to answer questions. Miles Brewster picks his way carefully through his words. The public have a right to know who fixed the cover-up.'

Platoons of reporters scoured Monterrey and Saltillo. People began coming out of the woodwork with fantasies.

A Mexican said he'd been in Saltillo police station and overheard conversation in a room next door. 'The man's voice was the same as President Lambert's. He was saying: "I'll give you a thousand dollars if you don't write down the passengers' names."' The story was blazoned around the world before someone discovered the man was four years old at the time of the crash.

A woman said she'd been a patient in the room next to Teresa's in the Monterrey hospital. 'I heard her voice cry out: "Do not leave me, Miles. Oh, Miles, do not leave me." Over and over. I never forget it. Never.'

A Saltillo garage attendant said he remembered putting gas in a truck and the driver saying he had just taken some people and a dead child to the hospital. No, he didn't know the truck-driver's name, but it was a blue truck, a Ford. 'I remember what he said as if it was yesterday. He told me they all rode on the truck's open flatbed, two of them hurt real bad and lying flat, lots of blood, and as he drove he could hear the beautiful Mexican woman they called Teresa crying with pain, and the American they called Frank kept telling her to shut up.'

A few hours after 'Frank kept telling her to shut up' was the lead story on every news report, guards at the mesquite barrier pulled it aside long enough to allow a car through. At the wheel was Speers Jackson.

In the whitewashed living-room the two men sat near Teresa. Pedro's boots were planted like tree trunks before him, fists pushed into his thighs. Speers leaned back, one boot resting on the other knee, as he went over the thing a second time.

'No quiero hablar con reporteros,' Pedro answered again, determined not to speak English, even to Speers.

'Es necesario – totalmente necesario,' said Speers, and for the rest of their conversation they all talked in Spanish. 'We have got to change tack,' Speers went on calmly. 'You both must speak to the reporters. Not many. Just a small group. Maybe two lots from TV. Two from the papers with their photographers.'

'Maybe they ask other questions,' Pedro said sullenly. 'You don't like that. I don't like that.'

Speers turned his open face to Teresa lying there, her eyes alert, and in the same unhurried movement, his expression bland, he returned his gaze to Pedro. A deep flush moved up Pedro's face.

'You will tell them only what you know about the accident, Pedro – that is all you will tell them. Nothing else,' Speers said. 'They already know about the money Miles Brewster pays into the Monterrey bank each month.

There's no need to add anything further to that. Teresa won't have to say much more than she said to Simon Fleet.'

Speers turned to her.

'I was impressed,' he said. 'You handled it well.'

She reached to the tiled floor and gave a little push to start the settee swinging again.

After a silence Pedro said in a surly voice: 'How much will I be paid?'

'I'll take care of that,' Speers replied. 'You know you can trust me.'

'*I* do not require payment,' Teresa said sharply. Daintily the monkey shifted its place on her lap.

Speers looked at her. 'You'll be offered plenty for your exclusive story before this is through,' he said.

'I shall say what I wish to say,' she replied. 'And I can only be sure of what I truly wish to say if I am not being paid for it.'

After Speers left, Pedro stood over the settee, bent elbows tight against his body, fists clenched before him. The gamey smell of his dungarees – like a butcher shop – mingled with the almondy scent of mimosa growing in a pot by the window.

'You never told me the passengers were anybody important – that he was a congressman. Even at the time, when it had just happened, when you were lying on that hospital bed, you never told me.' Self-pity mingled with his frustration.

'There are lots of American congressmen,' she replied. After a slight pause, she added: 'It wasn't important who he was,' and as she spoke the words her eyes became unreadable.

'Next you will tell me it wasn't important when he became President,' Pedro went on furiously. 'Maybe it would have been important for me to know that. Maybe it would have been me who first told the world that Miles Brewster' – he spat the name – 'had covered up that the President of the United States was there when the whole thing happened. It would have been worth a lot to me. Now it is too late.'

She met his bitter gaze defiantly.

'You're the only one' – his voice was close to a shout – 'who can make big money out of this now. And you refuse. You are a fool.'

'I have made you money for fifteen years,' she said coldly. 'You can go to the bank in Monterrey each month for the rest of my life. We both have been paid well.'

She gave a shove. Pedro watched the settee swing back and forth. After a minute he stamped from the room.

The media elected its representatives, and with their camera equipment they piled into a single van. The mesquite barrier was pulled aside to let it through. Guards by the front door watched impersonally as the group went into the house.

In the living-room, its windows overlooking the cordilleras, men and women were getting into position, intent and orderly, like a small crowd scene in a ballet. The sound man scowled and squinted out at the azure sky as a helicopter's rattle grew louder. 'For Chrissake,' he said urgently into his bleeper, 'do something about the geek filming from the air. The goddam chopper sounds like my mother's Mix Master on speed.'

Pedro glowered in a chair near his daughter, his feet in his best boots. He spoke his lines mechanically – they were familiar enough to him – and even though they would need translation for the worldwide television audience, anyone could tell from his face that he spoke from the heart, and that it was a vengeful heart.

Miles Brewster had arrived from the north, a gringo looking for a good time. Gringos treated Mexico as their private playground. No, Pedro had not met him before the accident. He first saw Miles Brewster lying on a hospital bed.

No, Pedro had not met the Lamberts. Until this past week he didn't know the passengers were anyone special.

Yes, Miles Brewster had paid money ever since. Why shouldn't he pay money for doing what he did? Maybe he still felt guilty. Anyhow, what did money mean to the gringo? Nothing. And all the money in the world would not make his daughter walk again.

That was all he knew, he said truculently, and truthfully.

The sound man had to adjust his receiver for Teresa's low voice. One camera stayed on the whole settee, and viewers would later point to the little monkey that scampered into frame and settled itself in the woman's lap. Another camera stayed in close-up. Her face had few of the signs of time you'd expect in a woman of thirty-seven. The dark hair braided atop her head like a jet coronet, the delicate features, the translucence of her eyes, all made her a cameraman's dream.

She answered the reporters with calm dignity. Matter-of-fact. No resentment. Even the most cynical of those journalists accepted that a woman like that would not mislead them. Like the public when they saw her on their screens a few hours later, they were impressed by her directness.

She'd been a schoolteacher at the time – teaching English. She still taught English to students who came here to the Lopez *estancia*. The ranch, not large today, was smaller then. And their house today was bigger than it used to be. Her mother had died when she was a child. Her mother's sister lived with them and brought her up.

She met Miles and the Lamberts at a grange evening. They were with the son of the owner of Las Ballas ranch. A big ranch, owned by one of the Spanish *hacendados*. The other side of the cordillera.

Evenings at the grange were always fun. Anybody could buy tickets, unless they were known to be trouble-makers. People had drinks. Talked to each other. Danced to loud music from a Mexican band.

'I danced with Miles. And with Frank Lambert,' she said. 'From the beginning I liked them both. I liked Nona too. She was very friendly.'

Yes, of course Miles told her that Frank Lambert was in the House of Representatives.

'They all gave me a lift home at the end of the evening. Miles and I arranged to go riding the next day.'

No, the Lamberts were not with him the next day. They had their own car, and they wanted to get to Mexico City. Miles stayed on at Las Ballas ranch, and they rode together each day.

'No,' she replied to another question, 'my father never met him – because my father was away. At Torrien. There's a big cattle market at Torrien.'

Yes, of course her aunt met Miles. She liked him very much. Sadly, her aunt was no longer alive.

Yes, she spent a number of evenings with him. They ate at the main hotel in Saltillo. Once in Monterrey. Various places.

'There was nothing very odd about a woman of twenty-two going out with an unattached man,' she said in a slightly mocking tone.

'Even though he was from a very different background from your own?' a New York reporter asked.

'I had thought Americans believed we are born equal,' Teresa replied, with a smile that made the cameramen want to dance.

Did she fall in love with Miles Brewster when first she met him?

'Fall in love?' she repeated quizzically. 'You mean as in fairy-tales?'

For a moment she seemed to turn it over in her mind. Then she went on:

'I quickly came to love him. He was a very attractive man. He remains so. He always treated other people with respect. But I always knew he would be returning to his own life. He never suggested anything else.'

'When you realised he was going back, did you resent him having seduced you?'

'Seduced me? Who gave you that idea?'

'Are you saying you didn't have an affair with him? We understand he moved into a Saltillo hotel for the last days of his vacation.'

Slowly her lashes came down over her eyes. When she lifted them she said calmly: 'I have nothing to say about an affair with Miles Brewster or anyone else. If you wish to speculate about any affair, that is for you. It's a free country.'

Then they reached the nub: the accident.

'Ah, the accident,' she said. She reached down to give the tiniest push. One of the cameramen swore beneath his breath. The monkey leapt nimbly to the settee's back where it perched to enjoy the undulating movement.

It had happened the day before Miles was to drive north. The Lamberts had returned to Las Ballas before continuing their own journey north to Frank's constituency. She couldn't remember why they all went in the Lamberts' car rather than Miles's. Yes, of course she now knew the car was registered in Nona's name.

'How could anyone today not know unless they were hermits?' Her tone made plain it was the most ridiculous question ever asked. 'But it wasn't of interest at the time.'

They had a picnic lunch high up on the cordillera. She didn't know how many bottles of wine. All of them were drinking. Miles took the wheel afterwards because by then he knew the road better than the Lamberts. She was up front beside him.

'He was driving too fast for the bends in that road,' she said, her voice even quieter than usual. 'We came around a sharp curve and it kept bending. The car skittered along the edge. Suddenly the little girl was in front of us.'

Then the screaming of brakes. The car shuddering. The car veering again. The plunge down the escarpment. The mesquite rushing at them.

She stopped speaking. The only sound was the *zikky-zikky* of a cicada somewhere in the room. She reached down and gave another little shove.

FORTY-SEVEN

The overwhelming jolt, noise, breaking glass, brief terrible pressure. But it was so fast she didn't remember feeling any pain. In the stillness that followed, she realised she was on the ground, the car on its side on her legs. She felt her face, and when she looked at her hand she saw the blood on it. She moved her hand over her body, then to her legs. That's when she realised she couldn't move them.

'It was absurd for that garage attendant to claim the truck driver said I was screaming in pain and that Frank Lambert told me to shut up. I couldn't feel anything where the pain should have been.'

Then the Lamberts were standing above her. Miles's face appeared, covered with blood. He was crawling. He couldn't walk. They couldn't get at the jack. The Lamberts had to try bodily to lift the car off her.

'You know how much a car weighs,' she said, 'but they kept trying. Whenever they got it up a fraction more, Miles shoved a mesquite branch further under it.'

She heard their grunts, like groans. Then the Lamberts got the car high enough so Miles could pull her until she was free. He was wet and sticky. It was like a dream, even though she always knew it wasn't a dream.

'Miles told me the Lamberts had gone for help. Then they were there again. A Mexican was with them. They took the back seat from the car and lifted me on to it. That's how they got me up the escarpment.'

All four, and the dead child, rode on the open flatbed of the truck. Miles was on his back near where she lay.

After that she remembered little. The white lights overhead in the hospital. Not much else.

'Did the Lamberts come to see you in the hospital?'

'I wouldn't have been aware of them,' she replied. 'I was very ill, in shock, I believe. They told me my spinal cord had been damaged. I do not even remember being moved from the Saltillo hospital to Monterrey. Only my father – and Miles – could visit me. Miles's bed was wheeled in from another room. He didn't stay long. He was very ill too.'

'How many doors of the car were thrown open?' a reporter asked.

'I am afraid I was only aware of my own,' she replied.

'We understand the wrecked car was removed from the escarpment. Who arranged that, and what became of the car?'

'I do not know the answer to either question,' she replied. 'The subject of removing the car was not one which greatly exercised my mind at the time.'

Then Miles had been flown to a hospital in Boston. Later, when she could be moved, she was flown to Boston too. The rehabilitation unit there was better than any in Mexico. Miles was in the same unit.

'Who paid?'

The question was not put aggressively, but its significance was none the less for that.

'Miles,' she replied.

When it became clear that no movement or feeling could be restored to her legs, she returned to her home in Mexico.

'Did you feel bitter when Miles Brewster didn't marry you after you were paralysed?'

'Why should I feel bitter that something we never intended before the accident did not occur after it? My home is Mexico. Miles's life is elsewhere.'

'When did you last see him?'

'Not so long ago.'

'When exactly?'

'Earlier this year? It is natural for friends to see one another from time to time.'

'How soon after the accident did you learn he would pay you and your father money for the rest of your life?'

'I can't remember when I learned that.'

'People today think it's a pay-off, *Señorita* Lopez – to make sure you won't reveal something Miles Brewster wants kept secret. People think someone bribed the police to keep the American passengers' names out of the formal report.'

'You know how many fantasies have been woven around this accident – only to be dismissed as ludicrous,' she replied, reaching down to get the swing going again. Not vigorously back and forth, gently.

'You have already said about the accident, *Señorita* Lopez, that it was something like a dream. Is it possible it has slipped your mind that Miles Brewster might have a reason – other than compensation for your injuries – for still sending monthly payments to you at that bank in Monterrey?'

There was something daunting in Teresa's dignity. It made the question impertinent and unnecessary to a number of people.

'Your question is meaningless,' she said. 'You might as well ask if it is possible I only imagine I cannot walk.'

In his chair opposite the television set, Speers rubbed a thumb across his mouth reflectively. It was a formidable performance. Yet he knew the spectre raised was not going to vanish, however impressive and beguiling the public would find Teresa Lopez.

A Texas billionaire announced he would pay for Teresa

Lopez to have the best treatment in America that money could buy until she was able to walk again.

Envelopes addressed to her were handed daily to guards at the barrier. Most contained requests for an exclusive interview, usually offering large payments. Some were from agents wanting to act on her behalf, for the customary commission.

That week she was on *Newsweek*'s cover. Looking out as well was a brown monkey with a perky mantle of ginger-coloured hair sweeping back from its brows.

The situation in Arabi was nearly untenable. Openly the dictator defied American and British soldiers whose presence on the border was intended to intimidate him. Each day President Lambert walked into his press conference, prepared to answer questions on whether he would authorise an air strike. Each day as soon as he finished his statement the first question was: 'Mr President, can you tell us why it never came out until now that you and Mrs Lambert were passengers in the car that killed the Mexican child and left a Mexican woman paralysed for life?'

In the music room Zoë sat with her elbows either side of *Newsweek*, staring down at the cover picture, riveted. It bore a startling resemblance to Frida Kahlo's self-portrait which she'd seen in Miles's office above the *Washington Express*.

The telephone made her jump. She ran into the next room to answer it.

'Are you OK, Zoë?'

'Oh, Jancie.' The despair in Zoë's voice said it all.

'Yeah. The press is pretty bad here too,' said Jancie.

'Did Teresa Lopez's interview make things any better for Miles on your side of the ocean?'

The pause that followed was so long Zoë thought the connection had been broken.

'Jancie?'

'Well, it pacified some people, yes. And certainly the Lamberts came well out of her account. I thought maybe she'd got them off the hook. But within twenty-four hours the media here were in full cry again, with the *Javelin* at the front of the pack. James has had the most terrific row about it with Lord Scrope. As Teresa herself said, why should Miles have married her just because he was responsible for her being crippled?'

Zoë bit her lip.

'Is that the *Javelin* line now?' she finally asked.

'One of its lines. I can't make out exactly what happened in Lord Scrope's office,' Jancie went on, 'but I think James resigned and then Lord Scrope induced him to stay on. James is very, very depressed. But not as depressed, I suppose, as Miles.'

'Have you talked with Miles?'

'I saw him and Marigold at a dinner party last night. They didn't look at all relaxed with one another. But then there was a definite strain in the air for everyone. Our charming Defence Secretary boomed out: "How're things down Mexico way, Miles?" But no one else mentioned it.'

Jancie gave a dry laugh.

'Nobody talks about anything else, yet ten of us managed to sit through that meal without referring to it.'

Zoë's free hand was over her eyes.

'I phoned him when the story first broke,' Jancie went on. 'He was composed, friendly, thanked me for my concern. But he doesn't want to talk about it. What about you?'

'You mean have I phoned him?'

'Yes.'

'I wanted to. But I decided he'd just as soon not hear from me – me now working for Gerald Scrope, and then phoning with my condolences.'

When they'd said goodbye, Zoë went back and stared at the cover picture again. The Victrola was now on the floor, the new fax machine put in its place, and she looked up when the mutter started. The sheet sliding out bore *The Monocle*'s heading. Those that followed were the Comment page her deputy proposed for that week's issue.

He had centred his piece on the issue of press morality. (*The Monocle*'s privileged independence from Lord Scrope's interference meant its deputy editor could write from a comfortable position.) His tone about Miles was snide.

Still, Zoë was forced to remind herself, everyone else seemed to have reached the same unpalatable conclusion as her deputy: Miles Brewster had connived at concealing the identity of his passengers in that crash. It was bad enough he was prepared to do that as a citizen, but the dishonour was magnified when he made himself an editor. An editor's job was to disclose the truth.

She gave a deep sigh. Would her own doubts about Miles's integrity hover for the rest of her life?

'Even if they did,' she said aloud to the portrait of her ancestor looking at her from under his ferocious brows, 'I sure as hell wouldn't cross to the other sidewalk if I saw him coming.'

Unless she said something publicly now, it would be the same as if she passed by on the other side. At least, that's what it would feel like to her. She had some decency left. She wanted Miles to know that.

Tossing the deputy's pages on to the sofa, she scribbled a note to him: 'Will fax my replacement in two hours. It will be the same length.' She put it in the fax machine and sent it over.

With a large pad of lined paper under one arm, she climbed the old staircase. Its yellow cedar bannister and steps scented the entire stairwell and always made her think of frankincense and myrrh. In the bedroom that once her parents used, the big cupboard had the same evocative smell. Her father's portable Olivetti was on a shelf at the back. She set the typewriter on a table looking out over the lake.

She headed the piece: 'A Reticent Man'.

She told the story again, writing it with great simplicity. There was scarcely an adverb in the whole piece. No one said *doubtfully*, or replied *stoutly*, or looked down *uncomfortably* – those qualifying adverbs which enable journalists to put their own gloss on the matter. The focus of public outcry – the Lamberts' role – was not the focal point of her account. Miles was.

She returned to those parts of the story that were needed to make her case.

'Supposing Miles Brewster, injured as he was, hadn't been determined to lift the car off Teresa. The Lamberts couldn't have managed it alone, and every minute her legs were trapped beneath that pressure meant her blood couldn't circulate.

'Supposing Miles Brewster hadn't arranged for her to be taken to the best rehabilitation unit in the United States. There was a rehabilitation unit in Mexico.

'Supposing he had made a financial settlement and then put the tragedy behind him. Teresa's account makes clear they never intended marriage and they remain friends.

'What do those actions say about the man?'

For a long time she sat with her chin in her hands, staring at the typewriter, thinking.

'What do his other actions say about the proprietor-turned-editor?

'An editor's duty is to tell the truth in his newspaper. But this is thornier ground than we like to admit. Normally he is not expected to retail his personal life. Normally he would not be admired for disclosing something told him in confidence. Normally friendship has a role as well – defensible in terms of decent human conduct, indefensible in the narrow journalistic sense.

'Any editor who tells you he has never been influenced by friendship is either lying or inhuman.'

She returned her elbows to the table, gazing unseeing at the keys, trying to get the jigsaw pieces into place in her mind.

'If the thing you are concealing concerns a crime, or it might disclose a significant weakness in an American president, is the balance of the dilemma altered? The answer has to be yes.

'But the terrible accident in Mexico was not a criminal act as we normally understand that term. There is no evidence that bribes were paid to conceal the Lamberts' identity.

'And their presence as passengers made no difference to the crash – although without their help afterwards, Teresa Lopez might not be alive today.

'Miles Brewster has always taken responsibility for what occurred on the road to Saltillo. He did not proclaim the tragic episode at the time or later. Until we make reticence an offence, that was the right of a reticent man.'

PART V

FORTY-EIGHT

People dressed for the White House dinner with especial excitement. Would the President or the First Lady refer to the threat hanging over them?

It was one of several large dinners the Lamberts had planned to demonstrate an outreaching attitude. Several heads of social services would be there, a few police chiefs, union leaders, educationalists. As well there'd be judges, a couple of generals, publishers, and one or two of the Lamberts' favourite Hollywood stars. Nona made sure every minority in the land was represented.

And the media. They were key players in any White House strategy, and if President Lambert decided to hit Arabi from the air, the goodwill of the media was essential. Television chairmen and leading newscasters, newspaper owners and the most influential editors had been invited along with a selection of small-town editors from across the country.

Invitations had gone out long in advance. Once the Mexico story broke and White House aides realised it was not about to go away, they agonized over the guest list. Was there no way to disinvite the most offensive of the press bloodhounds? What about that fucking Scrope? Why the hell should the bastard who started it all sit smirking in the State Dining-room? What about putting off the whole thing?

But the President was adamant. There was no way to duck out of it without looking as if he had something to hide. Nona agreed, and that settled it.

The invitation said seven-thirty. Her lip caught in her teeth, Zoë had just started on her hair. In the mirror an enormous flower arrangement loomed on a table behind her. Its card was written in fashionable florist copperplate: 'From Gerald Scrope.'

Her phone rang. It was the concierge.

'Excuse me for bothering you, Miss Hare, but I wanted to make sure you've already made arrangements for a car to take you to the White House.'

'I'll walk. It's only a block and a half,' said Zoë.

'I know, ma'am, but you'll be in evening dress.' He left the rest of his thought process hanging in the air.

'Thank you. I'd rather walk.'

When she left the hotel, the doorman tipped his hat, expectant.

'I want to walk, thank you.'

'Lord Scrope is waiting for you, ma'am,' the doorman replied, opening the door of a Cadillac at the kerb.

Was it a compliment or a threat? *The Monocle* had appeared that day, and he would hardly have been delighted by her Comment.

'Good evening, Miss Hare.'

However fine the tailoring of his Savile Row dinner jacket, it still conveyed a sense his energy would burst its cloth asunder.

'I'll have that,' he said, plucking her invitation from her hand and passing it to his driver.

'I didn't know you were even in America,' she said.

He was looking out his side of the car as limousines ahead moved forward like snails. Except for guests of honour, everyone now had to go in by the East-side entrance because of the anti-terrorist barriers at the front.

Zoë had lowered her window. A flash-bulb went off, and a face peered in. She heard a shout follow, and moments later another flashbulb at Gerald's window. Even Americans who couldn't care less which magnate owned what media chain had registered Lord Scrope as the Brit whose paper dug up the President's past.

As soon as they were inside the White House grounds, crowded with cars, Zoë said: 'Why don't we get out and walk? It's only a few yards.'

'Give me back the invitations,' Gerald said to the driver.

Once through the security hut and into the entry hall, they encountered a small press pool cordoned off – photographers, TV, scribblers – but these were present under sufferance and were polite.

A uniformed aide led them upstairs to the reception floor. As they walked along a red carpet on what reminded Zoë of a marble chequerboard, Gerald still hadn't spoken another word to her. Half her brain was trying to fathom his mood, half was absorbed in looking around her. She peeped in each open doorway they passed, recognising the President's Oval Office from pictures, uncertain about a blue room that followed, next a green one.

The hum of voices swelled when they entered the gold and white East Room where once Teddy Roosevelt's children rollerskated on the oak parquet and seven presidents had lain in state, three of them murdered.

'Zoë.'

It was Leila Sherman. Her cocktail party in Georgetown now seemed a hundred years ago.

'Do you know Lord Scrope?' asked Zoë. She introduced them.

Leila Sherman's face clouded for a moment. Then she decided to play it as if the *Javelin*'s bombshell and its repercussions were of no importance.

'You must be very pleased, Lord Scrope, with your new editor's début in *The Monocle*. It was a brilliant piece, Zoë, unlike anything else written in all this hysteria. Lots of people are talking about your Comment.'

Impassively Gerald looked around at other guests sipping California's most famous wines and looking over the shoulder of those they were talking to.

However deep her resentment of the man whose London paper had started the crisis, Leila did not expect him simply to ignore her. As one of Washington's most celebrated hostesses, she was accustomed to attention. When Gerald left off his survey, he saw her annoyance at once.

'You're the lady who footed the bill for Frank Lambert's presidential campaign,' he said.

After the briefest pause Leila replied: 'I was proud to play a small part in his achievement.'

'Are you still proud tonight, Mrs Sherman?'

'Nice to see you again, Zoë,' Leila said. 'I hope you find working for Lord Scrope is not too intolerable. He is the rudest person I have ever met.'

Declining to glance again at Gerald, she moved away.

'Lord Scrope.' It was the editor of *Newsweek*.

'You know Zoë Hare,' Gerald replied.

'I liked your piece,' the editor told her. 'You must have got to know Miles Brewster pretty well while you were on the *Dispatch*.'

'I wonder if he will show his face here tonight?' said Gerald.

Zoë's face coloured.

Suddenly the room was hushed, everyone looking towards the door. Zoë moved sideways to see around the people in front of her.

The President looked relaxed. The First Lady smiled too, but her face was tense. White House aides started taking guests up to the Lamberts.

The editor of the *New York Times* had engaged

Gerald's interest, and Zoë quickly slipped away. She was talking with a judge and his wife when an aide drew her aside: 'The First Lady would be glad to say hello, Miss Hare.'

Zoë was distinctly nervous.

'Congratulations on becoming editor of *The Monocle*,' Nona said brightly.

Zoë remembered that guarded look in her eyes.

'I wasn't sure what to make of your Comment this week, but at least it was original.'

Gerald's burly frame materialised beside them.

'Gerald Scrope,' he announced.

Nona's face became flint. She turned to the next guest waiting.

From her card Zoë knew she wouldn't be at the same table as Gerald, for which she gave thanks to whoever was above as everyone moved along the colonnade to the State Dining-room – fifteen round tables, ten places at each, white damask gleaming, cut-glass sparkling. Above the mantelpiece President Lincoln reflected benignly as he sat in a red chair. But it was the future of the President sitting amongst them that was in everyone's mind tonight.

Near the end of dessert, there was no formal calling for silence. President Lambert simply pushed back his chair and stood up, and a wave of silence moved of its own accord to the other tables. He looked as if he hadn't a care in the world.

'My friends,' he said, and then paused, his eyes moving about the room. 'And my non-friends.'

Nervous laughter fluttered at the tables.

'A speech would be inappropriate for this informal occasion, so I shall say only a few words. This evening was intended for some of us to meet others we haven't met before. I've always found I can learn something when I meet a person instead of just reading about them.' He paused.

People glanced at one another.

For several minutes he interwove banter and hard politics. A compliment to a hospital administrator present was followed by a reminder of the government's achievements in health reforms. After a friendly joke about one of the generals, he went straight on to a deadly serious remark about the Arabi crisis.

Guests selected for special mention either preened themselves as those nearby looked around at them, or affected modesty at being so honoured.

'Nona and I,' the President went on, 'are especially gratified that the English press baron, Lord Scrope – his London newspaper the *Javelin* may have come to your attention lately – felt able to be with us this evening.'

With masterly self-control, no one at Gerald's table looked at him.

'Nona and I are sorry Miles Brewster is not also with us this evening. We send him our good wishes in his trouble.'

His trouble, Zoë said to herself indignantly.

'And now you must enjoy the rest of our time together.'

The President sat down.

After a short silence louder than thunder, clapping ensued – enthusiastic (Leila Sherman), guarded (*Newsweek*'s editor). Sitting dead frontal in his chair, Gerald kept his fists either side of the dessert plate he had scraped clean before the speech began. Zoë sat silent.

At eleven sharp it was all over. As the guests poured out to find their cars, the real exchange of opinions about the President's closing words began. But Zoë made off on her own. She had just crossed East Executive Avenue when Gerald overtook her.

'We should have a nightcap, Miss Hare.'

'I don't feel like it tonight, Lord Scrope. I'm feeling slightly sick.'

They walked the rest of the way in silence.

In the hotel lobby she said: 'I'll say good-night. I have to get my key.'

When she came back to take the elevator, Gerald swung in beside her. They were alone. Side by side they stood, the only sound the whoosh of the elevator. Zoë's floor came first. As the doors were sliding apart, Gerald reached across her and jabbed a thumb on to the door-open button.

'You and I must talk, Miss Hare.'

Her expression made it unnecessary for her to answer.

'No, not tonight, Miss Hare. You are in your rabbit mould tonight. We will meet tomorrow for lunch. At one o'clock. In the Willard Room. Sleep well, Miss Hare.'

He released the button and removed his arm from blocking her.

Her phone was ringing as she turned her key.

'Hullo, Zoë.'

It was James Wharton, his voice slightly slurred. Drink? Fatigue? Stress? Maybe her voice sounded like that, and for two of the same reasons. (Drink had been served in moderation, which happened to suit Zoë as she didn't want to drink much.)

'I knew you wouldn't be asleep yet,' he said. 'The Chairman said you'd be at the White House dinner. Did he mention I'm in Washington with him?'

They both gave a weary laugh.

'Not that anyone,' James added, 'is ever actually *with* him. Simon Fleet's here too. I'm spending twenty-four hours pushing another defence contract with various brass hats. God knows what Fleet is doing – basking in his glory perhaps. I need to see you, Zoë.'

'Oh, James, what'll we do? I'm flying back to Vermont tomorrow. And I've got to have lunch with Lord Scrope before I go.'

'It's urgent.'

'Is everything all right with Jancie?'

'Yes and no.'

'She's not ill, is she?' Now she was really anxious.

'Not in the way you mean. But I need to talk to you.'

'I'll stay over tomorrow night and go north Saturday.'

FORTY-NINE

For a moment she didn't know where she was. She reached for her watch – 8.00 – and then lay gazing at the curtains' pattern of flowers, their petals washed out in the watery half-dark. Half-light, she muttered. Think positively, for Christ's sake.

She turned her head to look at the real flowers in the half-light. From Gerald Scrope.

She reached for the phone and ordered breakfast. 'On a tray, please.'

Then she resumed the position of a corpse laid out and emptied her mind. But images kept intruding. The President giving a friendly smile when he sent good wishes to Miles in his trouble. Miles when he'd had that warm, welcoming look, and then the cold withdrawal when she told him of Gerald's offer. *Newsweek*'s cover picture, now merged completely with Kahlo's self-portrait. The night with Peter at the Waldorf, two people huddling together for comfort. Gerald's thumb jammed hard on the door-open button.

She welcomed the waiter's rap at her door.

Soon after ten she crossed the lobby's mosaic floor purposefully, miming someone who knows where she's going. At least she knew her next port of call. Half-way through her second cup of coffee she'd decided how she would use the time before she met Gerald.

There must be a hundred taxis looking for business around the corner in 14th Street, but it seemed mean to deprive the doorman of his two bucks. Gerald, she bet, would have given him five, maybe ten. Then again he might give him nothing.

The doorman accepted her two dollars as if they were matched pearls. People in Washington had lovely manners whatever their position, in Maryland and Virginia too, really in all the South she'd seen. Much better manners than in London, she thought. She climbed into the taxi.

The *Express* looked smaller than she had remembered, the front door less prepossessing. But nothing had changed in the magic space that broke the ranks of office buildings opposite. The old magnolia still shaded the front steps. The blue clapboard showed no signs of peeling, the shutters looked like they'd just been spruced up. When she walked into the lobby of the *Express*, she had a rush of warmth, like someone coming home.

She hadn't told anyone she was coming. Quite a few people had already drifted in. The two she'd sounded out to come to *The Monocle* were the first to jump up when they saw her.

She chatted with journalists and secretaries she had liked best. All had seen the picture that morning in the rival Washington paper – Gerald deadpan as he looked out the car window, Zoë startled.

The editor that she had worked for was no longer there; a few weeks earlier he'd become editor of Gerald's American flagship daily paper in New York.

'There've been a lot of changes since you were here,' the features editor told her as they had a coffee in his office. 'Most of them bad. Until Miles moved to London, I hadn't really figured how crucial he was in the day-to-day running of this joint. We were all so awed by him, I guess, that some of us didn't realise the difference he made to morale. The new editor has brought in his own people over some of our best staff, who then took off. Nobody knows whether Miles is even aware how bad morale has got.'

'I thought he flew to Washington pretty regularly,' Zoë said.

'Yes, but it's not the same as when he was upstairs and could come down any time. We all knew the editor went up to see him at least once a day. Have you heard how Miles is taking his vilification? It must be rough. It's been damn uncomfortable, Zoë, I'm telling you, having to use his own paper to report his cover-up. Guess he should have known in the end a cover-up always comes out.'

'That's a dumb statement,' said Zoë. 'By the nature of things, you never know about cover-ups that don't come out.'

He grinned.

'Same Zoë. Always logical. By the way, I liked your Comment in *The Monocle*. Must have gone down a treat with Lord Scrope.'

'It crossed my mind you might jump the gun. At first I was displeased. Very displeased, Miss Hare.'

She had only just sat down at Gerald's corner table in the Willard Room.

'My second thought was it was good for *The Monocle*. People were talking about you before you even moved into the editor's seat.'

'Did you think my Comment was fair, Lord Scrope?' she asked, genuinely curious to know what he'd say.

'When people work for me they call me "Chairman", Miss Hare.'

Zoë swallowed.

'What do you want?'

She chose Maryland crab cakes – not just because no one in England knew how to make a decent crab cake, but because it was easy to eat. The strain of Gerald's company made it impossible to deal with anything normally so simple as cutting up a lamb cutlet, much less chewing it.

As soon as their order was taken, Gerald repeated her words: '"Any editor who tells you he has never been influenced by friendship is either lying or inhuman."'

She braced herself.

'What about the owner, Miss Hare?' he said. 'Do you see me as either lying or inhuman?'

'I wasn't aware you claimed never to have been influenced by friendship. Is that the case? Chairman.'

He swatted the air.

She said: 'When we had that second lunch at the Ivy, why did you tell me those things about yourself?'

She couldn't make out his expression as he looked at her.

'Maybe I like you, Zoë.'

He'd never called her that before. Neither said anything. He looked down to examine the Crab Imperial just put before him. He took up his fork and applied himself to his lunch.

Zoë started on her crab cakes.

After he'd pushed away his plate he said: 'You still want to believe Miles Brewster is superior to me – morally superior. You've always fallen for that stuff about a higher purpose, a greater good. Little Miss Clean.'

Zoë was damned if her face would show anything this time.

'I'm sure he believes he has higher motives than me. But you notice he gets his own way, don't he. Or he did until I caught him out.'

That hurt too. Yet his eyes were fathomable now. He wasn't trying to intimidate her. He was trying to convert her.

'You ought not to fall for them great ideals. In the end it don't help anybody. You ought to look at the world the way it is. Better for you if you did. Better for the world.'

He paused.

'For a girl who's got as far in the world as you have, you're still a baby in some ways, Zoë. I could teach you a lot.' His face softened. 'Even if hearts and flowers ain't my style.'

She gave a sudden smile.

'I can't speak for the hearts, but there's a bunch of flowers as big as a bear upstairs in my room,' she said. '"From Gerald Scrope."'

'When are you going back to Siberia?'

'Tomorrow morning. That leaves precisely five days of my famous restorative break before I move in at *The Monocle*.'

'Make it four,' he said.

She sat very still in her chair.

'I got some stuff I want to do in Washington,' he went on. 'Then tomorrow I'm going to the Eastern Shore.'

'I can't imagine you outside a metropolis,' she said.

'Come with me and you'll see a Gerald Scrope you never imagined.'

He didn't give her time to mount her defences.

'A Texas friend of mine has turned up in Washington. He's got a shooting lodge near some back-of-beyond called Tilghman Creek. He and I got things to talk about. You'd like him.'

He smiled.

'You needn't be Miss Rabbit again, Zoë Hare. He's got enough extra bedrooms. All very above-board.'

'I love the Eastern Shore,' she said, flustered. 'But I promised my grandparents I'd get back tomorrow. I can't phone them and put it off again.'

'Yes you can, Zoë.'

FIFTY

The restaurant was in a quiet street on the other side of the Potomac. James was already at a decent-sized table in the corner, so absorbed in his thoughts he didn't see her until she leant to kiss him.

He ordered a whisky for her and another large one for himself. He was drinking fast. Half-way through his second one he told her.

'I have to tell someone I trust – who loves Jancie.'

She had to concentrate on every word because his thoughts didn't proceed in an order and they came out in rapid bursts.

'Things were on a plateau with the Chairman. The two of us had evolved a working arrangement which was only intolerable from time to time. Then – it must have been just after you left – I refused to write a leader saying Alan Rawlston is Britain's saviour and should take over the helm – a view, incidentally, which is more widespread each day since you left. At least a third of the Prime Minister's backbenchers are now conspiring against him. The Chairman reached into his desk.'

James's face was grey.

'The video must have been in the bedroom of his flat. That great glass tower he lives in opposite Parliament. Rising like a cock. Like Fleet's. With Jancie.'

He passed a hand over his face.

Zoë put her hand on his arm. 'I don't understand, James.'

'They were stills. Of Fleet and Jancie. Like a piece of meat. That's what made them so disgusting.'

She took a deep breath.

'I showed them to Jancie that night. She'll never be free of him.'

Zoë kept her hand on his arm.

'When the Chairman gave them to me, I was too shocked to say anything. Just like a piece of meat,' James said again, his eyes vacant. 'In the morning I went in to see him before I cleared my desk. I told him if he wanted to sue me for breaking the contract, so be it.' He paused.

'And?'

'He closed and opened those eyes slowly. Then he said' – and here James spoke in Gerald's accent – '"It does not suit me, Ambassador, for you to resign at this time."'

Zoë withdrew her hand and took a long swallow of her drink.

'He reached in that monstrous desk again. This time he brought out a file of documents. Pages and pages of bureaucratic type, single space.'

James picked up the briefcase by his feet. He took out a file and turned to the first page. Zoë saw it was a photocopy. He ran a thumb down the edges.

'He turned the first half-dozen pages slowly. Very slowly. Wherever there was a break at the end of a section, I saw my scribbled signature.' He mimicked the flat vowels again: '"You authorised the export of those machine parts, Ambassador. That esteemed man of honour, James Wharton himself, saw nothing wrong in breaking the arms embargo on Arabi."'

Zoë's throat was dry.

'Scrope Electronics factories are scattered over America,' James went on. 'Last month he sent me to the one in Austin, Texas. Scrope Southwestern. My host was one of the nicest chaps you could imagine. Peter knows him. Even his name – Speers Jackson – made me smile. I still don't know his precise connection with Scrope, but he has *carte blanche* there. I found the Chairman had given me power of attorney to sign Customs declarations for an urgent road-shipment to Mexico. Pages and pages of technical jargon about machine-tool parts.'

He gave a short, harsh laugh.

'They included electronics parts which would – as the Chairman put it – guarantee Arabi's chemical weapons hit the spot. Thinking about it now, I'm sure he's been sending them out for some time. What his reason is for wanting me incriminated, God knows.'

She returned her hand to his arm.

'I've not reached the end, I'm afraid,' James continued. 'You know, don't you, that the reason the dictator hasn't used that supergun he's in love with is because he didn't have the essential electrical component. Well, he will soon. It was in that shipment I authorised.'

He flicked rapidly through the pages, then turned the lot around so she could read the final sheet. He ran a finger under a name. 'Pedro Lopez.' This time the brief laugh was wild.

'Nothing compared to the supergun component,' he said. 'Just a little joke at the end.'

'Is he the same one as Teresa's father?' asked Zoë.

'God knows. In this nightmare web he just might be.'

Sometimes James's words were his own, though they came out jerkily. Then he'd switch to Gerald's.

'"Cocaine dropped on to Texas ranches from the air is chicken-feed, Ambassador." Much, much more, it seems, comes over the border in trucks, hidden in whatever a shrewd operator deems safe if border officials decide to have a look. They inspect less than one in ten vehicles. To check more would paralyse cross-border commerce.'

He looked into Zoë's face and gave a tormented smile.

'"I should congratulate you, Ambassador," he mimicked, '"on your keen interest in cross-border commerce. But some things must be kept private. If any of this particular commerce became public, I would have to deny knowledge of what you have put your name to, Ambassador."'

He closed the file and pushed it at Zoë.

'You keep it, Zoë.'

'Why do I want it?' she asked, recoiling in her seat as if a rattlesnake had been put before her.

'Please, Zoë, keep it. Lock it away somewhere. I want to know it's safe if it's needed.'

After a few moments she said quietly: 'All right.'

There was another silence.

Then she asked: 'When you phoned last night, didn't you say you're here with Gerald Scrope?'

'Don't worry. As of next week I no longer will be his *chef de cabinet*. What a farce. I would have walked out last week, but I needed to clear my mind.'

She reached over and laid her hand for a moment on his cheek.

'Speers Jackson,' James said dreamily, as if trying to bring into focus someone on the outskirts of his mind. 'To be framed by such a pleasant man added to the shock.'

Neither of them had touched the plates of food growing cold. Zoë excused herself to go to the ladies' room. She got only as far as the wash-basin before she was violently sick.

With the file under one arm, she closed her bedroom door and pressed the bolt. Even before she turned around she sensed something different about the room.

She'd never seen anything like them except in a Georgia O'Keeffe erotic painting. There must have been at least a dozen, their petals not pointed like a lily which in some ways they resembled, but hollowed more like a tulip. They weren't too long in the stem, and they'd been clustered so they seemed to explode centrifugally, as if bursting from a core. Each one was already opened almost to the full, the moist, rosy inner flesh firm and taut as it spread wide, the stamen scarlet and thrusting.

She opened the envelope. Instead of a florist's showy copperplate, the card was written in a neat, somewhat crabbed script. 'This time from Gerald.'

FIFTY-ONE

She drafted her letter on the plane. When she got to the farm she'd type it. In the end it was short.

Dear Gerald

I was honoured when you invited me to become editor of *The Monocle*. I am sorry to give up my editorship before it has properly begun. But on reflection I find that however much I admire *The Monocle*, I do not want to work for Scrope Opportunities Ltd.

As ever,
Zoë Hare

It was more than a whim. The thought had first come to James when Concorde had been on the approach to Dulles.

He'd already planned to stay over for a day after he'd finished what he had to do in Washington. Most people he knew in the capital disappeared at weekends, but a few would be around.

Then the thought had come to him that what he really wanted was to be on his boat, sailing in the Chesapeake Bay, alone. A forty-foot racing yacht was big to handle alone. And much of his huge exhilaration in sailing came from being on wild open water with another man as crew, challenging wind and sea, each knowing his life depended on the other. But he'd taken the boat out on his own a number of times, he reminded himself, in the back rivers of the Eastern Shore, once on the Bay when it was fairly calm. So long as he used only the mainsail, it wouldn't be that difficult. It was odd: once he had the thought, it seemed to have been there a long time.

As soon as he had checked in at the Willard, he phoned the marina in Annapolis and told them to get the boat ready for Saturday morning.

He had always liked Annapolis. The eighteenth-century houses made from rosy brick unloaded by English schooners before they refilled their holds with tobacco waiting in bales behind the Custom House. The quiet elegance of the colonial State House where the Treaty of Paris with England was ratified. The sprawling severity of the Naval Academy commanding the river, slabs of white stone reflecting the morning sun, ranks of midshipmen's dazzling hats.

Spa Creek, where the boat was, lay just off the river. Everyone was glad to see him. The putt-putting of the motor was soothing as he moved from the inlet, lifting a hand to others on their way out – yachtsmen standing proud at their wheels as their crews busied themselves, a few watermen with nets piled on the bow of their flat oyster boats and crab boats. James's face was uncovered, and he liked the feel of the morning breeze on it.

When the water widened he locked the rudder while he hoisted the mainsail. He took the wheel again, and the white sail thwopped, billowing wide, and the boat skimmed across the slick waves, dipping to one side, then the other, as he tacked to catch the breeze.

Once on the Bay he made for the bridge, running fast with an incoming tide that would reach Baltimore an hour later. He looked up, as he always did, with pleasure at the twin spans above him, miles of steel linking the body of Maryland to its eastern limb, that flat land where time hardly moved and the old families still lived in the mansions at the neck of narrow back rivers, and on the far side of the peninsula the Atlantic crashed.

As he made for Love Point, the mainmast boom swinging over his head like a giant's club, he no longer was trapped inside himself. He was free of humiliation and the images that taunted him.

When he slackened the sail to turn into a pocket of the Bay, he smiled at a straggle of doll's houses where even this late in the year two or three elderly men, their faces the colour of charcoal, sat on the steps. Just beyond was a small waterside inn. A few stained-glass balls bright as jewels, bound with scraps of net, bobbed on the water's surface, marking where the new season's shellfish were trapped below. He and Jancie used to stay with friends who had a house near there. He secured the boom and tied up at the dock. The inn served freshly caught crabs and decent English lager.

But soon he was restless to get back to the boat. When the Bay grew wide, other yachts became bright triangles far away. At Love Point the waves swelled and he shouted aloud with exaltation.

He swung the boat around. He had booked to stay the night at the Crabshell Inn at Kent Narrows, and he wanted to get there in time to wash and have a Bourbon and an early dinner before returning to the boat for an evening sail. He loved skimming across impenetrable waters with the only light from stars and the moon. If he ran into anyone congenial at the Crabshell Inn, he might ask if they wanted to go along as crew.

He drank a fair bit of lager with his oyster stew, and the sense of well-being continued. He knew it stemmed from the boat, controlling the boat as he challenged the deep, controlling his destiny, not being at the mercy of a man who wished him ill.

The dining-room was fairly empty, and it was natural he'd be aware of the head waiter showing new arrivals to their table. James looked up to see a ravishingly pretty girl, a sexy vision. Immediately behind her was Simon Fleet.

Scarcely ten minutes later – still discussing the menu with the vision, showing off his knowledge of the Bay's succulent offerings – Simon was called to the phone. He'd already spotted James and stopped as he passed.

'What do you want to bet it's the Chairman?' he said to James, pulling down his mouth in a humorous grimace of despair. 'The first thing I was told when I joined the *Javelin* was that he's like Argos. "Wherever you are, one of his eyes sees you." '

Simon couldn't help grinning. It was the editor who had told him that. And on Monday it would be announced that Simon was replacing him.

Speers Jackson had invited a few people weekending on the Shore to come around for dinner that night at his shooting lodge, to meet Lord Scrope. They were carefully chosen for business – the Maryland senator on the Senate Armed Services Committee and his wife; Washington's most powerful lobbyist, Jock Liddon, with a girlfriend. It wasn't an easy drive for them: Speers's lodge was tucked away on Tilghman Creek, a duck hunter's paradise.

His lawn went down to a plank pier extending over the water, and all day the humid air had blurred the other shore and the duck blinds there among the scrub, and the water twisted out of sight behind a neck of land. Gerald was restless. He didn't think much of life outside the city at the best of times, and so far as he was concerned, the Eastern Shore of Maryland was the jungle, even when the poplars were stripped and mosquitoes biding their time.

Still piqued that Zoë hadn't come, he had the familiar urge to make someone jump through his hoop. He knew – he always knew – where he would find both his *chef de cabinet* and his editor designate. He would summon Simon only. That would fill James with uncertainty.

'On Monday I shall announce Simon Fleet is the new

editor of the *Javelin*,' he stated portentously as everyone settled down for drinks.

No one needed to be told who Simon Fleet was.

'Our host will not mind if I phone Mr Fleet and ask him to join us for dinner. He is staying at Kent Narrows with a friend, foolishly imagining he is without responsibilities for a night.'

Speers smiled amiably.

'But it will take him ages to drive here,' said the senator's wife. 'He has to get around all the inlets. Some of the roads are tiny.'

'That is for Mr Fleet to resolve,' Gerald replied, marching into the study.

'Tell him to hire a boat,' Speers called out.

On his return from the telephone Simon stoped at James's table. This time the expression of despair on his puck's face wasn't comic.

'Jesus. I've got to get to where he's staying. At the end of nowhere in some creek called Tilghman. "*At once*." It's bloody miles from here by those god-forsaken roads. The porter says it's faster by water. He's trying to get me a boat. And I can't bring my friend. That's going to go down well.' He cast a baleful eye at the girl sipping her cocktail decorously.

'I'll take you,' said James. 'My boat's faster than anything the porter's going to come up with. Wear warm clothes. I've got a life-jacket for you.'

The moon's crescent was blurred like a ghost, and the sky was dark above poplars that lined the shore like skeletons. James hoisted the mainsail.

'Get the storm jib up when we reach the Bay,' he directed Simon. 'We'll fly.'

Simon had been on many sailing yachts during his years posted in Washington, but he'd made sure they would be convivial outings in the long summer months. Unless circumstances dictated otherwise, he was always an idle crew. He knew how to get the bloody sail up and down, but he didn't get a high from it.

The jib thrashed against his cheek when it first whipped out and the wind snapped it taut. He clambered back and settled himself behind the mast, one sneaker placed either side of a cleat, sitting so his head was well below where the boom angled in to the mast. He looked at his watch. He had told her he'd be back long before midnight. She didn't take it well.

When they passed Windmill Island, the full blast of the north-west wind hit them, and the waves were suddenly enormous. The moon had vanished. Simon looked in vain for a star. As the boat's bow whopped against the waves, water flung over the deck. His lips tasted of salt. He looked at his trousers clinging to his legs. He wished to God he'd pulled a third sweater over his shirt. He was bloody freezing. He twisted around to shout at James. James looked bigger than Simon had remembered. A dark figure against a coal-black sky. The silhouette of the life-jacket made him look like an alien warrior.

Simon cupped his hands and bellowed: 'Have we gone too far?' He pointed to a little ribbon of lights off to their left.

James turned the wheel to catch more wind. The sails sounded like a train rushing through a tunnel.

Simon was shaking with cold. If he could get below deck – he hated being down in those narrow cabins: like being in a bloody coffin – he could get his jacket from where he'd stored it to keep it dry. He'd have to take off the Michelin-Man gear long enough to put his jacket on, and getting it over all these fucking sweaters wouldn't be easy. But he'd die if he didn't get another layer against the wind which was more penetrating each minute.

On his hands and knees he edged along the deck beside the mast, and a tremendous thrust of wind shoved the sails so far over that he saw the glistening mountains of water heaving just below where he lay clinging to the rail.

'For God's sake, man,' he shouted.

James spun the wheel. The deck lifted up so violently to tilt the other way that Simon was thrown to his feet. He scrambled for the cockpit but before he could reach it and jump below, the boom swung across it and smashed into the back of his head. Like a golf club whacking the ball and lifting it neatly into the air, the blow propelled him over the rail into the surging waters. Probably he never knew what hit him.

James gripped the wheel. He shifted his course to starboard of Tilghman Creek straight into the Chesapeake Bay. He was drenched but he didn't mind. The water was cold as death as it flung over the deck from one side, then the other, but it felt good on his face, and he couldn't tell what came from the sea and what came from the sky as the storm broke in its full power. He had challenged them and he would win.

When he saw Bloody Point light, the force of the wind must have been at least eight. He kept the mainsail's line tight. He was the one in charge of his destiny. He spun the wheel so the boat was at a right angle to the wind, and in the shudder before the boom could start its swing the stupendous gale crashed full into the sail. The taut canvas was nearly parallel with the water when he let go of the wheel. He gave a long shout of triumph and release.

FIFTY-TWO

Zoë hung up the clothes she'd worn to the White House. She'd type the letter in the morning.

After dinner they took their coffee into the music room. Television news had become hypnotic for Zoë. The first item on the news was just starting:

'A patrol of British soldiers in the West's peace-keeping troops on the Arabi border were ambushed by Arabi Muslims and forced to hand over their weapons. Thirty heavily armed gunmen held a machine-gun at the leader's head and made the six other members of the patrol lie face down while the Muslims stripped them. As a final humiliation, the British soldiers were forced to do push-ups in the road. The gunmen claimed to be independent fighters, but the British patrol leader was in no doubt they were attached to the dictator's army. They were armed with highly sophisticated weapons which appeared new and of a model the patrol leader had not seen before.

'In a separate incident three Arabi soldiers were shot and killed and five others captured after they fired chemical hand weapons into a group of civilians under the protection of UN troops. Preliminary examination of the weapons recovered from the Arabi soldiers indicates they are of recent design. Further examination may reveal whether key parts were manufactured in the United States or Britain.'

Zoë's face was intent as the next item brought up to date congressional reactions to the White House 'cover-up' crisis of confidence.

This led directly into the third item:

'The body of a key figure in the alleged White House

cover-up has been found floating in an inlet off the Chesapeake Bay following torrential storms that struck the eastern seaboard last night. Simon Fleet, thirty-five-year-old foreign editor of the London *Javelin*, was still wearing his orange life-jacket. He had received a massive blow to the head. Mr Fleet's investigation first brought to light that the President and First Lady were in the car with media magnate Miles Brewster at the time of the fatal accident on the road to Saltillo.'

Quick montage of photos.

'Mr Fleet had been sailing with the former British Ambassador to Washington, James Wharton. Hope has not been abandoned that Mr Wharton may still be alive.'

Both her grandparents turned in silence to Zoë. The newscaster was well into his next item on a racist attack in Los Angeles. Zoë got up and switched off the television. She sat down again and picked up her coffee.

'He's not still alive,' she said.

Tears started flooding down her face, and her coffee slopped into the saucer. She put it on the table and left the room.

They could see her silhouette where she stood at the edge of the drop to the stony shore.

A waterman in his oyster boat spotted the orange life-jacket two mornings later. It was lodged under the pier of a summer cottage. Peter identified the body. He'd never before seen a body that had been in the water for two days, he told Zoë afterwards. She flew to London that night.

The milkman was doing his rounds when she reached Kensington Park Road. Danny answered the bell. Their mother's bedroom door was still shut, he said. He knew she was glad Zoë could come, he said. He and Nell were just getting ready for school, he said. Their teacher had told them they should try and behave as if everything was normal. She'd said that would be best for their mother and best for them, he said. Danny was standing even more upright than most seven-year-olds, formal and dignified. He would carry Zoë's suitcase to her room, he said. As he reached down for it, he began to cry.

FIFTY-THREE

What happened on the boat? Of all the questions, that was the one Jancie couldn't let alone for any length of time. She and Zoë were lying on top of the bed, dressed but shoeless, propped against pillows, each sipping a whisky, gazing unseeing out the window opposite at the chimney-pots of the houses on the other side of Kensington Park Road.

Her bedroom, someone had said earlier to Janice. Horrible. It was *their* bedroom. She had got the whisky from the drinks table in James's study. If you were exhausted and in pain, it took less out of you if you talked lying down. Or you could just lie there looking out of the window, resting the pain.

'Everyone who knows about storms on the Chesapeake says it had to be an accident,' Zoë said. 'Fate roaming the world in those big boots. They're convinced the blow to Simon's head was from the boom. Knowing James, they're sure he was still at the wheel when the boat was swamped. Can you imagine James ever letting go that wheel?'

She looked at Jancie's profile and then returned her own gaze to the window.

'From James's viewpoint, Jancie, what a great way to die. Can you imagine any other way he would have chosen?'

Odd, Zoë thought. People tell cover-up stories all the time when they don't want to add to someone's pain. Peter was the only person she'd told what she knew. He said he'd have to see the policy before he could tell her, but life insurance often wasn't paid out if suicide could be shown. But that wasn't Zoë's biggest concern. If Jancie thought he'd meant to do it, God knows how she'd feel then for the rest of her life. It was bad enough without that.

'What I said to you that time,' Jancie said, 'about how I wouldn't be free of Simon until one of us was dead . . . Sometimes you say things because that's what you feel like saying at the time. But that doesn't mean they're true. I don't know if I meant it or not, even at the time.'

Without looking at her, Zoë put her hand on Jancie's for a moment.

'But someone hears you say it,' Jancie went on, 'and then makes it come true in a way you could never have imagined in your worst nightmare.'

Nell appeared in the doorway. When she and Danny got back from school, Zoë put them in charge of answering the bell.

'It's the man who takes Daddy to work in the morning,' Nell said. None of them noticed she used the present tense. They all did.

Zoë swung her legs off the bed. 'Back in a sec,' she said to Jancie. Nell led the way.

The driver had remained on the step.

'I have a letter for Mrs Wharton, ma'am,' he said. 'From the Chairman. I've been told to wait for a reply.'

He handed Zoë the envelope.

'If it's not convenient for Mrs Wharton to read the letter now, I can wait as long as you like,' he said. 'Or I can come back. Whatever you think.' He was unhappy and ill at ease.

'Wait,' said Zoë. 'I'll take it to her now.'

It was handwritten in Gerald's small script.

Dear Mrs Wharton,

Until the funeral is behind you, you may find it helpful

to have a car and driver at your disposal. I have instructed your late husband's driver to be on hand with the car at all times for the rest of the week.

Yours very sincerely
Gerald Scrope

Their faces were blank as they stared at the letter in Jancie's hand. She was the first to recover her wits.

'Tell him to go to hell,' she said, throwing the letter aside, turning her face towards the window again, her expression so stony it might have belonged to a statue of Anger. 'And give him back the letter. I don't want anything of Gerald Scrope's in this house.'

Folding it back into the envelope, Zoë took it to the driver still standing uncertainly on the front step. She handed it to him without explanation.

'We won't be needing you,' she said simply.

He tipped his hat and had started down the path when he turned back.

'I'd be glad, ma'am, if you would tell Mrs Wharton I am sorry for her trouble. A fine man.'

Jancie's mother and sister and brother-in-law arrived from Colorado. Zoë had booked them into a small hotel nearby. Peter flew in from Washington and stayed at the Hyde Park ten minutes away.

'I wanted to be here,' he said to Jancie. The bond of bereavement.

'Of course I'm not going to the funeral,' Marigold said. 'They were always your friends more than mine.'

Miles wasn't sorry. Each time he and Marigold went through the charade of appearing together in public, the bond that remained between them was further strained.

'I think we'll both be glad when today is over,' she said.

They were standing in his study. Through the open door they could see some of her cases standing in the hall, ready to be collected that afternoon. He looked at the beautiful hair in the cool morning sun coming through the window.

'I hope things go well for you,' he said.

'Thank you, Miles.' She hesitated. 'I wish whatever happened in Mexico could be cleared up. I don't enjoy the attacks on your integrity.'

'Thank you. I thought they might give you a sense of justification in leaving me for Gerald Scrope.'

'No.'

She kissed his cheek.

'I hope things go well for you,' he said again.

The funeral was at St Bride's off Fleet Street, still known as the journalists' church even though the famous ranks of press buildings were used for other things now. From their quarters elsewhere in London fifty or sixty journalists hurried in shortly before noon. Quite a few people came from Washington. Peter slipped into a pew in the middle of the church. Miles sat alone near the back. Lord Scrope did not attend.

Only the top of Nell's and Danny's blonde heads showed over the back of the front pew, one either side of Jancie. The family from Colorado and Zoë sat immediately behind. When everyone was standing up singing the seamen's hymn and they came to the line 'O hear us when we cry to Thee for those in peril on the sea,' Jancie began to shudder convulsively. Zoë reached out and touched her shoulder until Jancie got control of her body.

Outside the church Zoë saw Miles. He was standing apart. She went over to speak to him. Both were ill at ease.

'The BBC has given Jancie paid leave until she gets herself together, whatever that means,' said Zoë. 'I'm taking the three of them back with me to Lake Champlain for a couple of weeks.'

'Give her my love,' Miles replied.

They continued to stand awkwardly under Wren's curious steeple – its spire always looked to Zoë like the separate sections of a telescope pulled out.

'I don't suppose you happened to see my Comment in *The Monocle*?' she asked.

'I saw it. Thank you.'

'I mailed my letter of resignation just before I flew to London.'

She was sure she saw him swallow hard, but that was the only sign of any feelings that he showed.

Both turned away.

Late that night when Zoë left Jancie's bedroom and went downstairs, Peter was still there, sitting in an armchair reading a book of John Donne's poems he'd found on the shelves. He'd put a marker in front of the one called 'Death, be not proud'. He thought Jancie might find it helpful. He knew the attention span of the freshly bereaved is too short to take in anything much longer than a poem.

He and Zoë went out into Kensington Park Road to get some air together before he returned to his hotel, walking side by side along the empty pavement. Sometimes the quiet was broken when a car shot past like a courier focused on the next address on his list. After a while Peter put his arm around her shoulder.

'When this is all over,' he said, 'I think we'd better give some serious thought to getting married. Each of us needs the other.'

She rested her head against his shoulder as they strolled in the night.

FIFTY-FOUR

The day after the funeral they were all in the cab when Jancie said: 'I just want to check I locked the door.'

She got out and went up the path once more. When she returned no one said anything. The cab set off for Heathrow.

People could believe it. Or they could not. But they couldn't dispute the meaning of the goddam words. Miles got up from his chair and strolled into the conference room. It was packed with reporters and television crews.

He'd chosen to make his statement from the headquarters of his corporate empire on the top floor of the *Dispatch*. He didn't need anyone else to point out – and they all would – the irony if he sat at his editor's desk to speak about an event he had always tried to conceal.

'I wish to state that I regret the implications surrounding the car crash in Mexico fifteen years ago, for which I was entirely responsible. There were three people in the car with me: Teresa Lopez, Nona Lambert, Frank Lambert. The car belonged to Mrs Lambert. She and her husband were using it for their vacation. For no particular reason we decided to go in her car rather than my own for our picnic lunch in the sierras.'

Three Hares and three Whartons stared at the screen, Danny and Nell sitting on the floor drinking hot chocolate.

'It began as a happy occasion, and all four of us drank more wine than we'd intended. I was more familiar with the road than the Lamberts, and Teresa Lopez knew it well, so I took the wheel for the drive back. Teresa Lopez was beside me in the front seat. The Lamberts were in the back.'

Jancie said in a low anxious voice: 'It's the same so far as Teresa's account.'

Miles went on: 'The events surrounding the accident are like clear snapshots in my mind. I was driving too fast. The car began to skid on a bend and the outside wheels went on to the shoulder. I was pulling the car back full on the road when I saw the child ahead. I jerked the wheel so hard to the left that I thought I would miss her. But I felt the terrible thump and knew what had caused it.'

His pause was so fractional that people would have to replay their video-recording to be certain of it. His face and delivery were as impassive as a coroner's, Zoë thought.

'Between the effect of the brakes rammed on and the sudden turning of the wheel, the car was then careening directly towards a post supporting the power line. I spun the wheel the other way and before I could straighten it the car shot over the escarpment. When it hit the thicket of mesquite the doors flew open and the car turned on its side. Miss Lopez and I were thrown out. Her legs were trapped beneath the car.'

Again a fractional pause? Zoë wasn't sure.

'The trunk was jammed, the jack inside. Frank and Nona Lambert tried to lift the car, while I shoved the thin end of a mesquite branch beneath it. Each time they got it a little higher, I pushed the branch further until we were able to pull Miss Lopez free.'

His face was now damp under the television lights. This tugged at Zoë's heart.

'Frank and Nona Lambert climbed the escarpment to get help. They returned with the truck driver, who helped them get the car seat out, and they used that, like a sled, to carry Miss Lopez up the escarpment. I was unable to use one leg, so I began the climb on my hands and a knee. Frank Lambert and the truck driver came down again and got me on to Frank's back. Frank carried me on his back to the top. The truck driver drove us with the little girl's body to the hospital in Saltillo.'

This time his pause was deliberate, like a break between chapters.

'I like that part about the President,' said Danny.

'Miss Lopez and I were taken to the emergency unit. The statement to the police who came to the hospital was given by Frank Lambert. There was nothing that unusual in the Mexican policeman writing down the names of Americans by their initials. The following day Miss Lopez and I were transferred to the Monterrey hospital. The Lamberts made arrangements for the removal of Mrs Lambert's car to a scrapyard near Monterrey. They flew back to the United States a day or two later.'

Another chapter break. He was very good-looking, a number of viewers on both sides of the ocean remarked to each other, very much in command. But you couldn't tell what he was thinking.

Zoë held her breath.

Miles continued: 'Frank and Nona Lambert were not even peripheral to subsequent events.'

That was to be the key sentence, reported again and again to stamp and validate the argument that the Lamberts were peripheral to the whole sorry story.

'After a week I was flown to Massachusetts General Hospital where I remained for ten days. I was then moved to the rehabilitation unit. Three days later Teresa Lopez was flown to Boston to enter the same unit. Until then it was thought too dangerous to move her at all.'

Unsought images flashed across his mind. His shouts of rage as he sweated through excruciatingly slow hours with his weights and pulleys. Her sobs of frustration while he held her in his arms. Trying to will her to be able to move a toe. Silent days of depression. The crash and tinkle when she flung her tray to the floor. A weight lying on the grass when she hurled it through her shut window.

The sandy hair was wet, Zoë saw, where it edged his face.

'Two months later the doctors concluded there was no way to repair the damage done to her spinal cord, which had been severed near its base. Not long afterwards she was flown back to Monterrey and taken to her home.'

He looked around the room, his eyes lingering on one or two familiar faces among the political reporters, but he gave no sign of recognition.

'The financial arrangements were entirely of my own making and had nothing whatsoever to do with Frank and Nona Lambert. In the week after the accident, Mr Matthew Dunn, a senior partner in the Boston law firm in which my father was also a partner, Whitney, Brewster & Dunn, flew to Monterrey to act on my behalf. A payment of compensation for the death of Perdita Orozco was made to her parents' – again Miles's eyes moved over the intent faces – 'in full knowledge that nothing could compensate them for the loss of their daughter. Payments to Pedro Lopez on behalf of his daughter Teresa have continued for the express purpose of making less intolerable a life damaged cruelly and irreparably by my own actions.

'Have you any questions?'

Zoë was on the edge of her chair.

'Mr Brewster, the first police report, the one made at the hospital, records the presence of F. R. Lambert and N. T. Lambert. Who arranged for their names not to appear at all in the formal police report written later?'

'No one arranged it in the way your question suggests,' Miles replied. 'Police reports in Mexico vary as they do in the United States. There was no need to record the Lamberts as witnesses to the accident since I was never charged with a criminal offence. There was no reason for Mr and Mrs Orozco or Mr Lopez to want the case to come to trial, as the financial settlements I made were substantially higher than what was likely to have been awarded to them by a Mexican court.'

'Sir, some people believe the Mexican authorities were bribed not to take the case to court.'

'Some people will believe anything,' Miles replied. 'The Lamberts had no reason to bribe the police, and neither I, my lawyer, or anyone else bribed them on the Lamberts' behalf or on my behalf.'

Zoë's hands were clutched together.

'Mr Brewster, it is believed that what we call bribes are known as "arrangements" among some sectors of the police in Mexico. It is believed that a policeman, acting independently from the state, could well have suggested such an "arrangement" to you or your lawyer, representing it as common practice.'

'You will have to take your question to an academic writing a doctorate on Mexican jurisprudence,' Miles replied. Some of the faces confronting him relaxed for a moment into wry amusement. 'I can only tell you what occurred in my own case, and I have done so.'

'Sir, how many doors of the car were thrown open on impact with the mesquite?'

'I had a sense that the whole car exploded,' Miles replied, 'but I did not know until afterwards that probably all four doors flew open on impact.'

'Who told you?'

'I could see for myself that both doors were hanging

loose on the side of the car that was up. As for the doors on the side the car lay on, I had no reason to doubt that Miss Lopez had been thrown out of hers before the car flipped on to her, and Mrs Lambert had the impression that her door in the back came open before the car came to rest.'

'Sir, did it strike you at the time that the Lamberts were very lucky not to be thrown out of the back seat of the car as you and Miss Lopez were thrown out of the front seat?'

'I do not remember giving great thought at the time to the Lamberts' good fortune,' Miles replied.

Zoë gave a twisted little smile.

'Mr Brewster, who paid for the car to be removed to the scrapyard?'

'The Lamberts.'

'Sir, why did they bother to get the thing dragged up the escarpment and taken to the scrapyard? As it was a write-off, lots of owners would have abandoned it where it was, out of the way on the side of a mountain.'

'You reckon without Frank Lambert's sound business sense,' replied Miles drily. 'The scrapyard would have provided proof for the car insurers if they asked for it. You reckon as well without Nona Lambert's long concern for the environment. She wouldn't have dreamt of leaving that write-off to rust and clutter up a beautiful mountainside.'

Zoë clapped her hands silently, like a mime.

Those were key sentences of a different kind. They not only rang true for viewers but made them smile. The shift in Frank and Nona Lambert's favour began.

'He's got them off the hook,' Mr Hare remarked to no one in particular.

'Zoë, did you know when Miles killed Perdita she was the same age as me and Danny?' said Nell.

That made Zoë wince.

FIFTY-FIVE

Two days later a short report appeared on the *Javelin*'s front page:

'Mrs Miles Brewster has left the home of her husband, chairman and chief executive of the Brewster Media Corporation and editor of the *London Dispatch*. As soon as her divorce has been completed, Mrs. Brewster will marry Lord Scrope, chairman and chief executive of Scrope Opportunities Ltd.'

Marigold wanted her first name to be somewhere in the announcement. And she thought it no bad thing if her earlier marriage to the earl was mentioned. Gerald would have none of it. He wanted the stark statement that he had taken Mrs Miles Brewster from his rival. The *Javelin*'s sub-editors were instructed not a word could be altered or added.

'Anyone interested in going to Washington for twenty-four hours?' asked Zoë. 'I'm flying down tomorrow just for a night.'

'What are you doing?' Jancie asked.

'Some unfinished business.'

'Zoë's got a boyfriend,' singsonged Nell. 'That's why she's wearing her hair down.'

'I'm wearing my hair down, miss,' said Zoë, 'because I'm on Lake Champlain in the state of Vermont, and I don't have to pretend to be grown up. Although I'm getting there,' she added to her grandmother.

Nell and Danny giggled to one other.

'*Furthermore*, miss,' said Zoë, 'there are other reasons a girl might choose to go to Washington other than to have a tryst with some boyfriend. Ever heard of the Washington Zoo?'

No one else wanted to go to Washington. Jancie preferred to go down to the shore each day. When the lake was still, she liked to take the rowboat out alone, the only sound the pat of the oars.

Peter had tracked down Speers Jackson and found him due back in the capital. He would be glad, Speers said, to see Zoë Hare any time over the weekend at his place on the Shore. A car and driver were arranged by the Washington hotel where she was staying overnight, rather more modest accommodation than that laid on when she could put expenses down to her employer.

In the cold the pebbles' crunch resounded when they drove into the shooting-lodge forecourt. The man who came to the door was just as James had described him. An amiable Texan.

They sat in the living-room drinking coffee. Speers had chosen a high-backed rocking-chair for himself. He was mighty sorry, he said, about James's boating accident. 'Good man, James.'

Zoë's face hardened with anger.

'The day before it happened, he told me you set him up,' she said.

The crow's-feet at the corners of Speers's blue eyes crinkled.

'A harsh way to describe it,' he said with a good-humoured smile. 'I like to think of myself as a thorough man. Preparing for every eventuality.'

His eyes were untroubled.

'Preparing for a lot of things in life entails unpleasant acts, Zoë Hare. Think of what goes on in most people's kitchens before the perfect meal is served.'

Zoë's expression began to change. It made Speers think of a child studying a different species, rapt.

'You could argue that an agent has the clearest mind of all,' he went on. 'Seeing things from so many viewpoints. Uncluttered by conflicting emotions. Helping Lord Scrope deliver his products from Southwestern suited other interests of mine.'

'How long have you been' – she hesitated over the next word – 'helping him?'

'A few years now. The British Defence Secretary himself, Alan Rawlston, instructed Lord Scrope how the forms should be filled in to evade the Anglo-American embargo on Arabi. Who better than Rawlston to know the form? As you reminded us in your interview with him, he was Trade Secretary before he moved to Defence. At that time Scrope Electronics was exporting chemical-weapon components from Britain. Course I knew about that too.'

'Alan Rawlston showed Lord Scrope how to evade British Customs?'

Speers gave a kindly smile.

'Look at it from Rawlston's point of view, Miss Zoë. At Trade his job was to improve trade for Britain. At Defence he knows the dictator is our best bulwark against the really scary Islamic crowd. OK, America and Britain are just this side of outright war with Arabi. We have an embargo against sending arms to Arabi. That shows our heart's in the right place. And none of us *enjoy* arming the guy who hates our guts.'

He see-sawed a hand lazily.

'Alan Rawlston keeps his head and his heart separate. Getting those components to Arabi suited him just right. Suited us too. Scrope is one helluva fine electronics manufacturer, you know, Miss Zoë. More coffee?'

She shook her head. He poured out another cup for himself.

'"Nothing in the machine parts to be exported has been manufactured for military purposes." That was the message right through. But then the stuff from Britain had to stop. Things got too hot with British Customs. That's when yours truly stepped into the frame.'

He added more sugar to his coffee and gave it a stir.

'Lord Scrope was mighty glad to have my help. And that great barrel of mutton Alan Rawlston – don't think I'm being disrespectful: I have a lot of time for Alan Rawlston – was only too delighted that an arrangement could be made at Southwestern. The end purpose was the same. Only this time the stuff went via the arms dealers in Monterrey.'

'Did Gerald Scrope know your main line of business?' asked Zoë.

'Nobody spelled it out. He knew. Haven't you noticed he's got some sort of second sight? He'd come in handy in our business if he ever decided to move in full-time.'

Zoë's face had gone pale.

'Why did James have to be dragged in?' she asked.

'Lord Scrope got a funny feeling the Southwestern operation was going to blow. James Wharton's name on those documents would make a big difference if the shit began to fly. The shipment he authorised contained the essential component for that supergun the dictator has set his heart on.'

Speers's chair had begun to creak as he rocked – not every time, just sometimes.

'Why are you telling me all this?' she asked.

'Don't take offence, Miss Zoë, but there's no way you can show I played any part in these matters. Even so, and I hope you won't think me rude, I had a look in that shoulderbag of yours when you were admiring my view of Tilghman Creek. Also – you know how careful you gotta be these days – there'd be a funny little bleep inside this ol' jacket of mine if you, sitting here so close, were wearing something inside that jacket of yours. But I didn't really think you were the kind of lady who would tape a conversation surreptitiously.'

Zoë gave a wan smile.

'You know, that funny feeling of Lord Scrope's was right,' Speers said reflectively.

He rocked quietly, thinking about the thing. Then he went on.

'My contract with Lord Scrope *is* coming to an end. I'm cancelling it.'

'What do you mean?' asked Zoë.

'It doesn't any longer suit my main interest. It was all right for a while letting Arabi get stronger to hold back the fundamentalist mob – so long as we didn't broadcast what we were doing. But that supergun component was riskier than I like. The dictator is now too big a threat to my own country.'

He gave her a look that brought to mind a decent citizen who is going to put a wrong right, by God.

'And I've gotta let Lord Scrope understand he's not going to get Alan Rawlston into Number Ten Downing Street. If Rawlston was there, it would be goodbye to what remains of the Anglo-American relationship.'

He gave a half laugh, half snort.

'Don't forget,' he said, 'I've been as useful to Lord Scrope as he's been to me. He's made a lot of bucks out of it, plus the kick of the risk. You could say we were friends in a way. But I'm a patriotic American who doesn't like it when a foreigner – even if he's a friend – makes really vicious personal attacks on the American President. I kinda withdraw my friendship.'

After a few moments Zoë asked:

'Has the President known right along about the arms embargo being broken by Scrope Southwestern? About the components for Arabi's chemical weapons and nuclear programme?'

'Why don't I make us a drink before you set off back to Washington,' said Speers. 'Bourbon? Gin?'

She sat motionless until he returned with two highballs. When he was sprawled comfortably again in his chair, he answered her question.

'You still got some things to learn about life, Miss Zoë. You don't realise what an awful busy man the President of the United States is. We can't be bothering him with everything under the sun.'

Keeping his eyes on hers, he sipped his drink.

'If you'd mixed in different circles,' he continued, 'you'd know about the metric of covert operation.'

'I thought metric had to do with measuring distances,' said Zoë, a note of despair in her voice.

He smiled with understanding.

'In this case it means loyalty and deniability – protection in both directions. That's why I told you earlier you can't prove I played any part in these things.'

He looks so kind, she thought. Her own face was bleak. After a time she exhaled a long breath, like a sigh.

'James told me,' she said, 'those documents he signed included authorising Pedro Lopez to be responsible for the return journey of the trucks after they delivered the electronics in Monterrey. When Gerald put his horrible cards on the table, he told James that Pedro Lopez used the trucks to take cocaine back across the border into Texas.'

'Well, maybe, but you oughtn't get yourself too stirred up by these things, little lady,' said Speers. 'If it weren't Scrope Southwestern's trucks it would be somebody else's. If Pedro Lopez wasn't the mule, somebody else would be.'

'Did his daughter know? Teresa?' asked Zoë.

'There's no reason she'd of known about her father's sideline. Pedro didn't make a lot out of it. The ones high up make the killing. Hardly anybody else in drugs manages to keep the money. Especially the mules shifting the stuff. And Pedro was a glorified mule.'

Serenely he rocked his chair.

'Most of what Pedro made he lost in Monterrey. He likes the casinos. That's one reason Teresa had to acknowledge receipt of those cheques from Boston that Pedro collected in cash from the Monterrey bank each month.'

Zoë hadn't touched her highball.

'The thing about Pedro Lopez that made him so efficient at organising Southwestern's deliveries to the dealers – and bringing the trucks back again, sure – was he didn't need the money as much as most Mexicans, so he didn't have to take dumb chances when he was on the job. And he didn't need the money because of the payments from Miles Brewster for his daughter. Small world.'

The crow's-feet crinkled again.

'I could of told Lord Scrope long ago that the guy handling those trucks for Southwestern was the father of the woman Miles Brewster looks after. But nobody asked me. People get so fixed on using me for one purpose they never think of asking me about something else.'

After a silence between them, broken by a couple of creaks, Zoë asked: 'Did Gerald Scrope take a cut from the drugs deal?'

'Who's to say? Funny man, Lord Scrope. He likes grabbing things so much he might. Then again he might not. An unpredictable man.'

When she was leaving, Speers said:

'By the way, are you still in touch with Miles Brewster?'

'Why do you ask?'

'I could lend a hand in his newspaper's campaign to keep Alan Rawlston from toppling the Prime Minister. Martin Mather is a good friend to America.'

He handed Zoë a cassette.

'Being a curious young lady, I expect you'll want to play it before you give it to Miles Brewster. So you'll discover right quickly it's a recording of Alan Rawlston when he was still at Trade – explaining to Lord Scrope how to evade British Customs and export arms components illegally from Britain. Lord Scrope taped their conversation and gave me a copy. I made a copy from that. Want it?'

FIFTY-SIX

On her way back she stopped to make two more copies at an electronics place she knew from her days on the *Express*. In her hotel bedroom she grabbed her cassette-recorder from her suitcase. When she had played the tape through, she phoned for a courier.

She went to play it a second time and stopped. She had Speers Jackson's phone number on the Shore. He answered.

'About that thing you gave me,' she said, 'have you something similar about those trucks returning to Austin – about what was in them?'

An amused laugh at the other end of the line.

'Didn't that grandaddy of yours ever tell you about keeping a second shot in your locker?' said Speers. 'What I gave you will do the trick for now. I'll keep the other matter in reserve. You never know with these south Londoners. They got a lot of bounce in them.'

When the courier left with the cassette she phoned the *Dispatch*. Miles was at his desk. Their conversation was brief, no adornments. The envelope was marked for his attention only, she said. Her heart was pounding when she put the receiver back.

His voice hadn't been impersonal, not at all, but she wasn't sure what it had been. She lay atop her bed staring at the ceiling. In a way she was glad Peter, as usual at weekends, was back in the state he represented. She was overwrought and exhausted. She fixed for an early morning call, closed the curtains, undressed. When her call woke her, she couldn't remember having got into bed.

*

Three mornings later the *Dispatch* broke the story that the Defence Secretary, Alan Rawlston, while a minister of the Crown, had connived to evade Britain's arms embargo on Arabi. The transcript of the tape was electrifying. It even raised the question of whether his junior minister at Trade took the rap for Alan when things got sticky then.

It was plain the tape had been made in Alan's room at the House of Commons. Talk between him and Gerald was interrupted several times by the arrival of one or another MP whom Alan introduced. After the sound of a door being shut conversation between Gerald and Alan resumed.

Miles did not deign to write an editorial. The transcript of the tape spoke for itself.

That afternoon the Defence Secretary resigned.

A cabinet minister had guided Lord Scrope's hand in evading the arms embargo. In the event, the Director of Public Prosecutions found that there was not sufficient evidence against Lord Scrope to prosecute him successfully. Everyone took this explanation with a pinch of salt.

But every paper except his own mauled Lord Scrope's credibility. So did the public: 'The *Javelin* tells us to put our country first, and now we learn Scrope is helping that monster build up a chemical and nuclear arsenal.'

Some major advertisers withdrew their contracts with the *Javelin*. Others waited to see how the paper's circulation would be affected. Thousands of 'disgusted' readers cancelled their subscriptions. But news-stand sales didn't drop at all: people wanted to know what the *Javelin* would say next.

No one, however, could still take seriously Lord Scrope's campaign to get rid of Martin Mather. Everyone suddenly realised Mather was a strong and determined prime minister unlikely to be blown off his course. What the country needed, they all now said, was Mather's calm and vision to lead Britain through its financial difficulties, while at the same time enabling Britons to hold their heads high on the international stage.

Disgruntled back-benchers and manufacturers still called for the embargo to be lifted. 'We're a trading nation, for God's sake.' But with their two leaders discredited and their cause tainted, they knew they had lost a decisive battle.

'Rawlston' became a byword for dishonour.

'Bugger them all,' Gerald said to Marigold.

A few still felt something wasn't quite right in Miles Brewster's detailed public statement. But they had to accept there was not a scrap of evidence that the Lamberts' presence as passengers had been intentionally concealed. And Frank's conduct on the mountainside won respect from everyone. Nona's conduct too, though Frank was the one who carried Miles Brewster up the escarpment on his back.

Political damage remained, of course, particularly in the United States where it mattered most:

'It's disgraceful that Frank and Nona Lambert should have allowed themselves to be driven by someone full of drink.' – 'And with such a predictable outcome for innocent Mexican victims,' others added.

A shadow remained across the Lamberts. But the damage was containable as it would not have been had it come out while he was still seeking office.

Most Americans were relieved that the White House had weathered the storm.

The stain on Miles's integrity as an editor would never go away entirely. But emotions usually outweigh intellectual assessment. People were impressed when they saw him on television: not defensive, not whining, even humorous at the end ('that voice really gets you') when he jousted with his accusers.

Zoë's relief was immeasurable. Yet she was stuck with contradictions she couldn't iron out. It was plain that Miles would always have concealed the fact that the Lamberts were in the car if Simon Fleet hadn't forced his hand.

'Maybe I shouldn't have put him on that tall pedestal in the first place,' she said to Jancie.

They were drinking coffee in the bay window. The afternoon sun was pale. Frost coated the ground except where small boots had tramped across it.

'Not the first person to do that,' Jancie commented. 'First you set the statue on the pedestal. Then you blame the statue when it falls off.'

Zoë wondered if Jancie had anyone else in mind, but she didn't ask lest it force them to speak of Simon. They never referred to him now. Nor to Gerald Scrope if they could help it.

The person least impressed by Miles's television performance was Miles himself. What kind of fool was he, he rebuked himself scornfully, for taking it into his head to become the *Dispatch*'s editor? Hadn't he known it was inappropriate, that the moral obligations were different from the owner's?

But the thing couldn't be undone. He'd have to fucking live with it.

FIFTY-SEVEN

'Well, it's very beautiful once you get here,' said Peter.

He had phoned two nights before, on Christmas Day, to say whatever there is to say at Christmas when death stands in every room.

'Can you put me up for the night later this week?' he'd asked.

They were all glad to see him. Jancie had first got to know him during her time as British Ambassadress in Washington. He had just the right way of talking with Danny and Nell when he was in London for the funeral. Zoë's grandparents knew he was someone special in her life and were more than a little curious to meet him. There was a small bedroom not yet occupied, which must once have been a maid's room. Peter got that.

No snow had fallen as winter fastened its grip on the land. Where the lake had crept up the flat rocks and then been pushed back by the wind, a thin layer of ice glittered and crackled deliciously as the children stamped upon it. Wrapped up like Eskimos, they braved the rowboat with Mr Hare. (Mrs Hare said she would stay home, thank you, she had some things she had to do.)

'I guess it's far too soon for you to think about the future,' Peter said to Jancie as she walked between him and Zoë. In their boots they clumped through the pasture where once Fern had grazed.

'I'm taking the children back to London next week. I'll return to the BBC to start with. In time I'll have to think whether I want to stay there or move back here and get a job. Do you realise how long it's been since I worked in

American television? Probably I have more friends in London now than here. So I don't know.'

'That makes two of us not taking any decision yet on our futures,' said Zoë firmly.

'You're bound to have offers from newspapers in both countries, Zoë,' Peter said.

'Well, maybe. Let's hope so. But I wouldn't mind having a little respite from anything to do with the media for a couple of weeks.'

When they all left the dining-room that evening, Zoë said to Peter: 'How would you like to have a walk under the moon with me?'

It would be slightly easier to say something difficult if they were outside walking, she'd finally decided, instead of sitting in a room face to face. They took the dirt road that ran beside the lake where it bent around the Hare farm and narrowed before swelling big again.

'I'm not sure how we left things the last time we had a stroll,' she said. 'After the funeral,' she added unnecessarily. He realised at once what was coming.

'We were going to give some serious thought to getting married,' he said, taking her hand and pulling off its mitten before clasping it inside his jacket pocket.

Their boots resounded on the frozen road.

'Each of us has been a harbour when the other was being tossed around on the waters,' Zoë said uncertainly. 'But that's not the same thing as marriage. I think it might wreck the most beautiful friendship I have ever had with a man.'

She looked at him from the corner of her eye. He stayed in unreadable profile, as if they were discussing a theory of Einstein's as they walked through an evening almost as clear as day, the fields on one side white under the moon, on the other side gleaming inky water, a moon path across it.

'And it would be anyone's guess how your children would take to me. Nobody knows what I'd be like on the mother side of things,' she said awkwardly.

Their boots on the road, and waves lapping the shore, were the only sound.

'I think it's also likely,' she said softly, 'that what you feel for me now is mixed up by your life being turned upside down. I mean, even if I didn't have this feeling that marriage really isn't right for us, you'd be crazy, my lovely, lovely Peter, to take a big decision like that right now.'

'That's for me to judge, not you,' he said.

But he didn't try to persuade her. They knew each other well.

When they turned back she put her mitten on again. As they neared the house, its cupola irradiated like a ghost in the moonlight, she said: 'Are you going to keep in touch with Jancie? She needs a harbour too.'

He leant down and kissed her on the cheek, and they linked hands as they skirted the frozen ridges of the vegetable garden.

In the morning Jancie said: 'Why don't I take Peter to Burlington? – if that's OK with everyone.'

Two days before the Whartons were to leave, they woke to silent stillness. The snow had fallen in the night.

'It's too beautiful to mark with footsteps,' Jancie said.

'Will we sink all the way in if we do?' asked Danny.

By late morning boot tracks were sunk as far as the cottonwood, making a circle around its base, and individual pockets in the snow went to the edge of the cliff and back.

After lunch Zoë pulled her boots on again and went out alone, making a new trail to where the invisible path sloped through Hans Christian Andersen birches to the shore below. It was heavy going, but the cold wasn't as penetrating as it was before the snow. Her wool hat got too warm and she shoved it in her jacket.

When she reached the flat rocks that had been there for ever, she stopped, awed by the stillness of undulating white marked only where dark water lapped. Slowly she sank one boot in front of her, then the other. When she reached the highest mound she stood motionless, gazing across the lake to the red buoy where a seagull perched. It didn't move. She didn't move. Time did not exist.

Something made her turn. It can't have been a sound: the land was silent. Miles was standing with the snow nearly at his boot-tops.

When he was nearer he called: 'Next time could you have bigger feet?'

He put another boot forward and widened the pocket left by her.

When he reached her they stood apart, each face glowing, laughing, though no sound came from their mouths. It was as if they were feasting with their eyes.

After a time Miles said: 'I've only seen your hair loose once before.'

'How are you?' she asked. She could hardly speak.

'I'm all right.'

She turned her face towards the lake.

'Can you ever forgive me?' she asked.

'I forgave you in front of St Bride's Church.'

She looked at him again. 'What I did was not right. But it was not as bad as you thought.'

'I didn't make it easy for you,' he said.

She searched his face.

He repeated her words with a different inflection. 'What *I* did was not right,' he said. 'It can never be put right.'

She put a hand out and touched his arm. Her face was

tender when she turned back to the lake. 'When seagulls perch on buoys, do they normally fall asleep?' she asked.

'Did you know Marigold and I have separated? For good.'

'No. I didn't know.'

'She's marrying Gerald Scrope.'

'Oh.'

He touched the ends of her hair where it hung against her jacket, and then lifted some strands, rubbing them between his thumb and fingers.

She looked into his face again.

'Did you know that steeple on St Bride's is the tallest steeple Wren ever made?' she asked.

He took her in his arms.

After a time the seagull shook itself and flapped off.

FIFTY-EIGHT

'I'm thinking about the future,' he said. 'What about you – your work?'

They were sitting on the sofa in the music room, Miles's legs stretched out. The fax machine had disappeared. The Victrola was back on its stand.

'I'm not thinking about it yet,' said Zoë. 'Being home means cash isn't frantic the way it'd be if I were lolling about somewhere else.'

'You saw for yourself when you went down to Washington,' he said. 'Staff morale at the *Express* is abysmal – second-rate journalists brought in over good ones. The present editor is just not up to it. I want you to do it.'

'Do what?'

'Edit the *Express*. In that respect, anyhow, Scrope was quicker than me to realise what you could do.'

She was too stunned to speak. Nell came stumping in, boots leaving wads of snow behind her, snow melting in rivulets down a bright red cheek.

'Me and Danny agreed we wouldn't hit each other in the face. And he did.'

Miles chuckled and got to his feet.

'Come on,' he said, taking her hand, 'we'll have to put a wrong right.'

When he returned he and Zoë discussed his proposition.

Several times her eyes moved from his face to the framed photograph on the table. She stuck her legs out in front of her, her head on the back of the sofa. Then she sat up again.

'You'll go on being based in London?' she asked.

'For now,' he replied. 'Though that doesn't mean I won't be dropping in quite often to check up on how the editor at the *Express* is getting on.'

'I'll take that into consideration too,' said Zoë, her eyes sparkling.

'Well?' he said.

'Could I think about it?' said Zoë.

He looked at his watch, smiling to herself as they replayed the scene in his office nearly seven months before. 'It's now just past four.'

'OK, I'll let you know before supper.'

He exhaled a big breath when she told him.

'Could you start in two weeks' time?'

'Why not?' she said.

'There's something else.'

She tensed.

'I wanted to know your decision before I told you,' he said. 'I won't be there when you take over the *Express*, but within a couple of months I'll be moving my base back to Washington – upstairs in Corporate again, above the newsroom. How would the new editor feel about that?'

Zoë felt as if a band was pressing into her temples. If it came undone all of her would explode and fly in a hundred different directions. She jumped up and went out the front door. A path had been shovelled across the veranda. She stood there in her sneakers, arms wrapped around herself, hardly aware of the crisp cold as she looked at the lake.

Miles joined her.

'Does that prospect make you happy or sad?' he asked.

'I suppose it's happiness,' she replied. 'The problem is I've never felt anything like this before. So I'm not sure how to describe it.'

'I've been trying to work out how long I've loved you,' he said. 'I knew it when I was at World's End that evening. Before that, I must have known, but I never acknowledged it to myself. So it's hard to be precise.'

He put his hand through hers.

'God, it's like schooldays, visiting your girl's family,' he said, glancing through the glass pane of the veranda door at Mrs Hare sorting out some papers at her desk.

He spent the night in the room where Peter had stayed.

In the morning they went over more details. Zoë would start off in one of Washington's residential hotels. The person renting her apartment overlooking the Potomac had a contract for another three months.

'Peter will know some place. He's good on that sort of thing,' she said.

They drove alone to Burlington, Miles at the wheel. Half-way there she said: 'Would you mind if I went to see Teresa? I'd like to meet her.'

He took so long to answer that she turned and studied his profile.

'If that's what you want,' he replied. He glanced at her with a lop-sided smile. 'Which isn't the same thing as saying "Do what you like."'

He took a hand off the wheel to rest it over hers.

As they turned into the airport landing stage he said: 'By the way. We haven't begun to discuss a lot of things. It may need a lifetime together to get through it all. Don't take it into your head to marry someone else without mentioning it to me first. As soon as some things get straightened out, we need to have a talk.'

When she got back, Zoë went into the music room. No one else was around. From a shelf beneath the Victrola she took out a twelve-inch album, its spine now cracked. On the turntable she carefully placed *Tristan und Isolde*'s love duet. The ancient record crackled – it had crackled as long as she could remember – but the molten music moved her even more than in her girlhood, if that was possible. Or perhaps the difference was that this time her images were focused on two actual individuals. She got so carried away as the chromatic themes surged and yielded to each other that she stretched her arms above her in rapture.

The next day she made the drive again, Jancie beside her, Nell and Danny in the back with suitcases that wouldn't fit in the trunk.

Zoë smiled at the excited faces in her rear-view mirror. 'And I want no flip remarks from either of you about anything, my honeys.'

That Thursday Mr Hare drove her to Burlington.

Peter had found a short-rent apartment in a residential hotel on P Street near 16th. It was miniature, in fact, but had charm. And there were two large cupboards. Really all she needed, she reminded herself, while she got going on her new career. Day one was next Monday.

She went to bed early and dreamt a lot, half-waking, trying to catch the dream before it slipped away. In one dream Fate sat in a chair, wearing blue tonight. Zoë glimpsed the big boots, but Fate's head was too far away, out of sight.

Friday morning she flew to Monterrey.

FIFTY-NINE

Zoë went over to the windows. The view over the cordilleras, blue slopes stretching against a cloudless sky, made her draw in her breath. The almond scent from mimosa growing in a pot was delicious. After a few moments she returned to her chair near the swinging settee.

They had liked each other at once. Teresa's face was less like the Kahlo self-portrait than Zoë had expected. But the resemblance was still strong. Most of the time they talked about Miles.

'It was a romantic summer affair,' Teresa said. 'After the accident it grew into lifelong friendship.'

Miles had been to see her fifteen, perhaps twenty times since. They talked sometimes on the phone.

When dusk began to fall and the windows turned a deeper blue, Zoë stood up to leave.

Teresa said: 'Miles trusts you more than anyone in the world, now.'

Her pause before 'now' was so slight that Zoë wasn't sure it was there. Then she realised: he must have had total trust in Teresa all these years.

Neither spoke for a few minutes.

Then Teresa said: 'It's not the way it seems.'

'It never is,' said Zoë.

'When the car hit the mesquite,' Teresa said, 'the back doors were the ones flung open. That's how Miles and I were thrown out. The Lamberts were in the front. Frank was driving.'

Slowly Zoë sat down again. A cicada's *zikky-zikky* rended the silence.

In a low voice Teresa went on.

The lie had been decided when they were on the flatbed of the truck with the child's body, on the way to the hospital in Saltillo. Though she was aware of the truck jolting, she could remember no pain. She was conscious throughout.

Nona had raised it. Driving with too much drink inside him. Killing the child. It would ruin Frank's chance of reaching the White House. Miles had already told her that all three of them believed he would make a good reforming president one day. None of them needed reminding of what Chappaquiddick had done to Edward Kennedy's prospects, which all his family's wealth and single-mindedness could not restore.

If Miles had been driving, it would reflect badly on him, but his incipient career as a newspaper publisher would not be affected.

'You must remember we were all in shock. The Lamberts you can imagine. Miles was in agony, I believe, bleeding steadily. I was passive – it hardly seemed to matter who'd been driving – but even though I didn't take it in properly until later, I was a party to the decision to tell the lie.'

A policeman arrived soon after they reached the hospital. A blood test was taken of all four. Frank Lambert, she learned later, gave the description of what happened pretty well word for word as it appeared in that first police report.

'By the time we'd been moved to the hospital in Monterrey,' Teresa said, 'Miles realised the folly of a lie told for political advancement. It would have been better to tell the truth at the outset and face what followed. And who knows? The American public might even have forgiven it as a tragic episode in a young man's life. It *wasn't* the same as Chappaquiddick. But once the lie was told, it could not be untold without making things worse – not least by revealing that the would-be American President had panicked at the moment of crisis.'

When Zoë got back to her Washington hotel she found a message to ring Miles Brewster in London.

'You'll have to tell that residential hotel,' he began without ado, 'that you won't be staying the full three months until you can get back into your own apartment.'

'Why not?'

'You'll want to be moving somewhere else in a few weeks.'

'I see,' Zoë said, tilting her swivel chair back. 'Any place in mind?'

'The woman who owns that blue clapboard house across from the *Express* is moving to the Eastern Shore to be near her daughter. I bought the house from her.'

'*What?*' The swivel chair straightened abruptly.

'You might sometimes let Corporate use the first floor for singsongs, if you want, but the second floor would make a cosy dwelling for the editor to live. Only a few walls would have to be knocked about.'

Total silence at the Washington end of the line.

He chuckled.

'I thought you'd be pleased,' he said. 'Oh yes, one other thing. The editor would be expected to pay the company notional rent and of course carry her own expenses. When I move into that house with you, we'll have to think again.'

'I see,' said Zoë a second time, spinning her chair first one way, then the other, in her joy.

EPILOGUE

The streets were nearly deserted. From the car window Gerald recognised the gait in the glow of a street lamp. Miles was walking along the empty pavement in the same direction.

'Stop a couple of hundred yards in front of that bloke. Right here.'

He jumped out and stood under a lamp where he was clearly visible as Miles approached.

Miles stopped five feet away. They surveyed each other.

'How's it going, mate?'

'Good evening, Scrope.'

'I told you at the start, Brewster: nothing personal.'

Miles gave a wry laugh.

'We all got our roles to play, Brewster.'

Gerald was starting to shout though he stood absolutely still.

'Next time maybe it'll be the other way round, Brewster.'

'Whatever, Scrope – whatever the name of the game.'

Gerald raised one arm slowly in a mock salute, then swatted the air. Abruptly he got in his car.

Miles walked up the street, hands in pockets as he turned the corner.

READ MORE IN PENGUIN

In every corner of the world, on every subject under the sun, Penguin represents quality and variety – the very best in publishing today.

For complete information about books available from Penguin – including Puffins, Penguin Classics and Arkana – and how to order them, write to us at the appropriate address below. Please note that for copyright reasons the selection of books varies from country to country.

In the United Kingdom: Please write to *Dept. JC, Penguin Books Ltd, FREEPOST, West Drayton, Middlesex UB7 OBR.*

If you have any difficulty in obtaining a title, please send your order with the correct money, plus ten per cent for postage and packaging, to *PO Box No. 11, West Drayton, Middlesex UB7 OBR*

In the United States: Please write to *Consumer Sales, Penguin USA, P.O. Box 999, Dept. 17109, Bergenfield, New Jersey 07621-0120.* VISA and MasterCard holders call 1-800-253-6476 to order all Penguin titles

In Canada: Please write to *Penguin Books Canada Ltd, 10 Alcorn Avenue, Suite 300, Toronto, Ontario M4V 3B2*

In Australia: Please write to *Penguin Books Australia Ltd, P.O. Box 257, Ringwood, Victoria 3134*

In New Zealand: Please write to *Penguin Books (NZ) Ltd, Private Bag 102902, North Shore Mail Centre, Auckland 10*

In India: Please write to *Penguin Books India Pvt Ltd, 706 Eros Apartments, 56 Nehru Place, New Delhi 110 019*

In the Netherlands: Please write to *Penguin Books Netherlands bv, Postbus 3507, NL-1001 AH Amsterdam*

In Germany: Please write to *Penguin Books Deutschland GmbH, Metzlerstrasse 26, 60594 Frankfurt am Main*

In Spain: Please write to *Penguin Books S. A., Bravo Murillo 19, 1° B, 28015 Madrid*

In Italy: Please write to *Penguin Italia s.r.l., Via Felice Casati 20, I–20124 Milano*

In France: Please write to *Penguin France S. A., 17 rue Lejeune, F–31000 Toulouse*

In Japan: Please write to *Penguin Books Japan, Ishikiribashi Building, 2–5–4, Suido, Bunkyo-ku, Tokyo 112*

In Greece: Please write to *Penguin Hellas Ltd, Dimocritou 3, GR–106 71 Athens*

In South Africa: Please write to *Longman Penguin Southern Africa (Pty) Ltd, Private Bag X08, Bertsham 2013*

BY THE SAME AUTHOR

Dangerous Games

Georgie Chase is the tough, high-powered editor of America's top news weekly. Her husband Hugo Carroll is the nation's number one political columnist. Together, they're America's most envied couple – rich, glamorous, smart – and safe from the corruption that surrounds them, or so they believe.

Until ruthless lobbyist Jock Liddon and his amoral aide Lisa Tabor draw them into a sinister web of political intrigue, violence and sexual blackmail that stretches from the White House to Downing Street. As IRA terrorists and British power brokers compete for notoriety and political prestige, Georgie's friend Patsy and her husband Ian Lonsdale, a British Cabinet minister, are also ensnared by those willing to employ the weapons of love as well as hate.

'Susan Crosland is a brilliantly successful storyteller who keeps all the tensions going and still manages to surprise us at every turn' – *Sunday Telegraph*

'Crosland writes with an insight of life in the political fast lane. A sure-fire bestseller' – *Sunday Express*